BOU...

WITH ...

*Taken to his bed, but ~~he~~
can't buy her heart!*

Complete your collection with
all four books!

In February:
Blackmailed With Diamonds
In March:
Shackled With Rubies
In April:
Bound With Gold

Glamour, passion and jewels: what more can a woman ask for?

Four fabulous collections of stories from your favourite authors

February 2010: He can shower her with diamonds, but can he make her his bride?

Blackmailed With Diamonds

Lucy Gordon
Sarah Morgan
Robyn Donald

March 2010: He can bind her with rubies – but can he keep her for his own?

Shackled With Rubies

Lucy Monroe
Lee Wilkinson
Kate Walker

April 2010: He can chain her with gold – but can he win her love?

Bound With Gold

Susan Napier
Kathryn Ross
Kelly Hunter

MISTRESSES
BOUGHT
WITH EMERALDS

SANDRA MARTON
KATHERINE GARBERA
MARGARET MAYO

M&B™ and M&B™ with the Rose Device
are trademarks of the publisher.
Harlequin Mills & Boon Limited, Eton House,
18-24 Paradise Road, Richmond, Surrey TW9 1SR

BOUGHT WITH EMERALDS © by Harlequin Books SA 2010

Emerald Fire © Sandra Myles 1995
Mistress Minded © Katherine Garbera 2004
The Wife Seduction © Margaret Mayo 2000

ISBN: 978 0 263 87727 4

24-0510

Harlequin Mills & Boon policy is to use papers that are natural, renewable and recyclable products and made from wood grown in sustainable forests. The logging and manufacturing processes conform to the legal environmental regulations of the country of origin.

Printed and bound in Spain
by Litografia Rosés S.A., Barcelona

EMERALD FIRE

SANDRA MARTON

Sandra Marton wrote her first novel while she was still in primary school. Her doting parents told her she'd be a writer someday and Sandra believed them. In secondary school and college, she wrote dark poetry nobody but her boyfriend understood, though looking back, she suspects he was just being kind. As a wife and mother, she wrote murky short stories in what little spare time she could manage, but not even her boyfriend-turned-husband could pretend to understand those. Sandra tried her hand at other things, among them teaching and serving on the Board of Education in her home town, but the dream of becoming a writer was always in her heart.

At last, Sandra realised she wanted to write books about what all women hope to find: love with that one special man, love that's rich with fire and passion, love that lasts forever. She wrote a novel, her very first, and sold it to Mills & Boon® Modern™. Since then, she's written more than sixty books, all of them featuring sexy, gorgeous, larger-than-life heroes. A four-time RITA® award finalist, she's also received five *Romantic Times Magazine* awards and has been honoured with RT's Career Achievement Award for Series Romance. Sandra lives with her very own sexy, gorgeous, larger-than-life hero in a sun-filled house on a quiet country lane in the north-eastern United States.

CHAPTER ONE

SLADE MCCLINTOCH was at the reception desk of the Hotel Florinda when he first saw the woman. She was coming down the rickety wooden steps that led into what passed for a lobby, the expression in her blue eyes as cool as the white cotton dress she wore, and the sight of her was so incongruous that Slade almost forgot how annoyed he was with the rat-faced little man lounging behind the desk.

She paused on the last step, her hand on the banister. Tall, slender, her face a pale oval beneath a short, shining cap of golden hair, she was about as perfect a sight as a man could hope to see in New York or San Francisco, let alone in this God-forsaken town on the edge of the Peruvian jungle—and disapproval was etched into every line of her beautiful face.

Well, why wouldn't it be? Slade thought, with a lift of one dark eyebrow. The only thing attractive about the Hotel Florinda was its name. Nobody, not even the most dedicated optimist, could find anything to like in the cheap furnishings, smeared walls and worn floorboards.

Its singular claim to fame was that it was the only hotel in Italpa. That was why Slade was here. As for the woman—why *she* was here was anybody's guess. From the looks of her, she was probably a tourist who'd strayed from her group. There were increasing numbers of them down here lately, pampered rich folks happy to shell out whatever it cost to taste the dangers of the savage jungle—but at a safe and sanitized distance.

Whatever the woman was, she was as out of place in this grim setting as an Amazon orchid would have been in a tangle of sawgrass.

'A lovely flower, is she not, *señor?*'

The desk clerk leaned toward Slade over the scarred mahogany counter, a sly grin on his rabbity face. For a second, Slade wondered if he'd spoken his thoughts aloud. No. He was tired—but not tired enough to have begun talking to himself. Not yet, anyway, although if he didn't get some sleep soon…

The clerk bent closer. 'She is a sight to behold, yes?'

Adrenaline surged through Slade's veins. He worked in a world of men; he knew such speculative comments about women were commonplace, knew, as well, that, as such remarks went, the clerk's was mild and harmless. Still, he didn't like it. Maybe it was the man's shifty smile or the way he lowered one eyelid in an exaggerated wink.

Or maybe, Slade thought, forcing a smile to his lips, maybe it was just that he hadn't had any sleep in damned near fourteen hours.

'Indeed,' he said pleasantly. 'She is almost as lovely as this charming establishment—for which, I assure you, I have a reservation.'

The clerk pursed his lips. 'I will check again, *señor,* but—' His shoulders rose then fell in a gesture of eloquent distress. 'I still do not see your name on my list.'

Slade fought to keep the smile on his face. He had been patient, even gracious; he had played the game, which involved pretending innocence even as he slipped the sleazy little man a fistful of *intis*, and now, by God, he'd had enough.

Perhaps the clerk wanted a bigger bribe. Perhaps the reservation was truly lost. Perhaps a miracle had occurred and the Florinda had turned into a tourist mecca, booking suites and deluxe accommodations to high society. Hell, anything was possible here, on the edge of the Amazon.

Slade didn't give a damn. He was exhausted. He was short-tempered. He wanted a cold beer, a hot shower and a soft bed. He wanted the room he was entitled to, and he wanted it now.

He counted silently to one hundred while the clerk made an elaborate show of thumbing through a stack of papers.

'It is as I feared, *señor,*' the little man said finally. 'There is no reservation in your name. I cannot imagine what we can do to solve this problem.' His hand crept to the desktop where it lay palm up, fingers lightly curled, like a rhinoceros beetle that had been flipped on its back and awaited salvation. 'Unless you can, perhaps, think of some solution…?'

Slade smiled, his teeth flashing whitely against his tanned skin. He crooked his finger, motioning the clerk closer, and the man obliged, smiling slyly in anticipation of more *intis*.

'I can, indeed, think of something,' Slade said, very softly. His eyes, as cold as green glass, locked on the other man's and he whispered a few words in Spanish.

The clerk's smile turned sickly. He reached under the counter and came up with a key dangling from a brass tag.

'*Ay, caramba,*' he said in amazement. 'Look at this,

señor. I have found your reservation. Such a foolish error. You will forgive it, yes?'

Slade grinned. 'Certainly.' He reached across the scarred desktop, patted the clerk lightly on the cheek, and picked up the key. 'We all make errors from time to time.'

'You are most gracious, *señor*. May you have a pleasant stay at our humble establishment.'

Slade nodded as he turned away. A pleasant stay? Only if you believed in miracles, he thought as he strode across the lobby. The best he could hope for was that the roaches weren't bigger than rats, that the sheets would have been changed this month, that…

Damn! What room was he in, anyway? He hadn't asked, and he should have. The Florinda was four stories high, and that fourth floor would be the only one that was bearable. Scowling, he dug in his pocket for the key and held it up, trying to read the number on the worn brass tag. With luck, noise from the street wouldn't carry to the top floor. There might even be a breeze from—

'Oof!'

The collision was swift and forceful. There was a whisper of silken hair across his chin, the faint drift of jasmine in his nostrils. He reached out and clasped a pair of slender, feminine shoulders.

'Sorry,' he said, 'I didn't mean to—'

He stopped in mid-sentence. It was the woman he'd noticed a little while ago. Close up, she was more than beautiful. She was stunning.

'I didn't mean to run you down,' he said, smiling as much in appraisal as in apology, 'but—'

'That's quite all right.' Her tone was frigid, and if

moments before her face had registered disapproval, now it radiated disgust.

Slade's smile thinned, but hell, he could hardly blame her. He knew how he must look—the emergency call that had brought him here had taken him straight from a work site and the hours of travel that had followed would have done nothing to improve his appearance except to rumple his jeans further and add another layer of dust to his boots.

'If you'll excuse me,' she said pointedly.

He looked at his hands, still wrapped lightly around her shoulders.

'Oh. Oh, sure.' He let go of her and smiled again. 'Sorry. I—'

'You're wasting your time.'

Slade blinked. 'I beg your pardon?'

'I said, you're wasting your time. And mine. I am not interested in a tour of Italpa.'

'I didn't—'

'Nor am I interested in seeing the jungle by moonlight.'

'Well, I'm glad to—'

'And I certainly have no wish to buy a genuine shrunken head or a stuffed alligator or anything else you might want to sell me.'

Slade's eyes narrowed. 'That's a relief. I unloaded my last shrunken head yesterday.'

A snort of muffled laughter drifted toward him. He turned sharply and glared at the desk clerk, who flushed and looked away, but not in time to conceal the smirk that curled over his mouth.

A dull wash of color rose along Slade's high cheekbones as he swung back to the woman.

'Listen, lady—'

He was talking to the air. Her shoulder bumped him as she brushed past. He stood still for a moment, and then he turned, marched after her, and caught her by the arm.

'The first thing to learn about going slumming,' he growled as he swung her around, 'is that you ought to be prepared for what you're likely to find.'

Color flew into Brionny Stuart's face. She stared at the man, at this creature who smelled of sweat and dust. She'd seen his performance with the poor desk clerk, how he'd taken satisfaction in bullying a man half his size, and then he'd turned his attentions to her. Had her really expected her to greet him with a smile?

She gave him a slow, contemptuous look, one that went from his scuffed boots to the shadowy stubble on his face.

'I couldn't agree more,' she said coldly, and before he had time to react she turned on her heel and strode away. She could feel the man's eyes boring into her back and she had to fight the almost overwhelming desire to hurry her pace.

Stupid, she thought. What she'd just done was stupid! You didn't taunt a man like him in a place like the Florinda, but after a week in this miserable river town her patience was worn thin.

Professor Ingram had warned her about Italpa, about the bugs and the filth, the heat and the unsavory opportunists who hung around its mean streets, but he needn't have bothered. This might have been Brionny's first expedition as a graduate student but it was hardly her first time in the field. Her father, a prominent archaeologist himself, had taken her with him on digs from childhood on.

Henry Stuart had grumbled about the sort of men who

hung around places like Italpa, too. Liars, leeches and worse, he'd called them, looking to steal fortunes in antiquities from the scientists who found them.

Unfortunately, Brionny had had to learn that truth for herself.

Her blue eyes darkened as she remembered her seventeenth summer, when a dark-eyed Latin Lothario had wooed her under a Mexican moon, gaining her trust and parlaying it into a job at her father's dig site when two of his regular workers fell ill.

The end of the story had been painfully predictable. The man had made off with a fortune in relics, her father had been furious, and Brionny had been left heartbroken, humiliated—and a whole lot wiser.

Wise enough to be immune to the kind of smooth operator who'd just come on to her, she thought now as she peered down a grimy service corridor that deadended off the lobby of the Hotel Florinda. Some women might have found him attractive, with his green eyes and his broad-shouldered, lean-hipped body, but she certainly wasn't one of them. If anything, she was turned off by his sort.

Brionny sighed. Actually, the only man who interested her right now would be short, squat and whitehaired.

'Where the devil are you, Professor?' she muttered under her breath.

The Ingram expedition was leaving in the morning on its quest for the legendary Eye of God, and there were still checks to write and last-minute things to buy. And, since Professor Ingram was not just half the team but the only half with the authority to sign checks and approve purchases, nothing could happen without him.

Brionny paused outside what passed for the hotel dining room and pushed open the door. Mismatched wooden chairs leaned drunkenly against stained tables; rainwater dripped from a hole in the ceiling. Except for a procession of large black ants that marched determinedly up and down the far wall, the room was empty.

Damn! Where had Ingram gone? It was unlike him to disappear. The most positive thing Brionny could say about him, aside from his brilliance as an archaeologist, was that he kept to his schedule. He was impossible otherwise—autocratic, unpleasant, unforgiving—and more than willing to load her with work in the face of what she suspected might be a decline in his health. It was hard to tell; Ingram did not take kindly to personal questions.

'You are my assistant, Miss Stuart,' he'd said sharply just yesterday, after she'd thought she'd noticed him suddenly going pale at lunch, 'not my keeper.'

But then, she hadn't become Ingram's graduate assistant for his charm. He was a leading expert on Amazonian Indian culture; even her father had been impressed when she'd gotten the appointment. Of course, Henry Stuart would have preferred if it she'd entered the graduate program at the university where he was head of the archaeology department, but Brionny had made it clear she wanted to succeed on her own.

Or fail, she thought with a little sigh. Where the devil was the professor? She'd checked everywhere: in his room, at the market, in the town square, and now in the Florinda's public rooms—the lobby, the card lounge, the dining room...

Ahead, in a dimly lit hallway, a small neon-lit sign blinked on and off. 'AR,' it said, and she wondered idly how long it had been since the 'B' had gone dark.

There seemed little chance of finding Ingram in the barroom, but she knew she had to check.

A pulse of screeching music drifted from beneath a slatted, swinging door. She reached toward it, then hesitated. She thought of the man who'd come on to her minutes before. She remembered how he'd terrorized the desk clerk, how he'd looked at her as if she were something that had been gift-wrapped just for him, how his green eyes had turned to chips of ice when she'd rebuffed his unwanted advances.

It would be hell to find a room full of men like him on the far side of the door.

It would be worse to have Professor Ingram blame her for forfeiting their appointment.

Brionny took a deep breath, set her shoulders, and pushed open the door.

Music swirled around her, wafted along on a pungent breath of cigarette smoke and liquor fumes. She coughed, blinked her eyes against the artificial darkness—and felt her heart plummet to her shoes.

The good news was that Edgar Ingram was definitely not in the room. The bad news was that the men who instantly turned toward her made the man in the lobby look like a candidate for Boy Scout of the Year.

Brionny swallowed. Her mouth opened, then closed. 'Sorry,' she said briskly. She swung around quickly—but not quickly enough. A man had already slipped from one of the stools that ran the length of the bar and started in her direction.

'Buenas noches, señorita.'

She looked up. He was not tall, but what he lacked in height he made up in girth. He looked like a barrel, Brionny thought, with tree trunks for arms and legs. He grinned, flashing a smile that revealed shining gold teeth and clouds of bad breath.

Brionny smiled politely. 'I'm afraid I don't speak Spanish,' she said, lying without hesitation. 'If you'll excuse me—'

'Iss no problem, *señorita*.' Barrel Man grinned and put a beefy hand on her arm. 'I speak the Anglish perfect.'

'You certainly do,' she said brightly. 'Now if you'd just—'

'I buy you drink, yes?'

'No. No, thank you very much, I'm not thirsty.'

Her answer brought a roar of laughter. 'She no thirs'y,' he said to the room at large. The men who understood him chuckled, then translated for their fellows. Within seconds, everyone was laughing gaily. Brionny smiled too, although it wasn't easy.

'Would you let go of my arm, please?' she said politely.

Barrel Man chuckled. 'Why?'

'Why?' Brionny swallowed drily. 'What do you mean, why? Because-because—'

'We danze,' he said.

'No.'

'Yes.' His arm slid around her waist.

Brionny dug in her heels. 'No,' she repeated, her voice sharp. 'I have no intention of—'

She gasped as his hand dropped low on her hip.

'Dammit,' she snapped, grasping his wrist, 'don't do that!'

Barrel Man shot a sly glance toward his friends. 'Dammit,' he mimicked in a high, mincing voice, 'doan do that!'

'You have no right—'

His hand curved around her bottom. Oh God, Brionny thought—and all at once a dangerously lazy voice spoke from behind her.

'She's right, pal.'

Brionny and Barrel Man both swung around. The man from the lobby stood silhouetted in the doorway, his posture relaxed yet definitely threatening, shoulders back, arms flexed, legs slightly apart. He looked, she thought, as if he was ready to take on the world.

'Let go of the lady,' he said softly.

Barrel Man smiled. 'Why should I?'

The man smiled too. 'Because she belongs to me.' Brionny's head came up sharply. 'She's my woman,' he said, flashing her a warning look. 'Do you understand, *compadre?*'

Whether Barrel Man understood or not was debatable, but Brionny suddenly did. I can get you out of here, the man in the doorway was saying, but only if you cooperate.

As choices went, it was better than nothing.

She took a breath, smiled, and tossed her head so that her hair flew back from her face.

'Well,' she said, 'it's about time. Where have you been?'

He grinned. 'You see how much she loves me, *compadre?*' His smile vanished and he looked straight at Barrel Man. 'For the last time, man. Take your hand off her.'

There was a moment that seemed to stretch on forever. Everyone in the room seemed to be waiting, waiting—and then the man standing next to Brionny laughed and, with exaggerated care, lifted his hand from her backside.

'You mus' keep a better watch on your woman,' he said.

The man in the doorway smiled. 'You're right. I looked away for a couple of seconds and, *caramba,* she was gone.' He looked at Brionny, then raised his band and crooked his finger at her, just as he had done to the hapless desk clerk. 'OK, baby,' he said. 'Let's go.'

His eyes locked on hers and she could see the warning burning like a cold flame in their green depths. Don't do anything stupid, he was saying; this isn't over yet.

She stepped away from her admirer and walked toward him, her gaze locked on his face. He still had that lazy look about him but she could see how deceptive it was. He was ready for trouble, perhaps even hoping for it.

'Don't stop now, woman!'

She looked up, not realizing her steps had faltered until she heard that low-pitched warning. Her rescuer, it you could call him that, was still smiling, but she could hear the tension in his voice, see it in the way his eyes kept scanning the room behind her.

Her legs felt like lead. She took a step, then another, and he reached out impatiently, wrapped his hand around her wrist, and tugged her forward. She fell into the hard curve of his arm, her body molding against his side.

'Hello, lover,' he said, and he bent and kissed her, hard, on the mouth. 'Smile, lady,' he growled, his lips against her ear. 'Smile as if you mean it—unless you'd rather give our friend with the mouth full of nuggets another shot at getting lucky this evening!'

Brionny forced a smile to her face. 'You're despicable,' she whispered.

He grinned. 'She says I'm irresistible,' he called to the watching men, then added something in Spanish that made them roar with laughter as he led her out the door.

As soon as they were in the corridor, Brionny shoved her elbow into his ribs.

'You can let go of me now,' she said.

'You're welcome,' he answered, hustling her down the hallway at his side.

'All right. Thank you for your help. Now let me go.'

'When I'm good and ready.'

'Dammit, are you deaf?' She was trotting along on her toes, struggling as much to match his stride as to free herself from his unwanted embrace. 'I said—'

'I know what you said.' His arm tightened around her as he marched her toward the lobby. 'It's what *I* say that counts right now.'

'Listen here, mister, you may have saved me from— from an embarrassing situation, but that doesn't give you the right to—'

'Embarrassing?' He stopped dead and swung her around to face him, his eyes glaring into hers. 'Is that what you call that little scene I stumbled into? Hell, if that's all it was, I'll take you straight back to the boys and—'

'No!' Brionny spoke quickly, almost breathlessly. 'I—I wouldn't want to go back there.'

He nodded. 'I'm glad to see you've got some kind of brain in that head.'

She flushed. 'All right. I suppose I do owe you a thank-you, but that doesn't mean—'

'What in hell were you doing in there, anyway?'

'Look, I don't owe you—'

'You just got done telling me you did.'

She glared at him. 'I said I owed you my thanks, not an explanation, Mr-Mr—'

'McClintoch. Slade McClintoch. And I still want to know what you were doing in the bar. Come to think of it, what in hell are you doing in the Florinda?'

'I'm a guest here, if it's any of your business.'

'The Florinda doesn't have "guests", it has poor unfortunates who have no choice but to spend the night under its roof.'

Brionny smiled coldly. 'I couldn't have said it better myself.'

'Come on, baby, tell the truth. You're with one of those fancy tours and you went off on your own to see how the other half lives.'

'Damn you!' Brionny twisted away from him, dug furiously into her pocket, and pulled out her room key. 'Is this good enough to convince you that I belong here?'

He looked at the key, then at her. 'Either your travel agent's crazy or you are.'

'Thank you for that wonderful piece of information. Now, if you'll excuse me—'

'The next time you're desperate for a drink, go down to the corner, buy a fifth of tequila, and take it to your room.'

'Yes. I'm sure that works wonderfully for you, Mr McClintoch. But I happen to have been looking for someone—not that it's any of your business.'

Slade grinned. 'Yeah? Well, you sure as hell found someone, didn't you?'

'How dare you speak to me that way?'

'You're lucky I'm speaking to you at all. I could have taken one look at the mess you'd stirred up—'

'Me? I didn't stir anything up. Those men—'

Footsteps sounded in the hall. Slade looked up. The guy who resembled a barrel with legs was ambling toward them, flanked by a couple of his buddies. When he spotted them, his pace quickened.

Slade glanced at the woman, standing there with her room key dangling from her fingertips and fire blazing in her eyes.

'Shut up,' he hissed.

'I won't! Just who do you think you—?'

He cursed, snatched the key from her hand, and swung her up into his arms. She squealed and punched him in the shoulder as he strode into the lobby, hard enough so that he knew that beneath the curving softness of her body there was some surprisingly firm muscle.

'Put me down! Do you hear me? You put me down this minute!'

'*Señor.*' The voice and the footsteps accompanying it were closer. 'Hey, *señor,* has the lady change' her mind?'

The woman in Slade's arms was struggling harder now. And she was still mouthing off, calling him every kind of bastard, demanding he set her on her feet. If she didn't start behaving herself, he thought grimly, they were both going to be in trouble.

'Dammit, lady,' he growled as he made his way past the goggle-eyed desk clerk and started up the stairs. 'I told you to keep quiet.'

'I won't!'

'You will,' he said, and covered her mouth with his.

It was not a real kiss, it was simply a way to convince anybody who needed convincing of his ownership, to silence the damned fool woman until he dumped her in her room. It was the only way he could think of to get the both of them out of there without first having to take on The Barrel and Company, although Slade was beginning to think that might not be a bad idea, considering his growing irritation at how quickly a rotten day was getting steadily worse.

What the kiss wasn't supposed to be, he thought as he jammed her key into her door and elbowed his way into her room, was something that would turn him inside out. But hell, that was the way it felt. And when he kicked the door shut, dumped the woman on the bed and looked down at her, he took one look at her flushed face and glazed eyes and knew that that was the way it had felt to her, too.

'Damn,' Slade said softly, and he came down beside her on the bed and kissed her again.

CHAPTER TWO

Two weeks later, standing knee-deep in a tangle of reeds beside a jungle pool, Brionny thought of Slade McClintoch—something she did with regularity but certainly not with pleasure—and muttered a word that would have put Professor Ingram's hair on end, had he been there to hear it.

But the professor was back at their campsite, sitting propped against a tree, making yet another entry about the Eye of God in his personal journal while the native cook prepared lunch.

Making journal entries was all he'd done since they'd found the Eye two days ago. The professor wasn't well; Brionny was sure of it now. And it worried her. He was seventy if he was a day, and they were a million miles from nowhere. When she'd tried questioning him, he'd given her as sharp-tongued a reply as he had in Italpa.

'My health is my concern, Miss Stuart. Keeping records is yours. This is the find of the century and I want it well documented.'

There was no arguing with his logic. The Eye would make Ingram's reputation and go a long way toward establishing her own. That she couldn't seem to work up the proper level of excitement was entirely Slade McClintoch's fault.

'The bastard!' she hissed into the silence surrounding the pool.

It was ridiculous that remembering a man she would surely never see again should spoil such an achievement. Other expeditions had tried to find the Eye but with no success. Ingram had put in years of painstaking research and half a dozen prior field trips, most of them made before Brionny had been born. It had all paid off. He'd gone straight to the ruins of the Forbidden City, then to the statue that contained the emerald.

'Ahh,' he'd sighed as he'd wrenched the stone from where it had lain for centuries. 'Be grateful you were part of his extraordinary event, Miss Stuart.'

'I am, sir,' Brionny had said. She'd reached out, touched the stone—and suddenly thought of Slade McClintoch, whose eyes had blazed with fire like the emerald's when he'd come down beside her on the bed in her hotel room.

With a choked cry, she'd pulled back her hand. Ingram's bushy brows had risen in surprise.

'Superstitious, Miss Stuart?' he'd said with a hint of contempt.

Brionny had grasped at the excuse. 'No, sir,' she'd said, somehow managing to smile, 'but you must admit it's not every day you get to risk the Curse of the Mali-Mali, is it?'

Of course, she thought as she unstrapped the webbed belt at her waist and laid it beside the pool, she hadn't really meant it. She came from a long line of scientists who scoffed at superstition. The gear that hung from her belt was a link to her distinguished heritage—light in weight but heavy in tradition. The battered water canteen had accompanied her maternal grandfather through the jungles of Asia and Africa. The brass-handled camp knife had been with her father's father on his explorations in Central America. And the pearl-handled revolver had been her own father's companion on his expeditions to New Guinea.

'You never know what to expect in the field, Brionny,' he'd said solemnly when he'd handed it on to her.

Or in the bedroom, she thought, and her face flamed.

Dammit! How long was she going to be plagued by the humiliating memory of what Slade McClintoch had done to her? She sank down on a fallen log and began unlacing her boots. It was like having a film clip stuck in her head. All she had to do was let her guard down and it would start to roll.

She kicked the boots off and peeled away her heavy socks, her jaw tightening as she thought back to the way McClintoch had scooped her up, marched her through the lobby. The humiliation of it. And then he'd kissed her, the typical reaction of a primitive male trying to assert dominance over an assertive female.

And then—and then...

Brionny blew out her breath. And then he'd dumped her on the bed, and everything had gone wrong.

She remembered looking up, seeing the darkness of his eyes.

He's going to kiss me again, she'd thought, very calmly.

She should have slugged him. Or raked his face with her nails. Or kneed him in the groin. She should have done *something,* dammit! Even throwing back her head and letting out a yell would have been an improvement over what she *had* done—which was nothing. Absolutely nothing. She'd lain there like the log she was sitting on and-and—

She sprang to her feet, yanked her T-shirt over her head, and tossed it on a shrub. Who was she kidding?

If only she really *had* lain there like a log! But she hadn't. What she'd done was rise to the kiss like a trout to a well- cast fly.

And McClintoch, the bastard, had taken advantage of that instant of insanity. He'd drawn her close in his arms, slipped his tongue between her lips. Sometimes she thought she could still feel the hardness of his body pressing against hers, smell his scent, taste the heat of his mouth. She could feel the brush of his fingers as he lifted her blouse and cupped her breast...

'Damn you, Slade McClintoch!'

She yanked down the zipper of her denim shorts, pulled them off, and high-kicked them on to the shrub next to the T-shirt. At least she'd come to her senses before it was too late, recognizing what he was up to, that he was taking advantage of her disorientation and turning it into fun and games time for his own selfish pleasure.

There was grim satisfaction in recalling the glazed look on his face when she'd begun to struggle beneath him. It had been the look of a man who'd almost managed to snag a prize he knew he didn't deserve and suddenly saw it being snatched out from under his nose.

'No, sweetheart,' he'd whispered huskily, his breath a sigh against her lips, 'don't stop now.'

But she had, pounding her fists against the rock-hard wall of his shoulders, telling him to get the hell off her. When he'd drawn back and stared down at her as if she'd gone crazy, she'd rolled away from him, yanked open the drawer of the rickety bedside table, pulled out her father's revolver, and jammed it into his side.

Oh, that moment was worth remembering!

'Get up,' she'd said, while the color drained from his face, and he had, by God. He'd risen obediently to his feet, then tried to sweet-talk her into putting the gun down, into admitting that she'd been a willing participant in the kiss and not the outraged victim of his insufferable ego.

And then he'd moved, fast as lightning, his hand clamping down on her wrist, his leg thrusting between hers and sending her tumbling off balance. When it was all over, the revolver was in the corner and she was sprawled across the bed—back in McClintoch's arms.

'A word of advice,' he'd said with a mocking smile. 'A woman who pulls a gun should first learn how to use it.'

'I know how to use it,' she'd started to say, but he'd kissed her into silence, his mouth moving on hers with swift arrogance, although that time his kiss had done nothing but turn her rigid with fear.

She needn't have worried. McClintoch had rolled away from her and risen to his feet.

'Relax, baby,' he'd said with a contemptuous smile. 'I'd sooner sleep with an anaconda.'

Then he'd strolled to the door, opened it, and vanished from her life like a bad dream.

A bad dream, she thought, shuddering. Yes, that was what his brief intrusion into her life had been, a bad dream. And now, she thought as she stepped into the water, now it was time to set it aside and forget it had ever happened. She would concentrate on what came next—first the long trek back to Italpa and then the exciting business of bringing the Eye home to the museum in triumph. A year from now she'd have her doctorate, and Slade McClintoch wouldn't even be a memory.

She sighed, luxuriating in the silken feel of the water. It felt cool in comparison to the hot, breathless stillness

of the air. She glanced around before reaching behind
her and unclasping her bra, but there was nothing to
worry about. Who was going to see her? The campsite
was easily half a mile away. She drew back her arm
and the bra went sailing into the reeds.

'To hell with you, Slade McClintoch,' she yelled,
took a breath, and dove beneath the water. She came
up sputtering in the centre of the pool just as a pair of
scarlet macaws swooped overhead. The birds landed on
a branch, cocked their handsome heads, and shrieked.

Brionny pushed the wet hair back from her face.
'What is it?' she said, laughing. 'Do you think I'm being too harsh on the man? Believe me, I'm not. He's a
number one, *el primo* rat. That's just what I'd tell him
if I ever saw him again.'

Which, thank heaven, she would not.

Smiling, she fell back into the water and let herself
drift. She felt better than she had in days. Maybe it was
finally getting wet all over instead of just being soaked
with her own sweat. Maybe it was saying out loud what
had been bottled up inside her for two weeks. Whatever
it was, she felt free. It was as if she'd exorcized a ghost.
Slade McClintoch was gone, poof, just like that. She
would never think of him again, never—

'I don't believe it,' a voice roared. 'Dammit, woman,
what in hell are you doing here?'

No, Brionny thought, no, no, no—

She dug her feet into the sandy bottom, shoved forward, and stared across the water.

'Oh my God,' she whispered, and dove for cover.

It couldn't be. But it was.

Slade McClintoch was standing on a rise just across
the way.

*   *   *

No, Slade thought; no, it couldn't be.

But it was. It was the woman from the Hotel Florinda, Brawna Stevens, or Brianna Smith—dammit, what was her name? He'd asked the desk clerk before he'd left the hotel—

Brionny. Brionny Stuart. Her name had slipped his mind but nothing else about her had. The cap of shining golden hair. The eyes as blue as summer and as wide as a fawn's. The way the soft curve of her breast had felt, thrusting against his hand—and now the quickest glimpse of that breast, rising rounded and full, tipped with pale rose, a flower blooming softly against the green water of the pool.

His body tightened as memories rushed back. The feel of her in his arms. The heat of her, and the perfumed scent—

The unyielding obstinacy of her. The disdain. The ease with which she'd shoved a gun into his gut.

His face set in grim lines as he made his way toward the water. The woman was a spoiled brat. He'd grown up poor in a town owned by people like her; the contempt with which she'd treated him brought back a thousand ugly memories. He knew exactly how she viewed anyone she deemed unfit to exist on her social plateau.

The only unusual thing about Brionny Stuart was that she had a damnable ability to be in the wrong place at the wrong time. She'd managed it at the Florinda and she was managing it now, in the middle of the jungle, lolling around as if she were in a backyard swimming-pool where there was nothing evil lurking in the shadows.

Slade fought back the desire to spin around and check out the jungle behind him. There was no need to do it, not after he'd already done it a dozen times in the past couple of hours, ever since a Mali-Mali arrow had gone zinging into a tree just ahead of him. After enough years in places like this you knew when something was meant to kill you and when it was meant to warn. The arrow had been a message, but he wasn't sure how to read it. Was he being told to go back, or was he being warned away from something that lay ahead? He had to know, before he could send any of his people into possible danger, and so he'd gone on, not knowing exactly what he was looking for but certainly not expecting to find this.

Ahead, in the pool, the woman finally surfaced, just enough so her head and neck stuck up from the water. What in hell was she doing here? There was nobody cleared for this area but his surveying crew and a couple of archaeologists—bad news in itself, considering what they were after. It was touchy enough bringing a crew and equipment into the jungle. Letting a pair of dried-up scientists look for and maybe walk off with a sacred stone would only make matters worse.

Dammit, but this place was getting as crowded as Central Park on a summer Sunday. A construction crew. A pair of weasely mummies from some museum. And now whatever party of tourists the woman was with— God, what a mess.

Slade put his hands on his hips, glared at Brionny Stuart, and let her have the full force of his anger.

'Get out of that water,' he snarled.

Brionny's mouth firmed. 'You can't frighten me,' she said, wishing the words would make it so. Her heart was hammering so hard she was afraid it was going to explode.

He laughed in a way that made her blood go cold. 'Want to bet?'

'I'm not alone,' she said quickly.

'I agree. Your bath tub's probably teeming with life. Piranhas. Leeches. Water-snakes.'

'It isn't,' Brionny said quickly. Too quickly. He was trying to scare her, and she was helping him do it. 'I checked,' she said, with more assurance than she felt. 'Anyway, I didn't mean that. I meant that I didn't come down here by myself.'

Slade made an elaborate show of looking around. 'No?'

'No. My guides—'

'Come on, Miss Stuart, stop the bull. There's no one here but you and me. Now, get your tail out of there. Fast.'

'I'm not alone, I tell you. If you so much as take a step closer, I'll scream.'

'You'll…' He shot her a look that was part incredulity, part disgust. 'By God, lady, you have one hell of an inflated opinion of yourself. What do you think's going on here?'

'I know what's going on,' Brionny said, mentally measuring the distance from where she crouched to the bank where her pistol lay hidden among the reeds. 'You've been following me, and—' His bark of laughter cut her short. 'What's so funny?'

'You. You're what's funny. You think I've followed you for the past—what's it been since that night? Ten days? Two weeks? Do I look like some love-smitten boy?'

'You expect me to believe it's just coincidence that's made you turn up here?'

Slade glowered darkly and folded his arms over his

chest. 'One of life's lousiest lessons is that fate is not necessarily kind. Do us both a favor, OK? Get out of that pool before I come in and get you.'

Brionny looked toward the bank again. If he'd let her get to her clothing, that would put the pistol within arm's length.

'I'm counting to three, lady. One. Two. Th—'

'Let me get my clothes,' she said, nodding toward the adorned shrub.

'Go ahead.'

'Turn your back first.'

He glared at her, his face expressionless, then shrugged. 'Two minutes,' he said impassively.

He turned away, his long legs planted firmly apart. Brionny hesitated, then paddled furiously for the bank. Water cascaded from her body as she rose and stepped on shore.

'Ninety seconds and counting.'

The bra. Where was the bra?

'Eighty seconds.'

Never mind the bra. She grabbed her T-shirt, tugged it over her head with shaking hands. Her shorts clung to her wet underpants, then snagged as she zipped them up.

'Fifty seconds. By the time I turn around, you'd better be—'

He heard the click of the safety as she released it. Son of a bitch, he thought wearily, and raised his eyes to the sky.

'Turn around, Mr McClintoch.'

'Listen,' he said, 'you're making one hell of a mistake.'

'I said, turn around.'

He did, slowly, his hands lifted. Well, he thought,

despite what had happened in the hotel room, she was right. She knew how to use the gun. She was standing erect, holding it in a no-nonsense, two-handed grip. Her hair was plastered to her head, her feet were bare, she wore no make-up at all that he could see. Except for the sweet, lush outline of her breasts beneath the damp T-shirt and the long, curved line of her hips and thighs, she looked like a fourteen-year-old—a fourteen-year-old with a gun she wasn't afraid to use.

'Take it easy,' he said quietly.

She looked at the gleaming machete that hung from his belt. 'Drop that machete, Mr McClintoch, and then start walking this way.'

'Sure.' The machete fell to the ground. 'Just do me a favor. Put the safety back on, will you?'

Brionny waved him towards the foot trail that led back to camp. 'I said, start walking.'

'Sure,' he said again, and as he did he shot a horrified look over her shoulder and yelled, 'Look out!'

Even as she spun around, Brionny knew she'd been had. But the realization came a second too late. Slade was on her instantly, moving with the speed and grace of a big cat. They fell to the ground together, rolling over and over, his hand clasping her wrist, forcing the pistol up and away.

'Let go of me, you bastard,' she panted.

'Let go of the gun,' he said.

'No! No, I—'

His hand closed over hers. The shot was an explosion of sound, echoing and re-echoing across the little clearing. The macaws screamed and rose up with a whir of wings, and then there was silence. Slade was lying across her, one hand still clasping her wrist, the other clutching the gun.

'Now you've done it,' he said softly.

Brionny's pulse began to gallop. 'Yes, I have. They'll hear that, in camp; they'll come after me—'

He rolled off her and got to his feet. 'Get your shoes on.'

She stared at him while her heart slowed its gallop. 'What?'

'Come on, Stuart. We haven't got all day.'

She did as he'd ordered, her eyes still on his. 'Where are we going?'

'To your camp.' She watched as he checked the safety catch, then tucked the pistol into the waistband of his jeans. 'How far is it?'

'You mean you're not...you won't—?'

He shot her an amused look as he retrieved the machete. 'I know this is going to come as a disappointment, sweetheart, but I've no designs on your body—delightful though it may be.'

She flushed. 'Then why did you follow me? Why did you sneak up on me? Why—?'

'Where are you camped?'

'Up the trail. But—'

She stumbled as he put his hand into the middle of her back and pushed her forward.

'Do you think you can manage to talk and walk at the same time?'

'I can even manage it without you poking at me,' Brionny snapped, twisting away from his prodding hand. 'How about telling me what's going on, McClintoch?'

'Ah, how quickly we forget our manners. A little while ago I was ''Mister'' McClintoch.'

'Dammit, McClintoch—'

'Do you know El Kaia Gorge?' Brionny nodded.

'Well, I'm with the construction crew that's surveying on the other side of it.'

'You mean you work for the company that's going to build that road?' Her face registered distaste. 'I might have known.'

Slade's eyes narrowed. 'What's the problem, Stuart? Do people who put in an honest day's labor offend your delicate sensibilities?'

What offended her sensibilities was the thought of a road through the jungle, but there was no reason in the world to explain herself to this man.

'If you work on the far side of the gorge,' Brionny said coolly, 'then what were you doing crossing it?'

'Sorry, lady. If you folks had a "Keep Out" sign posted, I didn't see it.' His smile thinned. 'All I saw was an arrow, shot into a tree on the trail ahead of me.'

'Such poor aim,' she said sweetly. 'What a pity.'

'It wasn't poor aim at all,' he said, giving her another little shove. 'It was deliberate. The arrow was a warning.'

'Well, of course it was. Somebody was telling you they don't like the idea of that road, McClintoch. Surely you can—'

'It was a Mali-Mali arrow.' He flashed her a cool smile. 'Maybe you've heard of them.'

'I've heard of them.' Certainly she'd heard of them. Hadn't she just helped Professor Ingram make off with their fabled treasure?

'Then you also know they're not a tribe to fool with. They're tough and dangerous.'

'Don't be silly. They're just secretive and—'

'They're also headhunters—or didn't your guide bother mentioning that?'

'They used to be headhunters,' Brionny said, giving

him a pitying look. 'There's no proof at all that they still—'

'Listen, I'm not going to get into a debate here, Stuart. The point is they're angry about something.'

'Of course they are. Your road. Why else would they shoot at you?'

Slade grabbed her arm. 'Be quiet!'

'Why? Because I'm saying something you don't want to—'

She gasped as he clamped his hand over her mouth and drew her back against him.

'Look,' he said, his lips against her ear.

Brionny looked. She saw the campsite just ahead, and Professor Ingram still sitting at the foot of the tree, his notebook in his lap.

'So?' she said, around Slade's fingers, her voice automatically dropping to the same whispery level as his. 'I don't see—'

'I don't either. Where are the other tourists?'

'What tourists? There's just the professor and me.'

'The professor and…' He groaned. 'No. You can't be.'

'Can't be what?'

'Are you saying you're the archaeologists searching for the Eye of God?'

Brionny went very still. 'How do you know about that?'

'Don't answer a question with a question,' he said irritably. A woman. And an old man, he thought, staring at the professor's white hair. 'Didn't you people at least have the brains to hire native porters and guides?'

'We're not fools, McClintoch. We have seven men who—'

Who weren't there any more, she thought, staring at

the campsite. Where was everybody? When she'd left the cook had been preparing lunch, while the other men talked softly among themselves.

'Stay here.'

Slade's voice was low and taut with command. Brionny opened her mouth, prepared to tell him she didn't take orders, but then she thought better of it. Something was wrong. Very wrong. No sign of the guides, no sounds, no movement...

The hair rose on the back of her neck. Professor Ingram hadn't stirred in all the time they'd been watching him.

She watched as Slade circled the little camp, then carefully made his way into it. He squatted down beside the professor. After a minute he rose to his feet and turned to her, but by then she understood.

'He's dead, isn't he? she said, her voice quavering a little.

'Yes,' Slade said bluntly. 'From the looks of him, I'd say he had a heart attack.'

Brionny let out her breath. 'Then, it wasn't—he wasn't—'

'No. Your professor died a natural death.'

She nodded. It all added up. The way Ingram had looked the past months, the bouts of weakness he wouldn't admit to...

She swayed unsteadily. Instantly Slade was beside her, his hands clasping her shoulders.

'You're not going to be sick on me,' he said sharply.

Brionny swallowed and looked up at him. 'I know it's beyond you to understand,' she said shakily, 'but some of us have human emotions. I can't help it if I—'

'Yes. You *can* help it.' His hands tightened on her, and now she saw something in his eyes she could not

quite identify. 'Look around you, Stuart. The professor's dead from natural causes. But nothing else is natural here. Your Indians are gone. Your stuff's been rifled.'

'Rifled?' she said, staring at him.

'Rifled,' he said flatly. 'Take a look.'

He was right. Her backpack lay open on the ground,
the contents strewn around it. The professor's pack had
received the same treatment, and their storage boxes had
been torn apart.

'But—but who would do such a thing? And why?'

Slade's eyes bored into hers. 'Someone who wanted
something you and the professor had.'

'Our supplies? But they're still—'

'The Eye of God.'

Brionny's heart thumped. That was twice he'd mentioned the Eye. Was that what had brought him here?
Had he come looking for the expedition that had gone
after the emerald?

Her gaze skittered past Slade to where a dozen tin
cans lay spilled across the ground. The tea canister that
held the emerald lay undisturbed. It was a good place
to hide the stone, Ingram had said. No one would think
to look for it there.

'Well?' Slade's voice was harsh. 'Aren't you going
to check and see if whoever did this took your precious
stone?'

Brionny looked into his eyes. They were the same
color as the emerald and just as cold. Her heart thumped
again but she spoke calmly.

'How could they,' she said, 'when we never found
it?'

Slade's mouth narrowed. 'You're telling me the emerald wasn't in this camp?'

She nodded. 'That's right. We looked for it, but we didn't find it.'

'Then why did your men take apart your stuff and then run off?'

Brionny shrugged. 'The porters probably got scared when they realized what had happened to Professor Ingram. They're very superstitious, you know. And they probably went through our stuff to see if there was anything worth taking before they—'

'Doesn't that strike you as odd? Doesn't it worry you a little, Stuart?'

It did, but not half as much as finding herself alone in the jungle with a relic worth a fortune and a man with no scruples.

'What worries me,' Brionny said calmly, 'is how I'm going to get back to Italpa without a guide.'

Slade gave her a long, searching look. 'You're right,' he said. 'Getting out of here is our first priority. Pack up whatever you need and we'll get moving.'

She turned away and picked up her backpack. The tin tea box. She had to get to it without Slade seeing her.

'Do you know the way back to the river?' she said as she moved slowly across the campsite, mindlessly picking things up, stuffing them into the pack, her eyes never leaving the tea box.

'Heading for the Italpa would take too long. We'll backtrack on my trail, then cross the rope bridge at the gorge. There's a radio at the construction site; we'll call for a 'copter to come and get you.'

Would he take her safely to the construction site? Yes, why not? So long as he thought she'd found nothing, he'd probably be eager to get her out of here so he could come back and set out on his own search.

'Fine,' Brionny said. She glanced over her shoulder. Slade had grabbed a shovel from the expedition's equipment and was digging into the spongy soil. Quickly she reached for the tea box and dumped it into her pack. 'Well,' she said briskly, 'I'm ready.'

'Grab something to dig with, then, and give me a hand.' He looked up as she came toward him. 'We've got to bury your professor before the animals find him.'

Brionny shuddered as she reached for a trowel. 'Are you always this blunt, McClintoch?'

He grinned. 'Not to worry, Stuart. A stroll through the jungle, a trot across the bridge, and you'll have seen the last of me.'

Four hours later, Brionny came stumbling out of the dense trees panting, her clothing stained with sweat. Slade was standing a few feet away. Beyond him she glimpsed a gorge so deep and endless that it made her stomach rush into her throat.

'My God,' she whispered, 'I didn't think…'

She turned away, telling herself this was no time to give in to her fear of heights, reminding herself that she had only to make it across the rope bridge and she'd not only never have to look at Slade McClintoch again, but she'd be on her way back to Italpa—wonderful, sophisticated Italpa—and then to New York, bearing the stone that would memorialize Edgar Ingram and put her feet firmly on the path of academic success.

'I don't believe it,' Slade said in a flat, strained voice.

Brionny blinked. 'Don't believe what?'

He reached out, caught her by the wrist, and dragged her forward. She threw a desperate look toward the yawning chasm at her feet, then stumbled back, her eyes clamped shut.

'Take a look.'

'I can't,' she said. 'I have acro—I'm afraid of—'

'I know what acrophobia means, Stuart.' His arms swept around her and he drew her back against him, lending her trembling body the hard support of his. 'Open your eyes,' he demanded.

She took a deep breath, forcing aside the dizziness as well as the incongruous thought that it came as much from being in McClintoch's arms as it did from the swooning drop before her.

'What am I supposed to see?' she said, her eyes still tightly shut.

'Dammit,' he said angrily. 'Are you blind? Look!'

She did—and her heart dropped to her feet.

The bridge that was supposed to cross El Kaia Gorge was gone. Where there should have been swaying rope, there was only endless, empty space.

CHAPTER THREE

THE GORGE was impossible, at least two hundred feet deep and surely twice as wide. Brionny's gaze flew across it. What remained of the bridge hung drooping down the opposite cliff wall, swaying delicately in the wind.

Her stomach contracted into a hard, cold knot. Instinctively she clasped Slade's encircling arms. Her fingers dug into his muscled flesh as she fought the wrenching nausea that heights had always inspired.

Slade drew her closer. 'Easy, Stuart.' Step by step, he moved her back until the yawning gulf was no longer at her feet. 'There's nothing to be afraid of.'

'I know.' She swallowed hard. 'It's—it's completely irrational, but—'

'But entirely human.'

Brionny tilted her head back, just enough so she could see his face. He was smiling, but the smile was without derision.

'We all have our flaws, Stuart.'

She forced a smile to her lips. 'Not in my family,' she said, only half jokingly.

Slade's brows lifted. 'Ah,' he said, 'you're descended from a long line of saints, hmm?'

She laughed. 'Not saints. Scientists.'

'And scientists don't have irrational fears?'

'Well, it's not logical. I mean, when you understand what causes those fears—'

'Bull. Who pumped you full of such garbage, Stuart? You're as entitled to be scared of the shadows under the bed as the rest of us.'

The upside-down philosophy surprised her. Slade McClintoch was muscle and macho, a man who'd surely never been afraid of anything in his life, yet he was assuring her that it was OK to be exactly that.

'Anyway,' he said, 'I can make you forget your phobia.'

'You can?'

'Sure.'

'How?'

He smiled. 'Like this,' he said softly, and kissed her.

The kiss took her by surprise. There was no time to think; there was time only to feel the warmth of his lips and the answering warmth spiraling through her blood—and then sanity returned.

Brionny pushed him away. 'What are you doing?' she demanded.

Slade grinned. 'I told you. I'm helping you deal with your fear.'

'That's pitiful!'

'Really? I haven't had any complaints that I can remember.'

Her chin rose. 'Truly pitiful—that you should have to get your women by taking advantage of them in their worst moments.'

If she'd thought to insult him, she'd failed. He grinned again and shrugged.

'You know what they say. Whatever method works.'

'Well, this method's worked one time too many. Don't try it again.'

The grin faded from his lips, was replaced by a swift and dangerous smile.

'Threats, Stuart?' he said softly.

Brionny forced her gaze to remain locked with his. She was in no position to threaten him and they both knew it, but backing down would be an error.

'Promises, McClintoch. We'll be out of this place eventually. And when we are—'

He laughed. 'What will you do? Report me to the authorities for saving your pretty tail yet one more time?'

'You haven't saved anything yet,' she said coldly.'Or have your forgotten that we're standing at the edge of El Kaia Gorge—with absolutely no way to cross it?'

Her taunt hit home. There was pleasure in seeing the self-satisfied grin wiped from his face—but no pleasure at all in suddenly reminding herself of what she had, for a few minutes, managed to forget.

'Yeah.' Slade nodded. 'Let me take a look at what's left of that rope.'

She watched as he walked to the rim of the gorge, held her breath as he squatted down, grasped the short, swaying end of the rope, and drew it to him.

'Dammit,' he said softly.

'What's the matter?'

'I was right.'

Brionny took a hesitant step forward. 'About what?'

'The rope's been cut!'

'Couldn't it have just come apart?'

Slade looked at her as if she'd suggested the bridge might have been carried off by space aliens.

'Of course,' he said coldly. 'Between the time I crossed it this morning and now, all those heavy hemp strands got together, had a meeting, and decided they'd dissolve their partnership. Why didn't I think of that?'

'There's no need to be sarcastic, McClintoch. My explanation is at least as reasonable as yours.'

He waved the end of the rope at her.

'Do you see this?'

Brionny glanced at the rope, then folded her arms over her breasts. 'So?'

'So,' he said through his teeth, 'rope that comes apart by itself doesn't do it with such neat precision.'

She looked at the rope again. 'Neat' was the word for it, she thought. It had been severed as cleanly as a loaf of bread.

Her eyes flew to his. 'But—but who would—?'

'The "who" is easy.' She tried not to shudder as he flung the rope back over the cliff and stood up. 'The Mali-Mali.'

'You can't be sure of that,' Brionny said quickly.

'No.' He shot her a quick, mirthless smile. 'I can't be sure. Hell, can you imagine such poor manners? Whoever did this didn't even leave a calling card.'

'There's no reason to be snide, McClintoch.'

'No. And there's no reason to stick your head in the sand. Someone cut the ropes, and we don't have a long list of suspects.'

'I know that. But there's still no reason to assume—'

He swung toward her, his eyes filled with anger. 'You and Ingram found the stone, didn't you?'

Brionny blinked, 'What—what stone?'

His mouth twisted. 'Don't play games with me, lady. You know damned well what stone. The emerald. You and the old man found it, you took it, and the Mali-Malis want it back.'

'That's not true! I mean—I mean, we didn't take it. I told you, we didn't find it.'

'And that's still your story?'

'It's not a story. It's the truth. And you're wasting your time, McClintoch. You're trying to shift the blame, but you can't.'

'Me? Shift the blame?' He jammed his hands on to his hips. 'For what?'

'If—I repeat if—the Mali-Mali really are angry, it's at you. It was you they shot at.'

'I was a handy target. One outsider's the same as another as far as they're concerned.'

'So you say. But *you* were the target, not the professor and me.'

'The operative word is ''were''. Taking out the bridge puts us on an equal footing.'

'What do you mean?'

'What's the matter, Stuart? Can't your highly trained, upper-class brain process this information? Let me simplify it for you. The bridge is gone. We're stuck here, on this side of the gorge, while the Mali-Malis decide what they want to do next.'

Brionny stared at him. 'But—surely there's something we can do?'

Slade walked slowly to the rim and stared across it. 'So near and yet so far,' he said softly. 'The construction camp is only a couple of hours' walk.'

A couple of hours, Brionny thought, her gaze following his. A handful of miles to a field telephone, to civilization, to whoever was in charge of the company where Slade McClintoch worked, where he'd probably first heard about the easy pickings across the gorge, about the archaeologists who'd come after the fabulous emerald.

'Won't the construction company send someone after you when they realize you're missing?' Brionny felt a surge of hope. Why hadn't she thought of it sooner? 'They'll see that the bridge is out and—'

'No one knows I crossed El Kaia.'

'Someone must. Your boss. Your crew chief. Whatever the man in charge is called.'

Slade looked at her. This was the time to tell her that the man in charge was called Slade McClintoch...

No, the devil within him said, don't do that. Let the lady sweat a while; let her stop looking down her pretty nose at a man she obviously thinks is only slightly better than dirt.

He shrugged lazily. 'I didn't check with anybody before I took off.'

Of course, Brionny thought, she should have known better. Men like him came and went, taking jobs for a few days, walking off when they tired of the work.

'You'll be missed, though,' she said, trying to keep the desperation she suddenly felt from her voice. 'Somebody's bound to realize you're gone and—'

He shot her a pitying smile. 'Give it up, Stuart. No one keeps tabs on me.'

He turned away, jammed his hands into his pockets, and paced along the rim of the gorge.

'Damn,' he said, 'damn, damn, damn.'

'What about repairing the bridge?' Brionny said, more sharply than she'd intended. 'Is there a chance of that?'

Slade looked at her and laughed. 'Can you fly?'

'I already told you, McClintoch, there's no point in being sarcastic.'

'Then try using your head. How can we fix a bridge we can't reach?'

Her gaze flew over the wide chasm again. He was right. The bridge might as well have been on the moon.

'Well, what did people do before the bridge was here?' Slade gave her a look that made her bristle. 'Don't look at me that way,' she snapped. 'I know something about the history of this place, McClintoch. People from both sides of El Kaia have traded back and forth for centuries. Surely they didn't always have a bridge to walk across?'

'Yeah.' He smiled slowly. 'I suppose that's true. Hell, maybe you're not as useless as I thought.'

'Intelligence is never useless,' Brionny said coldly, 'but I wouldn't expect someone like you to understand that.'

Slade's smile narrowed. 'No. No, you're quite right. The only things I understand are sweat and hard work. All the rest is just so much garbage.'

'What a charming philosophy. I just— Hey. Hey!' Her voice rose as Slade bent down, grasped an end of rope, and began to ease himself carefully over the rim. 'What are you doing?'

'Putting my muscles to use. As you just pointed out, it's all I'm good for.'

He grunted softly as he began lowering himself. Brionny saw his muscles strain and expand under the soft, clinging cotton of his T-shirt. A rush of heat blazed through her blood. Vertigo, she thought, and looked quickly away.

'What's the matter, Stuart? I'm not going to fall, if that's what's worrying you.'

'The rope's not long enough to climb down, is it?' she said, ignoring the taunt.

Slade shook his head. 'Not by a long shot. But there's a narrow ledge ten or fifteen feet down—I can get that far. There might be something below it that I can't see from here, strong vines or maybe some footholds—'

'Footholds?' Brionny gave a choked laugh. 'Only if you're a mountain goat.'

'Yeah, well, I'm going to check it out anyway.' Slade squinted up at the sky. 'We've got a little time before it gets dark, enough to see if we have a shot at climbing out of here at first light tomorrow.'

'You're crazy, McClintoch. If you fall—'

'Oh, darling,' he purred, 'how sweet. I didn't think you cared.'

Brionny glared at him. 'Understand something. If you fall and break your head, I'm not coming down after you.'

He gave her a cocky grin. 'Ah, the sweetness of the woman,' he said. Clutching the rope carefully, he maneuvered down another foot. 'Come on, Stuart, think of how great it'll be to stand up there and say, "I told you so", if I go crashing to the bottom.' He looked over his shoulder, then shuddered dramatically. 'Just be sure you say it loud enough so I can hear you. It's a long way down.'

Brionny looked past him to the floor of the gorge. Panic clutched at her belly but she would sooner have died than let him see it. 'Go on,' she said, 'have a good time. There's no accounting for some people's tastes.'

She turned, marched to a mossy boulder, and sat down. With a display of elaborate unconcern, she slipped her arms from the straps of her backpack and set it at her feet. Then she unlaced one of her boots, took it off, and gently massaged her toes. When she looked up again, Slade had vanished from view.

Her shoulders slumped forward. Wonderful. She was stuck in the middle of nowhere with a man whose motives were suspect, and now he'd decided to play at being a human fly. Was she supposed to pray he made it down and back in one piece—or was she better off hoping she never saw his face again? Sighing, she jammed her foot back into the boot and laced it up. If Slade was right a tribe of head-hunting Indians wanted the emerald she carried in her backpack. If *she* was right, it was Slade himself who wanted the stone. Either way, she was in trouble.

She leaned forward and ran her hand lightly over the nylon backpack, her fingers finding and tracing the faint outline of the small metal box that held the Eye.

Only one thing was certain. She had the stone, and she intended to keep it. She wasn't about to lose it, not to a bunch of bloodthirsty savages or to a conniving adventurer.

Professor Ingram had devoted years of his life to finding the Eye. She had been privileged to have been with him when he'd finally achieved his goal. Now it was her responsibility to deliver the emerald safely to the museum, and that was what she would do.

She got to her feet, tucked her hands into the rear pockets of her shorts, and tapped her foot. What was taking so long? McClintoch should have been back by now. She hadn't heard any yells or shouts of distress, so he couldn't have fallen. Had he managed to find a way to the bottom? Come morning, would he expect her to sail over the edge the way he had, follow him down, down, down…?

She shuddered. It was best not to think about that, nor about what it would be like to claw her way up the other side. Instead, she'd concentrate on what it would be like once she was out of the jungle. She smiled. The museum officials would be delighted. Her father would be proud. Her doctorate would be guaranteed...

Where in hell was McClintoch? How long could it take to see if there was a way to the bottom of the gorge?

She took a deep breath, then moved forward a few steps, trying not to think of the chasm ahead or of the man who might lie crumpled at the bottom of it. She didn't like him, but she certainly wouldn't want him to break his neck.

'McClintoch?' she said.

There was no answer. She frowned and took another couple of steps forward. Thickening shadows were beginning to crowd the gorge, turning it from a deep valley into a mysterious slash in the face of the earth.

A chill ran along Brionny's skin. She thought of the first night she'd spent in the rainforest, how nothing had prepared her for the blackness that had suddenly enclosed the campsite. Professor Ingram had looked across the glowing fire at her and given her one of his rare smiles.

'Incredible, isn't it, Miss Stuart?' he'd said.

It had certainly been that. The night had seemed like a living, breathing creature, one with a somewhat malevolent intent. She'd shifted her camp chair closer to a pool of yellow light thrown by one of the butane lanterns.

But there'd be no lanterns tonight. And if Slade didn't hurry, he wouldn't be able to see clearly enough to climb back up.

'McClintoch?' she said. The word came out a whisper, and she cleared her throat and tried again. 'McClintoch? Can you hear me?'

Dammit, where was he?

Something rustled behind her and she looked around, her eyes scanning the perimeter of the jungle. The trees seemed black, almost ominous. The sounds of the night were picking up now, the hiss and hum of insects mingling with the growing chirrup-chirrup of the tree frogs. Soon there'd be other noises too—the growls and grunts of the hunters, the shrill cries of their prey—

Brionny turned a furious face to the gorge. 'Dammit, McClintoch,' she yelled, 'where in hell—?'

A sudden, awful roar burst from the jungle behind her. Brionny screamed and swung around, heart hammering in her breast, then screamed again as a hand fell on her shoulder.

'Easy,' Slade said. 'Easy, Stuart. It's only me.'

She spun toward him. 'Where in God's name have you been?'

His brows lifted. 'That's a hell of a greeting.'

'Do you know how long you have been gone?'

'No.' He grinned. 'I forgot to take along a timer.'

Enraged, she struck out blindly, punching him in the shoulder.

'You bastard! Is everything always a joke with you?'

'Hey. Take it easy.'

'Why?' She punched him again, harder. Slade caught her wrists in one hand, imprisoning them against his chest. 'Why should I take it easy?' she said, her eyes flashing. 'Do you know what it was like to sit here and wonder if you'd fallen and broken your stupid neck?'

'Would it have mattered? You weren't about to come after me if I had. You made that clear, remember?'

'You're damned right I did! And—and it would have served you right if you *had* fallen!'

'Let me get this straight. Are you ticked off because I could have gotten hurt—or because I didn't?'

Brionny stared at him. 'I-I—'

He moved closer to her, still holding her hands in his. She could feel the slow, strong beat of his heart under her fingers.

'Well?' His voice was soft. 'Which is it, Bree?'

'Stop trying to reduce this to-to—'

'To logic.' He smiled. 'But you're a scientist. You pride yourself on logic, don't you?'

His eyes were fixed on hers. How green they were, how deep and smoky.

'You're—you're confusing me, McClintoch.'

'Am I?' He smiled, as if the possibility pleased him.

Brionny swallowed. What was happening to her? The heat of his body was becoming her heat; the hardness of it made her want to lean against him. Her eyes closed and she took a breath, inhaling his clean male scent, the faint musk of his sweat.

'Bree.' One of his hands slid up her throat, framed her face, tilted it up to his. 'Were you afraid I'd been hurt?'

She touched the tip of her tongue to her lips. 'I—I'm not inhuman, McClintoch.'

'Ah.' He nodded and touched his forefinger to the centre of her lower lip. 'That's nice to know.'

'And—and I didn't much relish the possibility of being left here alone.'

'I see.' The tip of his finger traced the seam of her mouth. 'In other words, given the choice between tolerating my intolerable presence and tolerating only your own, you'd sooner cast your vote for me.'

'Yes. No. Dammit, McClintoch, don't do that!'

'Don't do what?' His finger stroked across her lip again. 'This, you mean?'

'Please.' Was that hesitant voice really hers? Why

did it sound that way, as if she was asking for one thing but wanting another?

'Please, McClintoch—'

'Slade. My name is Slade. Don't you think we know each other well enough to be on a first-name basis?'

'We don't know each other at all!' she said, desperately trying to ignore the feel of his finger moving against her flesh. 'We don't—'

'Well, then,' he said, 'we'll just have to remedy that, won't we?'

He bent his head and kissed her, not as he had that first time at the Florinda, nor even the way he had a while before. This kiss had nothing to do with control nor even with passion. It was a soft, almost gentle kiss, the faintest brush of mouth against mouth, and yet Brionny felt as if she was being turned inside out, as if she might lift off the ground and float into the darkening sky.

Slade's arms went around her. 'Bree,' he whispered, and his mouth dropped to hers again.

'No,' she said, but what was the point? She was saying one thing and doing just the opposite, linking her arms around his neck, letting him gather her close. She whimpered as the tip of his tongue traced the path his finger had followed moments ago. His teeth nipped lightly at her lip and she sighed and opened her mouth to his.

'Yes,' he whispered, 'oh, yes!'

His hands cupped her bottom; he lifted her to her toes, drew her forward, and fitted her hips to his. He moved, rotating gently against her, and the world seemed to stand still.

'Please,' she whispered, just as she had a little while ago, only now she knew what she was asking him to do. He did, too. His hand slipped under her shirt. Brionny gasped at the heat of it, at the feeling of his fingers cupping her naked breast. His thumb brushed across her nipple, lightly, lightly—

A deep roar exploded from the jungle again, this time so close that it seemed to shake the ground they stood on.

It was like being doused with a shower of icecold water. Brionny's eyes flew open. She stared up at Slade, shuddered, then dug her fists into his chest.

'Let me go,' she demanded.

'Bree.' His voice was thick, the words slurred. 'Bree, listen—'

'Don't "Bree" me, you—you cheap opportunist!'

'What?'

'I warned you not to try this kind of thing again.'

His hands fell away from her. 'The return of the ice princess.'

'The return of sanity, you mean.'

He smiled tightly. 'Some day, sweetheart, that little hot and cold act's going to get you in deep trouble.'

'Just keep away from me, McClintoch. Can you manage that, do you think?'

'With pleasure,' he said coldly.

'I hope so, because the next time you try anything—'

'You're repeating yourself, Stuart, and anyway I haven't got time to listen.' He brushed past her and, before she could stop him. snatched up her pack and put his arms through the straps. 'Well?' What are you waiting for? Let's get going.'

'Get going where? Didn't you find a path down the cliff?'

'The cliff wall is absolutely smooth below the ledge.'

'Then—then what are we going to do?'

'What do you think we're going to do?' he said impatiently. 'We're going to retrace our steps, pick up the trail you and Ingram took coming in, and follow it back to the river.'

'That's impossible!'

'I couldn't agree more.' In the near-darkness, she could just see the look of disgust on his face. 'The thought of spending the next week with you doesn't thrill me, either.'

'Ten days,' she said, trying to keep her voice under control. 'Ten days, McClintoch. That's how long it takes to walk that trail.'

He shrugged. 'Have you got a better idea?'

Brionny put her hand to her forehead. 'There's got to be something else we can do,' she said, and all at once Slade could hear the desperation in her voice. 'There's got to be.'

He looked at her. The haughty, don't-touch-me look was gone. In its place was not just desperation but fear. She looked, he thought, as she had when he'd first seen her that morning in the lagoon—innocent and scrubbed and younger than her years.

For a moment he thought of taking her in his arms, of telling her that she didn't have a damn thing to be afraid of. He wanted to tell her that he wasn't the villain she obviously thought he was, that he'd never hurt a woman in his life and he sure as hell wasn't going to start with her. Most of all, he wanted to tell her that he didn't give a damn for the emerald he was certain she'd found.

But then he thought of the way she'd looked at him that night at the Florinda, of how she'd looked just moments ago, after she'd realized she'd almost come to life in the arms of a man like him, and his heart hardened.

'The only thing you can do,' he said, 'is make damned sure you keep up the pace—unless you want to stick around and see if that jaguar phones in his dinner reservation again.'

'Jaguar? Is that what…?' She took a deep breath. 'Then—then why are we heading into the jungle? Why don't we camp here for the night?'

'What a great idea, Stuart. Why didn't I think of that? We can stay right here, in the open, with the gorge at our backs so that if the jaguar comes to dine we have nowhere to run. Oh, and we can make things simple for the Mali-Mali, too. I mean, if it turns out I'm right and we're not on their popularity list, they can dispose of us the same way they disposed of that bridge.'

Brionny's eyes widened. 'You don't mean—you can't mean—'

'I noticed a small clearing on the way here. It wasn't much, but it's a lot safer than this.' He gave Brionny a quick, cool smile. 'Your choice, lady. You can tag along and take your chances with me or you can sit here and wait to see what strolls out of the trees first—the jag or the guys with the arrows.'

He turned without waiting for her answer and strode off into the jungle.

Brionny watched him go. Some choice, she thought bitterly. Slade had her pack. Her pistol. Her supplies.

And her emerald.

Oh, yes. It was one hell of a choice, but it was hers to make. Gritting her teeth, she set off after him.

CHAPTER FOUR

THE POSSIBILITY that Slade had lied, that he'd designed an elaborate charade for her benefit, didn't strike Brionny until they were half an hour into the jungle.

At first, she was too preoccupied with trying to match his stride to think of anything. Then, gradually, her legs found the right rhythm and she fell in behind him, near enough to reach out and touch him had she wished—which, of course, she had no desire to do—but not so near that she would be subject to any more lectures or commands.

'Don't fall behind,' he snapped, when she paused to fix her shoelace.

'Aye, aye, Captain, sir,' she said. 'Any other orders?'

Slade shot her a cold glare. 'Yes. I don't like women with smart mouths.'

He turned away and Brionny made a face at his rigid back. What he didn't like were women who couldn't be bullied. Or intimidated. Or scared out of their socks with stories about hungry jaguars and tribes of bloodthirsty headhunters.

And, just that quickly, it came to her.

Suppose he was lying? Not about the jaguar—she'd heard the cat's roar loud and clear, and anyway it was no secret that this stretch of virtually unexplored jungle was home to a considerable number of the big, handsome animals. But that stuff about being pursued by headhunters—what proof did she have that it was true? Yes, the rarely glimpsed Mali-Mali were rumored to have once been headhunters, but that was a long time ago. And it wasn't as if McClintoch had produced the arrow he claimed had been shot into a tree ahead of him on the trail.

As for the bridge at El Kaia Gorge—someone had cut it, all right. Someone had deliberately hacked the swinging ropes in two, probably with a machete.

Slade had a machete. He could easily have cut the ropes himself.

How long would it have taken to do the job? One minute? Two? He'd had plenty of time; she'd come straggling out of the trees at least three or four minutes after him.

He had asked her about the Eye of God and she had denied having it. Maybe he hadn't found her denial convincing. Maybe he thought she at least knew where the emerald was. It he wanted the stone badly enough—and she was certain he did—wouldn't he try almost anything to get information from her? Scaring the wits out of her, then making her totally dependent on him for survival, would be a damned good start.

Brionny stared up the trail. Slade was a dozen yards ahead of her now, his figure vivid in the bright moonlight, marching along as if he owned the world. A knot of rage ballooned in her chest. It was all too neat and tidy: the ravaging band of headhunters supposedly stalking through the jungle, the rope bridge destroyed by vengeance-driven savages... She'd bet everything that none of it was real, that Slade had invented the tale for her benefit.

The only thing she had to fear was him!

This morning she'd awakened in a neatly kept camp,

the junior member of a prestigious scientific team that had achieved the impossible. Now she was a second-class citizen, slogging along on the heels of a self-styled Indiana Jones who barked out orders and expected her to jump.

She might have the academic credentials, but Slade McClintoch had all the tricks—and all her resources.

Brionny glared at his steadily retreating figure. Her gun was tucked into the waistband of his jeans. Her backpack rode easily across his broad shoulders. He had everything of hers that would ensure survival in the jungle—not just the gun but the supplies in her pack, the bags of dried fruits and nuts, the water-purification tablets, the matches, the maps...

And he had the emerald. It was tucked inside the pack, just waiting for him to find. And when he did—when he did...

What unbelievable stupidity had made her stuff the Eye into a box of tea? A man searching for an emerald would go straight for it, just as she had when she'd sought a place to hide the stone. And then it would all have been for nothing—the professor's years of research, his death in the steamy jungle, her future—all of it would be wiped out.

Slade would steal the stone and take off. By the time she found her way to civilization—assuming she did—he'd be long gone, and the Eye would be in the hands of some greedy unscrupulous collector, traded for enough money to keep Slade McClintoch in whiskey or women, or whatever it was men like him wanted, for a long, long time.

Anger made her incautious. Marching along blindly, her mind crowded with unpleasant images and her blood pumping with fury, she didn't see the fallen tree that lay across the narrow trail. Her foot caught in a root and she tumbled to the ground.

Slade stopped and swung towards her as she scrambled to her feet.

'What's the problem?' he snapped.

'No problem,' Brionny shot back. 'Don't worry about me, McClintoch. I assure you I can take care of myself.'

'Am I to assume there's some deep meaning in that remark, Stuart?'

'I don't much care what you assume.'

He smiled tightly. 'You're pushing your luck, lady.'

'My luck ran out the night you and I bumped into each other in The Hotel Florinda.'

'Funny, but I've been thinking the same thing.'

Brionny dusted off her shorts. 'Then you ought to be more than happy to agree to my plan.'

'Let's hear it.'

She smiled brightly. 'You go your way and I'll go mine.'

'You really are a mind-reader, Stuart. As soon as we get to Italpa, that's exactly what we'll do.'

'I don't want to wait until we get to Italpa.' She strode forward and thrust out her hand. 'Give me my pack and my gun and I'll be on my way.'

'On your way to where, if you don't mind my asking?'

'Get that tone out of your voice, dammit! Do you think I can't find my way to the river? I have a map in that pack. I don't need your help, not for a minute.'

'That's not what you said when we found Ingram dead and the camp ransacked.' His voice rose in cruel parody of hers. '"What worries me is how I'm going to get back to Italpa without a guide"' you said.'

'I was in shock. I'd forgotten I had a map. And

you're the only one who thinks that camp was ransacked.'

He laughed. 'What'd they do, Stuart? Check it for souvenirs?'

'Stop trying to change the topic, McClintoch. I want my stuff, and I want it now.'

Slade gave her a pitying look. 'Don't be ridiculous. You wouldn't have a chance on your own.'

'Your concern for my welfare is touching, but—'

'Don't flatter yourself, lady. It's my welfare I'm concerned about. Two people have a better chance of making it out of here than one.'

'Meaning?'

'Meaning two sets of eyes and ears offer greater protection.'

'Against the bloodthirsty savages tracking us?' Brionny smiled coldly. 'I'll take my chances. Just hand over my things.'

'What have you got in this pack?' Slade demanded.

She felt her heart kick into her ribs. 'What do you mean?'

'Come on, Stuart, it's not a difficult question. What's in here? Food? Matches?'

'Get to the point, McClintoch.'

'We've got a ten-day walk ahead of us, a handful of resources, a map and a gun. Assuming I let you go off on your own—'

'Assuming you *let* me? Who died and made you king?'

'Assuming I did,' he said with airy disdain, 'how do you propose we split those things up?'

'Why should we split them up? They belong to me.'

Slade's eyebrows rose in mock disbelief. 'Where's your sense of morality? Are you saying you'd just watch me set off alone, without any supplies or weapons?'

'You're a big boy, McClintoch. You got yourself into this mess—you can get yourself out of it.'

He put his hands on his hips. 'Is this the same woman who told me she wasn't entirely without human feelings?'

Color flooded her cheeks. 'This is a ridiculous conversation!'

'Yeah. It is.' He settled the pack more firmly on his shoulders. 'Sorry, Stuart. Whether we like it or not, we're stuck with each other until we reach the river.'

'What you mean is I'm stuck with you,' Brionny said angrily, 'because you've requisitioned my supplies for you own use.'

'If that's the way you see it.'

'Is there another way to see it?'

Slade sighed. 'Even with a mountain of supplies and a gun in each hand, you'd never make it back to Italpa on your own.'

She looked as if she wanted to slap his face, Slade thought as he turned on his heel and set off along the trail again without giving her a chance to answer. Not that he cared. This wasn't about winning popularity contests; it was about survival.

Would she fall in line and follow after him? He smiled grimly to himself. Sure she would. She hated his guts, but she wasn't stupid. No matter what she said, she had to know he was right, that she needed him to make it back to Italpa.

He sighed wearily. On the other hand, she was dense as stone when it came to some things. The emerald, for instance. The Mali-Mali seemed convinced she had it, or had it stashed. He had no reason to doubt them. He didn't doubt the Indians' ability to keep them from reaching Italpa alive, either.

The messages had been easy to read. A trade, the Mali-Mali were saying. Free passage to civilization for the Eye of God.

Slade thought it sounded more than fair. The problem was convincing Brionny Stuart. Even after she'd seen what the headhunters had done to the rope bridge at El Kaia, she'd refused to tell him the truth.

But she would, eventually. It was just a matter of time. She was pigheaded and stubborn, but she wasn't dumb.

And, much as he hated to admit it, she was also beautiful. He liked his women in soft chiffon and delicate high heels, wearing discreet jewelry and smelling of Joy. Brionny Stuart was dressed in faded denim shorts, boots and an almost shapeless cotton T-shirt. She wore no jewelry, and the only things she smelled of were sweat and herself, and still she was sexier and lovelier than any woman he could think of.

His body tightened as he remembered that glimpse of her he'd had as she'd floated in the jungle pool, her hair drifting like yellow petals around her face, her breasts rising from the water like ivory globes tipped with the palest pink silk.

Dammit, what was wrong with him? He wasn't a boy, given to sweaty fantasies. He'd been busy as hell lately, yes, flying from one on-site emergency to another, but he hadn't lived like a monk. There'd been women. Hell, there'd always been women, attracted first to his muscles and then to his money. Heaven knew, there was nothing special about this one—unless you were turned on by snotty, ill-tempered bitches. Brionny Stuart had a cold heart and a sharp tongue and a grim determina-

tion not to tell him what she knew about the Eye of
God, even if it meant that the two of them might end
up as miniaturized *objets d'art* hanging on the wall of
some Amazonian thatched hut—

'Ouch!'

He swung around. She was dancing from foot to foot,
waving her hands in front of her face. Anyone who
didn't know better would think she'd lost her mind.

'Mosquitoes?' he said, almost pleasantly.

The look she shot him was filled with fury.

'Of course mosquitoes,' she snarled. 'There's repel-
lent in my pack, if you'd let me get at it.'

'Dousing yourself with bug spray once they start biting is useless. You should have done it hours ago.'

'Thanks for the advice. Now give me the bug spray.'

Slade shook his head. 'I don't want to stop now. You
can use the stuff when we make camp.'

'And when will that be?' Brionny blew an errant wisp
of hair from her forehead. 'If you figure on doing another million miles before then, tell me and I'll drop
out now.'

'Keep your voice down.'

'I'm tired, I'm hungry, and I've given enough blood
to the mosquitoes to win a medal from the Red Cross.'

'I said to keep your voice down.'

'Listen McClintoch, I don't know where you get this
Genghis Khan complex from, but—'

She gasped as he caught hold of her shoulders.

'I get it from my basic instinct to survive,' he
growled. 'You've got a pocket full of degrees—aren't
you bright enough to figure out that you're making too
much noise?'

'Sorry. If I'd known human speech would disturb
your thought processes—'

'Have you forgotten about the Mali-Mali?'

'Oh. Right.' Brionny gave him a dazzling smile. 'The little men in grass skirts.'

'Actually,' Slade said coldly, 'they probably wear bark cloth.'

'Of course. Bark cloth. And plugs in their earlobes. And in their noses.' She shot him another bright smile. 'Just like in *National Geographic*.'

'Are you making a point?'

'Just that it's late, I'm tired, and I'm fed up being *smorgasbord* for the bugs.'

'I couldn't agree more.'

'Well, then...?'

'We'll stop when I decide we've put enough distance between us and anybody who might be following.'

Brionny nodded. 'The cannibals,' she said. 'Sorry. I keep forgetting.'

Slade's eyes narrowed. 'Come on, Stuart. You've spent snough time rubbing your academic credentials under my nose. What's with this sudden show of ignorance about Amazon tribes?'

'I'm just deferring to the man with all the information. That *is* you, isn't it?'

'I'm too tired to play games, lady. If you have something to say, say it. Otherwise, shut your mouth, grit your teeth, and hang on another few minutes. If I remember right, the place I figure on stopping at is just ahead.'

Brionny's eyes rounded with exaggerated surprise. 'A place the vicious headhunters won't know?'

'A place they won't find, if we're lucky. Anyway. I suspect they're more interested in tailing us for a while than in attacking.'

'How good of them to keep you informed.'

'Dammit, what's this all about?'

Suddenly she felt incredibly tired, too tired to go on with their verbal warfare. It had been a long, wearing day, and it wasn't over yet.

'Nothing,' she said. Sighing, she slumped back against a tree, slid down its length and plopped down on the ground. 'I need a breather, McClintoch. Just five minutes.'

He gave her a long, measuring look. Something that was a cross between admiration and pity welled inside him. He could see that she really was exhausted. Actually, that she'd managed to push this far was more than he'd expected.

'All right,' he said, after a moment. 'You sit there while I take a look around.'

Brionny nodded. 'Fine.'

He looked at her again. Her legs were drawn up and her arms lay limply across her knees. Her head was tilted forward so that the softly vulnerable nape of her neck lay exposed. There was a welt on her arm from a mosquito bite or a thorn, and he fought down the impossible urge to bend and put his lips to it.

Slade swallowed hard, forced himself to look away. The brush alongside the trail was a bramble-filled tangle. He could see a thick tree trunk rising perhaps fifty feet from where he stood. Was it the place he remembered?

He looked back at Brionny. She hadn't moved, except to let her head droop even further forward. That was how he felt, too, tired to the point of collapse. Neither of them could go much further tonight.

'Stuart?' She looked up. 'Will you promise to stay put?'

She laughed wearily. 'Do I look as if I could go anywhere?'

No, Slade thought, she certainly didn't. With a grunt, he dropped the pack from his shoulders.

'I'll be right back,' he said, and stepped into the bush.

The instant the dense foliage closed around him, Brionny sprang to her feet. Heart pounding, she pounced on the pack and all but ripped it open. She'd never dreamed she'd get lucky like this, that Mc-Clintoch would just drop the pack at her feet and walk off.

She hadn't lied about staying put. She was worn to the point of collapse and besides, she wasn't foolish enough to try and make a break for it at night.

But the emerald, she thought as she fumbled for the tea box, the emerald was a different story entirely. She could dig it from its hiding place, put it somewhere else.

But where? Her hand closed around the stone. Where could she hide the thing? It was only twenty or thirty carats in size, not huge, but bulky enough to—

Only twenty or thirty carats, she thought, biting back a gurgle of hysterical laughter, and only worth—what? A million dollars? Twice that? More?

'Stuart?' Brionny's heart leaped into her throat. She looked up wildly, her eyes sweeping the wall of brush. 'Stuart,' Slade hissed from somewhere behind it, 'do you hear me?'

'I hear you,' she said. Where to hide the emerald? *Where?*

'This place looks OK. Grab the backpack and come on through.'

Think, Brionny, think!

Swiftly she dug into the pack again. There was a package of tampons at the bottom. Her hands shook as she opened it, shoved the emerald deep inside, then closed it again.

She shut the backpack and was just rising to her feet as the bushes parted.

'What's taking so long?' Slade demanded.

Could he hear her heart trying to pump its way out of her chest? Brionny gave what she hoped was a lazy shrug.

'I told you, I'm tired. It took me a while to get myself together.'

She looked more than tired, Slade thought; her face was white with strain, her eyes dark pools of exhaustion—but whose fault was that? It was her fault they were on the run from a tribe of savages.

'My heart breaks for you,' he said coldly, 'but we've got more important things to worry about than you needing a night's sleep.'

'Forgive me, McClintoch.' Brionny's voice dripped with sarcasm. 'I keep forgetting. The jungle's alive with enemies. They're behind each tree, under each leaf—'

The breath whooshed from her lungs as he grabbed her and yanked her hard against him.

'This isn't a game,' he said harshly. 'And I won't permit you to act as if it is, not while you're playing with my life as well as your own.'

'You're right,' Brionny spat, 'this isn't a game! And I'm tired of pretending it is. Who are you kidding, McClintoch? The only thing we're in danger from is your over-acting.'

'Are you crazy, woman?'

'No.' Her jaw shot forward. She hadn't meant to tell him she was on to him, but what point was there in letting him go on playing her for a fool? 'And I'm not the impressionable jerk you think I am, either. This whole incredible story of yours, about the natives and—'

She cried out as Slade's hand whisked across her mouth. His arm went around her waist, inflexible as steel. In one swift movement he lifted her from her feet, jerked her off the narrow trail, and into the dense underbrush.

Branches tore at her hair; brambles raked her cheek. She kicked against his shins, yelled silently against his palm. Her teeth sank into his flesh, but though he cursed her under his breath he didn't let go.

And then, suddenly, she heard the sound.

A pulsebeat, deep and primitive, throbbed through the jungle.

She went still in Slade's arms.

'Do you hear it?' he whispered into her ear.

Brionny nodded frantically. His hand fell from her mouth and he drew her back with him through the bushes until they were standing in a small clearing. The drumming sound intensified, and Brionny turned without thinking and burrowed into Slade's embrace.

'Easy,' he whispered, while his hand stroked gently down her spine.

'What—what is it?' she said, her voice trembling.

'Our pals are sending a message.'

Of course. They were listening to the sound of hands drumming on a hollow log. How could she not have recognized it? A shudder went through her as she answered her own question. It was one thing to read about this ancient form of communication in a textbook but quite another to hear it yourself, in the humid darkness of a rainforest.

'It—it doesn't sound the way I expected,' she whispered.

Slade nodded. 'It never does.' His arms tightened around her. 'It goes right through you, doesn't it?'

Oh, yes, it certainly did. The drumming seemed to be all around them, defying her to tell where it was coming from. She knew only that it was the most primitive and frightening sound she'd ever heard. It was like listening to the heartbeat of some great, primordial creature, waiting out there in the darkness.

Brionny shivered again. Slade drew back a little, took her face in his hands, and lifted it to him.

'It it helps,' he whispered, 'I don't think it's the prelude to an attack.'

She made a sound that was supposed to be a laugh. 'Don't tell me. They're using Morse Code and you learned to read it in your days as a Boy Scout.'

He smiled. 'It wasn't such a hot idea to be Boy Scout where I grew up. Wearing a good guy's uniform was bad news in my neighborhood.'

Brionny pressed her forehead against his shoulder. 'Then how do you know what they're saying?'

'I don't. But if they wanted to rush us, they'd have done it by now.'

'Well, that's reassuring.' She looked at him again. 'So, what kind of message do you think it is? "Dear Jane, I'll be late, don't hold dinner"?'

Slade laughed softly. 'Something like that.' His thumbs moved lightly across her cheekbones. 'I think they're sending out word that they know where we are, more or less, and that everything's under control.'

'Wonderful.'

'It is, when you consider the alternative.'

'An attack, you mean.' Brionny took a deep breath. 'You're sure they're not planning one?'

'I can't be sure of anything, Bree. But I can make a pretty good guess. The tribes I'm familiar with—'

'The tribes you're familiar with?'

He shrugged. 'I've traveled a bit through this part of the world and I've been in a few other places where primitive peoples still exist.'

Yes, she thought, looking at him, at the hard, masculine planes of his face, the sweep of dark hair, the proud yet sensual mouth, he would be a man who traveled in such places. He was a man drawn to adventure and the endless search for treasure, committed to nothing more than following the sunrise.

Why did the thought make her throat tighten?

Slade drew in his breath. 'The drumming's stopped.'

'I guess the telecommunications office shut down for the night,' Brionny whispered, trying for a smile to match the quip, but she failed miserably. Slade drew her closer.

'We'll be OK,' he said. 'They've had plenty of chances to hurt us, if that's what they wanted to do.'

'What *do* they want, then?'

The emerald, he thought, but somehow he couldn't bring himself to say it when she already looked so frightened.

'Maybe they just want to remind us that they're out there.'

Brionny stared at him. Was he telling her the truth? Or was he taking advantage of whatever set of circumstances had put that jungle drum corps within hearing?

She thought of that night at the Hotel Florinda, when he'd kissed her and the world had spun out from under her feet. She thought of the moment at the edge of the gorge, when he'd kissed her again and the taste of him had been more dizzying than the sight of the ground plunging away to infinity.

She barely knew this man; she didn't like him or respect the way he lived—and yet he was taking subtle control of her life.

'My God,' Slade said quietly. His eyes were narrowed, fixed to her face, and dark with sudden understanding. 'You think I made all this up, don't you?'

Brionny hesitated. 'Well, it's—it's all kind of—I mean, it's so strange, you know? The bridge, the arrow, and now the drums...'

He let go of her, so abruptly that she staggered back.

'The arrow came close enough to damned near part my hair. And you saw the bridge yourself; you saw the way the ropes had been severed. And those drums— what do you think, Stuart, that I've got a tape player in my back pocket?'

'No, of course not. I just—look, I'm trying to be completely honest with you, McClintoch. You can't blame me for expressing some doubts.'

'Doubts?' he said, anger and indignation sharpening his voice. 'Hell, lady, you're not expressing "doubts", you're labeling me a liar—and I damned well don't like it!'

Brionny stiffened. 'And I don't like having stories about headhunters and warning arrows and heaven only knows what else dropped on my head by a man who comes sauntering out of the jungle without so much as a how do you do!'

'My manners never were the best,' he said, flashing her a cold smile. 'Next time, I'll wait for a proper invitation.' He took a step forward, and Brionny fell back. 'Since you've got all this figured out, Stuart, why not tell me the rest? Why would I invent this whole elaborate story just for you?'

In for a penny, in for a pound, Brionny thought, and took a breath.

'It you thought I had the Eye of God,' she said, 'and if you wanted it badly enough, you might do anything to try and take it from me.'

Silence stretched between them, taut as a drawn string. Slade was still glaring at her, his broad chest rising and falling rapidly, and suddenly she knew that all he had to do was tell her she was wrong and she'd believe him. Not even the greatest magician could have staged the events that had been happening during the past hours. Everything was too well choreographed for one man to—

Slade snatched the backpack from the ground. 'You're wrong,' he said.

Brionny sighed. 'I believe you, McClintoch, and I'm sorry if—'

'I don't think you *might* have the emerald,' he said coldly. 'I'm *sure* you have it. And I'm not going to try and take it from you—I damned well *am* going to take it.' His mouth twisted in a smile that was not a smile at all. 'Any questions, Stuart? If not, I'd like to settle in for the night.'

CHAPTER FIVE

BRIONNY STARED at Slade, at the narrowed green eyes that were so coldly focused on hers. She felt a flutter inside her breast, a whisper of what might have been disappointment—but then Slade's lips curved into a self-assured smirk and she knew that the only thing she felt was overwhelming relief.

All the cards were on the table now. She didn't have to go on wondering if Slade was the villain in this piece or if he was her savior. He had identified himself for her, confirming what she'd suspected—that he was a man with the ethics of a snake and the determination of a pit-bull.

He wanted the Eye of God; he was sure she had it and he would do whatever it took to wrest it from her. Her only safety lay in steadfast denial that she had the emerald. It was her only protection against his stealing it and abandoning her in the jungle.

Slade was still smiling, that same damnably smug grin that made her yearn to slap it from his face. Instead, she smiled too, as if they were both in on some terribly amusing joke.

'Well,' she said, 'now that you've made your position clear, I suppose I ought to state mine. I'll make it easy for you, McClintoch, and put it in the simplest terms possible. I do not have the emerald. I have no idea where it is. But, I assure you, if I did, I'd sooner choke than tell you. Any questions?'

The smile disappeared from his face as he clasped her shoulders.

'Not a one,' he said with soft menace. 'But I do have an observation that might interest you. Keep pushing me and you may not like where you end up.'

'I don't like being threatened,' Brionny said coolly, despite the sudden frightened race of her heart. 'And I don't like being manhandled, either.'

'Manhandled?'

She dropped her gaze to where his fingers dug into her flesh. 'Manhandled,' she repeated in a frigid tone.

They glared at each other. The woman was impossible, Slade thought grimly. Her perfect little world was verging on collapse, but rather than admit it she'd decided to blame it on him.

'People like you amaze me,' he said. 'You go through life acting as if the world were created for you to command—and then you accuse the rest of us of not knowing how to behave.'

'On, give it up! The only thing you know about people like me is that if you hang around us long enough you might get a shot at stripping us bare.'

Slade laughed again, but now his laughter had a soft, suggestive sound to it.

'What a creative thought, Stuart. That's the best idea you've had yet.'

A wash of color rose under Brionny's skin. 'You know what I mean,' she snapped. 'You want something you think I have—'

'Damned right I do.'

'Face the facts, McClintoch. You're out of luck.'

'Back to square one,' he said flatly. 'You're going to keep insisting you don't have the emerald.'

'I can't help it if you don't want to deal with the truth.'

'Your story might impress me more if the Mali-Mali weren't after you—or do you think that band concert we were just treated to was for kicks?'

'Assuming you're right—if those were drums—'

'*If* they were drums?' He gave a bark of laughter. 'What else could they have been? Castanets?'

'If they were drums,' Brionny said firmly, 'maybe they were serenading you.'

'Me?'

'Come on, McClintoch. Don't sound so all-fired innocent.' She gave him a look that she hoped blazed with accusation. 'Remember that company you worked for, the one putting in the road? Maybe the locals don't like the idea of the jungle being desecrated.'

'Putting in a desperately needed road isn't a desecration. If you'd ever had the worry about getting to a doctor or a hospital or a decent school, you'd understand.'

'Slade McClintoch,' Brionny said, 'candidate for this year's Albert Schweitzer Fellowship Award!' She planted her hands on her hips and glared at him.

'What I don't want to be,' Slade said sharply, 'is Martyr of the Year. If you've got half a brain in that beautiful head, you'll take my advice. Give me the stone—'

'Hah!'

'Give me the stone, and I'll return it to the Mali-Mali.'

'Why, Mr McClintoch,' Brionny said, giving him a look of wide-eyed innocence, 'I've misunderstood your motives. You don't want the Eye for yourself. You want to return it to its rightful owners.'

'Dammit, Stuart! Will you stop being a fool?'

'You're the fool, not me, if you think I'm going to believe you're really Robin Hood in disguise.'

Slade stared at her, his jaw set, and then he grabbed the backpack from the ground and began yanking open the straps that kept it closed.

'What do you think you're doing?'

He sank down on a log, the pack in his lap. 'Figure it out, Stuart. What does it look like I'm doing?'

'That's my stuff,' she said, reaching toward him. 'You've no right to—'

He brushed her hand aside. 'Stop me, then.' He looked up, smiling tightly. His voice was soft as velvet, yet somehow rough with menace.

Don't react, Brionny warned herself; don't do anything.

She shrugged, as if the sight of him examining the contents of the pack weren't important.

Go ahead,' she said casually. 'Throw your weight around.'

Helpless to stop him, she watched as he sifted through her things. Her extra socks looked incredibly small in his hands. When he picked up a pair of white cotton bikini panties and looked at her, brows lifted, she didn't give an inch. 'My underwear,' she said coldly. 'I'd offer to lend, but I doubt we're the same size.'

Slade grinned. 'Let's see what else we have here that might be useful.'

'Just some stuff to eat and some personal things,' she said, with a show of disinterest. 'If you want something in particular, ask.'

'I already did. I want the emerald, remember?'

'Well, you won't find it here,' she said with more conviction than she felt.

'In that case, I'll just have to settle for whatever I— Aha!'

Brionny's pulse skittered. 'Aha, what?'

'Bug goop,' he said, tossing a plastic bottle to her. 'Better put some on before there's nothing left of you.'

She nodded, then sank down on the log beside him, watching with growing apprehension as he continued his hunt.

'What's this?'

'Penicillin tablets. The museum people thought it would be a good idea if—'

'This?'

'Aspirin.'

'What's in here?'

'An antibiotic. Honestly, McClintoch, if you'd just let me—'

'You've got a regular pharmacy here, Stuart. I'm impressed.'

'I'm delighted to hear it. Are you done messing with my property?'

'Well, well,' Slade said softly. 'And what have we here?'

Brionny went very still. He was holding the little tin tea box in his hands and looking at her as if he were a cat who'd found the key to the mouse hole.

'It's tea,' she said, when she could trust herself to speak.

'Tea?' He smiled gently. 'I thought there was nothing in here but personal stuff and first aid equipment.'

'Well—well, the tea is personal.'

'Do tell,' he said, very softly.

Brionny nodded. 'I like tea,' she said, her voice steady.

'Oh, yes, you must—if you were willing to carry your own supply instead of trusting it to one of the porters.'

'What's your point, McClintoch?'

'No point at all. I like tea myself.' His thumb toyed with the box cover. 'You won't mind if I open it, then, and take a sniff?'

His smile made a mockery of the polite request. You bastard, Brionny thought, you miserable bastard...

With one swift motion, he yanked the cover from the box and upended it in his lap. Tea leaves spilled out, trickled across his thighs, and fell on the ground. Slade looked down, then lifted his eyes to Brionny's.

'It's tea,' he said flatly.

'Yes.' She smiled sweetly, trying to still the race of her heart, trying not to think about how close she'd come to disaster. 'Did you expect to find something else?'

He glared at her, slammed the container shut, and dumped it into the pack.

'Are you satisfied now?' Brionny said. 'You've pawed through my things, acting as if you owned the wor—'

She swallowed. Slade was holding something else in his hands. It was the package of tampons.

Her mouth went dry. Say something, she thought fiercely; say something before he opens it.

'They're tampons,' she said briskly. He looked at her and she smiled coolly. 'Do you need me to explain what they are? Or would you rather dump the contents all over yourself so you can make an in-depth analysis?'

It was wonderful to see the quick flood of crimson that sprang out along his high cheekbones. His eyes dropped from hers. He looked at the tampon package as if it were liable to go up in flames, frowned, and tossed it into the pack.

'I thought you had something to eat in here,' he said gruffly, shoving the pack at her.

Casually, as if her pulse-rate weren't somewhere off the charts, Brionny nodded.

'I do.' She pulled out a couple of plastic containers. 'Nuts. And dried fruit. You get your choice.' She hesitated. 'Or do you want to spill it out and check to see if any of the raisins are emerald-green?'

Slade rose to his feet. 'I just hope you're still laughing when our drummer pals get tired of following us and decide to move in for a closer look,' he growled.

Brionny's eyes suddenly seemed very large in her pale face, and Slade almost regretted his sharp words. But then he looked past her, to the shadows surrounding the little clearing, and he knew the only thing worth regretting was Brionny Stuart's damned determination to hang on to her ill-gotten prize, even if it meant both their necks.

There wasn't any question in his mind now. The determination of the men following them, plus the woman's dogged declarations of innocence, had convinced him. She had the stone. But where? It wasn't in her pack. Was it, then, stashed somewhere on her?

He looked at her again. She was nibbling at the trail mix, bent on ignoring him. He watched as she lifted her hand to her lips. The tip of her tongue dipped delicately into her palm, and he felt his entire body tense.

What would it feel like if that tongue dipped into his mouth? Would she taste as he remembered, sweet and clean and fresh? Would she sigh and lean into him as she had the last time he'd kissed her; would she wind her arms around his neck so he could feel the softness of her body?

Damn! It was the emerald he wanted, not the woman. Where could she have hidden it? Did she have it tucked into a pocket or sewn into her clothing?

The only way to find out was to search her.

His breath caught, seemed to knot just in the back of his throat. He could imagine ordering her to stand, to take off that shirt that clung to her like skin, to peel off her shorts and underpants...

No. First he'd pat her down. Lift your arms, he'd say, and when she did he'd lift his too, he'd put his hands against hers and begin moving his fingers slowly along her skin, down her arms, her shoulders, to her breasts. He'd feel the weight of them against his palms, cup them while he watched her eyes darken as they had that night at the Florinda. Then he'd kneel before her, run his hands slowly over her hips and her buttocks, bring his fingers gently between her thighs while his thumb moved lightly against her.

Finally, when he had stroked every part of her through her clothing, he'd rise to his feet. Take your clothes off, he'd say softly, and he'd watch while she lifted her arms again and drew off her T-shirt, and when her breasts were free he'd bend and touch his lips to her nipples, draw them into the heat of his mouth...

Brionny looked up when Slade groaned. His face was pale, the cheekbones suddenly prominent as if he was in pain.

'McClintoch?' He didn't answer and she got to her feet. 'Are you OK?' She laid her hand lightly on his shoulder and he jumped as if she'd touched him with a hot poker.

'Let's go,' he snarled. He grabbed the pack and slung

it over one shoulder. 'We've wasted enough time on nonsense.'

So much for treating a rat with a show of kindness, she thought, and her lips curled with distaste.

'I was only asking if you were ill,' she said icily.

'Come on, Stuart. You'd be glad to see me collapse in a heap.'

Brionny's eyes snapped with anger. 'Yes, but it's probably too much to hope for. Well? What's your next order, General?'

'We make camp.'

'Where?' She swung in a half-circle, then stared after him. He was striding purposefully across the little clearing. 'Hey. Where are you going?'

The sniping had gone on too long, Slade thought wearily. He had one sort of enemy behind him and another sort beside him, and just now he was damned tired of both.

'To bed,' he said. 'I suggest you get your tail over here and do the same.'

'But—what are you doing?'

'For a woman with a bunch of fancy degrees, you certainly ask a lot of dumb questions. What does it look like I'm doing?'

He was standing beneath the branches of an enormous tree, gazing up into them as if he had all night to spend in contemplation of their leaves.

'I don't know,' Brionny said honestly. 'Is there something up in that tree?'

He laughed. 'You might say that, yeah.'

She tilted her head back, her gaze following his. 'I don't see anything.'

'Look again, Stuart. Right there—see? That forked branch maybe fifteen feet up?'

'So?'

'So,' he said, flashing her a quick grin, 'that's our hotel room for the night.'

She stared at him as the blood drained from her face. 'You're not serious.'

'I'm dead serious.'

She looked up. And up again. The tree was huge, taller and bigger in circumference than any she'd ever seen. It was something that might have sprung up after Jack had planted the magic beans.

Brionny took a step back. 'I am not going to climb that thing,' she said with conviction.

Slade sighed. 'I forgot. Your fear of heights.'

'Yes. My fear of heights. How good of you to remember.'

'Look at the tree, Stuart. Between the knotholes and the vines there are lots of places to grab.'

'Forget it, McClintoch. I'm not climbing that thing, and that's that.'

'You only have to make it to that forked branch. Once you get up there, you're home free. The branch is as wide as a sofa.'

'Forget it, I said.'

'Look, I know you're afraid—'

'I am not afraid.'

'You just admitted you were. And—'

'It's not a fear, it's a phobia.'

'Much more impressive. But I'm not interested in a discussion of phobias right now. I just want to see you get your butt up that tree.'

Brionny folded her arms. 'Well, you're in for a long wait. I'm not going to do it.'

To her surprise, Slade shrugged. 'OK. Have it your way. Sleep on the ground, if you want. It's your choice.'

She nodded. 'Exactly.'

'Just try not to make any noise, will you?' He brushed past her and gave the tree an assessing look. 'The wild pigs have sharp ears.'

'What wild pigs?'

'Of course, you can't do anything about your smell.'

'What smell? I don't—'

'They have such damned good noses. They can pick up a scent miles away.'

He's just trying to frighten me, Brionny told herself firmly.

'That's nonsense and you know it,' she said. 'Pigs won't—'

'Oh, and if you should hear any roaring—'

'Roaring?' she said weakly.

'We passed a stream a couple of miles back, remember? It wasn't very big but I'd bet it's got a fairly healthy caiman population. Once the frogs and the cicadas shut down for the night, you should be able to hear the big guys staking out their territory.' He smiled cheerfully. 'It's mating season.'

'I don't think—I mean, caimans don't—'

'Roar? Sure they do. They're like 'gators and crocs. Nobody's sure if they roar out of passion or because they're in a bad mood.' He shrugged. 'It's the rotten mood part you might want to remember.'

Brionny swallowed hard. 'None of this is true,' she said with determination. 'You're making it up to scare me.'

Slade grabbed a vine, put his foot on a knot of wood, and climbed a couple of feet before he paused and looked down at her.

'As for the jag—he should be done hunting in another couple of hours. With any luck at all he'll have found

a capybara or two to fill his belly, and he won't be the
least bit interested in you as an entrée.'

'I don't think this is funny, McClintoch!'

'Oh, by the way—if the guys who play the drums
should stop by to say hello, don't wake me. I'm not
much on conversation once the moon goes down.'

'Damn you,' Brionny said furiously. She stomped toward the tree, her face uplifted and angry in the waning
moonlight. 'You win. I'll climb this miserable thing.'

Slade chuckled softly, dropped to the ground, and
held out his hand. 'Ah Stuart,' he said, 'your eagerness
to sleep with me is overwhelming.'

Flushing, she lunged at one of the tightly wound
vines and began to climb.

'I hate this place. I hate you. I hate—' Her hand
slipped, but before she could slide backward Slade
caught her around the waist.

'Easy,' he murmured. 'Don't be afraid. I've got you.'

'And one fine recommendation that is,' she snapped.

But he did have her, his hands firm and steadying,
his murmured reassurances helping to guide her, until,
at last, she was sitting on the forked branch, trying to
pretend the ground wasn't a million miles away.

'Relax,' Slade said as he scurried up behind her.

'I am relaxed. I am completely relaxed.'

'If you spend the night sitting like a statue, you'll be
stiff in the morning.'

'Listen, McClintoch, maybe you can pretend this is
a four-poster bed, complete with feather quilt and soft
pillows, but I—' She gasped as Slade's arms went
around her.

'Come here,' he said gruffly. 'Stop struggling, Stuart.
There's nothing personal in this.' He laughed softly, his
breath stirring the damp curls at her temple as he drew

her back against him. 'Just think of me as your seat belt.'

'And what am I supposed to think about the branches above us?' she said, trying not to notice how closely she was plastered to the hard male body behind her. 'When you were having such a good time describing the wildlife on the ground, you forgot about the wildlife in the trees. How do you know there aren't snakes up here with us?'

Slade sighed. 'Do us both a favor and try and relax, OK? I promise you, we're safe. There's nothing to worry about.'

But there was, Brionny thought uneasily. There was the way it felt to be held so tightly in Slade's arms, with the beat of his heart against her back and the heat of him surrounding her.

'Will you loosen up, Stuart? Take a deep breath. Good. Now let it go.' He shifted his weight so that she was lying back in his arms. 'If you were really a hotshot scientist you'd know that a tense body falls at double the rate of a relaxed one.'

It was impossible not to laugh. 'What?'

Slade laughed too. 'You don't buy that, huh?'

'You must have slept through general science, McClintoch.'

He smiled. 'Something like that.' What was the point in telling her that he'd slept through most of his high school science courses because practical experience had by then taught him at least as much as any of his teachers knew? 'Just take it easy. You're not going to fall.'

'My head agrees. But my stomach doesn't. It's doing loop-the-loops at the thought of being up this high.'

'You flew to Peru, didn't you?' Brionny nodded.

'Well, how did you manage to survive the flight? Tran-
quilizers?'

'No. I don't like taking stuff like that.' She hesitated.
'It'll sound silly—'

'Try me.'

'Well, I made myself fall asleep. It's what I always
do when I'm up in a plane.'

'You make yourself fall asleep?'

'I told you it would sound silly,' she said defensively.
'But it works.'

'How do you do it?'

She sighed. 'I tune out my surroundings. You
know—I pull down the window shade so I can't see
out, I get the flight attendant to bring me one of those
little pillows so I can put my head back, I burrow under
a blanket, and I tell myself I'm really not up in the air
but that I'm—' She made a little sound of distress as
Slade turned her in his arms. 'What are you doing?'

'I'm putting you across my lap,' he said in a no-
nonsense voice, 'and there's no point in complaining
because, believe me, I'm only doing it for our safety.'

Brionny felt the heat of his body encompass hers. Her
nose brushed his cheek; her hand slipped across his
chest.

Safe, she thought. Safe?

'That—that makes no sense. There's no reason to—'

'There's every reason,' he said firmly. 'If you don't
get any rest, I won't either. And tomorrow we'll both
need our wits about us.'

'Yes, but this—'

'Look, we don't have a window shade to pull down,
nor a pillow. But you can put your head against my
shoulder and close your eyes.' His hand came up, his
fingers warm as they tunneled into her hair, and he

brought her cheek to his chest. 'Now. Where shall we pretend we are? Do you have any preferences?'

Brionny gave a little laugh. 'Anywhere but a mile up in a tree.'

'OK. I've got it. It's summertime, and we're sitting on my aunt Bessie's wooden swing.'

'Come on, McClintoch—'

'The swing is very old. And it needs to be oiled. It creaks when it moves.'

'Look, I appreciate what you're trying to do, but it won't—'

'The moon is up.' Slade's voice whispered against her skin. 'It's a warm night, and the wind's coming in soft and easy from the south. We've been sitting out here for hours, just talking and counting the stars. Now we're both getting sleepy. "I'm tired, Slade," you say, and I say, Well, why don't you just put your head on my shoulder and close your eyes?'

'McClintoch, really. This is interesting, but—'

'A second ago you were calling me Slade.'

'No, I wasn't.'

'Sure you were. "I'm tired, Slade," you said, and I told you to put your head down and close your eyes.'

She couldn't help smiling. 'Nice try, but that wasn't me talking, it was you, speaking for me.'

'Me? Putting words in your mouth?' He smiled too, and drew her closer. 'Come on, give it a shot. Put your head on my shoulder, take a deep breath, and relax.'

With a little sigh, she did as he'd asked. Amazingly enough, she felt the tension begin easing from her body. Gradually she became aware of Slade's scent, sweaty and male. And exciting—but how could that be? What on earth could be exciting about the smell of sweat?

The way he was holding her was exciting too. She

had never imagined feeling so safe in a man's arms—
and yet feeling so aware of herself as a woman. Her
skin felt so sensitized, and so hot where his touched it.

Her hand lay against his chest, her fingers lightly
curled into the damp cotton of his shirt. His cheek was
against her temple. He needed a shave, she thought suddenly; she could feel the faint abrasion of his shadowy
beard against her skin. What would happen if she put
her hand to his cheek and let her palm play softly over
the light stubble? Her heart gave a thud, then another,
and she shifted a little in Slade's arms.

'Comfortable?' he whispered.

Brionny nodded, although that wasn't quite the way
she'd have described how she felt. Slade's throat was
inches from her mouth. What would his skin taste like?
she wondered. And his lips—how would they feel on
hers? His kisses this morning had seemed as hot and
fiery as the sun. Now, with the moon slipping from the
sky and the blackness of night settling around them,
would his kisses taste of coolness and of the dark?

Brionny shut her eyes. She could imagine going
down into that darkness with Slade, letting him carry
her into a bottomless whirlpool where there was nothing
but him and the night and the feel of his body against
hers...

'Bree.'

She lifted her head and looked into his eyes, as deep
and green as the jungle. His hand stroked her cheek.

'You're tensing up again,' he said softly.

'This isn't working,' she said shakily. 'I think—'

'You're not supposed to be thinking.' His voice was
husky, but it sounded as if it was somehow shot through
with silver. 'You're supposed to be relaxing. That was
the whole point of this, remember?'

The truth was that she was having trouble remembering anything.

'McClintoch—'

His mouth brushed lightly against her temple. 'My name is Slade.'

She swallowed. 'Slade. Please—'

He smiled. 'I like the way you say my name,' he whispered.

Their eyes met again, and what she saw in his made the breath catch in her throat.

Slade murmured her name, tilted her face to his, and kissed her.

CHAPTER SIX

IF ONLY Slade had kissed her with passion, or even with anger—with any of the fiery emotions they'd sparked in each other since they'd met—Brionny knew she could have handled it. She could have shoved him away, slapped his face, done what women had always done to humiliate men who took advantage of a woman's momentary weakness.

But he was kissing her with a sweetness that was almost unimaginable. His lips moved gently on hers, silk against satin; his hands cupped her face, his thumbs gently tracing the delicate bones. An unpredictable kiss, she thought hazily, from an increasingly unpredictable man.

She knew the kiss was meant to be a distraction, a calculated assault on her senses to divert her from reality. And it was working, she thought as he drew her closer. She could feel her fear slipping from her, falling away into the night. The trouble was that something just as dangerous was replacing it. Her mouth was softening under Slade's, her pulse-rate was quickening. Her hands were spreading on his chest, her fingers curling into his shirt.

With a little moan, she twisted her face from his. She waited, struggling for composure. When she thought she'd regained it, she looked at him and managed a strained smile.

'Thank you,' she said, as if he'd given her some aspirin for a headache. 'I'm OK now.'

Slade stroked damp tendrils of hair back from her temples. 'You're not afraid?'

'No, not any more.' She smiled again, a little less tremulously. 'Your diversionary tactic worked. I feel much calmer.'

It wasn't true. She felt anything but calm. He was tracing the lobe of her ear, his finger moving lightly along the tender flesh, and, though she'd tried to put some distance between them, how much distance could you manage when you were sitting in a man's arms?

His fingers dropped to the neck of her T-shirt and traced a path that encircled her throat.

'Do you?' he said softly. 'Feel calmer, I mean.'

'Absolutely.' Brionny cleared her throat. 'And you were right about this branch. It's so wide that I can't possibly fall.'

'No, you can't.' He looped both arms around her. 'I'd never let it happen.'

His arms were a strangely welcome fortress. It took effort not to lean back in his embrace.

'In fact,' she said, 'I—I don't even feel woozy about being so high.'

Slade chuckled. 'All that reassurance from one kiss? I'm flattered, Stuart.' His smile tilted, grew soft and lazy. His gaze dropped to her mouth. 'Just think how reassured you'd feel if I kissed you again.'

'No,' she said, her voice breathy and high-pitched. She cleared her throat again. 'I mean—it's not necessary. Really.'

'It's OK,' he said solemnly. 'I'm willing to make the sacrifice.'

Her eyes flashed to his. 'Don't make fun of me,' she said sharply.

'Me? Make fun of you?' He wore the angelic expression of a choir boy with a frog tucked in his back pocket. 'I wouldn't do that.'

Brionny ran the tip of her tongue over her lips. Was he flirting with her? If he was, he was wasting his time. She wasn't into that kind of male-female banter, not on the ground and certainly not here, in the branches of a tree in the Amazon with a man like Slade McClintoch.

He touched his forefinger to her mouth, drawing it gently along the curve of her lips, leaving a trail of fire in its wake.

'I was just thinking, Stuart...an experiment always has to be repeated before it has validity. Isn't that right?'

'If you expect me to find that amusing—'

'I expect you to treat this with scientific detachment.' He laid his finger against her lips again. A tremor went through her as he began to trace their outline. 'Such a sweet mouth,' he whispered. Her lips parted slightly. His fingertip slid inside and moved gently over the damp inner flesh. 'Just think of this as our treehouse lab,' he said. He was still smiling, but his voice had grown thick, the words softly slurred. 'I have no personal stake here. It's all in the interest of science.'

'It isn't. You know it isn't. And—and—' She caught hold of his hand as if she were catching hold of reality before it slipped away completely. 'Slade. You aren't listening.'

'Of course I am.' His fingers curled around her wrist. He lifted her hand to his mouth, pressed a kiss against the palm. 'I'm listening harder than you can imagine.'

'You're not,' she said, trying not to tremble at the feel of his lips against her skin.

'Of course I am.' He turned her hand over, kissed the inside of her wrist. There was no lightness in his voice now, no teasing tone at all. 'I'm listening to everything, sweetheart, even to the things you're afraid to say out loud.'

'You're talking nonsense,' she said shakily. 'Slade, please, you have to stop.'

A murmuring sigh of pleasure whispered from her lips as he kissed her.

'Is that what you really want me to do, Bree?'

Her head fell back as he pressed his mouth to her throat. What *did* she want? Not this, she thought desperately. Surely not this. Even if Slade wasn't lying about the headhunters—and that was a damned big 'if'—he was still the sort of man she knew better than to trust, a man dropped into her path by a fate with a bad sense of humor...

But what happened to all that logic when he kissed her?

'Tell me what you want,' he whispered, but it wasn't really a question for he was already kissing her deeply, hungrily, and she was kissing him back.

Her lips parted and his tongue slid against hers. He tasted like spring mornings and summer rain, like the first cool snowflake dropping from a winter sky. He tasted of fire and of flame, and when he drew up her shirt, baring her skin to the soft night air and to his caresses, Brionny moaned against his mouth. Heat pooled between her thighs as his thumb rolled across her nipple.

'Slade,' she whispered, 'Slade, please...'

He groaned, lowered his head, put his mouth to her

breast. His tongue laved her skin, and she cried out as his teeth closed lightly on the aching nub of flesh. He drew it into the warmth of his mouth and she felt her last hold on reality slipping away.

What was happening to her? She had never felt like this before. Hers was a world of cool scientific thought and careful investigation. There was no room in it for madness—and surely what she felt now was madness. Pull back now, she thought desperately; pull back before it's too late.

Instead, her hands swept into Slade's hair. She grasped his head and dragged his face to hers, her mouth hot and open against his. He was trembling too—she could feel it—and the realization sent a lightning shaft of pleasure curling through her blood.

'You are so beautiful,' he whispered.

She was—but it was such a pathetic way to describe her that Slade almost groaned with despair. Words had never been his strength; he was a man whose thought processes ran to problem-solving, not poetry, and those rare times when mathematical formulae hadn't worked, muscle always had.

Now he cursed the moments he'd read Euclid instead of Shelley. A perfect sunset was beautiful, or a warm summer morning. But the woman in his arms was much more than that. She was everything female, as mysterious and as lush as the jungle that surrounded them, yet she had a clever mind, as agile as any he'd ever known. She had a face a man dreamed of, a body that was perfection. Her lips were soft and yielding, tasting of honey, and she had set him on fire. He burned as he never had in all his years; he knew that only the exquisite sweetness of her body closing around his could ease his pain.

He arched her back over his arm, touched the tip of his tongue to her nipple, and she made a strangled sound of pleasure that set his blood to pounding in his ears. He took her hand from his chest, stroked the palm with the tip of his tongue, then slid it under his shirt.

'Touch me,' he whispered.

Touch him. Oh, yes, Brionny thought, that was what she wanted to do. She ached to touch him, to explore the hardness of his body. She thrust her fingers into the soft mat of hair that covered his chest, danced them across the hard layers of muscle that were so hot beneath her hand. She stroked his flat, taut abdomen and then hesitated, wanting to touch him even more intimately but afraid to do it, afraid of this sudden, driving need that was so terrifyingly new.

Slade clasped her wrist, brought her hand down his body, over the straining denim of his jeans to his aroused maleness, and she gasped at his heat, at the power she had unleashed.

'Feel what you do to me,' he said thickly.

She knew what she did to him, knew what he did to her. But it was wrong. It had to be wrong—although at the moment she couldn't remember why, couldn't remember anything but the feel of being in Slade's arms.

'Wait,' she said urgently. She caught his wrist, stilled his hand against her breast while she fought for control. 'Please, Slade. We—we can't—'

'We can.' His voice was low, fierce with elemental need. 'All I have to do is—' He lifted her, brought her across his lap so that she was straddling him. He cupped the back of her head, brought her mouth to his and kissed her. He put his lips to her ear, whispering what he wanted to do to her.

The husky words sent fire racing through her blood.

When he lifted his knees, she eased back against his upraised legs, her eyes closed, her heart hammering, riding the hardness of his body, luxuriating in the feel of him against her and under her. Her hips lifted, moving instinctively to welcome that full male pressure.

His fingers moved against her shorts and the zipper hissed open. Slade spread his hand against her belly, his touch silken on her warm skin as it brushed lower and lower...

A roar rent the night. The sound was primitive and terrifying, and Brionny froze in Slade's arms.

'The jaguar,' she whispered.

'It's all right, sweetheart.' His voice was gruff, impatient. 'He's not going to bother us.'

She sat up straight, her spine stiff with tension. 'But where is he? He sounds so close!

Slade cursed softly. Then he sighed, reached for her, and drew her into his arms. Brionny buried her face against his shoulder as he soothed her, his hand stroking gently against her back.

'The jag's made his kill by now,' he said. 'He's not interested in us.'

'But that roar—'

'It was a roar of self-satisfaction. The cat's no different from any other predator.' Slade smiled, pressed a kiss against her temple. 'He has what he wants, and now the world belongs to him.'

Brionny went very still. It was such a simple analogy—and such a humiliating one. The jaguar had made its kill—and Slade had almost made his.

He wanted the emerald—the emerald he was certain she had. He would do anything to get it—and, with her eager assistance, he almost had.

That was what this seduction scene had been all about.

God, how could she have been so stupid?

A taste as bitter as ashes filled her mouth.

'Let me go,' she said in a low voice.

'Sweetheart, trust me. There's nothing to be—'

'Trust you?' Brionny's voice rose. 'Trust *you?* I'd sooner trust a whole nation of headhunters!'

'Bree, I promise, the cat won't—'

'Damn the cat!' She pulled away from him, shifting off his lap and out of his arms, angry enough to ignore the drop beneath them as she scooted back along the branch. 'And damn you, Slade McClintoch! You're disgusting! I wish I could—I wish I could—'

'What?' His voice had gone cool and flat. 'What do you wish you could do, lady? Take back the last few minutes? Pretend you'd never lowered yourself to my level and trembled in my arms?'

'If I was trembling, it was only because—because I was forcing myself to endure—'

'Oh, yeah. Right. You sure as hell were ''enduring'' me, Stuart.' Anger at himself for wanting her made him cruel and reckless. 'That's what those little sounds you made were all about. That's why you were rubbing against me as if—'

'Don't be insulting, McClintoch! I went along with it just to see how far you'd go to get what you want.'

Slade's mouth twisted. 'Meaning I was making love to you so you'd tell me where you've hidden the emerald?'

'Making love? Is that what you call the way you were pawing me? Maybe it wows the belles in Italpa, but—'

Slade's hand flashed out and caught hold of her wrist.

'Don't push your luck,' he said. 'We're in the middle

of nowhere, and there's nothing that stands between you and whatever's out there—except me.'

'You seem to have forgotten that whatever's out there is following the both of us.'

She could see the chill flash of his smile, even in the darkness.

'Ah, but that's only a temporary condition, isn't it, sweetheart?'

'I'm not good at riddles,' she snapped. 'If you've something to say—'

'It's simple, lady. I have your supplies. I have your gun. And, sooner or later I'll have your emerald.'

'I've told you and told you, I don't have—'

'Skip the lies, Stuart. I'm going to get that stone and when I do this little game we've been playing will take on a new set of rules.' Slade let go of her and leaned back into the forked branch. 'Is that clear enough?'

It was clear, all right. Once he got what he wanted— *if* he got what he wanted—she'd be on her own. Whether she got back to civilization or not would be her worry.

It certainly wouldn't be his.

'Well?' Slade's voice was gruff. 'Don't tell me you haven't got some kind of snappy comeback. If there's one thing I've learned about you, it's that you've always got to have the last word.'

Brionny's chin rose. 'There's no advantage in having the last word over someone who's not up to the challenge,' she said coldly. 'I'm going to try and get some rest. I'd appreciate it if you'd shut your mouth and do the same.'

If her feet had been on the ground, she'd have pivoted on her heel and marched off. Instead she did the best she could, shifting her weight recklessly, swinging her leg across the branch, and turning her back to Slade.

She would ignore him for the rest of the night. She wouldn't sleep, of course. For one thing, her adrenaline was pumping like crazy, and then there was the fact that she was sitting in mid-air, with the ground an awfully long way down, something she'd somehow managed to forget until now.

Slade seemed to read her mind.

'If you try to sit balanced like that all night,' he said with a resigned sigh, 'you're almost certain to fall off.'

'Thank you for worrying about my comfort,' she said primly. 'But I'm fine.'

'You're perched out there like an acrophobic Humpty Dumpty, Stuart, which is pretty stupid when you consider that the whole idea of climbing up here was so we could relax and get some rest.'

'Your concern is touching, but—'

'Concern? Listen, lady, once we're out of here you can walk a tightrope across El Kaia Gorge, for all I care. But for now, while I'm in charge—'

'Put your mind at ease, McClintoch. You're not in charge. And I've no intention of falling.'

He laughed unpleasantly. 'Neither did Humpty Dumpty.'

'I can't possibly fall because I won't be asleep,' Brionny said, ignoring his puny attempt at humor. 'So you see—' She yelped as Slade reached forward, put his arms around her, and dragged her into his embrace. 'How dare you? Let go of—'

'Relax. I've no evil designs on your body.'

'Dammit, McClintoch! Let me go!'

His arms tightened around her. 'How can I steal the

Eye of God from you if you fall out of this tree and get eaten by a jaguar?'

'You said the jaguar was—'

'I know I did. But you can't believe anything a man like me says, Stuart, remember?'

'You won't get any argument from me,' Brionny said tightly.

'Exactly. Now, lean back against me, shut your eyes, and go to sleep.'

'Sleep? Like this?' She folded her arms over her breasts. 'You have to be kidding.'

'Well, I'm going to get some sleep. What you do is your business.'

'In that case, let go of me.'

'With pleasure, once the sun rises and we're on the ground again.' Slade tugged her unyielding body back into the cradle of his, then brought her head to his shoulder with a firm hand. 'Until then, you can sit here and count the ways you hate me.'

'There aren't enough hours in the night for that!'

'Or you can stop being an ass and relax.'

'It would be easier to relax with the jaguar.'

'I wouldn't wish you on the cat. Your claws are more lethal than his.'

'Honestly, McClintoch—'

'I warn you, Stuart, my patience is wearing thin.'

'Your patience? What do you mean, your patience? I'm the one who—'

Slade caught her chin in his hand, turned her face to him, and silenced her with a hard, swift kiss.

'Keep talking,' he said, 'and I'll just have to think of some other ways to shut you up.'

Brionny's hands knotted into fists. 'I hate you,' she

snapped. 'Do you understand? I *hate* you, Slade Mc-
Clintoch!'

'Yeah.' He yawned, put his head back, and shut his
eyes. 'I understand completely.'

'I hope so,' she said angrily, 'because—'

A soft, rasping sound purred from Slade's throat.
Brionny stared in disbelief, then rolled her eyes to the
sky.

Damn Slade McClintoch to hell! Wasn't it bad
enough that she was trapped in his arms for the balance
of the night? Did he have to snore, too?

She was just going to have to sit here and endure it.
She wouldn't even be able to relax. Relaxing would
be... She yawned, then yawned again. Relaxing would
be—it would be—

Her head drooped against Slade's shoulder. She gave
a deep sigh and fell headlong into sleep.

'Bree?'

'Mmm.'

'Bree. Wake up.'

Brionny sighed. What a strange way to have fallen
asleep, she thought drowsily. She was half reclining
against something unyielding yet incredibly comfortable; her arms were enclosing not her pillow but something warmer and far more pleasant.

'Sweetheart.' A voice whispered softly in her ear,
stirring the tendrils of hair that curled back from her
cheek. 'Bree, you have to wake up now.'

Slowly, her lashes lifted from her cheeks. In the early
dawn light Slade's face was a breath from hers. He had
a look on his face that was impossible to define, like a
man caught midway between heaven and hell.

'Bree.' His gaze swept across her face. 'Bree, I want you to listen to me.'

How could she listen when she was trying to figure out how she'd ended up lying in his arms? With a flurry of limbs, she tried to put some distance between them but his hold on her was like steel.

'I might have figured you'd try and take advantage of me the one second I let down my guard! Just because I dozed off it doesn't mean you're free to—'

'You've been asleep the whole night,' he said, his voice low and humming with a strange kind of tension.

Brionny snorted. 'Don't be ridiculous. I'd never—'

'Listen to me, Bree.'

'Why? So you can invent more lies?' She slammed her fist against his shoulder. 'Let go!'

'Will you listen to me?'

'Get your hands off me first.' Slade muttered a word that made her cheeks turn scarlet. 'You have no principles at all, McClintoch. A man who has to resort to such subterfuge—'

She gasped as his mouth dropped to hers. She struggled wildly against his kiss. Then, slowly, she went still. Her breath quickened—and Slade took his lips from hers and pressed them to her ear.

'In a little while,' he whispered, 'we're going to have company.'

She drew back and stared at him, seeing for the first time the grim look in his eyes.

'The jaguar?' she said.

'No such luck,' he said, and hesitated. He could see doubt creeping into her eyes. She knew what he was going to say, and she didn't want to hear it.

Damn! Moments before, he'd heard the drums again, heard the change in their rhythm, and he was certain there was going to be an attack soon. Still, there was a possibility he could turn things around—if he could convince Brionny that he was telling her the truth.

But how? How could he change the doubt in those blue eyes to belief? It had to be done quickly. There was no time to waste on another round of argument.

There was one chance. He could do what Brionny was sure he'd been doing all along. He could lie, though he didn't much like the idea...

'I hope this isn't going to be another story about the Mali-Mali,' she said coolly, 'because if it is—'

Hell, Slade thought, lying to her was better than letting her sit here like a target in a shooting gallery.

'Listen to me,' he said. 'I don't want to frighten you, but I saw something a few minutes ago.'

She stared at him, eyes watchful. 'What?'

'Two of their scouts. They were out there, just past those trees.'

She followed his pointing finger. He could see the change coming over her face.

'Are you sure?'

Slade drew her closer, hating himself for what he was doing yet praying it would do the job.

'Positive.'

She nodded. 'At least we have a gun.'

'Yeah, I thought of that.' This was easier, because this was the truth. 'Trouble is, I could only get a couple of them before—'

'If you're not a good shot,' she said quickly, 'I am.'

'That's not the problem.'

'Then what is?'

'We don't know how many headhunters there are, but we're certainly outnumbered. And our visitors will be bristling with poisoned darts, bows and arrows—against our one gun.' Slade tried to smile. 'The odds aren't in our favor.'

Brionny knew he was right.

'Then what do you suggest?'

Slade hesitated. 'There's one thing that might work.'

'What is it?'

'You're not going to like it.'

She smiled a little. 'I don't like the idea of being turned into a Mali-Mali pincushion either. Try me.'

He drew a breath. 'If you give up the stone, we might just have a chance.'

She didn't like it. The doubt came back into her eyes and she shook her head, an automatic denial on her lips.

'I don't—'

That was as far as she got. A sound interrupted her, carried toward them on the still morning air, a soft rustling, as if an animal—or a man—was moving stealthily through the trees.

Slade's heart slammed against his ribs. 'Shh,' he murmured.

Brionny sank back into his arms, her eyes fixed on the tangle of greenery at the far side of the clearing.

Was someone coming? The leaves and vines were so thick, the sun so faint as it tried to penetrate them, that it was almost impossible to see anything, but she thought—she thought she could see—

She managed only one swift intake of breath before Slade's hand clapped over her mouth.

Below, branches and leaves shifted delicately, exposing bits and pieces of the face that hid within them. Brionny had a glimpse of dark eyes set in a broad face—and then it was gone.

She swung toward Slade, her mouth trembling. He nodded grimly and put his finger to his lips.

The time for negotiation was over.

Quickly he grabbed the backpack, jumped noiselessly to the ground, and held up his arms. Unhesitatingly Brionny dropped into them. He wanted to hold her close, ease the fear from her eyes, but there wasn't time.

'We'll be fine,' he whispered, wishing he really believed it. He kissed her gently before setting her on her feet. 'I won't let anything happen to you, sweetheart. I promise.'

He took her hand, the clasp of his fingers firm and comforting, and drew her swiftly into the trees.

CHAPTER SEVEN

THEY HAD been traveling through the rainforest for hours before Slade held up his hand.

'If you hear the Mali-Mali,' Brionny panted, 'I don't want to know about it.'

'Stuart—I think I know where we are!'

She would have laughed, but she didn't have the energy. 'So do I. We're smack in the middle of a big blank space on the map.'

'I read something about a mining company that came in here a few years ago.'

'So?'

'So, our luck may be improving.'

This time she did laugh. 'From what, McClintoch? Desperate to just plain awful?'

Slade pushed a tendril of damp hair back from her smudged face. 'Can you hang in a little longer?'

As if there were a choice, she thought. 'Sure,' she said, and followed after him, deeper into the jungle.

Miles later, she came staggering around a bend and stumbled into him.

'Slade,' she moaned, 'I can't go another step. Don't you think the Mali-Mali must have given up by now? If they were still after us, they'd have—'

'Listen!'

'Listen to what? I don't…' Brionny frowned. 'What is that?'

'Water,' Slade said, grinning like a schoolboy. 'Running water. If I'm right, it's a branch of the river.'

'Here?' It was too much to hope for. 'But—but it can't be.'

'That mining report mentioned a tributary that's supposed to cut through the forest somewhere in this vicinity.' Slade took her hand and they moved forward. 'It's not on the map so I wouldn't have wasted time searching for it, but going this distance cross-country may have put us right in line for—'

'Oh, Slade—look!' Ahead, a brown stream arrowed between sloping banks of dense vegetation. And tucked snugly against the nearest bank was a small, tin-roofed structure. 'A house!' Laughter bubbled from Brionny's throat. She turned and went spinning into Slade's arms. 'That means people, and a radio, and a boat—'

He shook his head. 'Don't expect miracles, sweetheart. It's probably just an old supply shed.'

Her face fell a little, but she kept smiling. 'It's still a miracle. The river, and a roof over our heads for the night—we can stay the night, can't we?'

He hadn't planned on it. Sunset was still hours away. If he worked fast, there was time to cut down some saplings, lash them together to form a raft—but how much further could he push Brionny? She'd already shown more courage and stamina than any woman he'd ever known.

She was probably right. If the Mali-Mali hadn't caught up to them by now, surely it meant they'd given up.

He smiled. 'OK. We'll get a good night's rest. First thing tomorrow morning, we'll build ourselves a raft.'

'A raft.' She sighed happily. 'And then, Italpa.'

'Yeah. We're almost home free,' Slade said, with just

a shade more conviction than he felt. He put his hand under her chin, dipped his head, and brushed his mouth over hers. 'To success.'

Their eyes met, and something deep inside his gut knotted. Slowly, he bent to her again, giving her time to make the choice—and she did. Brionny gave a little sigh, tilted her head back, and offered him her lips.

How could she deny this moment? she thought as Slade's head dropped to hers. They had teetered on the brink of incredible disaster and come through unscathed. Surely a gentle, brief kiss to celebrate their victory over the headhunters wasn't dangerous…?

It was like touching flame to dry kindling. Slade groaned as their lips met—or was it she who made that soft, impassioned sound? It didn't matter. Her arms wound tightly around his neck as he gathered her to him, his mouth opening in demand over hers. His hands slid down her spine, cupped her buttocks, and lifted her into the hard heat of his body.

Sensation swept through her in a dizzying rush. 'Slade?' she whispered.

'Yes, sweetheart.' He took one of her hands, kissed it, then brought it between them. He placed it against his chest and she felt the thudding beat of his heart. 'Tell me what you want.'

The question was simple, but the answer was complex. What did she want? Every time Slade touched her she was swept away on an emotional roller coaster, and she was never sure how she would feel at the end of the ride.

Brionny's head drooped. 'I don't know,' she said honestly. 'I'm too tired to think.'

Slade nodded. He had hoped for a different answer, but she was right. This was no time to think of anything but survival. He took a breath and clasped her shoulders gently.

'Well, I know what I want,' he said, smiling. 'A bath in that river, another gourmet dinner of dried fruit and nuts, and the chance to curl up on the floor in that elegant shack and sleep for the next twelve hours straight. How does that sound?'

Brionny's face lit. 'It sounds like heaven.'

Hand in hand, they made their way to the shack. Slade motioned her behind him as he slowly pushed open the door. It was dirty, hot and musty—but it was safe.

'Welcome to the local branch of the Hotel Florinda,' he said, with a grin.

Brionny shuddered as she stepped inside. 'The Florinda's a four-star establishment compared to this.'

'Come on, Stuart, where's your spirit of adventure? We've got four walls, a roof, a cot bed—' He dropped the pack to the floor and walked slowly across the room. 'Some kind soul's even left us a couple of tins of food.'

With a weary groan, Brionny sank down on the edge of the cot. 'Tinned ptomaine,' she sighed.

Slade chuckled. 'What you need is a nap. Tell you what. I'll scout around outside while you curl up here for a little while. How does that sound?'

'No.' She started to struggle to her feet. 'No, if you're not going to rest yet, I'll—'

Gently, he pressed her back down on the cot. 'It doesn't take two people to check the area,' he said. 'I only want to see if whoever built this place left behind anything else we might be able to use. OK?'

Brionny fell back on the cot. 'OK. You do that, and I'll see what I can do to make this place a little more liveable.'

He smiled. Her eyes were already closing. 'Good idea,' he whispered. He waited until her lashes lay against her cheeks, and then he went out the door.

She came awake in a rush, heart pounding. 'Slade?'

Silence greeted her. The shack was still and hot. Brionny frowned, sat up, and thrust her hands into her hair. How long had she been sleeping? Five minutes? An hour? Her watch had stopped working during their flight through the jungle; she had no idea what time it was or how much had passed.

She rose stiffly to her feet. Every muscle ached, and she groaned softly. Where was Slade anyway? He'd said he'd be just outside, but she couldn't hear anything out there except for the omnipresent chirp of insects.

Maybe insects were the only things out there. Maybe Slade was gone. Maybe something had happened to him. The headhunters might have come creeping out of the jungle, or—

She swung toward the door as it flew open. Slade stepped into the room.

'Hi,' he said. 'How are you feeling?'

Her breath caught. He was shirtless and shoeless, dressed only in his jeans, and they were soaking wet, clinging to his long, muscular legs and narrow hips like a second skin.

He'd been swimming, she thought dizzily. Water gleamed in his dark hair, droplets of it dappling his golden shoulders and glinting in the swirls of hair that covered his chest.

Brionny's throat constricted. How beautifully male he was, how perfect. Her gaze drifted down his torso, taking in the well-defined muscles, the hard belly. A dark arrow of hair led down to his jeans, dipped under the opened waistband, disappeared behind the taut, wet denim...

Heat shot through her, piercing her breast and pooling deep in her loins.

'Bree?'

Her eyes shot to his. His smile had faded; he was watching her with the intensity of a jaguar stalking its prey.

'Bree,' he said again, his voice a husky whisper, and he started toward her.

She shook her head and took a step back. 'Slade, don't.'

'Bree, sweetheart.' He reached out for her, his hands hard but his smile persuasive. 'Why should we go on playing this game?' Her eyes closed as he brushed soft kisses along her face. 'We both know what's been happening. We've known since the day we met at the Florinda...'

His arms were tightening around her. He kissed her, his mouth hot, his tongue insistent. She was melting, she thought desperately, melting in his heat...

But she had melted before, in the arms of a man like this one, a man who'd also known just the right words to whisper, just the right places to touch and kiss...

She tore her mouth from Slade's.

'Stop it,' she said sharply.

His head lifted. His eyes were dark and puzzled. 'Bree?'

'Don't ''Bree'' me,' she snapped, and wrenched free of his embrace. 'I swear, if you touch me again—'

'If *I* touch *you* again?' Color flared across his high cheekbones. 'Who are you kidding? You were all over me, lady, with about as much subtlety as a cat in heat!'

Her hand shot through the air and exploded against

his cheek. He caught her wrist and dragged it behind her back.

'I warned you before about this little game you play, Stuart. How many times do you think you can turn a man on and off before you get in over your head?'

'Listen, McClintoch, when we reach Italpa—'

Slade smiled tightly. 'Don't you mean *if?*'

'When we do,' Brionny said with cold determination, 'you're going to get what's coming to you.'

He laughed. 'I already have. These couple of days in your company have been like a lifetime sentence in hell. The Mali-Mali don't know how lucky they were, being denied the pleasure of your gracious presence, Stuart.'

Brionny yanked the door open and marched outside. 'Why don't you open one of those tins and have something to eat?' she said, flinging the words over her shoulder. 'With luck, you'll get food poisoning.'

'Stuart.' Slade's voice called after her. 'Stuart! Where do you think you're going?'

She turned and looked at him, her smile as cold and unforgiving as her eyes.

'For a swim, McClintoch. Any objections?'

He glared at her. 'Just don't take too long.'

'Why?' she said sweetly. 'Are you afraid I'll use up all the warm water in these magnificent accommodations you found us?'

'I was thinking of the possibility of intruders, Stuart. Caimans or piranhas or such.' He folded his arms across his naked chest. 'Snakes, too, but hell, what is there to worry about? There's nothing out there with fangs sharper than yours.'

Brionny's chin lifted. 'Just remember that,' she said.

She turned, kicked off her boots and, still dressed, dove into the water.

It was warm, almost unpleasantly so, but at least it would wash away the dirt and sweat.

Damn Slade McClintoch, she thought furiously. The man was impossible. The sooner they parted company the better.

She ducked under the water and came up, tossing her wet hair back from her face.

How dared he accuse her of playing games? She wasn't the one. It was he who—

Something bumped gently against her calf. She held her breath and looked around her. There was nothing to see except some branches, carried by the current. That was what she'd felt—a branch or—

Something bumped her leg again. And again. And—

A long, sinuous body, as thick around as a man's thigh or the trunk of a tree, broke the surface of the water beside her. For an instant Brionny stared at the huge snake, enraptured by its cold beauty, and then a scream burst from her throat.

Slade called her name. She heard him dive into the water.

'Get to shore,' he shouted, and she obeyed blindly, falling to her knees among the reeds.

She scrambled to her feet and stared out at the river. The water was churning, turned to foam by Slade and the snake. It was impossible to see anything clearly...

Everything went still. There was nothing visible, not the snake—not Slade. Brionny began to tremble.

'No,' she said. Her voice rose in panic. 'Slade, no—'

He rose from the water, gasping for breath. Brionny flew to him as he stumbled to shore and threw her arms around him.

'Slade,' she sobbed, 'I thought the snake had—'

'You damned fool!' He caught her by the shoulders and shook her, his eyes blazing with fury. 'You could have been killed!'

'I only went for a swim,' she said in a choked voice. 'You said—you said it was safe.'

'The hell I did!'

'Don't yell at me,' she said—and, to her horror, she burst into tears.

Slade glared at her. 'Stop it,' he growled. 'Dammit, Stuart, did you hear me? I told you to— Oh, hell.' His arms swept around her and he held her to him so tightly that she could feel the thudding beat of his heart. 'Bree, sweetheart, don't cry.'

But she couldn't seem to stop. The weariness and terror of the past days had finally overcome her; she buried her face in his shoulder and wept and wept, her arms looped around his waist.

Slade pressed his lips to her hair. 'It's OK, sweetheart. It's all over now.'

'I'm sorry,' she said brokenly. 'I've been nothing but trouble, and I know it.'

'Shh.' Slade swept her into his arms and carried her into the shack. He sat down with her in his lap on the cot. 'Shh,' he said again, rocking her gently. She gave a little sigh and wiped her nose, and he smiled. 'Better?'

'Yes.' She hesitated. 'I never saw that horrible thing until—'

'Hush, sweetheart. I should have stopped you from going into the water but I was so—so—'

'Angry, I know.'

'Not angry.' His arms tightened around her. 'I saw the way you looked at me when I came through that doorway. I knew what you were feeling, how your heart was racing—'

Her cheeks turned pink with embarrassment. 'I don't want to talk about it.'

'And then I saw you regret those feelings. I saw you judge me—and find me wanting.'

'It—it isn't that simple, Slade. I know you think it is, but—'

'Hell, I don't think it's simple at all. It's what happens to me whenever I look at you.' He made a sound that was not quite a laugh. 'I'm never sure if I want to turn you over my knee and paddle you or take you into my arms and make love to you until neither of us has the strength to move.'

Color flew into her face. 'Is—is that really how I make you feel?' she whispered.

Slade groaned softly. 'Here's how you make me feel,' he said, and kissed her.

Brionny held still for an instant, and then she sighed, wound her arms around his neck, and kissed him back.

It was Slade who ended the kiss. 'This situation's a mess,' he said, 'and I'm to blame. I've been so stupid and stubborn—'

'Not you. Me.' She laid her palm against his cheek, loving the feel of his beard-roughened skin. 'You've saved my life more times than I can count, and, instead of being grateful, I pay you back with—'

'Dammit, I don't want your gratitude!' Slade tumbled her back on the mattress and glared down at her. 'Brionny, we have to talk.'

'Yes. I suppose we do.' She gave a muffled yawn. 'Sorry. I'd forgotten how nice a real bed feels.'

He couldn't help grinning. 'Hey, Stuart, you already had half an hour's sack time. It's my turn, remember?'

She smiled and held up her arms. 'How about if we share?' she said softly.

'Bree, please. Just stay awake for another few minutes. There's so much I need to tell you—'

Brionny looped her arms around Slade's neck. 'Can't it wait a little while longer?' she whispered sleepily.

With a muffled groan, he came down beside her and gathered her into his arms. The truth about himself had already waited this long, he thought; what did another few hours matter?

'Why not?' he said.

Slade's eyes closed, as did Brionny's. Within seconds, they were asleep.

Brionny awoke to heat, blazing heat that encompassed her.

Her eyes opened slowly; it took a moment to orient herself. The shack, she thought, that was where she was—with Slade.

Slade. Brionny's breathing quickened. It was his heat she felt. Some time during the hours they'd been sleeping, she had turned on to her back while he had rolled on to his belly. Now they were lying entangled, his leg across hers, his arm draped over her in a gesture that was as possessive as it was protective. His hand was lightly curved over her breast. She felt her nipples harden, felt an answering constriction deep in her womb. She swallowed and shut her eyes. It was only a physiological reaction. She had done enough experiments to know that you couldn't control nerve and muscle responses.

Slade murmured in his sleep, rolled on to his side. His hand moved against her breast, his fingers brushing lightly over her swollen flesh. She bit back a soft whimper. Just a physiological reaction, she told herself desperately, that was all it was...

'Brionny. I thought you were a dream.'

Slade's voice was low. It sent a tremor of longing down her spine.

'Slade. I—I didn't mean to wake you.'

'I felt the heat of your skin, smelled its perfume.' He moved a little, rose up so that he was looking down into her face. 'I felt the softness of you here, under my fingertips—'

'Slade—it must be late. Shouldn't we—shouldn't we—?'

'Bree.' He took his hand from her breast, curved it under her chin. 'I want to make love to you.'

She looked up at him, at the eyes she had once thought cold, the mouth she'd thought insolent. He lowered his head slowly and kissed her, his lips catching at hers, shaping them to his desire.

Brionny stirred beneath the kiss, and her breathing quickened.

Slade drew back. 'Tell me you want me too, Brionny.'

Maybe it was the darkness, lightened only by the moonglow streaming through the window. Maybe it was the sensation of being suspended in time and space. Whatever it was, Brionny knew that the time for denial was over.

With a little cry, she reached for Slade and brought his mouth to hers.

His kisses were gentle at first, soft touches that were like the brush of butterfly wings, but as she began to return them they deepened, grew more intense. His tongue slipped between her lips, slid along the soft inner lining of her mouth.

Brionny made a soft, urgent sound in the back of her throat and ran her hands up Slade's naked chest, exploring the soft mat of dark hair that covered it, skimming over the taut pectoral muscles, the flat washboard abdominals.

Slade groaned, caught her hand, brought it to his lips and pressed his open mouth to her palm.

'Do you have any idea how much I want you?' he whispered.

She smiled. 'Tell me.'

He did, but not with words. He showed her by kissing her deeply, his tongue moving against hers in long, hot strokes. He kissed her at the soft place just behind her ear. When she shivered, he smiled against her skin, then trailed his lips the length of her throat.

He drew back a little, stroked his hand lightly over her cotton shirt, shaping her breast, cupping it, and then he dipped his head and took the fabric-covered nipple gently between his teeth.

Brionny cried out and arched against him.

'Slowly,' he whispered, 'slowly, love. There's no rush.'

He drew her flesh into the damp warmth of his mouth, teasing her with soft kisses and softer bites until she was moving blindly against him, and then he sat her up and slipped the shirt over her head.

'Beautiful,' he said, cupping her breasts in his hands. His thumbs moved gently against her nipples. 'I've never forgotten seeing you in that pool,' he whispered, 'the soft ivory and pink of your breasts. I wondered if they would taste as sweet and silken as they looked.'

She trembled as he traced the fullness of her flesh, first with his hands, then with his lips. He rubbed his cheek against the tender skin. It was days since he'd shaved; his beard was soft, feathery light, its touch so electrifying that she cried out. He touched his tongue to one rosy crest and she held her breath, waiting for the moment when he would take a deeper, hungrier taste. When he did, when his teeth closed lightly on the puckered bud, flame shot through Brionny's body and pooled like liquid fire between her thighs.

'Sweeter,' he whispered, 'sweeter than honey.'

He moved up over her, kissing her mouth while his hand slipped over her belly. He undid the button at her waistband and she whimpered as his fingers slid inside her shorts. His hand moved down and down, and finally his thumb stroked across her, sliding with agonizing slowness against her nylon-covered flesh, and she arched against his finger and cried out his name.

'Do you want me to touch you?' he whispered. 'Tell me what you want.'

Were the words an echo of some darker time? It was too late to wonder or to think. Brionny whispered her answer in shameless abandon, lifting her hips so that Slade could ease away the rest of her clothing.

Then he drew back. She watched as his hands went to his jeans. Slowly, he slid them from his body.

He was perfect, as she had known he would be. The broad shoulders and muscled chest tapered to a narrow waist and hips. His legs were long and muscular—and his sex was proud and exciting, rising from the dark, lush hair that surrounded it.

'You're beautiful,' she whispered, and he smiled. He ran his hands over her again, as if to memorize every soft curve. Gently, he parted her thighs. He kissed the softness of her skin, breathed in her scent, buried his face against her and kissed her intimately until she cried out. Then he lifted his head, looked at her face, watched her as he slid his fingers against her slick, wet flesh.

Brionny arched toward him in ecstasy. She reached

for him, needing to touch him as he was touching her. Her fingers curled around him, as far as they could. He was hot, like flame, as hard as steel yet with the smoothness of silk, and she stroked him, her rhythm matching his until, with a startled cry, she exploded against his hand.

Slade growled his triumph. He bent and kissed her, taking her soft moans into his mouth, and then he drew back.

'Bree,' he whispered.

Her lashes fluttered open. She looked at him, at his dangerous smile, at the dark green fire of his eyes. Slowly he leaned forward, not to enter her but to brush the fullness of his sex against her swollen flesh. Sensation shot through her again, arrowing from her dewy center to every part of her body, and she knew that what had just happened was only the beginning.

'I want to see your eyes as you take me inside you.'

'Slade,' she sobbed, 'Slade, please—'

But he was relentless, moving himself back and forth against her until she was mindless with abandon. Then, at last, he entered her.

Brionny clasped his head, dragged his mouth down to hers. Slade was filling her beyond anything she had ever imagined, not just physically but in a million other ways.

She cried out as he began to move, pulling back slowly then rocking forward, his hands beneath her, cupping her buttocks, lifting her to him. He caught her mouth with his, his tongue duplicating the motions of his body. Suddenly she tensed, dazzled with pleasure yet terrified, knowing he wanted to take her to a place so high that she might reach it and tumble off into space.

'Come with me,' he whispered. 'Come with me, love, come—'

There was no way to resist. Sobbing his name, Brionny gave herself up to him, riding his passion and making it hers. She shattered in his arms, bursting into a million pieces as bright as sunlight, soaring up and up into the sky. Then, slowly, she drifted to earth again, safe in Slade's embrace.

He kissed her throat, nipped lightly at her skin, and began to roll away, but she held him close, loving the weight of his body on hers. She wanted to feel the slowing beat of his heart, the silken dampness of his skin.

'You're wonderful,' he whispered.

She smiled as she stroked her fingers through his hair. 'It wasn't me,' she said, 'it was—' It was because I love you, she'd almost said.

The thought stunned her. Did she love him? Was that why what she'd felt in his arms just now had been so incredible?

She was willing to admit she'd misjudged him. He might be an adventurer, a man who chased dreams, but he certainly wasn't evil, he wasn't—

'It was what?' he said.

Brionny sighed. 'It was you,' she murmured, unwilling to give voice just yet to that last, confusing thought.

Slade kissed her and rolled on to his side, still holding her close.

'Shut your eyes, sweetheart, and sleep. We'll need all the rest we can get before morning.'

Brionny's smile dimmed. For just a little while, she'd forgotten their situation.

'Slade? Do you really think we've lost the Mali-Mali?'

Maybe, he thought.

'I hope so,' he said.

'What—what if we haven't? What if they come after us again?'

It was a good question, and it needed a good answer.

'Then I'll do everything in my power to protect you,' he said.

He kissed her, then drew her head into the crook of his shoulder. Brionny snuggled against him. She was almost asleep when Slade whispered her name.

'Bree?'

'Mmm?'

'You never did tell me where you hid the Eye of God.'

She hesitated. She knew what he was asking. Do you trust me now? he was saying. Do you trust me with your secret, now that you've trusted me with your body?

She took a deep, deep breath. 'It's in the box of tampons. I didn't think you'd look there.'

He smiled, and then he laughed softly. 'No. It's the one place I'd never have checked.' His arms tightened around her. 'Go to sleep now, sweetheart.'

It took a while. She felt strangely uneasy. But, eventually, she did.

She dreamed she was entering a great hall, one that looked like the museum's but was a hundred times bigger. People were rising to their feet and applauding—the Mayor, the director, the members of the board—but she brushed past them, looking for just one face.

'Señorita?'

She was mounting the steps to the podium now, where the Eye of God waited, glowing like emerald fire.

'Señorita. Habla usted español?'

The audience was waiting for her to speak but she couldn't, not until she found Slade.

But it wasn't Slade she saw as she came abruptly awake. There was a stranger standing over her, a tall, cadaverous-looking man in a black suit. Heart racing, she clutched the tattered blanket to her throat and sat up.

'Wh-who are you?' she stammered. 'What do you want?'

The man raised his hands, as if in benediction. 'Do not be afraid, *señorita*. I am Father Ramón, of the Mission of San Luis.'

'The mission of…?' She could see his clerical collar now, and the cross swinging from his neck. Brionny blew out her breath. 'You scared the life out of me, Father.'

'That was surely not my intention,' he said solemnly.

'But-where did you come from?'

'Our mission is just upriver, *señorita*. Some of my flock were out hunting. They stopped here, as they have done before, and found something most unexpected.' Father Ramón came closer, his eyes politely fixed on a point just beyond Brionny's shoulder. 'How have you come to be here, *señorita?*'

'It's a long story, Father, and we'll be happy to tell it to you as soon as—'

'We, *señorita?*'

'Could you just turn your back for a minute, Father? I'd like to-to dress before—'

The missionary turned away. 'Of course. Forgive me for intruding upon you, but when my people said there was a *gringa* here—'

'Don't apologize, please.' Brionny dressed quickly, ran her hands through her hair, and cleared her throat. 'You can turn around now.'

'We thought you might be ill,' he said as he swung toward her.

'No, no, I'm fine.' She peered past him, trying to see outside. 'Didn't Slade answer any of your questions?'

'Who?'

'The man—' She felt her cheeks pinken. 'The man I'm traveling with. We had no idea we were so close to civilization, and... Where is he, anyway? Oh, he must have been so pleased to see you!'

'There is no one here but you, *señorita.*'

'Don't be silly.' Brionny brushed past Father Ramón and stepped into the sunlight. An handful of Indians dressed in Western clothes stared at her. 'Slade?' She frowned as she turned in a little circle. 'Slade, where are you?'

'*Señorita,*' the missionary said firmly, 'you are alone here.' He hesitated. 'Perhaps you *have* been ill. There are some jungle fevers that cause hallucinations and—'

'The Mali-Mali! They must have taken him!'

'The headhunters?' Her made the sign of the cross. 'They have not raided for years, thanks be to God.'

Brionny turned toward him, her face flushed. 'I'm telling you, they've taken Slade! Your men must go after them!'

'*Señorita,* calm yourself. Had the savages been here, they would have left signs to inspire fear in others. It is their custom.'

'To hell with their custom! If Slade's gone, it's because they took him!'

'Blasphemy will not help, *señorita.*'

'Neither will sanctimony! I saw them, I tell you.'

'What did you see, *señorita?*'

'Indians. Well, an Indian, but—'

'Why would you not see an Indian?' the priest asked with a little smile. 'There are many of them who live here, in the Amazon.'

'Father, please. While you stand around insisting nothing's happened to Slade, the Mali-Mali could be—'

'*If* there had been a man with you, and *if* the savages had taken him, do you think it likely they would have left you behind?'

Brionny's mouth opened, then closed. There was logic in his argument. But if Slade hadn't been taken away...

A coldness crept around her heart, squeezing it like an icy fist. She spun toward the door and flung it open.

Hours ago, a million years ago, Slade had undressed her and then himself. He'd flung his clothing into the corner.

Now that corner was empty. Slade's shirt, his jeans, his shoes—everything was gone. All that remained was her gun and her backpack. It lay upended, the tampon box ripped open and the contents a spill of white across the dirt floor.

With a cry of despair, Brionny buried her face in hands,.

'You see?' she heard the missionary say gently. 'It is as I suspected. You are ill, *señorita.* Let me help you.'

But no one could help her, Brionny thought as Father Ramón led her from the shack.

Slade was gone, and so was the Eye of God.

CHAPTER EIGHT

BRIONNY SAT sat in her stuffy basement office, her fingers resting lightly on her computer keyboard, her eyes scanning the pages of her report as it flashed across the monitor.

...set within a niche on what had been an altar in the Forbidden City...

...smaller than the size we'd imagined but larger than...

...deep green in color, with no imperfections or striations visible to the naked eye...

The words blurred together. She muttered under her breath, hit a key, and the screen went blank.

The report was no good. She had an appointment with the museum director in less than an hour and what would she hand him? Surely not this piece of fluff.

She'd been writing the thing for days, and it still sounded more like a travelog than a scientific rendering of how she and Professor Ingram had found the Eye of God.

No. No, that wasn't really true. The report was perfectly fine—to a point. She'd had no trouble describing what had led up to their locating the emerald, nor had it been difficult to depict the stone.

The problem had started when she'd tried to explain what had happened to it after that.

'How could you, of all people, have been such a fool?' her father had said, when she'd told him what had happened—and she hadn't told him anything but the essentials: that she'd thrown in her lot with a stranger, and that he'd ultimately made off with the treasure she and Professor Ingram had found.

Her mother had hushed him, pointing out that Brionny's only choice had been to combine forces with the stranger, that she'd been left alone in the jungle and that there'd been headhunters pursuing her—

'You mean,' Henry Stuart had said, displeasure thinning his lips, 'she *thought* there were headhunters pursuing her.'

'That's enough, Henry,' Eve Stuart had said, her eyes snapping out a warning—but it really hadn't mattered.

Her father was right. The story about the Mali-Mali had been an outright lie, nothing but the cheapest fiction—and she'd fallen for it. She'd let Slade McClintoch spin a web of deceit that a child could have seen through. He had turned her to clay in his treacherous hands and then he had stripped her of her dignity as a scientist—and as a woman.

If only she could forget that long, humiliating night she'd spent in his arms, the things she'd done, the things she'd let him do…

Brionny shoved back her chair and jumped to her feet.

'Damn the heat in this place!'

She glared at the ancient air conditioner, chugging away uselessly in the wall, as if the machine were to blame for her mood. He couldn't fix it, the janitor had said when she'd complained; there was no money for buying new units for the basement.

And the basement, Brionny suspected, was where she and her career were going to stay—unless she lucked into a miracle.

Maybe she could force the window open. It was hot outside, but hot air that was fresh would be better than the recirculated stuff that was pumping through her office.

The window wouldn't budge. Layers of paint had mixed with years of soot to form an impenetrable bond. She gave the sash a last, angry thump with the heel of her hand.

'Damn,' she said. Her shoulders slumped. 'Oh, hell,' she muttered, and she gave a tired little laugh and plopped herself down on the wide sill.

Was this really what she'd been reduced to? Cursing windows and air conditioners and storming around her steamy cubicle of an office like a frustrated rat in a maze?

None of that would put her career back on track.

'What happened was not your fault,' her mother kept saying.

But it was.

She was already being talked of as the woman who'd let the Eye of God slip through her fingers.

Yesterday the girl in the next office—a graduate student in geology—had introduced Brionny to her boyfriend.

'This is Brionny Stuart,' she'd gushed, 'the-girl-who-lost-that-fabulous-emerald-in-the-Amazon.'

It had been said just that way, all in one breath, as if the designation were part of her name, as if she had no other identity and never would have.

Even that had been an act of kindness, because saying she'd 'lost' the stone was a polite euphemism for the truth, which was that she'd been stupid enough to let an opportunistic stranger steal it—and nobody even knew exactly how he'd managed that.

Not yet, anyway.

Brionny shuddered. Would she ever live down the disgrace? Maybe not, but she wouldn't go down without a fight. She'd take Slade with her, see to it that he was caught and tossed into prison for a long, long time.

'It's just too bad they don't guillotine people for what you did, McClintoch,' she muttered, her flushed face taking on a look of grim determination.

She'd tried taking the first step. She'd gone straight to the police after she'd finally reached Italpa in a dugout paddled by Father Ramón's Indians. Unfortunately, the lone policeman on duty had seemed more interested in admiring her legs than in taking notes—but surely things would get moving now.

This morning she was meeting with Simon Esterhaus, the director of the museum. He'd been away when she'd returned from the Amazon, so there'd been no one to take her official report, but he was back now, and, as his secretary had made clear, this meeting with Brionny was at the top of his agenda.

Brionny glanced at her watch, then rose from the sill and dusted off her skirt. Ten minutes to zero hour, she thought, and tried to calm her suddenly racing pulse.

'The director will expect you at ten-thirty,' Esterhaus's secretary had said crisply. 'He wishes to talk with you privately before his eleven o'clock appointment arrives.'

'Someone will be joining us, you mean?'

'That is correct, Miss Stuart. Please be prompt.'

The woman had broken the connection before
Brionny could ask any questions, but it hadn't really
been necessary. She could make a pretty good guess at
who the third party at the meeting would be. Esterhaus
had obviously contacted the authorities—the New York
police, perhaps, or a firm of private investigators.
They'd expect her to tell them everything.

Her stomach clenched as she closed her office door
behind her. She would do that, she thought, her heels
clicking sharply against the tile as she made her way to
the stairs to the Great Hall. She would tell them everything—everything but the final, ugly truth: that she'd
gone willingly into Slade's arms, that he'd made love
to her, that she'd told him—*told* him!—where she'd
hidden the Eye of God.

Brionny's face flamed scarlet.

There was no need for anyone to know those details.
No need at all.

'Be prompt', the secretary had warned, but Brionny was
kept cooling her heels in the waiting room for more than
half an hour.

An act of intimidation, she decided. Not that any was
necessary. She was nervous to begin with, and the director had a formidable reputation. The staff joked that
he had a calculator where he should have had a heart.

Now, as she finally entered his office, she saw that it
had all the trappings of power. The room was enormous,
its furnishings elegant. Choice relics from the museum's
vast collection adorned the walls and tables, and what
seemed like an acre of magnificent Persian carpet
stretched between the door and his Queen Anne desk.

Esterhaus smiled politely.

'Come in, Miss Stuart.' He waved a bony hand to a

chair opposite his desk. 'Sorry to have kept you waiting.' He tilted back his chair and steepled his fingers beneath his chin. 'Well, let's get right to it, shall we? I know the basics of what happened in Peru. What I need now are the details.'

Brionny nodded. 'Yes, sir.'

'How unfortunate, my dear, that your very first expedition for us should have ended so badly for you.'

A good shot, Brionny thought. In one sentence Esterhaus had established both her guilt and the tenuousness of her position.

'I myself have never had the pleasure of going into the field.' He smiled, showing feral white teeth. 'But then, my area of expertise is so dull compared to the exotic nature of yours.'

Shot two, and straight across the bow. Esterhaus had neatly pointed out that it was administrators such as he who kept scientists such as she in business.

Cut to the chase, Brionny told herself. She cleared her throat and shifted forward in the chair.

'Mr Esterhaus, I know how distressed you must be at the loss of the Eye of God. Exhibiting it would have brought us great prestige.'

'You are direct, Miss Stuart. I admire that. Yes, you're quite right. An exhibit of the emerald would have brought us prestige, and a lot of money—surely enough to have justified the cost of the expedition.' Esterhaus's chair tilted forward, and he tapped a finger against a stack of papers on his desk. 'Professor Ingram was so sure he would be bringing the stone back that I'd indulged myself in a little judicious daydreaming.' His teeth glinted again in a rapacious smile. 'You'd be amazed at the admission fees the public's willing to pay to see something so ancient.'

'Sir, no one is sorrier than I for what happened, but—'

'What *did* happen, pray tell? As you said a moment ago, you lost the stone.' Esterhaus smiled again, but his eyes were flat and cold behind his spectacles. 'Such a quaint way of putting it, don't you think? One may lose a pen, or a wallet, but losing a priceless relic—well, it's not quite the same thing, is it?'

'I assure you, Mr Esterhaus, I safeguarded the stone as best I could, but circumstance—'

'Your rescuer, that missionary—what was his name?'

'Father Ramón.'

'Father Ramón. Yes. I'm afraid the message he sent us was not terribly clear.' Esterhaus moistened the tip of his index finger and began shuffling through his papers. 'I have a transcript of it here somewhere...' He looked up, frowning. 'I'm sure you know what he said, Miss Stuart. Ramón thought you might have been delirious. He said you were raving about headhunters, and about a man who was supposedly with you.'

Brionny swallowed. 'I wasn't delirious. I—I'd had reason to believe there were headhunters after us, and—and there was a man with me.'

Esterhaus's brows arched. 'Indeed?'

She hesitated, wondering if Esterhaus could hear the pounding of her heart. 'He was the one who—who stole the emerald from me.'

The director took off his rimless eyeglasses, held them to the light, then popped them back on his nose.

'I must say, Miss Stuart, I'm delighted you've decided to be up front about this.'

'Sir?'

'Taking up with a strange man, letting him get a priceless relic in his hands—those were very poor decisions to have made. I admire your honesty in admitting your errors.'

His tone, and his smile, made it clear that the only thing he admired was the swiftness with which they'd come to what had to be the heart of the interview.

'That isn't exactly accurate, sir. I didn't "take up" with this man. Professor Ingram was dead, my guides had abandoned me, and a tribe of headhunters was—'

'There was never any danger from headhunters. Father Ramón's message makes it clear that he explained that to you.'

'I know that now, Mr Esterhaus. But at the time I thought—'

'How did this man take the stone from you, Miss Stuart?'

'He—he just did.'

'By force?'

Brionny flushed. 'No. Not—not by force.'

'By intimidation?'

'No, sir. He—uh—he simply found it, and—'

'Found it? You mean you'd hidden it?'

'Yes.'

'But not terribly well, hmm?' Esterhaus pursed his lips. 'When he took the stone, did you try to stop him?'

'I couldn't. He took it during the night, sir. I was asleep, and—and...' Her throat constricted. 'I did what I could, Mr Esterhaus. I reported the theft to the police in Italpa—'

'The police in Italpa,' Esterhaus said with a little laugh. 'A waste of time, Miss Stuart. A joke! I've no intention of involving them in such serious business.'

Brionny nodded. 'I can understand that, sir, but I did try to—'

'It would be appropriate for me to ask for your resignation at this moment. You know that, of course.'

'Mr Esterhaus,' she said, fighting to keep her voice neutral, 'I know I made some errors in judgement, but I promise I'll do whatever I possibly can to—'

The shrill of Esterhaus's telephone silenced her. She waited while he took the call.

'Good,' he said, 'very good. Ask him to wait just a moment, please.' He smiled as he hung up the phone. 'Did my secretary tell you about the gentleman who'll be joining us this morning?'

'No, not really. She only mentioned that someone would be—'

'Unfortunately he was unavoidably delayed, which means I'll have to curtail my plans to meet with the two of you together.' Esterhaus shot back his cuff, looked at his watch, and frowned importantly. 'I have a luncheon appointment with the Mayor,' he said, and smiled. 'But you'll be able to manage without me, I'm sure.'

'Yes, sir.'

'He'll need to know everything you can tell him about your unfortunate experience in the Amazon, Miss Stuart. Do you understand?'

Brionny flushed. Not everything, she thought. 'I'll—I'll do my best,' she said.

'It's vital that you do. With sufficient information, I have reason to believe we have a good chance of recovering the emerald.'

'That's wonderful!' Brionny's face lit with excitement. 'I'd like nothing better than to see the man who stole it caught and—'

'Your personal need for vengeance is not the museum's concern,' Esterhaus said coldly. 'Recovering the stone is our sole interest.'

'But it's the same thing, isn't it? Catching the thief and getting back the Eye—'

'Think, Miss Stuart, think! There are circumstances in which the one might cancel out the other.'

'I don't understand, Mr Esterhaus.'

The director sighed. 'If we can take the thief to trial, we will. But if we have no choice but to buy the stone back—'

'Buy it back?' she said, her voice rising.

'It is entirely possible we may have to negotiate for the emerald's return.'

'But—that's blackmail. It's ransom. It's—'

'It's business,' the director said sharply, 'and it's done all the time.'

Brionny wanted to tell him he was wrong—but she couldn't. Occasional whispers surfaced about a museum or gallery recovering a stolen object by 'buying it back' from the thieves who'd stolen it. The excuse was always the same—that the principals involved hadn't realized they'd been dealing with crooks—but no one really believed that.

'Even if you wanted to make such a deal,' she said slowly, 'how do you know the emerald hasn't already been sold on the black market?'

'I have it on good authority that the thief is lying low with the stone.' Esterhaus stood up and came around the desk. 'You see,' he said as Brionny got to her feet, 'we've had the most incredible good luck.' Smiling, he clasped her elbow in his skeletal hand. 'The gentleman you're about to meet contacted me several days ago.'

'While you were away?' Brionny threw him a bewildered look as he led her toward the door.

Esterhaus nodded. 'He was in Peru when the emerald disappeared.' They had reached the door, and he let go of Brionny's arm and put his hand on the knob. 'He's privy to some inside information.'

Brionny's heart thumped. 'Can he lead us to the thief?'

'He believes he can, and that's where you come in. He'll need you to help him identify the man—and the stone, too.'

A chill as cold as the grave whisked across the nape of Brionny's neck. It made no sense, but she could feel the hair rising on her skin.

'Therefore, Miss Stuart, as of this date, you are relieved of your duties at the museum.'

She paled. 'You're dismissing me? But I thought you said—'

'I am reassigning you. You will devote yourself to helping find the thief and the emerald. When the stone is safely in my hands, I shall wipe the slate clean and see to it that you are awarded your doctorate.' The director smiled benevolently. 'How does that sound, my dear?'

It sounded like the best news she'd had in weeks. So why was that chill dancing across her skin again?

'Sir,' she said quickly, 'wait a minute. Who is this man you—?'

Esterhaus flung the door open. Framed in it was his secretary's desk. The woman's flushed face was tilted up to an unseen figure standing beside her.

'Oh, go on,' she said, giggling happily, 'you don't really mean...'

Esterhaus cleared his throat. His secretary gave a startled jump.

'Mr Esterhaus. I didn't hear you, sir.'

Esterhaus took Brionny's arm and drew her forward. 'Miss Stuart,' he said, 'I'd like you to meet—'

But Brionny knew. She knew even before the man turned toward her.

It was Slade.

He had traded his jeans for a perfectly tailored gray suit, but everything else about him was the same, from that whipcord-hard body to the cool, emerald-green eyes.

Brionny made a choked sound. Esterhaus frowned.

'Miss Stuart?'

Slade laughed politely. 'I don't think I mentioned it, Esterhaus, but Miss Stuart and I have met before.'

'I don't believe it,' Brionny whispered.

Slade's eyes, cold with derision and warning, met hers.

'Surprise,' he said softly.

She spun toward Esterhaus, whose expression was puzzled. 'I didn't realize you two knew each other,' he said.

'Knew each other?' Brionny gave a cackling laugh. '*Knew* each other? Mr Esterhaus, this man—'

'Certainly we know each other.' Slade's voice was silky. He reached out, took Brionny's limp hand, and clasped it in his. It seemed a simple, friendly gesture; only she could feel the almost painful pressure he was exerting. 'Miss Stuart and I met in Italpa. We were guests at the same hotel and—' he shot Esterhaus a knowing, man-to-man smile '—we ran into some—ah—some personal problems, I'm afraid.'

'We didn't,' Brionny said desperately, 'we never had any personal prob—'

'I think she might still be annoyed with me, Simon, if you get my meaning.'

Simon? *Simon?* Brionny tried to wrench her hand from Slade's, but his calloused fingers gripped hers like steel.

'Mr Esterhaus,' she said desperately, 'you've made a terrible mistake. You said the museum had been contacted by a gentleman, but you were wrong! Slade McClintoch is—'

'Now, now, Bree.' Slade chuckled as he stepped to her side and slipped his arm around her shoulders. His fingers bit into her flesh. 'We don't want to wash our dirty linen in public, do we, sweetheart?'

'Mr Esterhaus, dammit, this man—'

'That is enough, Miss Stuart.' Esterhaus's eyes were like chips of ice in his bony face. 'Whatever happened between you and Mr McClintoch in Italpa is your problem, not the museum's.' He looked at Slade and smiled. 'I look forward to swift and satisfactory progress.'

'Of course, Simon.'

Brionny made one last, futile effort. 'Wait,' she said.

The door to Esterhaus's office slammed in her face. With a little cry of fury and despair, she swung toward Slade. The polite smile he'd worn for the museum director was gone, replaced by a look of arrogance and utter contempt.

'You bastard,' she whispered, and he laughed coldly.

'I'm delighted to see you again too, sweetheart,' he said, and he put his hand in the small of her back and marched her past the desk of Esterhaus's goggle-eyed secretary, across the museum's Great Hall, and down the wide marble steps into the street.

CHAPTER NINE

THE INSTANT they reached the pavement, Brionny spun away from Slade and came to a stop. She was trembling with anger; her face was as pale as ivory, except for a flag of crimson high on each cheek.

'You fraud,' she said. 'You liar! You—you—'

'You really should try working up a new routine, Stuart. That litany's getting kind of dull.'

'You've got one minute to explain what you think you're doing, and then I'm going to march straight back to Esterhaus's office and blow your pathetic little cover story to smithereens.'

A smile tilted across Slade's mouth, although his eyes remained cold.

'Threats?' he said, his voice soft as silk.

'Promises, McClintoch.'

'You'll change your mind after we talk.'

'We have nothing to talk about.' Brionny put her hands on her hips. 'Unless you want to talk about your prison sentence.'

His mouth tightened into a hard line. 'This isn't the place for this discussion.'

'Ah. Where is the place, then? The local police station? The court house? Perhaps the director's office?'

Slade moved closer to her. There was a sense of tightly controlled anger about him, and it took all her concentration not to step back.

'Do you see that car at the curb?'

She looked past him. A bright red sports car was pulled up next to a 'No Parking' sign.

Her gaze flew to his. 'I see it.'

He smiled thinly. 'It's mine.'

'How charming. Am I supposed to applaud, or what?'

She saw a tiny vein throb in his temple. 'Walk to the curb and get into that car,' he said.

'Walk to the curb and...' Brionny tossed back her head and laughed. 'What do you think this is, Mc-Clintoch, a *Godfather* movie? You don't give orders to—Hey. Hey!' She grimaced as his hand clamped around her wrist and he began hustling her toward the car. 'What are you doing?'

'What does it look like I'm doing?' he said grimly.

Brionny slammed her fist against his shoulder.

'I'll scream!'

'Be my guest,' Slade growled. He held her tight against him, opened the car door, and thrust her into the passenger seat. 'Scream your head off. This is New York, remember? Nobody will notice—and if they do they'll pretend they didn't.'

Brionny glared at him. 'What's the reason for this, McClintoch? Have you gone from theft to kidnapping?'

His eyes narrowed. 'I suppose you'd have no trouble believing that.'

'You're damned right. You're capable of anything, and we both—'

His kiss silenced her in mid-sentence and landed, hard, on her parted lips.

Caught by surprise, she had no time to turn away. There was time only for her to feel the firmness of his mouth, the coolness of it—and to realize, with absolute horror, that she had not forgotten anything of how it felt to have his lips on hers.

'Do you really want to recover the Eye of God?' he asked softly.

Brionny licked her lips, trying not to notice the taste of him that now lay sweet on her tongue.

'Of—of course,' she said.

He smiled. 'I have a proposition to make to you, Bree, one I'm certain you'll find interesting.'

His voice was soft, almost husky. Her throat worked as she swallowed. 'What—what sort of proposition?'

He smiled. It was the same sexy smile he'd given her the time they'd first met, a lifetime ago, in the Hotel Florinda.

'I'll tell you all about it if you come with me quietly.'

'You're crazy, McClintoch. Why would I go with you any way at all?'

His smile grew even more intimate. 'I can think of at least two reasons. One, your boss handed you over to me for an indefinite period of time.'

'He didn't "hand me over" to you,' she said indignantly. 'I'm not your property!'

'Two,' he said calmly, 'it's the only way you're going to hear what I have to say.'

'I know what you have to say!'

'Yes. It's one of your finer qualities, Stuart. Knowing things in advance, I mean.'

Brionny folded her arms. 'What's the sense in playing games? There's no need for us to make a big thing out of this. You have a proposition to make to me— make it.'

'Aren't you even going to ask me if the Eye is safe?'

She blew a strand of hair off her forehead. 'Is it?'

He grinned. 'Safer than it was in that tampon box.'

She knew she was blushing but she kept her gaze steady on his.

'I'm not authorized to make any deals.'

'Deals?'

'You know what I mean. I've no idea what Esterhaus is willing to pay for the stone's return. You'll have to take it up with—'

'What if I told you I didn't want money for the stone?'

She stared at him. He was looking at her in a way that made her dizzy. His emerald eyes were hot, like flames; it was insane, but she could almost feel the lick of heat against her skin.

There was a strange knot of tension forming in the pit of her stomach. She'd felt like this standing at the edge of El Kaia Gorge in Slade's arms, almost overcome by a heady mixture of excitement and fear, the two mixed so closely together that it had been impossible to tell where one ended and the other began.

'I'd—I'd tell you to take it up with Esterhaus,' she said, 'not with me.'

Slade smiled, though the smile never reached his eyes. 'I don't think you'll want me to do that.'

'Well, you're wrong. That's just what I want.'

'You haven't even heard the proposition yet, but you're certain you want it dumped on the director's desk?'

She wasn't certain of anything except the bone-deep knowledge that she was being drawn into something way beyond her depth.

'Yes,' she said, 'I do.'

Slade shrugged. 'OK, Stuart. It's your choice.'

Quickly, before he could change his mind, Brionny swung her legs out of the car. Slade leaned toward her.

'Of course,' he said slyly, 'you realize we'll have to tell old Simon everything.'

'Exactly. Starting with the fact that you're the rotten crook who stole his emerald!'

Slade smiled. Her suit skirt had ridden well above her knees, and he was taking his time appreciating the view.

She tugged furiously at her hem.

'Don't do that,' she snapped.

His eyes met hers. 'Why not?' he said pleasantly. 'After all, we're going to get into much more intimate detail in Esterhaus's office. You want to tell him everything? Fine. I'll tell him all he needs to know—including the fact that you told me where to find the Eye of God after we'd made love.'

Color rose beneath Brionny's skin. 'He doesn't need to know that at all! And—we didn't make love. You seduced me, McClintoch, so you could steal that emerald!'

'We can leave out some of the more intimate details, I guess.' He ran his finger down her cheek. His eyes had gone dark, as silken-soft as his voice. 'Those little sounds you made when I kissed your breasts, or the way you reached for me when you wanted me deep inside you again.'

Brionny twisted her face away from his hand. 'Esterhaus called you a gentleman,' she said, her voice trembling. 'But I don't think you even know the meaning of the word.'

Slade's voice hardened. 'You don't *think*? Come on Bree, you're usually a hell of a lot more positive than that. You're the expert on who and what I am, remember? You sized me up from day one.'

'The only thing I know about you is that you belong

in jail. And I'm not going to rest until that's where you are!'

'This is getting tiresome, Stuart. Make a decision, please. What's it going to be? Truth and confession time in the director's office—or a friendly little chat alone with me?'

Brionny looked at Slade without speaking. It was inconceivable that she'd ever, even for a moment, imagined feeling something for this man. He was everything she'd thought him to be and worse.

'This proposition of yours had better be worth hearing,' she snapped.

He laughed. 'It is. In fact, I suspect you'll find it fascinating.' He slammed her door, came around the car, and climbed in behind the wheel. 'I can hardly wait to hear your reaction.'

He hit a button on the console and the locks on the doors snicked down into place.

Trapped, Brionny thought, and the car shot into traffic.

'I'm not going in there!'

Slade had pulled into a drive outside one of Manhattan's priciest bits of real estate, and now Brionny was sitting with her arms crossed and an expression of defiance on her face.

'Don't be ridiculous. Of course you are.'

'You said we were going to a restaurant. You never mentioned a word about taking me to an apartment.'

'I said we were going to lunch, Stuart. The days when ladies swooned at the prospect of setting foot inside a man's home are long gone.'

She looked from him to the glass skyscraper and laughed.

'This is your home? Come on, McClintoch. You don't really expect me to believe this is where you live.'

'Frankly, I don't give a damn what you believe, as long as you don't give the doorman a scene to remember for the rest of his life.' His gaze flicked past her. 'Good afternoon, Hodges.'

A man in a blue and maroon uniform was looking in at them and smiling.

'Afternoon, Mr McClintoch.' He put his hand to the brim of his cap. 'Ma'am.'

The door swung open. Brionny sat still for a second, and then she muttered something under her breath, gave the doorman a bright smile, and stepped from the car.

Slade took her arm as he came up beside her. 'Would you ring the Golden Phoenix and ask them to deliver the meal I ordered, please, Hodges?'

'Don't bother, Hodges.' Both men looked at Brionny. Another falsely polite smile curved across her lips. 'I'm afraid I won't be staying long enough to eat.'

Slade's fingers bit into her arm but he nodded. 'You heard the lady, Hodges.' He kept a tight grip on her arm as he led her under the portico, through the elegant lobby, and into an elevator.

'Afraid I'll bolt and run?' she said sweetly.

The elevator doors slid shut, and he let go of her and lounged back against the wall of the car.

'Too bad you decided to pass on lunch,' he said pleasantly. 'The Golden Phoenix does a terrific Peking duck.'

'How nice for the Golden Phoenix.' Brionny smiled tightly. 'But I don't care much for private luncheons.'

Slade breathed out a weary sigh. 'I know what you're thinking, and you can relax. Seduction isn't on the menu.'

'You've no idea what I'm thinking,' she said, her eyes fixed on the flashing floor numbers. 'It's your safety I had in mind, Slade, not mine. With witnesses around, I'd be less likely to shove you out the nearest win—'

The doors slid open, and she caught her breath in shock.

A marble entry foyer as large as Simon Esterhaus's office stretched ahead. Beyond it was a living-room almost the size of the museum's Great Hall.

'Whose apartment is this?' she whispered.

Slade laughed. 'Don't you mean, are we going to be arrested between dessert and coffee?' He tossed his car keys on a table and moved past her. 'What would you say if I told you it was mine?'

'I'd ask what bank you'd robbed,' Brionny said drily, 'and, in your case, it probably wouldn't be a joke.'

He smiled. 'Let's just say it's mine to use whenever I'm in New York.'

'It belongs to someone you know?'

'Yes. That's right. It belongs to someone I know.'

'Well, it's certainly nice to have friends who live in the right places.' She walked to a wall of glass that looked out over the East River. 'That's an impressive view.'

Slade shrugged his shoulders. 'It's OK. I prefer my place in Connecticut. Trees, rolling hills—'

'Is that where you live? Connecticut?'

'Why do you sound so surprised, Stuart?'

'I don't. I just—' Brionny looked at him. She had never thought of him living anywhere, she realized; she'd imagined him bouncing from country to country with no real place to call his own. And yet she had no difficulty picturing him in a sleek, contemporary house on a verdant hillside in Connecticut; he didn't even seem out of place here, in this apartment that might have come off the pages of *Better Homes and Gardens*...

'How about some wine?'

She blinked. Slade was holding out a glass half filled with a dark, ruby liquid. She hesitated, then took it from him. She didn't want the wine, but she did want something to hold on to, something that would make her feel less as if she was walking through a surrealistic dream.

'So.' Slade sipped his wine, then smiled. 'Do you really like my—my friend's apartment?'

Brionny nodded. 'I like the things he collects, too.' She nodded toward a series of glass shelves that housed a dozen or more tiny terracotta figures. 'I've never seen so many of those under one roof.'

'They're just clay,' Slade said lazily.

'They're pre-Colombian relics and worth a fortune. You probably don't...' She fell silent, and he chuckled.

'Ah, Stuart, you have a face that's so easy to read! You're sorry you said that. Now you're afraid I'm going to toss the figures into a suitcase and steal them!'

Faint spots of color rose in her cheeks. 'You knew they were valuable,' she said stiffly.

Slade grinned. 'Did I?'

'It doesn't matter to me if you steal everything in this place. Come to think of it, everything's probably stolen to begin with. Your pal most likely collects black market antiquities.'

'Really.'

She looked around the room, at the small Van Gogh on the far wall, the Klee over the fireplace, at the Egyptian cat that guarded a shelf displaying exquisite jade figures.

'My God,' she whispered, 'there's a king's ransom here!'

'And all of it stolen?' Slade asked politely.

Brionny glared at him. 'You think it's funny, don't you?'

Amusement fell from his face like a discarded mask. 'I think it's incredible how you set yourself up as judge and jury. I promise you, Brionny, the man who lives here is not a thief.'

'You're a fine one to give character references, McClintoch. Not that it matters to me. I'm only interested in the Eye of God.'

'Isn't that the truth?' Slade said pleasantly.

Brionny swung toward him. 'You said you had a proposition to make me, McClintoch. Suppose we get to it?'

He nodded, his eyes suddenly cool. 'I agree. The sooner we can agree on terms the better.'

Terms? Brionny thought. What did he mean? He couldn't really think she'd believed him when he'd said he didn't want money for the emerald. Of course he wanted money. Why else would he have stolen it in the first place?

Why was he being so mysterious? And why had he involved her? Was it because he figured he could trust her not to turn him in, that she had no choice but to do his bidding in order to protect herself?

Slade poured himself more wine. He took a drink, then looked at her.

'My price is non-negotiable.'

She nodded. 'I expected it would be. Well, I can't promise anything—'

A crooked smile eased across his lips. 'You'll have to.'

'I don't have the authority. Esterhaus didn't—'

'I told you, Esterhaus hasn't got a thing to do with this.' Slade put down his glass and walked toward her.

'If you knew the slightest thing about how museums operate, you wouldn't say that. Esterhaus is the only one with the power to approve whatever amount of money you request.'

He took her wineglass from her fingers and set it aside.

'You really weren't paying attention before, Stuart. I said I don't want money for the emerald.'

'Of course you do,' Brionny said, a little breathlessly. Why was he standing so close to her? 'Otherwise—'

'That's a hell of a habit,' he said softly. He smiled and stroked his thumb lightly across the fullness of her mouth. 'You're always so positive you know what I want—but you never bother checking with me to see if you're right.'

His touch scalded her. She wanted to move away from it, but where was there to go? The table was at her back, and Slade—Slade was so close that she could see that his eyes had turned a heated mix of turquoise, emerald and jade.

'And you're always right, aren't you, Bree?' His voice fell to a whisper. 'Just as you were right to have me locked in a roach-infested cell in Italpa—because I'd stolen your precious Eye.'

That he'd been locked up by the Italpan police was a shock. She waited for the elation that should have followed it, but all she felt was a strange hollowness.

'I didn't think they'd even filed my report. How—how did you make them let you go? Did you bribe them?'

His mouth twisted. 'Why ask me? You already know the answers you want to hear.'

His thumb was still moving gently against her flesh. She jerked away from his touch.

'Don't do that!'

'Why?' His smile was chill. 'Does it make you remember things you'd rather forget?'

'It makes me remember how much I dislike you,' she said sharply. 'Now, can we please get down to business?'

Slade stepped back. He tucked his hands into his trouser pockets, and walked slowly to the window.

'You want to know what price I've set on the emerald,' he said.

Brionny nodded. 'Yes.'

He swung around and smiled. 'Nothing you can't afford, Stuart.'

'It's not a matter of what I can or can't afford, Slade. The museum—'

'But it is,' he said. His smile vanished. 'You're going to buy the stone from me. Not Esterhaus or the museum.'

She laughed. 'Me? I haven't got the money to—'

'I'm not talking dollars.'

'You're not?' Why was her heart beginning to pound? Why was he looking at her like that, as if he were a cat and she were a canary, trapped in a cage with a paw-sized opening?

'The Mali-Mali barter for the things they want. You must know that.'

'The Mali-Mali!' Brionny's eyes flashed. 'Let's not talk about them, McClintoch, not if you want me to be in the right mood to listen to your so-called proposition.'

He showed his teeth in a quick smile. 'I'm just giving you some background, so you'll understand that what I'm about to suggest has historical validity.'

Brionny flung her hands on to her hips. 'Dammit, will you get to the point?'

'Here it is, then, Stuart.' He paused, and she found herself holding her breath, waiting for him to speak. 'We're going to barter, you and I. I give you the emerald—and you give me one night.'

It was a joke. It had to be a joke.

But Slade wasn't laughing. He wasn't even smiling any more.

Brionny shook her head. 'You're crazy!'

'It will all be very civilized. Dinner, dancing, a pleasant evening on the town—'

'You can't really mean this, Slade.'

'That's the price, lady. Take it or leave it.'

'But—but why?'

His mouth twisted. 'You always know what I'm up to, Stuart; figure it out for yourself.'

Brionny snatched up her purse and started past him. 'I won't even dignify this with an answer.'

'The hell you won't,' Slade growled, catching her by the arm. 'You'll survive the deal. You might even enjoy it. Think about the night we spent in that jungle shack.'

Heat swept into her cheeks. 'That night was an obscenity! If you hadn't lied to me about the danger we were supposed to be in—'

'I see.' His voice was soft as velvet. 'It was fear that drove you into my arms, hmm?'

'You know it was!' Humiliation made her reckless. 'Nothing else would have made me sleep with a man like you!'

She saw his face and wanted to call the words back,

but it was too late. Slade said something ugly, pulled her into his arms, and crushed her mouth under his. When he let her go, Brionny wiped the back of her hand across her lips.

'I only wish the headhunters had been real,' she said, her voice trembling, 'so they could have put an arrow through your heart. Why does it mean so much to you to humiliate me?'

Slade looked at her for a long moment, and then he turned and stood with his back to her, his gaze riveted on the scene below.

'You're beginning to bore me, Stuart,' he said. 'Do we have a deal or not?'

Brionny closed her eyes. She thought of Professor Ingram, who'd given his life for the Eye of God. She thought of the generations of Indians who had worshipped it. She thought of the long line of archaeologists standing like watchful, ancestral shadows behind her.

And she thought of the one person responsible for the emerald's loss, the one person who now had the chance to set things right...

Slade turned to her. 'Well?' he demanded impatiently. 'Is it yes—or is it no?'

A shudder went through her. She took a deep, deep breath and said the only thing she could.

She said yes.

CHAPTER TEN

BRIONNY STARED at her reflection in her bedroom mirror.

Her dress was midnight-blue lace, an expensive bit of gossamer she'd bought on impulse at a sale months before and never worn. It had thin straps and a short, above-the-knee skirt. Sterling silver hoops swayed from her earlobes; a silver chain glinted against the soft, rising curve of her breasts. On her feet were slender-heeled silver sandals.

She looked as if she was dressed for a special date with a special man. Her throat closed. In truth, she was dressed for a charade.

At least she'd realized that truth before the night began.

She thought back to what had happened this afternoon. Within seconds after she'd caved in to Slade's ugly demand, she'd known she couldn't go through with it. She hated herself for it, but at least she'd gone to him willingly that first time. But selling herself to him—that was different. The price was too high, no matter what the pay-off.

She'd turned to him to tell him that, but Slade had spoken first.

'You disappoint me, sweetheart,' he'd said slowly. 'I expected a lecture on my lack of morality, or an appeal to my better nature. And how about some girlish tears? A desperate plea for compassion?'

And, in that moment, she'd realized that it was all a sham. He would never give her the emerald. It was worth far too much money and he'd risked too much to get it.

Slade was lying, but there was nothing new in that. Lying was what he did best. He'd set up this whole ugly little exercise to make her pay for the night he'd spent in jail in Italpa.

The realization had sent a swift, fierce sense of power sweeping through her. Knowing his game, she could afford to play it—but by her own rules.

She would turn the game back on him. She had already taken the first step, even though it had been by pure good luck.

Accepting his obscene offer—seeming to accept it, anyway—had denied him the pleasure of watching her grovel. Now she'd deny him everything else.

And so she'd squared her shoulders, looked straight into his cold, lying eyes, and told him that people like her never pleaded for anything.

It had been the perfect exit line. She'd stalked out, head high—and between then and now she'd planned her strategy.

She would go out with him this evening. She would be polite and proper—so polite and proper that it would make his head spin. But she would never miss the chance to insult him—as politely as possible, of course. And when the end of the night came, if he was fool enough to try and take her in his arms, she would tell him that he wasn't the only one who could lie through his teeth and get away with it.

'You must be crazy,' she'd say. 'I wouldn't sleep with you if you offered me the Hope diamond.'

And then she'd offer him her own proposition. He could hand over the emerald to her and she'd keep his secret. She'd tell no one that Slade McClintoch was a thief.

If not, she'd turn him over to Esterhaus.

How stupid she'd been, thinking Slade could blackmail her! What he held over her head was nothing compared to what she could tell the world about him.

He was the one with everything to lose, not she. It had taken her a while to figure it out, but now that she had—

The doorbell sounded. Brionny's heart gave a fluttering beat.

Was it really time already?

She took a deep breath and made her way through the living-room.

Be polite, she reminded herself, be chillingly polite, and she flung the door open like a queen greeting her subjects.

'Good evening,' she said. 'You're right on—'

The words died on her lips. Slade was wearing a black dinner suit that had surely been custom-tailored to make the most of his height, his powerful shoulders, his hard, lean body. The white ruffled shirt beneath the jacket set off his tanned, angular face, the softness of the ruffles somehow enhancing the overall aura of masculinity that surrounded him.

'Good evening.' His gaze moved slowly over her before returning to her face. 'You look beautiful.'

Brionny pulled herself together and managed a brittle smile. 'Really?' she said. 'This old thing? It's terribly out of date.'

'These are for you.' He held out a nosegay of flowers, a magnificent riot of reds, corals and pinks. 'The color choice was sheer luck, but I'm glad to see it complements your dress.'

It would have complemented anything, she thought, her fingers itching with the desire to touch the lovely blossoms. Instead, she shook her head.

'How unfortunate. I'm afraid I don't like flowers, Slade. I'm allergic to them.'

His eyes narrowed, as if he was slowly catching on to what was happening.

'What a shame,' he said.

'Yes, isn't it?'

'It must have been hell for you, down there in the Amazon. Traipsing through a jungle filled with all sorts of flowers, I mean.'

'Oh, it was. Except for the time I spent with Professor Ingram, my entire stay in the Amazon was hell.'

Slade's lips drew back from his teeth. 'Nicely done, Stuart.'

Her smile was the equal of his. 'Thank you,' she purred.

She took her purse from the table. You don't know the half of it, McClintoch, she thought, and swept past him.

It was going to be one hell of a night.

Slade's red sports car wove swiftly in and out of traffic.

Where were they going? Not to the apartment he was staying in; they'd left Manhattan behind half an hour ago. Now they were speeding along a highway that traveled the length of Long Island.

Damn, but the silence in the car was oppressive. She

was tempted to ask Slade to put on some music, but—

As if on signal, he reached toward the built-in compact-disk player, hit a button, and the poignant strains of a Rachmaninoff piano concerto filled the car. She almost laughed. A man like him, pretending to like such rich, romantic music? Who was he trying to impress?

'Is Rachmaninoff OK?' he said.

Brionny folded her hands in her lap. 'If you like that sort of thing.'

'You don't?'

Of course she did. She always had. But that wasn't the point, not tonight.

'His work's been played to death.' She gave him a polite little smile. 'What CD is that? One of those things they sell on TV, ''Rachmaninoff's Ten Greatest Hits''?'

To her surprise, he laughed.

'''The Best of Bach'', you mean, or ''Beethoven's Hit Parade''?' He flexed his hands on the steering wheel. 'Those old boys would spin in their graves if they knew how their stuff's marketed today—they'd spin at 78 RPM, of course.'

Brionny stared at him. She wanted to laugh—it was a funny line, and it evoked a funny picture. In fact, she almost did laugh. But at the last second, thank goodness, she remembered that she couldn't.

Slade pulled the disk from the player. 'Let's try something brighter. How about Vivaldi?'

Vivaldi. Her favorite composer. Such beautiful, lyrical music...

'Every film maker for the last ten years seems to have used Vivaldi,' she said, flashing him another chill smile. 'Not that I blame them. Vivaldi's music is so—so accessible.'

The arrow seemed to have missed its target. Slade simply shrugged.

'Choose something you prefer, then. There are other CDs in the glove compartment.'

Well, she'd walked right into that. Brionny sighed and popped open the compartment door.

'I'm sure you'll find something you like. I have fairly eclectic taste.'

'Eclectic' wasn't the word for it. Her eyebrows rose as she shuffled through the disks. The Beatles. Borodin. Eric Clapton. Gershwin. Billie Holliday…

'Billie Holliday?' she said aloud, before she could stop herself.

Slade glanced at her. 'You probably never heard of the lady. She was a blues singer a long time back, maybe the greatest that—'

'—Ever lived.' Brionny bit her lip. 'I—uh—I know.'

Damn. Why was she talking so much? She stabbed the CD into the slot. Billie Holliday's soft, quavering voice drifted from the speakers.

'Do you like jazz, Stuart?'

No harm in answering that.

'Yes.'

'All kinds?'

Of course, all kinds.

'I never thought about it,' she said.

'Modern?'

Well, maybe not modern. Too much of the music seemed self-indulgent. Unless it was Miles Davis or Chet Baker—

'I don't,' Slade said, without waiting for her to answer. 'Care for most of the modern stuff, I mean. Unless it's Davis or Baker, I get bored with all those self-serving riffs.'

Brionny swung her head toward him. Was it some sort of parlor trick, this seeming ability to read her mind?

No, of course it wasn't. She turned away, looked out into the night. Lots of people liked jazz. It just seemed surprising that Slade would—

'I'm surprised you like jazz, Stuart.'

'Are you?' she said, as if the question were too dull to consider.

'Well, it's so unstructured.' Slade flashed her a quick smile. 'I'd have thought you'd prefer—'

'It isn't. It only seems that way if you don't understand it.'

Slade nodded. 'I agree. I met this guy once—'

What did she care whom he'd met? And how had she let herself get drawn into this foolish conversation?

From now on, she'd be silent.

'...Club Blue Note. Ever been there?'

Once. The night had been a fiasco. The club had been wonderful, smoky and dark just like the music coming from the tiny bandstand, but her date had despised it. Too crowded, he'd said, and the noise was awful.

'Once,' she said. 'It was crowded, and the noise was awful.'

'You're probably right. Anyway, the place to go, if you want to hear the best blues, is the old Chicago Red Slipper.'

'Oh, have you really been to the Red Slipper? I've read about it, but—'

Brionny flushed, clamped her lips together, and turned away.

'But what?'

'Nothing,' she said, very coldly.

'Come on, Stuart. What were you going to say?'

'This wasn't part of the deal,' she said, even more coldly. 'All this—this silly chitchat…'

'I'm writing the rules tonight, Bree.' His voice was soft, but she could hear the steel in it.

'You didn't say you expected conversation, Slade, only that you expected—'

The tires squealed as he turned the wheel sharply and brought the car to a sudden stop on the shoulder of the road.

'Behave yourself,' he warned. He reached to her and curled his fingers around the nape of her neck. 'Otherwise the deal's off. Understand?'

The deal's off anyway, Brionny thought, and she smiled.

'Certainly,' she said.

Slowly, his hand fell away from her. He took a deep breath and clamped his fingers around the steering wheel.

'I made reservations at a place on the North Shore of the island. Five stars, elegant décor, *boeuf en croute*, a pair of violinists playing softly in the background…'

'Are you waiting for me to tell you it sounds wonderful?'

'I've been there a dozen times. The food's always excellent, the music's unobtrusive, and the service is impeccable.' He reached for her hand. She almost yanked it back, then she decided it would be better to let it lie boneless in his. 'But I know this little place on the ocean,' he murmured, his fingers lacing through hers. 'They serve the best ribs and jazz this side of the Mason-Dixon line. How does that sound?'

Like a place a man would take a woman on a real date, Brionny thought, and a tremor went through her.

Slade brought her hand to his lips. She caught her breath as his mouth grazed her skin.

'We'll go there instead,' he said. 'You'll like it.' He put her hand back into her lap and stepped on the gas.

It was, as he'd said, a little place by the sea.

What he hadn't said was that he was taking her to an old Victorian house with a widow's walk and lots of gingerbread outside, and wonderful smells and overflowing baskets of flowers inside.

This was no out-of-the-way café. It was an expensive hideaway its devotees had protected from the food critics, and you probably needed to make reservations weeks in advance—and then hope they might be honored.

The hostess, a small black woman with skin the color of rich coffee and a broad, generous smile, saw Slade as soon as he and Brionny entered. She came sailing through the line of people waiting to be seated and threw her arms around him.

'Ellen,' he said, kissing her cheek.

'Slade.' Her voice was as Southern, as soft as a ripe Georgia peach. 'We haven't seen you in months.'

'This is Brionny Stuart. I've told her you've got the best food and the best music in the world.'

Ellen laughed as she shook Brionny's hand. 'He exaggerates,' she said. 'The best in this hemisphere—I'm not sure about the world.'

She led them to a table beside a window, with a view out over the moonlit ocean.

'Now,' Ellen said, plucking the 'reserved' sign from the center of the table, 'let me tell this young lady what to order.'

Slade grinned. 'Ellen wants to make sure you don't get the wrong idea and think this place is a democracy.'

Brionny smiled politely. 'That's all right,' she said. 'I'm really not very—'

'Nonsense,' Ellen said briskly. 'Of course you're hungry. And you'll eat. No one comes to Ellen's Place without eating. The food's much too good for that.'

'Well, I—'

'You can't be dieting,' Ellen said, eyeing Brionny critically. 'You're too thin as it is. So what's the problem, child? Are you piqued at something this big man did?'

Brionny's cheeks colored. 'No, no, of course not. I just—'

'The fried chicken is delicious, and so are the barbecued beef and the pork ribs. You'll have to try all three, and then you'll have some Creole coffee and a slab of my sweet potato pie.' Ellen softened her command with a grin. 'Don't panic. I'll tell the kitchen to send out small portions.' She patted Brionny's shoulder, waggled her fingers at Slade, and hurried off.

Brionny looked at Slade. 'Is she always so reserved?'

He grinned. 'She's not kidding, you know. She'll come back and scold you if you don't clean your plate.' He leaned forward, his eyes on hers. 'Well, what do you think?'

She looked around. Their table was very private, set with a blue and white checked cloth, heavy white napkins and handsome silver flatware. It was lit by the soft glow of a candle in a crystal holder. Across the room, on a small bandstand, a handful of men in tuxedos were playing the sweetest, most wonderful blues she'd ever heard.

This was a magical place, a marvelous place...

'Bree? Do you like it?'

She swallowed. 'It's—very nice.'

'Very nice, huh?' Slade smiled. 'See if you can stay with that lukewarm description after we've been here a while.'

She tried. She really did. But how could she? The food was ambrosial. The music was superb. And Slade—Slade was—

He was a man she had never met before.

He knew which ale went best with ribs, which wine would complement the chicken. He knew the names of the tongue-twisting spices that had lent depth and smokiness to the dark, rich beef, and the intricacies between one kind of barbecue technique and the next.

Over the chicken, he told her a story about Machu Pichu that made her smile. Over the ribs, he told her how he'd once confused the Japanese words *tatami* and *tisumi* with near-disastrous results, and made her laugh. Over the beef, he told her how he'd almost been thrown out of Boston University for a night that started with too much beer and ended with twenty fraternity brothers making a drunken, naked dash into a snow bank.

She didn't smile or laugh. She just stared at him.

'You went to Boston University?'

Slade's smile was stilted. 'An illusion shot to hell, Stuart? You figured me for a high-school dropout.'

It was the perfect time to say yes, that was precisely what she'd figured—but she couldn't.

'Actually—actually, I never thought about it.'

'It's OK. My mother had that same look on her face when I told her I'd wangled myself a scholarship. Nobody in our family had ever taken a university degree; I think she'd have accepted it better if I'd told her I was going to be the first McClintoch to go to the moon.'

He was still smiling, but there was a tension between them again. It was just as well, Brionny thought; for a little while, she'd almost forgotten why she was with Slade tonight; she'd almost forgotten what sort of deal they'd made, what she intended to do...

He reached out and touched his forefinger lightly to the corner of her mouth. His touch sizzled against her skin and she jerked back.

'Just being helpful,' he said. 'You had a spot of sauce on your lip.'

She stared at him, her pulse suddenly racing in her throat. He smiled, pushed back his chair, and rose to his feet.

'Come,' he said softly.

He was holding out his hand and moving in rhythm with the soft Gershwin tune the band was playing.

'No,' she said quickly, 'I don't—'

Slade reached for her, and before she could figure out a way to stop it from happening she was in his arms.

She didn't want him to hold her so close, but the floor was small and crowded. His hand came up and cupped her head, and he tucked her face into the curve of his shoulder.

Brionny's eyes closed. The feel of him, the smell of him were so painfully familiar. Memories flooded her senses: she knew his hair would be silken under her fingers, knew his skin would taste salty and warm.

God, she thought, oh, God, if only this were real...

What was the matter with her? This could never be real. She hated Slade, hated everything he stood for...

'Bree.' His mouth was at her temple; she could feel the soft whisper of his breath against her hair. 'Bree—I have to tell you something.'

What could he possibly tell her? More lies, she

thought, and she began to tremble. Soft, sweet lies this time, judging by the way he was holding her, by the way his hands were moving softly along her spine, lies he hoped would draw her down into a whirlpool of desire and give the evening the perfect finish.

But it wouldn't happen. And it was time he knew it.

'Bree,' he whispered, and she yanked herself out of his arms and looked at him.

'I want to go home.'

'Now?' There was bewilderment in his green eyes. 'But it's still early.'

'No, it's not,' she said. 'It's late. Later than you ever imagined.'

She started to turn away and Slade reached for her, caught her by the shoulder harder than he'd intended, and swung her toward him. People around them on the tiny floor cast sidelong looks, but he didn't notice.

'No,' he said sharply, 'no, you're not leaving, dammit. You're going to listen.'

'To you?' She laughed. 'What could a man like you possibly say that a woman like me would want to hear?'

Behind him, someone gave a muffled giggle. Slade spun toward the sound, his cheeks flushed, but no one met his eyes. When he looked for her again, Brionny was stalking from the dance floor.

Damn her! And damn him, for having thought she'd seen him, really seen him, for the first time, for having been about to tell her everything—who he was, what had really happened to her precious emerald...

He drew a breath. She had saved him from making a complete ass of himself, he thought grimly. He owed her something for that.

He reached the table an instant after she did, peeled

some bills from his wallet, and dropped them on the cloth.

'Let's go,' he growled, and he took her arm. She made a little sound and he knew he was hurting her but he didn't much care. Out of the corner of his eye he saw Ellen staring at him, but he didn't much care about that either.

The heat in the parking lot was oppressive. Beside him, Brionny was trying to break his hold, but she didn't have a chance.

What a fool he'd made of himself tonight! Determined to humble Brionny Stuart, convinced he owed her a lesson for the pain she'd inflicted on him, he'd forced her into an unholy contract and then ended up trying to please her instead.

How in hell could one woman who stood for everything he despised always end up making him lose his self-control?

'I'm speaking to you, McClintoch!'

He looked at her. They had reached his car; he was holding her against it and she was looking at him through eyes that blazed with contempt.

'Forgive me, my lady,' he said. His teeth glinted in a shark-like smile. 'I didn't hear you.'

'I said I'd rather go home by taxi.'

'Would you?'

'Yes. This night is at an end.'

Slade laughed. He opened the car door and pushed her inside.

'No,' he said, very softly, 'no, sweetheart, it is not.'

She was frightened now; he could see it in her face, although she was doing her best not to show it. Quickly, he got behind the wheel, put the car in gear, and sent it sliding out of the gravel lot.

She swung her head toward him. His profile was blade-sharp, his mouth thin. Her hands shook a little, and she folded them quickly into her lap.

'This display of machismo is boring,' she said. Her voice, at least, was steady. 'And it's not impressive.'

'I'm not interested in impressing you, Bree.' He looked at her, his smile terrifying in its emptiness. 'We made a deal, remember?'

'The deal's off,' she said sharply.

'Don't be silly, sweetheart. Don't you want that emerald?'

'Why don't you tell the truth for once, Slade? You just wanted to—to bring me to my knees. You know it's money you want for the emerald, not me.'

'Ah,' he said, 'Brionny Stuart, she who knows all, speaks again!' His voice hardened, became like the sting of a whip. 'Well, you're wrong, lady. We made a deal, and you're going to live with it. You're spending the night with me.'

'Slade, damn you—'

He reached out, dumped the Billie Holliday CD from the player, stabbed in the Rachmaninoff, and turned up the volume. Music, loud and dramatic, filled the car with sound. Speech was impossible.

Brionny gritted her teeth. She hadn't pleaded this afternoon; that was what this was all about. He wanted her to plead now.

She'd sooner burn in hell.

Let him put on an act. He was angry, he was trying to scare her, but so what? No matter what else he was, Slade was not a man who would force a woman into his bed.

Cars lined the curb in front of her apartment building. Slade shot into a space beside a fire hydrant. He slammed his way out of the car, clamped his hand around Brionny's wrist, and marched her up the four flights of steps to her apartment.

'The key,' he demanded, holding out his palm. When she didn't move, he pushed her back against the door, took her purse from her and dug through it until he'd found what he wanted. Then he undid the lock and shoved her inside.

He's trying to scare me, Brionny told herself, that's all he's doing.

When he unbuttoned his dinner jacket and dropped it across the back of the sofa, she decided things had gone far enough.

'That's it,' she said. 'You've made your point. You're stronger than I am, and—'

He laughed. 'Haven't we had this conversation before, sweetheart?' He reached out and took hold of her shoulders. 'Don't fight me, Bree. I don't want to hurt you.'

At last, fear flooded through her veins. 'No,' she said. 'Slade, don't—'

His kiss was punishing and painful, forced on her unwilling mouth with a pressure that made her head fall back.

'Stop it,' she panted, struggling frantically against him.

'Hell, sweetheart, I'm disappointed. I thought ladies of your class never tried to squirm out of an agreement.'

She cried out as he kissed her again, his mouth fierce and hot.

'You're hurting me! Slade, please...'

All at once, the terror in her voice cut through the blind rage that had almost overcome him.

He went absolutely still. 'Bree?' he said. 'Bree...'

His eyes swept over her face. He saw the tears on her lashes, saw her mouth, bruised and swollen from his kisses. He looked at her arms, at his fingers biting deep into her flesh, and he groaned with despair.

'Dear God,' he said. 'Bree, sweetheart, forgive me!'

He gathered her to him, pressing soft kisses to her hair, to her throat. He murmured her name, over and over, and stroked his hands over her back.

'I'm sorry,' he whispered, 'I'm so sorry...'

With a little sob of desperation, her arms went around his neck. She brought his head down to hers and kissed him, her mouth open to his. She didn't understand it, but fear had given way to something else, something that was always there when she was in Slade's arms, a desire so sharp and sweet it was like a pain in her heart.

The emerald, she thought as his hands began moving over her, the damned emerald! If only he'd really give it to her, she could return it to Esterhaus along with some made-up story about how she'd come by it, and all this would be behind them. There would be time to explore these feelings, this incredible, wonderful emotion she'd felt ever since she'd met him...

'Bree.' Slade kissed her deeply. 'I have to tell you...' She moved in his arms, just enough to lean back and look up at him. The action sent her hips against his and he groaned and shifted his aroused body against hers. 'Hell, it's going to have to wait.'

'No,' she said urgently, 'it can't wait. I have to talk to you, Slade.'

He swallowed hard, took a breath, and took a step back.

'You're right. This conversation is long overdue.'

Brionny put her fingers over his lips. 'Don't say anything until you've heard what I have to say. Please.'

He gave a choked laugh. 'Hell, we'll have to take turns. OK, sweetheart. You first.'

She drew a deep, steadying breath into her lungs. 'Slade? Did you mean it when you said you'd give me the Eye of God?'

He tensed. 'The emerald? That's what you want to talk about?'

'Yes! Of course. It's the most important thing we—'

'Sure it is.' Slade looked at her, at the soft mouth and beautiful eyes that offered a promise of warmth that was a lie, and he felt a coldness seeping into his bones. 'Business before pleasure, right?'

Brionny's face paled. 'You don't understand.'

'But I do.' He let go of her, knowing that if he didn't he might put his hands around her lovely, fragile throat and squeeze. 'I understand completely—and because you made the evening interesting I'll even give you an honest answer.' His eyes, flat and bright as green glass, met hers. 'I never had any intention of giving you the emerald, sweetheart.' His lips drew back from his teeth. 'A night with you, for the Eye of God? Not even the Mali-Mali would have made such a poor trade.'

Slade picked up his jacket, flung it over his shoulder, and walked out into the night.

CHAPTER ELEVEN

EARLY IN the morning, the museum was so quiet that Brionny's footsteps seemed to echo like gunshots as she made her way through the Great Hall.

She had always liked the museum at this time, just before the crowds invaded. One of the privileges of being on staff was that you could flash your ID at the guard at the gate and enter the building early, either for some quiet time at your desk or simply to stroll the halls and enjoy the treasures of the world in privacy.

That was what she was doing now, taking a last, peaceful look at the artifacts she loved, because she knew that the next time she came to this museum it would be as a paying patron.

But it would be worth it. By this time tomorrow, the museum would have its emerald.

And Slade would be where he belonged, in a prison cell.

At seven, she'd telephoned Simon Esterhaus at his home. His voice had been muzzy with sleep and gruff with the displeasure of being awakened. After she'd identified herself, his tone had sharpened.

'Have you news of the emerald, Miss Stuart?' he'd said.

Brionny had taken a deep, deep breath.

'I know who has it, sir.'

'Wonderful!' Esterhaus's joy had been almost palpable. 'That's wonderful news, my dear. Tell me everything.'

'I will, Mr Esterhaus. But—but not over the telephone.'

'Of course, Miss Stuart. I'll see you at ten. I take it Mr McClintoch will be with you?'

'No. He will not be with me, sir. I'll be alone.'

If that had struck Esterhaus as odd, he had not said so. Now, in just a few minutes, she would meet with him in his office—and this nightmare would finally come to an end.

She glanced at her watch, turned, and made her way slowly across the hall. The huge front doors were just opening and the early arrivals were filtering in. Students clutching notebooks, tourists, families with children whose squeals turned quickly to excited whispers when they spotted the impressive Tyrannosaurus Rex rearing up in the center of the Great Hall.

The anteroom to Esterhaus's office loomed ahead. Brionny came to an abrupt halt, her heart hammering. Then, before she could lose courage, she strode purposefully through the open door.

Esterhaus's secretary looked up from her desk.

'Good morning, Miss Stuart. The director is expecting you.'

Brionny tried to smile, but her lips felt stuck to her teeth. She nodded, marched to the door to Esterhaus's office, knocked lightly and opened it.

It was like a replay of her last appearance here. Esterhaus was seated at his desk, thumbing through a stack of papers. He looked up, frowned, and motioned her forward.

'Sit down, Miss Stuart.'

Brionny sat. She waited for him to say something more; when he didn't she cleared her throat.

'Mr Esterhaus. Sir. I—I have news about the Eye of God.'

Esterhaus took off his eyeglasses, massaged the bridge of his nose, and leaned back in his chair.

'Yes, so you said, Miss Stuart, but I think I should tell you—'

'Sir, please, this is—it's difficult for me to talk about. I'd appreciate it if you'd just let me—just let me say my piece. I'm sure you'll have questions, and I'm more than willing to answer them, but—but—'

Esterhaus sighed. 'Of course. Please, say whatever you wish.'

Brionny ran the tip of her tongue across her lips. She had gone over her speech dozens of times; it was the only thing that had kept her sane during the hours of the night.

She cleared her throat.

'Sir. You know—you know that there was a man traveling with me when the emerald was taken from me. And you know that—that I thought we were in grave danger from headhunters.'

'Miss Stuart—'

'The missionary thought I'd been hallucinating, but—'

'But he was wrong. The headhunters were dangerously real.'

Brionny blinked. 'No. They weren't real at all, Mr Esterhaus. Perhaps I didn't make that clear when we spoke, but—'

'An advisory reached me yesterday from Peru, Miss Stuart.' Esterhaus popped his glasses on his nose, thumbed through the papers on his desk and selected one. '"To Simon Esterhaus, Director,"' he read, '"from the Minister for...blah, blah, blah. Please be advised that permits for the purposes of archaeological and anthropological digs will be temporarily suspended due to..."'

He whipped off his glasses and looked at Brionny. 'The point of all this bureaucratic mumbo jumbo, Miss Stuart, is that some rarely seen Indian tribe's suddenly come creeping out of the jungle. The Mori-Mori, something like that.'

'The Mali-Mali?' Brionny said, eyes wide.

'That's it. Apparently they went on the warpath just about the time you located the Eye of God.'

She swallowed convulsively. 'Because the professor and I took the stone?'

'No, no, it's nothing to do with that.'

'The road, then. They must be angry about the road that's going through the jungle, and—'

'It's not that either. According to this directive, the— what did you call them?'

'The Mali-Mali,' Brionny whispered.

'The Mali-Mali are stirred up over some internal problem, a battle between two warring factions that's been broadened to include anyone who gets in their way.' His sharp little teeth showed in a quick smile. 'Primitive, but not without a certain definite parallel in our own world, don't you agree?'

Brionny sat back in her chair. Slade had not lied, then—at least, he had not lied about the headhunters. But he had lied about everything else—about wanting her, about trust, about caring...

'Miss Stuart?'

She blinked. 'Sir?'

'I was saying, if that's all you wanted to tell me—'

'No, it isn't. There's—there's more, Mr Esterhaus.'

The director sighed. 'Go on, then, Miss Stuart.'

'I—I think you have the right to know that I bear sole responsibility for the loss of the Eye of God, sir.'

Esterhaus's brows lifted. 'I thought you said it was stolen from you, by your traveling companion.'

'Yes. It was.' Brionny hesitated. The hard part was coming—and yet this wasn't the worst of it, not by a long shot. 'But—but he'd tried to get it from me before, many times.'

'Go on.'

She looked up. Esterhaus was watching her with a little smile on his face. Oh, God, she thought, God...

'I'd refused to tell him where it was, you see, because I knew—I knew he would steal it. And then, that last night...' Brionny took a shaky breath and stared past the director, her eyes focused on the wall. 'That last night, I made a terrible mistake. I told him where he could find the stone, I told him where I'd hidden it, and—and—'

Her voice broke. She gave a sob and buried her face in her hands.

Esterhaus shoved back his chair and hurried toward her. 'Miss Stuart, my dear young woman, you were under an incredible amount of stress. In the circumstances—'

'Dammit, Mr Esterhaus!' Brionny looked up, her eyes streaming. She dug into her pocket for a tissue, blotted her eyes, and blew her nose noisily. 'Will you please stop interrupting and let me get this over with?'

Esterhaus drew back. 'If that is what you wish, Miss Stuart, but I assure you it isn't necessary. If you'd just listen to me for a moment—'

'No,' she said fiercely, rising to her feet, '*you* listen

to *me*, sir! I have something to tell you, and, and—I know where the Eye of God is,' she said.

Esterhaus smiled politely. 'Go on.'

Brionny frowned. She'd certainly expected more of a reaction than that.

'It won't cost us a penny to recover it, because we won't have to buy it, you see; we'll only have to have the thief who took it arrested.'

'Miss Stuart—'

'Don't you want to know his name?'

'No, not really, Miss Stuart. You see—'

'What do you mean, "not really"?' Her face, pale but for the slashes of color in her cheeks, took on a stern cast. 'I want the thief tried, convicted and imprisoned. I want him to spend years in jail. I want him to be old and feeble by the time he gets out.'

Esterhaus was smiling again, in a manner that was almost paternal.

'Ah,' he said. 'I think I'm beginning to understand.'

'Good,' Brionny said. 'You'd better understand. And you'd better be prepared to bring charges against— against—'

After a moment's silence, Esterhaus his throat. 'Against?'

Brionny stared at him. I can't tell him, she thought, I can't!

She had spent the endless hours of the night deciding which punishment Slade deserved more, immersion in boiling oil or being tied to the rack, reminding herself that she would have to be satisfied with seeing him handcuffed and led off to prison—and now, with her chance finally at hand, she couldn't do it. She couldn't condemn Slade to a cell and to years of confinement.

'Miss Stuart?' Esterhaus said gently.

Brionny looked at him, her eyes bright with unshed tears. 'I can't tell you,' she whispered.

'Well, then,' Esterhaus said, even more gently, 'if you can't tell me the thief's name, how will we recover the stone?'

She stared at him while her brain processed the question. It was a good question. An excellent one.

And she had no answer.

'I'll find a way,' she whispered, blotting at her eyes with the now useless tissue. 'I'll go to—to the thief, and—and I'll plead. I'll get down on my knees and beg him to give me the stone, so I can return it to you. I'll offer him anything, anything—'

'Anything, Bree?'

She spun around. Slade was standing in the doorway, dressed as if he were back in the jungle, in jeans and a cotton shirt and dusty, well-worn boots. His hands were on his hips, and he was watching her with absolutely no expression on his face.

'McClintoch,' Esterhaus said happily. Brionny watched as he hurried across the room and grasped Slade's hand. 'It's so good to see you.'

Slade smiled tightly. 'We only saw each other two hours ago, Simon,' he said, his eyes never leaving Brionny's face.

'Of course, of course.' Esterhaus laughed. 'But the man who gave the museum such a gift will always be a welcome visitor in my office.'

Brionny tried to speak, but her throat was dry. She forced moisture into her mouth, then swallowed.

'Gift?' she whispered. 'What gift?'

'I've been trying to tell you, Miss Stuart. The Eye of God is safe in the museum vault.'

'What? But how—?'

'Mr McClintoch telephoned me just after you did this morning. He told me that you and he had recovered the Eye of God.'

'He told you…?'

'He explained that the thief had agreed to return the emerald at no cost, provided we agreed to keep the matter quiet.' Esterhaus put his finger to his lips. 'I assured Mr McClintoch that there was no problem with that, of course.'

'Of course,' Brionny said lamely.

'It means,' Esterhaus said, smiling at her, 'that we will never know the name of the thief, nor even how he came by the stone—'

'But I told you that much,' Brionny whispered.

'Did you?' Esterhaus shook his head. 'I'm afraid I've so much on my mind this morning, Miss Stuart, that I wasn't paying full attention.' He looked from Slade to Brionny and cleared his throat. 'In fact, I have an appointment in just a few minutes, so if neither of you minds…'

'Neither of us minds,' Slade said, his eyes still on Brionny.

The door swung shut and they were alone.

Slade spoke first. 'I heard that last part,' he said as he walked slowly toward her. 'That you'd get down on your knees, if you had to, and beg the thief to give back the stone.'

Brionny flushed. 'Why do you sound surprised? You were the one who kept saying I'd do anything to get the Eye back.'

'Not quite. You didn't tell Esterhaus I was the man who'd stolen it.' He moved forward again until they were a breath apart. 'Why didn't you?'

'That's my business, McClintoch.'

He reached out and touched her hair, his hand gentle and light. 'For a woman who couldn't wait to have me locked up in Italpa, that's one heck of a change in attitude.'

Brionny moistened her lip with the tip of her tongue. 'Were there—were there really roaches in the Italpa jail?'

Slade smiled. 'Big enough to lasso, Stuart, but it was just as well. Trying to stomp them to death kept me from thinking about what I'd do to you when I saw you again.'

'What *you'd* do to *me*?' Brionny's voice rose with indignation. 'That's very funny McClintoch. You stole the emerald from me, and —'

'I took it from your pack while you were sleeping.'

'Damned right you did!'

'I took it because I woke up and heard the Mali-Mali drums in the jungle.'

Brionny's eyes widened. 'What?'

'I thought, If only I'd spent the last hours of daylight building a raft, we might have a chance.' A fleeting smile curved across his mouth. 'And then I thought, Hell, those hours with Bree in my arms were the best hours of my life. I figured if I had to die I was ready.' His eyes darkened. 'But I didn't want you to die, sweetheart. I decided there had to be a way to stop those bastards.'

Without thinking, Brionny put her hand out and touched Slade's arm.

'And?' she whispered. 'What did you do?'

'I took the emerald from your pack. I kissed you and stepped outside. Everything was still—even the sound of the river seemed muted. The drumming had stopped.'

He smiled again, but Brionny could see the tension in the smile. 'Not a good sign, I figured.'

'No,' she said, caught up in the story. 'No, I suppose not.'

'I had to do something and do it fast. So I rubbed myself all over with mud—for camouflage—and made my way through the trees. I ended up right in the middle of twenty or thirty Mali-Mali. I figured I was as good as dead anyway, so I stuck out my hand, let the rising sun glint off the Eye, and told the bastards to come and get it if they had the guts.'

Brionny stared at him. It was an incredible story, so unreal that if any other man had told it she'd have known it was an outright lie. But it was easy to picture Slade doing just what he'd said, going off to save her, daring the savages to take him on.

'The emerald and my head would probably be sitting in some Mali-Mali village this minute—except that the Indians went crazy when the light hit that stone. They leaped into the air, yelling like banshees. *"Woowie"*, somebody screamed, or something like that. It scared the hell out of me and I screamed back. The next thing I knew, they were racing off like the wind—What's so funny?'

'My God, Slade!' Brionny's shoulders were shaking with laughter. 'They thought you were a *woo-ya-hoo*. A demon! No wonder they ran.'

'Yeah.' A grin tilted across his mouth. 'well, whatever they thought, it worked. I waited a couple of hours, but there wasn't a sign of them.' He took her hand and brought it to his chest. 'I figured it was safe to go back to you, that there was no risk they'd sneak back and follow me...' He drew a deep breath. 'But when I got to the shack, you were gone.'

Brionny nodded. 'Yes. Father Ramón—'

'Had found you. Yes, I know that now. But then—then, I couldn't imagine what had happened. Had you stumbled into the river and become dinner for another snake? Had the Mali-Mali doubled back and taken you?' His arms swept around her and he held her to him with fierce determination. 'I searched for two days, praying to find you—and afraid of what I'd find if I did.'

'Slade—I didn't know—'

'Eventually, I stumbled into Father Ramón's village. He told me he'd sent you upriver with his men. I went after you—but I was too late. You'd left for the States.' His smile was swift and hard. 'And the police decided to put me up in jail as their guest.'

'Oh, God,' Brionny whispered. 'I'm so sorry! I didn't know—'

'It was an interesting couple of days, Stuart, I'll say that.

Impulsively, she reached up and kissed his mouth. 'I love you,' she said fiercely. 'I'd never want anything bad to happen to you...'

Her hand flew to her mouth, but it was too late. The words she hadn't even permitted herself to think were in the open.

Slade smiled. 'Do you, now?' he said, very softly.

Brionny's cheeks flamed. 'Finish your story,' she said, her chin uplifted. 'How did you get out of jail?'

'It wasn't easy. It took me two days just to get word to my office in Rio to tell them to fly somebody down and sort things out.'

'Your—your office in Rio?'

He nodded. 'Later, one of my vice-presidents pointed

out that I'd have been better off calling my New York office, or the one in Miami— Bree? What is it?'

She had gone white as a sheet. 'What—what are you talking about, McClintoch? What offices in New York and—and Miami—and—and—?'

'Rio,' he said helpfully. 'Well, of course we have offices in Houston and LA too, but—'

Brionny closed her eyes, then opened them again.

'I take it you're—you're not talking about opening offices to—to supervise the theft of—of antiquities,' she said in a faint voice.

Slade chuckled. 'No, sweetheart, I'm not. I suppose I should have told you sooner—hell, I tried to tell you sooner... I'm President, CEO, and the guy generally in charge of Worldwide Construction.'

'Worldwide Con... The company building that road in Peru?'

'Yeah,' he said with a modest smile, 'that's the one.'

Brionny slammed her fists against his shoulders. 'You bastard! You let me think—'

'I let you think what you wanted to think,' he said, catching hold of her wrists. 'You took one look at me and saw a bum.'

'I—I—' She stared at him, and suddenly she knew the truth. 'I—I saw a ghost,' she whispered. 'Someone hurt me, a long time ago, and—and I thought I saw him again when I saw you. It was wrong, I know that now, but—'

'Yeah.' He blew out his breath. 'I guess I looked at you and saw a ghost, too, a specter from my childhood, when I was always the kid who had to prove himself over and over...'

Brionny reached up and kissed him again. It was a

longer kiss this time, and when it ended they were both smiling.

'Slade?' Brionny moved closer into his arms. 'Were you really going to—to demand payment from me last night?'

He brushed a soft kiss over her mouth. 'That was the plan. At least, I told myself it was. I think I really had some crazy idea that if I got you in my arms again I could make you admit you loved me as much as I loved you, but—'

'Do you?' she whispered. 'Love me, I mean?'

'Yes,' he said, 'with all my heart.'

'You'd better mean it. Because if you don't—if you don't, I'll—I'll—'

Laughing, Slade scooped her into his arms. 'What will you do? Whip out your gun and shoot me?' He kissed her, then let her down slowly to her feet. 'Darling Bree. Will you marry me?'

Would she marry him, her handsome renegade? Of course she would. He might not have stolen the emerald, but he had surely stolen her heart.

'I should tell you that you weren't entirely wrong about me,' he said. 'I've spent most of my life bouncing from one construction site to another—but if you marry me I promise to settle down.'

Brionny kissed him. 'You don't have to,' she sighed. 'To tell you the truth, McClintoch, I think I'd like to try my hand at being a bum for a while.'

His arms tightened around her. 'I'm supposed to be in Bora-Bora next week. How does that sound for a honeymoon, Stuart?'

'It sounds wonderful.'

He kissed her again, and when the kiss grew deep

and heated he drew back and gave her an unsteady smile.

'I think we should carry on this conversation in a more private setting. I happen to know this apartment on the East Side with a great view of the river.'

Brionny laughed softly. 'I love places with views of the river.'

And, with that, Slade swept Brionny into his arms and carried her out of the director's office, through the Great Hall, and down the wide marble steps of the museum to the street.

MISTRESS MINDED

KATHERINE GARBERA

Katherine Garbera has had fun working as a production page, lifeguard, secretary and VIP tour guide, but those occupations pale when compared to creating worlds where true love conquers all and wounded hearts are healed. Writing romance novels is the perfect job for her. She's always had a vivid imagination and believes strongly in happily-ever-after. She's married to the man she met in Walt Disney World's Fantasyland. They live in central Florida with their two children. Readers can visit her on the web at www.katherinegarbera.com.

Don't miss Katherine Garbera's next great romance. *The Moretti Seduction* **is available now from Mills & Boon® Desire™!**

Prologue

"**P**asquale, you've done well," Didi said as I materialized in front of her desk.

"Babe, call me Ray." No one had lived who'd called me by my given name when I'd been on earth, but Didi was different.

I didn't like the body-disappearing thing, but it beat the alternative, which was me going to hell. I'd been a *capo* with the mob until I was betrayed by one of my lieutenants and killed. My dying prayer for forgiveness had brought me here to Didi—one of God's seraphim, some sort of high angel.

The deal I'd cut was to unite in love as many couples as enemies I'd murdered in hate. I was going to be doing this gig for a long time. *Madon'*, some days it wasn't half-bad, but Didi had a way of getting on my nerves and under my skin.

And when she was giving me a compliment I certainly didn't trust her. She'd sent me to earth in a woman's body one time. Not a hot-looking chick, either, but some old broad.

"There was a reason I was called Il Re on earth," I said to her. *Il re* is Italian for "the king." Yeah, I had the ego and the attitude to carry that off. Didi was always reminding me there was only one king up here, but after successfully uniting three couples, I'd decided to call myself the king of hearts.

"And that reason was…?"

"Don't be smart, babe. You know it's because I'm good at what I do."

"What'd I tell you about calling me babe?"

"Did I call you that? *Madon'*, I'm sorry, Didi. I know you don't like it." I enjoyed giving her a hard time. She looked as if she'd been working in this office too long. Today she was wearing another one of her ugly suits. This one was the color of cooked salmon.

"What's up next?" I asked.

A large pile of colored file folders appeared on her desk next to the jar of Baci chocolates.

"Pick one," she said.

So far I'd pulled from the top and the middle of the pile. I reached for a blue folder about three-quarters of the way down and Didi took it from me. The remaining pile disappeared.

"So where am I going this time?" I asked. What I really wanted to know was if I'd be a man. But asking her that made me feel like a *babbeo*.

She handed me the folder. The location was an island in the Caribbean. Life was looking up. And this couple, Adam Powell and Jayne Montrose, already worked together.

"No problem."

"Don't start thinking about your tan yet, Pasquale. This one is different," Didi said.

Hell, they all were. Didi had yet to give me one assignment that was easy. Matchmaking—Holy Mary!—was hard work.

"How?"

She smiled. My gut tightened. I didn't trust her when she was acting all happy.

"I'll be accompanying you this time."

"*Madon',* is this some sort of punishment?"

"No, babe, it's your reward."

She disappeared before I could respond. Freakin' matchmaker to the lovelorn was one thing. Partnered up with a prissy, bossy angel? Oh, *merda,* this was going to be one hell of an assignment.

One

Adam Powell bit back a curse and tossed his cell phone onto the leather seat next to him. His plane was ready to leave, his guests would be here any moment and Isabella had chosen now to tell him that she wasn't getting what she needed from their relationship.

Frankly, he couldn't *give* her anything else. If diamonds, furs and a brand-new Jaguar weren't good enough, she'd have to look elsewhere.

Normally, being without a mistress wasn't any big deal. He was a grown man; he could live without sex. But the coming two weeks were important to his company. Adam had been trying to acquire La Perla

Negra Resort for the last five years and had been getting no where.

The owner, Ray Angelini, refused to sell his resort to anyone. Out of the blue, Adam had received a call last week inviting him to come to the resort to discuss the possibility of a sale. He had jumped at the chance.

Angelini had asked Adam to bring his wife, which had led to an awkward conversation. Angelini wanted a happily married couple to run the resort, as he and his wife had been doing for the last twenty years.

Adam had always believed in doing anything to close a sale, but pretending to be married was going too far. He told Angelini he'd bring the woman he'd been living with. Angelini had warned him that unless he believed Adam was a man who understood love and relationships there'd be no sale.

"I understand they're both a crock," he muttered.

He left his seat in the back of the jet, exiting the plane. He'd have to make up some excuse for Isabella, and see if Jayne Montrose, his executive assistant, could find another woman who'd meet him in the Caribbean.

Damn, it was hot. New Orleans in the summertime was no one's ideal place to be. The humidity soaked into his skin. He threw his head back, breathing through his teeth. It reminded him of the days when he'd worked the swamp in his uncle's old pirogue, taking tourists for jaunts to see gators and swamp lilies.

God, he'd come a long way from that boy. He intended to go even further, and no woman was going to throw him off track for long.

"Ooo, someone looks pissed," said Jayne, coming up behind him.

He'd hired Jayne because she was sassy and smart. She made life at the office flow smoothly, and in the downtime always made him laugh. "Don't give me any lip, Montrose. Isabella is not going with me and the Angelinis are due in less than fifteen minutes."

"I'm sorry. I told you not to count on her," Jayne said. She reached into the large bag she always carried and drew out a sheaf of papers. "I need your signature on these before I leave for vacation."

"You can't leave on vacation until I find a woman to accompany me to the Caribbean."

"Listen, boss, we've been over this before. I don't procure women for you," Jayne said. She narrowed her eyes and handed him a Mont Blanc pen to sign the documents she'd brought.

Jayne wasn't a particularly tall woman, but she carried herself like an Amazon. Some of the hotel industries' toughest figures backed down when Jayne negotiated with them. Hiring her had been a stroke of genius, and Adam secretly feared someday she'd get tired of working for him and move on.

"I only asked you to get a phone number one time," he said.

That had been a big mistake. Jayne had almost quit

over the matter, and he'd had to do some fancy talking to convince her to stay. Jayne had a strong core
of morality and integrity, and she'd do just about anything he asked her to as long as it didn't compromise
her own values.

"Once was too many times as far as I'm concerned," she retorted tartly.

Jayne was the best personal assistant he'd ever had.
She'd been with him longer than any of her prede-
cessors—almost eight months now.

He studied her as he signed the papers she put before him. Her short cap of brown hair was tucked
behind her ears, framing her heart-shaped face. Her
eyes were a cool blue, radiating both intelligence and
humor most of the time. Her mouth, strictly speaking,
was too large for her face. She should have had thin
lips, but instead had a lush mouth that made men
think of kissing her.

Since Adam had a zero-tolerance policy toward
fraternization in the workplace, he tried to avoid looking at her mouth. But he wasn't very successful.

"Why are you staring at me?" Jayne asked.

"I'm not staring at you," he said, signing the last
of the papers.

He'd have to cancel the trip and stay home. There
were other resorts in the Caribbean. None as elegant
as La Perla Negra, but he'd find another property to
buy.

"Listen, Jayne, I'm going to have to cancel your

vacation. Without Isabella, Angelini won't talk to me.''

Jayne's eyes narrowed again. ''I haven't had more than a day off since I started working for you.''

''You can have time off in a week. I need you here to help me handle this. I'll make it worth your while.''

''How?''

''Name your price,'' Adam said. Early on in life he'd realized everyone had a price. Especially for things they didn't want to do.

She rolled her eyes. ''Let's handle it now. Get out your little black book and call another one of your lady friends.''

''I don't have a black book. That's a cliché and women don't like it.''

''You used to have one, right?''

''No,'' he said. He'd never had a black book. He'd never had any problem remembering phone numbers. Strictly speaking, Jayne was right. He could probably make a few calls and find another woman, but he didn't want to. He was tired of the whole thing. And he'd been hoping that Isabella would prove to be different. That perhaps she'd fill that hole that had always been empty inside him.

None of them would be the right fit for this trip to the Caribbean, anyway. Angelini had to be handled carefully, and Adam didn't want to risk anything else going wrong. He needed someone who understood what was at stake. The perfect solution would be for Jayne to go with him.

"Jayne?"

"Yes?" She shoved the papers he'd just returned to her into her bag. Her hair fell forward over one eye and she shifted the tote impatiently to her left hand, tucking her hair behind her ear again.

"Want to come with me and be my mistress?"

A flush spread up her neck. Her mouth opened the slightest bit and for the first time he noticed how creamy her skin was.

She shook her head. "No."

"Why not?" Aside from the phone number incident this was the first time Jayne had said no to him.

"I can't be your mistress—what about Powell International's policy toward fraternization?"

"You wouldn't really be my mistress. We'd act like we were involved. We're not really fraternizing. It would be business."

"That won't work. I don't like to pretend to be something I'm not. I have to take these papers back to the office now, and I booked a nonrefundable airline ticket to Little Rock."

"I'll reimburse your airfare and book you a first-class ticket for the week we return," Adam said.

"I don't know…" She bit her lip and dug in her purse, pulling out a pair of sunglasses and putting them on. "No, Adam, I'm sorry, but I can't postpone my trip to Arkansas."

"Jayne, you're my last hope," Adam pleaded. "I've waited five years to talk to Angelini."

Two hours later, Jayne didn't want to analyze the reasons why she was sitting next to Adam on his jet, bound for the Caribbean. He had said they'd work out the details when they arrived at the resort, which she didn't like. She was a planner. She liked every detail set in stone before she took any action. That way there were no surprises and she could better manage her own experiences.

She'd been determined to say no to Adam's request, but in the end she'd been unable to. So here she was, eating caviar, which she hated, and drinking Moët with the Angelinis. She'd been on Adam's corporate jet twice before, both times to make sure that his every comfort was seen to. In fact, she'd been there this afternoon, arranging for Isabella's luggage to be stowed in the bedroom at the back.

The Angelinis were a very odd couple. Didi was slim and wore a slightly baggy dress in a shade that didn't really flatter her. Ray was short, a little pudgy and balding, but smiled with an effortless charm that immediately put Jayne at ease. They'd invited her and Adam to call them by their first names.

Ray and Didi had flown to New Orleans to see Adam's operation firsthand. Jayne had given them a tour around the city and taken Didi shopping while Adam worked his magic, convincing Ray of all the advantages of joining Powell International. Jayne had a bad feeling that she may have made the biggest mistake of her life in agreeing to come with Adam. She'd been falling in love with her boss since the first week she'd started working for him.

It wasn't his Cajun good looks that drew her, though his thick black, curly hair made her fingers tingle to touch it. Or his wealth, because she'd grown up in a world where money was the only factor in happiness. Or his intelligence, because she'd graduated summa cum laude from Harvard Business School and counted some of the smartest people in the world among her friends.

No, what drew her to Adam Powell was the way he held himself apart from everyone. In her heart she recognized the lonely soul that mirrored her own. But she'd been content to not do anything about it, just secretly dream of her boss and continue working for him.

This trip changed everything. She should have said no. She *would* have said no if any man but Adam had asked her. She'd be on her way to Arkansas right now. She would have accomplished a week's stay in another of the fifty states and be well on her way to achieving her current travel goal to see all of them.

The Angelinis were talking quietly together. Adam put his arm around her, drawing her close to him. He pressed a kiss against the top of her head and she froze. She wasn't going to survive two weeks of this.

Her hand shook and a drop of champagne spilled from her glass.

"Relax," Adam whispered against her temple.

She tried, but she couldn't. He took the champagne flute from her and put it on the table next to his chair.

Then he lifted her hand to his mouth and licked the spilled liquid from her skin. Shivers of white-hot desire spread throughout her body. Adam watched her with those crystal-gray eyes of his.

She saw something there that told her the lust she felt wasn't totally one-sided. Did that mean he had deeper emotions where she was concerned? Was she willing to risk her heart to find out?

She wasn't sure. She'd never been much of a risk taker. She liked to plan and slowly, methodically, move toward her goals.

But she was edging nearer to thirty, and marriage, which had always seemed not important, was becoming more and more a focus for her. She'd tried to make it to the altar once and fallen short. Adam was here now and she knew she might regret it later, but she was going to use the time they had together to explore her fantasies and maybe come out a winner. There wasn't a goal she'd set for herself that she hadn't achieved without planning and hard work.

Decision made, she rested her head on his shoulder. She wasn't sure how to handle Adam. He wasn't like the other men she'd dated. Those relationships had been based on common interests and some really good sex, but none of those relationships had an eighth of the intensity she'd just experienced with Adam's mouth on the back of her hand.

He held her loosely and she closed her eyes, pretending to rest. But closing her eyes was a huge a mistake. She was overwhelmed by Adam. His warm hard body cradled hers. His fingers made idle patterns on her shoulder. And his scent—that spicy, woodsy, masculine scent—surrounded her.

Jayne opened her eyes and stood up. There wasn't an action plan big enough, safe enough, for her to put Adam in it. She wasn't going to be able to do this. Despite the fanciful dreams she'd harbored, she knew that if she and Adam had any kind of personal relationship it would end eventually and she'd be out of a job. Jayne looked around the plane and felt the walls closing in on her. Didi and Ray sat across from her, smiling warmly. Suddenly Jayne stood up.

He raised one eyebrow in question, and she said, "I have to—"

"Change? Yes, you do." Turning to Ray and Didi, he said, "I hope you'll excuse us. Jayne hasn't had a chance to change from her day at the office."

"Of course," Ray said with a smile.

Jayne wondered what exactly she was going to change into. Isabella had about three inches in height on her and at least six inches in bustline. None of her clothes were going to fit.

Adam used his hand on her waist to guide her toward the back of the plane. Once they were inside the bedroom, he let her go and ran a hand through his hair.

"God, this is a mess. I don't think they're buying us as a couple."

"It's not going to help when I come out wearing this outfit."

"Don't worry about the clothing. I had a wardrobe delivered while you ran back to the office to drop off the papers."

She glanced at the bed for the first time and realized it was covered in boxes. She was touched. She knew it was the same thing he did for every one of his mistresses, and it shouldn't matter. But no man had ever bought her clothing before. Adam had an eye for women's bodies and had mentioned to Jayne that nine times out of ten he was right on the mark. He'd guessed her size to prove it.

"You can use Isabella's suitcases for your clothes. I'll leave you to change."

"Adam?"

"Yes?"

"I'll do my best to make this work."

"I know you will, *chère*."

"*Chère?*" Her heart beat too fast when he called her that in that throaty, masculine way of his.

"It's an endearment."

"I know. Why are you using it on me?"

"We're supposed to be lovers."

She tried not to let it bother her—"supposed" to be lovers. This is a big game of pretend, Jayne, don't forget it, she told herself. "Can I call you stud muffin?"

"If you want me to spank you," he said.

"That's a little kinky, Adam."

He closed the gap between them. Once again she was surrounded by his body heat and his scent. He leaned closer to her and his breath brushed her lips. She grabbed his shoulders for balance as the plane hit an air pocket, jostling them together.

Adam wrapped her in his arms and held her steady until the plane settled down. Jayne was cushioned against his hard chest, and his arms around her were so strong. He held her in a way that promised he'd be able to help her with any burdens she carried. And for a minute she was tempted to let the line between fantasy and reality blur. She leaned her cheek against his chest and listened to the heavy beating of his heart.

"Okay, *chère?*" he asked.

She nodded, unable to speak. He framed her face with his hands and looked deep into her eyes, making her feel as if all her secrets were laid bare before him. She blinked and tried to focus on the present. Fantasy, she reminded herself. This was all one big fantasy.

He cupped her face in his big hands and tilted her head back. She stared up into his dark eyes, every sense on hyperalert. Every feminine instinct screamed for her to reach up and touch him. To bury her hands in his thick black hair and pull his face closer to hers. To bring that mouth of his down to hers and then take the kiss that she'd been craving since the first day she'd walked into his office.

"I never said thanks," he said, his voice a husky growl.

She swallowed and licked her suddenly dry lips. His eyes narrowed and she felt tension move through him. "Are you saying it now?"

He nodded.

"You're welcome," she said.

He lowered his head even more and his breath brushed over her cheek. Oh, God, was he going to kiss her? She shifted to her tiptoes so that only a breath separated them, and she heard Adam groan.

Abruptly he dropped his hands and walked out of the bedroom. Jayne turned toward the boxes of clothing, telling herself that her heart was beating faster because of the charade and not because of the sexual arousal pumping through her veins.

Two

Adam paused outside the doorway. After months of ignoring that made-for-love mouth of hers it was damn near impossible to resist tasting her. And he knew it was only a matter of hours before he gave in and took the kiss he'd been dreaming of since the first day they'd met.

Adam cursed himself for forgetting his own rule. Every time he forgot it he had to relearn painful lessons. Lessons he'd vowed to never forget. And dammit, Jayne Montrose wasn't going to make him compromise.

He'd almost kissed her. And with the bed right there he wouldn't have stopped until he was buried deep inside her curvy little body. That mouth, which had tempted him for so long, had been so close, and only at the last minute had sanity intruded on the moment, forcing him to pull away.

Jayne was his assistant. She took care of everything for him. His office wouldn't function smoothly without her and he wasn't about to let his body screw that up now. He'd already proved time and again that he didn't think well when his hormones were involved.

He wouldn't have believed that Isabella thought they were heading toward something more permanent. But in the end he'd been wrong again. This thing with Jayne was going to have to work because he needed the acquisition of this resort as much to distract himself from the mess his personal life had become as he did to become more successful.

When Adam emerged into the jet cabin the Angelinis were arguing, so he held back until Ray glanced up and gave him a look that seemed to say *women!* Adam agreed.

"Jayne will be out in a moment." Adam returned to his seat, trying to banish from his head the images of Jayne changing.

"Why are you interested in La Perla Negra?" Ray inquired.

Adam's reasons were deeply personal and he wouldn't share them with anyone. Especially not the owner of the resort.

He planned to gut the entire resort area and turn it

into the most commercial tourist destination he could come up with. His reasoning was sound from a financial perspective, but from a personal one it would finally, Adam hoped, lay to rest the demons that had haunted him for a long time. Perla Negra had been the place where his father had fallen in love with his secretary and then left Adam and his mother.

"I'm looking to expand our presence in the Caribbean," he said at last.

"We enjoyed our stay at your Rouge Mansion in the French Quarter."

"I'm pleased. The Rouge was my first hotel."

The door opened behind them and Adam glanced over his shoulder and sucked in his breath. He'd asked Jean-Pierre to send the usual wardrobe over, never thinking of the impact. He told himself it was only because he was used to seeing Jayne in shapeless suits and sedate heels that she looked so damn sexy now.

The floral print dress was slim fitting and cut to a respectable length, but the scooped neckline revealed the ample curves of her breasts. He clenched his hands into fists to keep from reaching for her. This was Jayne, dammit, not some femme fatale.

She cleared her throat and awkwardly crossed her arms over her chest. There was an unexpected vulnerability in her eyes that made him want to stand up and protect her. To vow to always shelter her. A vow he knew better than to make because only fools or weak men made promises to women. And Adam wasn't weak.

She didn't look ready for a vacation, she looked ready for his bed. Her hair was tousled and she'd applied some sort of shiny lip gloss on her mouth. It took all of his control not to go to her and plunder those lips. She didn't need any makeup to enhance that feature.

To prove to himself that she had no impact on him, he deliberately turned away.

"Ah, now you look like you're ready for a vacation," Ray announced.

Jayne dropped into the chair next to him. "I feel ready for one, Ray. I haven't had time to read the file on Perla Negra. I think that means Black Pearl, right?"

What was that fragrance she was wearing? It didn't smell like Chanel or any of the other perfumes he was familiar with. Against his best judgment Adam leaned closer to her, inhaling the scent.

"It does. There's also a legend around the black pearl. Want to hear it?" Ray asked.

"Yes," Jayne said.

Adam closed his eyes and turned away. She was his employee. He wasn't going to act on any feelings he had toward her. He faced the Angelinis, trying to focus on whatever conversation they were having, but it was nearly impossible. Hell, he and Jayne were play-acting. He'd done enough pretending over the years that this should be a walk in the park.

From this angle he could see the curve of Jayne's breast, and when she tilted her head to listen more closely to Didi, he smelled the fragrance of her shampoo.

Didi's eyes lit up as she leaned forward in her seat, as well. "It involves a pirate, a maiden and a fortune lost at sea."

"Sounds like my kind of story," Jayne said.

Adam could scarcely pay attention. For the first time a woman was taking precedence over business. For the first time Jayne wasn't just his girl Friday, but a desirable woman. For the first time a woman was making more than his pulse beat faster, because he realized that Jayne used the same mechanisms he did to hide from real life. The job.

Knowing how important her work was to her, he was determined to make sure their stay didn't become more than a charade. Because he could never keep Jayne on staff if he took her to his bed. It would compromise the standards he'd set in the workplace and the code he'd followed since his father had run off with his secretary years before.

Adam listened to Ray and Didi tell a tale of forbidden love and piracy. He'd read about it already in the resort's literature, which the Angelinis had forwarded to him.

La Perla Negra, a strand of precious black pearls,

had been stolen from a Franciscan abbey by the devious pirate Antonio Mantegna. Along with the pearls, Antonio stole Maria Boviar, the only daughter of a wealthy nobleman. Maria and Antonio were rumored to have been lost at sea.

But the Angelinis at La Perla Negra Resort and Spa claimed that Antonio and his beloved Maria had made their way to the small Caribbean island that was now home to the resort. And that the strand of black pearls Antonio stole was hidden somewhere in the resort.

"Wow, do you offer tours of the resort to try to find the pearls?" Jayne asked.

"We don't have anything formalized, but there *is* a treasure map in every room," Ray explained.

"The real treasure isn't the pearls, Jayne," Didi said.

"What is it then?"

"The treasure is said to be whatever you desire the most."

"Sounds like fun, doesn't it, honeybun?" Jayne put her hand on Adam's arm.

He looked into those pretty blue eyes of hers and saw mischief sparkling in them. Well, at least she hadn't called him stud muffin. He reached out and tucked a strand of hair behind her ear. Her eyes narrowed and she sucked in a breath. She wasn't immune to his touch. A swift rush of triumph swamped him. He knew it would be better for both their sakes if she wasn't aware of him as a man, but he was primitive enough to like it.

"It does, *chère*. We'll have to check it out."

"See that, babe? I told you we'd found the right couple," Ray said.

Adam smiled to himself. He wasn't sure why Ray thought they were the right couple, but it sounded as if he wasn't going to have any problems closing this deal. Unless he counted Jayne and the desire she'd stirred to life inside him.

La Perla Negra rose out of the lush tropical foliage like a queen from a more elegant time. The main building was constructed in California Mission style. Spanish tile roofs gleamed red in the sunlight. Fourteen cottages dotted the landscape around the main resort. The suite they were given had a private balcony overlooking the ocean. One of the other walls was entirely made of glass and looked out over a cove that housed the resort's marina. Jayne slipped off the strappy sandals she wasn't used to wearing and let the thick carpet soothe her tired feet.

As soon as the door closed behind the bellboy, she glanced over at Adam. He'd removed his jacket and loosened his tie. His hair was disheveled from running his fingers through it. This was Adam in work mode. He might look sexy but he'd be all about business, except there wasn't really any work to be done here.

She glanced wistfully at the beach. She wanted to

change out of this dress into something comfortable and go walk on the sand. She'd never been to the Caribbean before. She hadn't planned on international travel until she'd completed her visits to all fifty states.

But this was nice and she vowed to enjoy her time here. Even though she was working she planned to enjoy the island. Could she convince Adam to go with her?

And where was the treasure map? She really wanted to search for it.

The silence once they were alone was charged with awareness. She stared at the man she'd wanted to be close to for so long, and couldn't think of a single thing to say.

"Well, honeybun, what do you think?" she asked.

Adam raised one eyebrow. "That you had better stop calling me that."

"Don't like it?"

"Listen, Miss Sassy, I'm still your boss."

"Are you saying you'll fire me if I call you that again?" she asked him, knowing Adam well enough to be certain he wouldn't.

"Would that make you stop?"

"No," she said.

He threw his head back and laughed. She felt pleased deep inside when she made him laugh. Adam didn't laugh often enough. Most times he was focused so intently on work that he rarely had time for any sort of fun.

Their suite was set up with a sitting area and desk in the main room. She hadn't explored further but there was a doorway that she assumed led to the bedroom. Probably the standard issue double beds were inside. And while she wasn't looking forward to being that close to temptation at night, at least she'd have her own bed.

"What's first on the agenda?"

"I want to make some notes to send back to the office. Did you bring your computer?" he asked.

Clearly, the beach was out of the question right now. And this wasn't a real vacation. "No."

"You can use mine. I have a few ideas. Do you mind if I dictate them to you?"

"No problem, boss. Let me get things set up."

She crossed to his computer bag and started setting up his mobile office, assembling the laptop, printer and fax machine on the large mahogany desk. Adam arranged the chairs and grabbed some snacks from the minibar. It looked as if this was going to take a long time.

"Tell me about yourself, Jayne."

"Tell you what?"

"Something that I can use when we have dinner with the Angelinis tonight."

"Like what?"

"Something only your lover would know," he

said. He sprawled back in his chair, long legs stretched out in front of him.

"Why don't you give me an example?" she asked, balking at the intimate question. Her lovers—and it was barely a plural term—knew little about her. Jayne had learned early on to hide her real thoughts and feelings. Men who said anything about her usually remembered her intelligence and her humor.

"I'm generous," Adam said after a few minutes had passed. Jayne realized she wasn't the only one with barriers. But then, that was one of the first things she'd noticed about him.

"I already knew that."

"How?" he asked, arching one brow in a devilish way.

"I'm usually the facilitator of your generosity."

"Facilitator?"

"That's the résumé spin on having to do your shopping."

He gave her one of those half grins of his that made her forget to breathe. She turned back to the computer and opened a file to distract herself. She labeled it Perla Negra.

"It's your turn."

Something only her lovers would know? She really didn't want Adam to know anything about her that was intimate or personal. She had a feeling that only by keeping a wall firmly between them was she going to survive these weeks together.

"Well, I think that was cheating, but I'll go with it. I like to be outside," she said at last. It wasn't something she'd shared with Ben, whom she'd been engaged to, but Adam was different.

"Why?" he asked.

"I like the feel of the wind in my hair and the sun on my face. We spend so much time in air-conditioned buildings, but I like the heat of New Orleans in the summer. The way it seeps into my skin...I don't know, it makes me feel like I'm really part of the city."

Adam watched her with narrowed eyes and she blinked and looked away. She'd said too much. God, what had she been thinking? "What about you, honeybun?"

"The heat means something to me, too," he said after a moment. "It reminds me of my childhood."

"I don't know much about that time of your life," she said at last. Very little was known about the man. He was a legend in the hotel business because he'd carved his success with his bare hands, buying a rundown old hotel with the money he'd earned drag racing in small towns in the South. He'd turned that hotel into a first-class resort and then used that to launch his international company.

He shrugged and looked away. "I don't like to rehash the past."

"Then why do you like the heat?" she asked. Okay, she didn't really need to know this, but if she had an action plan to make Adam fall for her, number one would be to figure out what made him tick.

"I didn't say I liked it."

She thought about it for a minute. No, he hadn't. "Why is it important, then?"

"It reminds me of the vow I made when I was fourteen."

"What vow?"

"One secret, *chère*. That was our deal."

"Is that the way your domestic arrangements usually work?"

"Why should you care about that?"

"You started this. If I'm pretending to be your mistress I should know the score."

"You're right. We should discuss the details of our arrangement. You're different than other women I've known."

He was watching her so intently she felt heat spread down her arms and over her body. "Smaller chest?" she suggested.

He gave her one of those vague half smiles. "I don't think so."

Her eyes widened when she realized he was really seeing her. It was as if he were peeling away the layers of clothing and revealing the body she'd always been too shy to put on display. Not too shy, she thought. Too afraid to put on display. She'd never wanted to be like her mother, who used her feminine form to open doors for herself and make life easier.

"How do your lovers treat you?" he asked her at last.

"They treat me like a friend and not an object."

"I haven't objectified you."

"Every item of clothing in that suitcase will."

"You usually dress in frumpy clothes, Jayne. Why?"

"Hey, don't turn this around to me. We're talking about you."

"I like the female form," he said with a shrug.

"I *don't* like mine," she said after long moments had passed.

"Women," he growled.

"What's that mean?" she asked.

"Just that your mouth has been driving me crazy for months and you're worried about how you look in a dress that fits you."

Her mouth. It was an ordinary one, one more plain thing on an average body. "What's so special about my mouth?"

"It's made for kissing," he said.

She swallowed. He leaned forward, closing the gap between them. His breath was minty and she closed her eyes for a minute, remembering that moment on the plane when she'd been surrounded by his body heat. Was he going to kiss her?

Did she want him to? Deliberately she pulled back. She needed to get this back on track, focusing on work. Adam was more complex than she'd dreamed and their time together so far was too…intimate. She had to make a decision. Did she want to become Adam's lover or keep her job?

He became all-business after that, giving her a much needed escape from the intense physical awareness. And in the imaginary box in her head, next to the item that said Adam, she put a big exclamation point and the word *danger*.

Adam congratulated himself for getting things back on a business focus with Jayne. That moment on the plane had been an aberration, and that instant when he'd confessed that her mouth drove him crazy had been simply a brief bit of craziness. He knew how to handle himself around the women he worked with.

Hell, he'd had a hard time keeping his eyes off her mouth. She bit her lower lip when she typed, which he'd never noticed before. Or, at least, never perceived it to be an arousing habit. But having mentioned his obsession with her mouth, he didn't intend to let the subject drop. He wanted to know what she tasted like, and wouldn't be able to rest until he had kissed her.

Jayne followed him into the bedroom and stopped abruptly when she noticed the bed. It was a sumptuous king-size one with a duvet in shades of deep blue. The same color as her eyes.

The rest of the room was done in the same hues. There was an overstuffed chair and ottoman near the window. The sheer curtains stirred in the breeze and a ceiling fan circled lazily.

Immediately, Adam felt the tension he'd brought with him from New Orleans start to dissipate. This was a room that begged the people in it to stop and stay for a while. To cast off worries and relax. Forget about rules and regulations and indulge. Jayne paused beside him and he knew exactly *how* he wanted to indulge.

He'd carry her to that big bed and lay her in the center of it. Then slowly peel away all the layers of clothing covering her luscious body until she was totally bare. Then he'd start with that mouth of hers that he'd been dying forever to taste and explore.

"Well, maybe we should talk about the sleeping arrangements, honeybun," Jayne said.

She sassed him when she was nervous, he realized. She dropped into that shy, quiet mouse mode when he was getting too close to the truth, but when he was scaring her she got mouthy.

But he knew that Jayne wasn't really his mistress, even though she played the part of one. And he was her boss, so he needed to walk a fine line here. Not only for the court of law but with his own conscience, because he'd always believed people who couldn't keep their mind on business shouldn't be in the workplace.

"I'll take the couch," he said gruffly, then was surprised at the scratchy sound of his own voice. Because what he really wanted to do was take her on the couch or any other surface. Damn, he shouldn't be this horny for this woman.

She moved past him into the room. She opened the French doors and stepped out onto the balcony. Adam followed her. A rainstorm was moving over the ocean and a cool breeze blew across his face.

He tipped his head back, imagining that the real world had disappeared and he and Jayne were the only ones who existed.

For a minute, he stood on the threshold studying her. She stared at the horizon and he knew she was searching for answers, just as he was. In his quest to keep business first he'd made a serious miscalculation, one he was going to regret for a long time.

He'd erred on the side of familiarity and factored in the control he took for granted, never considering Jayne outside the office, in this tropical paradise. She called to him just as Eve had beckoned Adam, and he knew that—like his namesake—he was going to follow her on the path of temptation. But he didn't want to lose his Eden.

And Adam had no doubt that his Eden was the world he'd carefully created for himself. The world he'd learned to take for granted because it was intentionally devoid of any of the emotions that made life sticky. Emotions like lust, desire and temptation.

All the things that Jayne called from him without even realizing it. Not things, he thought, emotions.

Those damn feelings he'd never been able to control, despite his experience watching his mother's heart break when his dad had left them. Despite his own experience when he'd been twenty and trusted the wrong woman. Despite all the couples he'd seen cheat on a spouse with a co-worker. He still wanted Jayne.

Damn the consequences, his hormones urged. But his mind knew that a price always had to be paid, and he hadn't decided yet if the price for a few weeks with Jayne was too high.

"Chère?"

She turned toward him and he saw something in her eyes he didn't understand. The wind blew her hair across her face. One silky strand caught on her lips. She reached up to brush it aside and it blew back again.

"We're going to have to share the bed. House-keeping will notice if we don't," she said at last.

He'd thought the same thing. But he knew that if Jayne was in his bed he'd be unable to sleep. Unable to breathe. Unable to do anything but pull her into his arms and kiss that mouth of hers that had been tormenting him for so long.

That strand of hair brushed her face again. This time he caught her hand before she could tuck the lock away. With his free hand, he reached up and swept it back behind her ear, then smoothed his thumb over her lower lip.

"I..."

He tapped his finger against her mouth, stopping the words he wasn't sure she could find. "I've put us in an untenable situation."

"Why untenable?" she asked, tipping her head back.

He leaned a little closer, desperate to taste her. Her breath caressed his face with each exhalation.

Wisdom be damned. "I want you, Jayne."

Her pupils dilated and her breathing speeded up. She watched him with an intensity that made him want to measure up in her eyes. But deep inside, he realized he knew little of what standards she used to measure men.

He doubted he'd be able to meet her needs. Even his mistresses, women he'd chosen because of their materialistic natures, had eventually needed emotions that he'd been unwilling to give them.

Jayne pulled out of his arms. "I'd better go make sure that fax went through."

He should just let her leave. That would be the wise choice, but he couldn't. He didn't know why, but she called to something deep inside him that he'd thought he'd forgotten long ago. "Jayne?"

She pivoted to face him. Her eyes were wide and questioning. Her skin was flushed with arousal and he felt an answering pull in his groin. Yes, his body said, take her now and end all this superficial double-talk.

"Have I misread the signals here?" he asked at last.

She shook her head.

She turned away and he let her go, still unsure that he should let anything develop between them. Not only because of the vulnerability he'd glimpsed in Jayne's eyes, but because of the protectiveness it called from him.

Jayne tugged at the protectiveness he had hidden beneath his armor of cynicism and he wasn't going to let her glimpse it.

Three

"Jayne?" Adam's voice was deep and commanding. She fought against the pull he had over her. Forced herself to take another step before she glanced over her shoulder at him.

She wasn't sure what to say to him. It was one thing to imagine having an affair with him, something else entirely to actually do so. In his eyes she saw a deep passion that she'd never really glimpsed in any of the men she'd dated. Just his gaze alone brought her body to readiness. Her pulse beat faster, her breathing came quicker and her center contracted.

If he lifted his hand and crooked his finger, she'd come to him. She'd bare herself to him and take whatever he had to give. She'd stop thinking about all that was wise and sane and just indulge that part of her that had been quiet and lonely for too long.

She bit her lower lip, fighting against her own urges and the potent power in his gaze. She slid one foot forward before realizing what she was doing. She stopped.

Though she always perceived herself as brave and adventurous, she knew deep inside that she was much too practical to ever really do anything that had a high risk potential.

And sleeping with Adam had risk written all over it. Not just on the job front, but on the emotional level. There was a reason she'd felt safe fantasizing about Adam; he was strictly off-limits. She didn't like to examine her own motives in life too closely but knew herself well enough to acknowledge that every relationship she'd ever had had been structured to make her feel safe. And safety came from not risking her emotions.

''What?'' she asked at last.

He leaned back against the railing, his shirt pulled tight across his muscular chest. A breeze danced past, blowing a strand of hair across her face and obscuring her view for a moment. She hesitated, then pushed her hair back behind her ear. She'd learned early on that hiding from the things that scared or excited her the most was never a good idea.

''Should I have kept silent?'' he asked.

Yes! she wanted to scream. ''It would have made the next two weeks easier.''

''Not really,'' he argued. He crossed his arms over his chest and she wished she could mirror his casual pose. But she had neither his experience nor his charm. Her coping mechanisms were smart-ass comments and a quip. And somehow she doubted either one was going to help her through this situation.

What had he said? Something about the next two weeks being hell?

He was right, but she didn't want to admit it. She'd spent a lifetime filling in for everyone. She was an emotional fill-in for her mother, for all the emotion her mom could never coax from her wealthy lovers. For her fiancé, Ben, Jayne had been a substitute for the woman he'd really loved, and when Carrie had returned he'd left her. For Adam, Jayne was a fill-in for his mistress, a temporary scratching of an itch. She was warm and female, but was she willing? The fact of the matter was she wanted nothing more than to crawl into bed with Adam.

For once in her life, she wanted to take what she yearned for, and say to hell with the consequences, the way her mother did. But Jayne had paid the piper one time too many to totally allow herself that freedom.

''Honeybun...'' She tried for the light, flippant tone she'd managed so easily before, but it escaped her.

The heart of the matter as far as she was concerned was that she was tired of filling in for others. For once she wanted to have a starring role with Adam.

"Don't get sassy, *chère*. I know you do that when you're nervous. I'm just asking for some honesty here."

She froze. He was the first person to ever call her on that behavior. She crossed her arms over her chest. "You're asking for more than I want to give you."

"Why?" he asked in the silky tone of his that made her want to confess her deepest secrets. He moved toward her with measured steps and she fought the urge to inch backward.

"I need more than you've ever been willing to give your women."

"I'd never group you with any other woman," he said, stopping in front of her. A thrill went through her. He framed her face with his hands, staring down into her eyes. She wondered what he was searching for and if he'd find answers there.

She was touched that he'd said she was in a class by herself. But she knew he'd diverted her question. "I'm serious. I can't enter into a relationship knowing it's not going to last."

"I can't, either," he said, dropping his hands but still remaining close to her.

She knew what he meant. No one started affairs with the intent of ending them. But their own situation was unique. They had two weeks in the Caribbean to enjoy each other. Working together after they'd slept together wasn't something either of them would be able to abide.

"But yours never last," she pointed out.

"You're alone as well."

"Touché." She was alone for a very different reason. She was searching for the missing piece to the puzzle that was her life. And she wasn't willing to try to make the wrong one fit. She had a careful list of traits she was looking for in a man, and she had to be honest. Adam fit the bill on some, but not all of them.

The phone rang before they could continue their conversation. Adam looked as if he was going to ignore the interruption.

"I'll get it," Jayne offered hastily.

"Stay here. We're not finished with this discussion."

Adam left the balcony, and she heard the low rumble of his voice talking on the phone. She hugged her arms around her chest, feeling so much more alone than she'd ever let him know. He was close to offering her something she'd craved for a long time, and she wasn't certain if her plan for life would hold up to a real temptation. It had hurt her when Ben had walked away, but not very deeply because she'd never let him glimpse the real soul beneath the public facade. She'd been unable to hide from Adam from their very first meeting.

Suddenly she couldn't wait any longer for him. She had to get away before she did something really stupid and gave in to the wild impulses flowing through her. There were stairs leading down from the balcony to the beach, and she quickly unfastened the gate and hurried down them.

She wasn't running away...not exactly. She knew she'd have to face Adam, and he'd want an answer to the question left unspoken between them. But she needed to think and plan. Because if she became his mistress she wanted to be prepared for a time when she'd be alone again.

"Jayne?"

She paused near the bottom of the stairs to the beach. The call hadn't been important—not compared to what was happening with Jayne. Just his office informing him they'd received the fax.

"Not now. I need to clear my head before dinner."

"Wait, I'll go with you."

"Why? In case the Angelinis see me?"

He hadn't thought of that, but it was the perfect excuse to go with her. "Yes."

She made a strangled sound and started moving again. Adam hurried to join her. He'd never seen his ultra-efficient assistant like this.

"What's up?"

"Don't be solicitous," she said.

He reached out and grasped her arm. Her skin was

soft and smooth. The full curve of her breast brushed his finger and he realized he'd trade his whole kingdom for an afternoon alone with Jayne. And that was very dangerous.

For a minute everything else in the world dropped away. The sea breeze filled his nostrils and the roar of the surf filled his ears. They were alone in the world, man and woman, and nothing mattered but that.

Her mouth was opened on a sigh and he knew she felt something when he touched her. He leaned toward her, needing that mouth under his. Needing it as he'd needed nothing else since he'd decided that life was better lived alone.

Alone… He pulled back abruptly, dropping his hand. A sheen of tears appeared in Jayne's eyes for a second, then she blinked and wrapped her arms around her waist. He'd been called a ruthless bastard more times than he wanted to admit, but this was the first time he'd really felt like one.

He cursed under his breath and pivoted to face the ocean, staring at the endless water. If he were a different man he'd take Jayne out on a yacht and disappear with her. Forget about the hotel business and promises made when he'd been too young to understand that passion and emotion weren't easily controlled by even the strongest men.

The silence between them felt tense and Adam knew he was to blame, but he didn't know what to say to Jayne. She was so much more vulnerable than he'd have guessed. God, he'd screwed this up royally.

He should apologize but couldn't find the words. "We have to get past this."

"I'm willing to do my job."

"It has to be more than a job or we'll never pull it off."

"It can never be more than a job, Adam. *Never*."

"Why not? I'm very good at acting the part. The Angelinis will never imagine I'm not the most devoted of lovers."

"I don't want you to pretend to be interested in me. I might forget the ruse and then we'd both be in trouble."

Jayne walked away, and he stood there watching her solitary figure. Instincts he didn't know he had rose in him. He wanted to protect her.

Even from himself?

He ignored the question. It wasn't his intent to hurt her. He just wanted…the same damn thing his father had wanted when he'd come here with Martha all those years ago.

Cursing, Adam deliberately turned away. For the first time he understood a little of what had motivated his father, and he didn't like it.

He'd been toying earlier with asking Jayne to really be his mistress, but he knew now he couldn't. What kind of man took what he wanted at the cost of the innocents in the world? Adam had no doubt that

Jayne was one of the innocents. There had been something in her eyes that had made him feel every inch
the cynical bastard he'd known he was from the moment they'd met.

Adam wasn't in their suite when she returned, and
Jayne was honest enough to admit she was relieved.
She took a shower, dried her hair and then gazed at
her face for a minute. She'd made some important
decisions on her walk.

Realizing at age twenty-eight that she'd spent most
of her life running and hiding wasn't a very comfortable discovery, but it was the truth.

There were two times in her life when she'd wanted
to act on her feelings and hadn't. The first had been
the one occasion when she'd met her father. She'd
been twelve and she'd wanted to ask him if she could
call him dad. But she'd hidden in her room and refused to talk to the tall dark stranger who had given
her half her genes. He'd never visited her again, and
she still felt regret.

The second time had been with Ben, when she'd
felt him slipping away from her. She'd wanted to ask
him if he had doubts about marrying her, but in the
end had kept silent.

This time she'd decided that hiding wasn't an option. She wanted Adam as more than a two-week
lover. And she knew the risks involved with the leap

she was about to take. During her shower she'd put together a rough plan.

She knew she'd have to start looking for another job right away. Because working together would be... difficult if things didn't pan out.

She put on the plush terry-cloth robe the hotel had provided and applied her makeup with a deft hand. She knew about fashion from her mother, and used all of those tricks now. A little voice deep inside pointed out that she wasn't exactly being herself, but Jayne ignored it. Being herself had gotten her a high-paying job and a lonely town house.

Maybe it was time for a change. She grinned at herself in the mirror, pretending not to notice that her eyes were strained and the makeup made her face seem strange and foreign. She exited the bathroom. Adam was in the process of pulling on his dress shirt. He pivoted toward her as she emerged. She'd thought she was ready to see him again. She'd been wrong.

His chest was bare and muscled. A light dusting of hair covered it, tapering to a thin line that disappeared into his waistband. God, he was gorgeous. Her gaze swept over him time and again and she knew she should look away, but couldn't.

''I didn't realize you were back,'' she said at last. What an idiot, she thought. Obviously Adam was going to have some doubts about her intelligence if she didn't snap out of this dreamy state.

When he gave her one of his wry half grins, she

realized she always accepted them as signs of real emotion, but perhaps they weren't. "I am. We need to talk before dinner."

That was the last thing she wanted to do. She'd been too chatty earlier. She knew she'd let him see too much of the real woman behind his handy little assistant today, and she didn't want to feel that vulnerable again.

"I don't think so. I just needed some time to adjust to being your pretend mistress."

"That's part of the problem," he said.

She couldn't endure another conversation on the topic, so she crossed to the armoire where the clothing Adam had purchased hung. Jayne usually chose clothes in shades of black, beige or white because they went together. Adam's mistresses apparently didn't worry about that, nor about the amount of luggage they brought with them. There was an entire rainbow of clothing hanging there.

"What's part of the problem, Adam?" she asked, congratulating herself on totally ignoring the fact that he had a scar above his left nipple. Where had he gotten it?

"Pretending. Frankly, you're not very good at it."

"No, I'm not," she said, allowing herself a small smile. "But I think I can handle it now."

"Do you?"

"Yes," she said. Her fingers fell on a boldly colored wraparound skirt and the gold taffeta, sleeveless blouse that went with it. She held both items to her body and glanced at herself in the full-length mirror on the armoire door. Then she took a deep breath, because she was about to take a huge leap and knew from past experience that there would be no one to catch her if she fell. And she'd probably be free-falling for a while.

"What do you think? As good as Isabella?" she asked, pivoting to face him.

He raised one eyebrow. "I can't tell with the robe."

"Didn't she wear one?"

"Yes, but it wasn't made of terry cloth and it never really covered her body."

Oh, man. It figured she'd screw this up. Jayne tipped her chin down and then glanced back at Adam. There was a new tension in his body as he stared at her.

She walked over to the settee and placed her outfit on it. Then she reached for the tie at her waist. It wasn't the smooth move Jayne had intended, for she'd knotted it tightly. Finally the belt was free and dangled at her sides, but the robe stayed closed.

She didn't know if she could do it. In fact, she couldn't. She must have island fever or something to have thought she could—

"Chère?"

She felt like a little mouse the moment before a big eagle swooped in for the kill. But steeling herself, she tipped her head to the side and gave Adam a once-over that left no inch of him unexplored. "Honeybun, you look good."

She'd expected him to throw his head back and laugh, but instead he took a few steps toward her, then reached out and touched her face with gentle fingers. She longed to touch him as well, but despite her new resolve, she had a lifetime of scruples keeping her hand firmly by her side.

"I don't think I've ever seen you wear makeup," he said softly.

He brushed his thumb across her cheek, starting a chain reaction deep inside her. Sensation spread down her neck, across her chest, making her breasts feel heavy and full. It continued downward, pooling in the center of her body. She closed her eyes briefly, which made each stroke of his thumb feel more intense.

Then he slid his hands down her neck and pried her fingers from their death grip on the lapels of her robe. He held both of her hands in one of his while using his free hand to cup her jaw and tilt her head up toward him.

In his eyes, she saw a million messages, but couldn't decipher even one of them. He leaned in close and brushed his lips over hers. She shut her eyes once more and quieted the inner voice that said she was in deep water and there was no sign of a life-guard. Instead she indulged in kissing the man who'd made a place for himself inside her quiet soul.

Four

Passion had always been the one area where Adam considered himself an expert, but Jayne made him feel as green as a boy with his first woman. Instead of smooth and practiced, he was grasping and hungry, thrusting his tongue past the barrier of her teeth and taking her mouth the way he longed to take her body. Deeply, thoroughly, leaving no space unexplored.

He slid his hand down her neck to the opening of her robe. Freeing her wrists, he held her loosely, grasping her lapels and slipping his forefinger under the terry cloth. Stroking gently, he moved it closer and closer to her breast.

She moaned deep in her throat, and something savage was unleashed inside him. It felt as if he'd never been with a woman. All the finesse he'd carefully cultivated over the years to protect himself from this kind of emotion was gone—stripped bare so that nothing was left but the rough-edged man who'd grown up in the swamp. The man who'd had to leave that life behind for vengeance.

He didn't want to dwell on that. Not now, when he finally had Jayne's made-for-sin mouth under his. She tasted just as he'd expected her to taste.

Headily, he drank from her lips, pulling back only when he became aware of the low sounds coming from her throat. He lifted his head to glance down at her. Her eyes were heavy and her mouth—damn, her mouth was wet and lush. Her lips were redder than usual and he couldn't help it, he had to see if her nipples had also darkened.

He pulled the sides of her robe away and stared down at her body. She was wearing a pale green bra of lace and silk, which hardly contained her straining breasts. Each breath she took thrust them into stark relief—miles of creamy skin framed by the light colored robe.

His erection, hard before, strained even more. He skimmed his gaze down her body, over the small swell of her belly to the matching mint-green panties covering her. He swallowed and reached out, caressing her from neck to navel.

''Do I look like your mistress now?'' she asked.

He didn't want to talk. Didn't want any reminders that this was Jayne standing in front of him and not some woman he'd made arrangements to have in his life for three months.

But because it was Jayne and not some other woman, talking in the middle of this seemed right somehow. "Not yet."

"Not yet?" She took a half step back from him and slid the robe down her arms, holding it there, and angling her hips to one side to pose like a centerfold. "How about now?"

"Jesus, woman," he said, and closed the gap between them. He freed the front clasp of her bra, peeling back the cups to expose her breasts. Her nipples were the same color as her lips, and hardened under his gaze.

"Now?" she asked huskily. But there was little of the vamp that had been present just moments earlier. In her place was the shy Jayne he always sensed beneath the surface.

He took her hands from the sides of her robe. "Not yet."

He rubbed the rough terry cloth over her nipples until she bit her lip to keep from crying out, and then lowered his mouth to once again kiss her. Kissing Jayne was an addiction he doubted he'd ever recover from. Only when her hips began lifting toward his did he break the kiss and step back.

"Now," he said.

She stood there in front of him, her robe open and her bra pushed out of the way. She should have looked vulnerable in that moment, but Adam knew the person with the real weakness was himself. He stared at her. A lifetime of scruples meant nothing when he was faced with the very real temptation of this woman.

He struggled against the emotions running rampantly through him, and settled on the one thing that had never let him down: lust.

He pulled her to him again. This time when he lowered his head, he thrust his tongue deep into her mouth. She met each thrust of his tongue with one of her own. God, she tasted sweet.

Her hips rocked against his and he nestled his hard-on into the notch of her thighs. She was so hot he could feel her through the layers of her panties and his dress trousers.

She rocked against him and he slipped his hands down her back, tracing her spine and then clasping her hips. Holding her still so he could rub his cock against her. He groaned and threw his head back. She felt incredible, just as he'd known she would.

"Adam?"

"*Oui, chère.* That's it," he said, moving against her, feeling her body pick up a rhythm that had only one surcease—in climax. He rubbed his chest against her breasts. Her nipples stimulated him and he gritted his teeth to keep from coming in his pants.

She called his name again and he traced the curve where her legs met, finding her humid warmth and teasing that opening before slipping one finger under her panties and touching her. He thrust into her body and felt her tighten around his finger. He added a second and placed his thumb over her pleasure bud, until he felt her clenching around his fingers.

He lowered his head and swallowed the sounds she made as she came, then cradled her against his chest and tried to ignore the throbbing in his groin. Adam knew there was no justifying what had happened here. They'd taken a step that couldn't be undone.

Jayne clung to Adam dizzily. Her body still throbbed from the sensations he'd evoked in her. A sheen of sweat coated her skin, and as satisfying as her climax was, she ached to have him take her. Ached to have him possess her, and maybe, in some small way, possess him as well.

She didn't know what to say. With the men in her past she'd been in control of herself. Adam had sent her carefully ordered world topsy-turvy and she was floundering. She didn't like it.

He tipped her head back, gazing down at her with those gray eyes of his. She searched for some kind of emotion there and found tenderness. He stroked one finger down the side of her face, then cupped her jaw gently, rubbing his thumb over her bottom lip.

She'd never felt so cherished by a man—by any

man in her entire life—as she did by Adam at that moment. He bent and lifted her in his arms, carrying her toward the king-size bed.

"Chère—"

His PalmPilot beeped. For a moment Jayne didn't know what it was. A meeting reminder. She'd scheduled a conference call for Adam with his vice-president, Sam Johnson. Let it go, she thought. And in her mind this became a sort of test. She schooled her expression to reveal no emotion as he set her on her feet. He left her side, glanced at his PalmPilot, and picked up the phone, his gaze never leaving hers and still filled with that tenderness she didn't really understand.

Then he glanced away and reached for his notepad. He turned from her and sank down on the bed, jotting notes and speaking into the phone in that rapid-fire way that meant he was angry. She knew in an instant that he was scarcely aware of her presence anymore.

She'd been dismissed. Finally she felt like a mistress, and it wasn't a feeling she particularly liked.

She felt used and cheap. She felt...aching and angry, and only her own self-control allowed her to turn away from him at that moment when she wanted instead to confront him.

She took the clothing she'd removed from the wardrobe and entered the bathroom. The woman she saw in the mirror was one she didn't recognize.

Her lips were full and flushed from his kisses. Her

hair fell around her face in disarray. Her nipples were still hard and her skin was exquisitely sensitive.

She ignored the urge to go back into the bedroom and rail at Adam. Instead, she calmly refastened her bra and dropped the robe to the floor. She donned her skirt, which ended at midcalf, and then put on the blouse. Other than being cut a little lower in front it was almost something she'd wear.

She fixed her hair, touched up her lipstick and hung up her robe before leaving the bathroom. Adam was still on the phone when she emerged. He didn't glance up from the notes he was making, and Jayne told herself it was nothing personal. Nothing that a pretend mistress should get angry about, but it didn't change the fact that she was riled up.

She found the shoes that matched her outfit and stalked out of the bedroom. She didn't know what to do now. Was she supposed to sit around and wait for him? Her mom would know, but Jayne wasn't calling her mom.

Instead, she explored the room in hopes of finding the treasure map.

There was a laminated notecard with typed instructions. She read the note, went to the reproduction print hanging on the wall and pulled on the frame carefully. It swung out from the left side and the map was in the pocket on the back of the frame. She read the legend again. And though Didi had done a nice job with the storytelling, the one on the map was more elaborate. Something out of a pirate romance novel.

The promise of finding your heart's desire was quixotic. How many people *really* knew their hearts and themselves well enough to find what they desired more than anything else? Jayne knew that if she were honest with herself she desired two things at this moment—Adam's head on a platter and a repeat of what had just happened, but with a different conclusion.

She couldn't stop the wild race of emotions through her body and she bounced between sexual frustration and a deep feeling of rage that she didn't know how to restrain.

The light on the extension blinked out and she knew he was off the phone. She waited for him to come to her, but he didn't. She heard the rush of water in the bathroom and realized he was getting ready for dinner.

She put the map down and entered the bedroom, skimming his notes. They were neatly written and had several instructions on them for her. Either what had happened between them was so commonplace in his world that it had no effect on him, or he had better mastery of his emotions than she did.

She hoped for the latter, but life had taught her that just because she wanted something to be true didn't always mean it would be.

"Good, you found my notes. I need you to send a few e-mails. I think we have time before we have to meet the Angelinis for dinner for you to do that."

He had buttoned his shirt and turned away from her to tuck it in. She felt as if she'd just dreamed the sensual encounter they'd had less than thirty minutes ago. He was acting the way he always acted around her.

Let it go, Jayne, she told herself. But she couldn't. She'd put something on the line here and she'd thought, maybe foolishly, that Adam was doing the same. Why the hell wasn't he as deeply affected by that embrace as she had been? Had he seen that damn flaw of hers that every man in her life had found? Why couldn't she fix it so she never had to feel this way again?

"*Chère,* you okay?"

"Don't."

She picked up the notepad and crossed the room, escaping to the living room. She'd send his damn e-mails and gather her wits. She needed to confront him about this, but not now when her blood felt close to boiling and her temper was about to get the best of her.

As she brushed past him, the scent of his aftershave wrapped around her like a lover. Making Adam fall in lust with her was incredibly easy. Making him fall in love with her was a different matter altogether.

* * *

Adam watched Jayne leave their bedroom and clenched his fists. Dammit. He looked for something to kick but didn't want her to see how deeply she'd affected him.

He thrust his fingers through his hair and stood there for a moment. He'd hurt her. God, if she looked at him with those wounded eyes one more time, he'd forget the good sense that the beeping PDA had brought back, and take her to bed.

He'd love her six ways from Sunday and not let her leave the room for the rest of their time here. To hell with business deals.

But his meeting had interrupted him before he'd gone too far. That kiss—hell, he needed another one—was going to be an aberration. He'd decided earlier against asking her to be his mistress in truth. And nothing had happened to change his mind.

He straightened, quickly knotted his tie, shrugged into his dinner jacket and smoothed down his hair. He'd put on too much aftershave, trying to drown out the scent of Jayne, which had permeated the bathroom. He'd been unable to resist burying his face in the robe she'd worn. Her scent was nearly irresistible to him.

He paused in the doorway. Jayne sat at the table where they'd worked earlier. She was typing at the computer, but her ire was clear in every movement she made. The outfit he'd ordered for her looked incredible. Though he knew it was hard on his libido, he was glad to see her dressed in clothing that fit and enhanced her feminine form.

"Almost done?" he asked.

"Sure thing, honeybun."

All of the teasing was gone from her voice, and he knew that if he took her down to dinner with the Angelinis now, they'd know something was wrong.

"You work too hard," he said, keeping his tone light. He walked over to her and put his hands on her shoulders, massaging them. But the feel of her soon had a pronounced affect on his body. He hardened and had to close his eyes for a minute, tipping his head back to reclaim his control.

"You're my boss," she said.

He removed his hands and sank down in the chair next to her. She finished typing the e-mail and then sent it. He noticed she'd checked off several items on the notepad and put the in-process symbol next to a few more. Some of the items had names written next to them and he realized in the time it had taken him to change she'd delegated his entire list of to-do items.

She shut down the computer and turned to face him. "How do you do it?"

"Do what?" he asked. He wondered how she'd accomplished so much so quickly. But he shouldn't be surprised. Jayne was the only assistant he'd ever had who kept pace with him in the office.

"Turn off your emotions. I can't do that."

"I don't."

"You do. I'm still...never mind. I'm mad at you."

"I know," he said. He had a feeling she was still frustrated sexually, as well. That one brief climax wasn't enough to have satisfied the passion that ruled her under that calm surface. And he'd never meant to stop before they'd made it to the bed and he'd taken possession of her.

"You treated me like...your mistress. I didn't appreciate it."

Adam struggled against what she was saying. Jayne was unique because for so long he'd felt safe with her. Her humor had made it impossible for him to keep his usual distance, and now he wished he had.

"I..."

"I don't like it, Adam. It's one thing for me to pretend to be involved with you, but I'm not cut out to be like one of your women. I won't be dismissed and ignored when business crops up."

He thrust his hand in his hair again and then realized what he was doing. He reached instead for Jayne, but she flinched when he touched her this time. Protecting himself was coming at too high a cost. And he didn't want Jayne to have to pay it.

He wanted to fight dragons for her. He wanted to protect her. To be her damn white knight. Where the hell had that come from?

He didn't know. But he knew that the feeling was the truest emotion he'd felt in a long time. And he knew that he couldn't tell Jayne. He'd feel even more foolish—no, vulnerable.

"I don't know any other way to act," he said.

"What, women only fall into two categories—lover or co-worker?"

"Yes. And don't say it with such disdain. I don't notice a man hanging around in your life."

"I date."

"Yes, but you never involve them in your life. They fit neatly into a category, as well."

"I wouldn't have done what you did. I don't even know how. How do you do it, Adam? How do you turn off your body like that?"

He couldn't. Didn't she realize it was all an act? One he'd fought hard to master a long time ago, when he'd realized that he wasn't immune to the weaknesses his father had. When he'd learned that women wielded a power far greater than any female ever realized. Especially Jayne who was a temptress worthy of her own legend. She had the ability to make him lose control. To lose his focus on work.

"Practice," he said. He glanced down at his watch and noted they didn't have a lot of time before dinner. He stood, and Jayne rose as well.

"What kind of practice?"

"Believe me, you don't want to know."

"I need to. I need some explanation. Because if all that before was you scratching an itch…"

He said nothing, just watched the emotions roll

across her face, realizing Jayne had no shield. And he didn't want to teach her to use one.

"It wasn't," he said. "It meant too damn much, which is why you should be grateful to Sam. I leave nothing but destruction in my path when it comes to personal relationships," he told her, and walked out of the room.

Five

"**A**dam?"

He paused but didn't turn around. It should have made words easier to find, but didn't. She hurried after him and took his arm in her grasp, making him face her. His muscles clenched under her fingers and she wished she'd taken more time earlier to explore his body.

"What?"

"You can't just walk away after saying a thing like that."

"I have to. Don't get your hopes up, *chère*."

"What hopes?"

"That what we have here can mean anything once we return to the real world."

The softest look came across his face and he cupped her jaw with a gentle hand. Tilting her head, he dropped a kiss on her lips. It was feather soft and it confused her. Adam was telling her something with this embrace. But she didn't understand.

It felt like goodbye. Then he dropped his hand and moved past her on the path. She touched her own lips, watching him leave.

A rush of joy flooded her and she knew it was foolish to let his comments mean that much to her. But they did. She steeled her heart and warned herself that the sight of him walking away from her was one she should get used to. But she didn't feel angry anymore.

Instead, she was conflicted with emotions about the complicated man who was so much more than a boss. His words made her ache for the boy he must have been. She'd felt many things for the complex man she was half in love with, but sympathy wasn't one of them until now.

She'd suspected there were dark secrets from his childhood that drove him to be so successful. He spoke little of his parents, and Jayne had imagined he'd had an upbringing like hers. She'd never suspected that he'd experienced the other side of the coin. Because in her heart she suspected his father must have left Adam and his mom for a woman like her mother.

Jayne ached deep inside in the emotional place that

reminded her she wasn't as mature as she wanted to be. The place that made her remember what it felt like to watch her father through a slated-wood closet door. That place that was still recovering from Ben's departure and didn't want to ache again.

She locked the door to the suite and headed toward the main hotel building, where the bar and one of the restaurants was housed. She had to get her focus back on work. It would be nearly impossible to ignore Adam, but that was the only way she was going to be able to survive these two weeks in the Caribbean.

The cobblestone path was lined with verdant bushes that smelled like the inside of a florist shop. She stopped by a hibiscus and plucked a bright red blossom, tucking it behind her ear. She was tired of being one bloom that never opened to the sun. Tired of living her life on the sidelines. Tired of not taking the biggest risk life had to offer.

Mentally she started a to-do list for when she returned to New Orleans. She'd have to find another job and prepare Adam to have a new assistant.

She finally reached the building and crossed the lobby. Standing in the shadows, she observed Adam, who sat alone at the bar. There was a tension in him that she hadn't noticed since the first few days she'd started working for him. She knew he was in a bad space, and that she was partially responsible for that. Ben had told her one time that just looking into her eyes made him feel guilty. She didn't really understand what he'd meant by that.

But for some reason, her code of morality shone around her, and many people had a difficult time lying to her. She also knew that she'd made things as difficult as possible between herself and Adam earlier. She'd wanted him to feel a little of the pain and indecision that was swamping her.

It looked as if she'd succeeded. He tilted back his head and drained his whiskey glass in one swallow. She knew he was drinking single malt. It was his favorite.

She knew so many superficial things about him that she'd been able to convince herself she loved him. But only now did she realize how much she still had to learn.

"How do you like my island, *amica?*"

Jayne turned to face Ray Angelini. He wore a well-tailored suit and held a cigar loosely in one hand. He appeared much more at ease here than he had on the plane.

His island was turning into her own personal proving grounds, Jayne realized. She had to face herself and make some tough decisions.

"It's very nice. Adam has already started making notes on the resort. He's so excited that you're talking to him about selling it."

"I know he is, but I don't want your business opinion. How do you like the romance of the island? Didi thinks some couples need to be pushed along, but I think each relationship has its own timetable.''

Jayne felt as if she was under a spotlight. She knew that if she said the wrong thing she might ruin this deal for Adam. And Perla Negra was important to him. ''Adam and I have found that. We worked together for a while before we started our relationship.''

''I can see you two are very close. Let's go join your man.''

Adam wasn't *her* man. Not really, but that didn't stop her pulse from racing as they approached him. Everything solidified in her mind and she wished he would be her man. Nothing would thrill her more. Love was the grand adventure she'd been searching for for a long time. And Adam was just the man to give it to her.

Adam watched Jayne like a man with an addiction. He took another swallow of his wine and knew he'd had too much to drink. He'd had three glasses of whiskey before she'd joined him.

And once they'd sat down at dinner he'd continued to drink more than eat. God, she was lovely tonight. She had a red flower tucked behind her ear, and she seemed to glow from within. He wasn't sure where that had come from because when he'd left her she'd seemed shattered and angry.

He felt the weight of that on his shoulders and reached again for his wineglass before realizing that getting drunk wasn't the solution. He picked up his water glass instead and drained it, signaling the waiter for a refill.

Ray had ordered for them all and they were dining on some of the best seafood Adam had ever tasted. And he'd grown up on the Gulf, so it was hard to impress him. But the resort's chef was first-class and the food was impeccable.

For all that, Adam barely tasted it. His concentration was solely on Jayne. Something had changed in her tonight and he wasn't going to rest until he'd figured out exactly what.

"I looked at the treasure map this afternoon. It's pretty easy to follow," she told him when silence fell between them.

Jayne had kept the conversation going all evening. Adam wondered bitterly if he should give her some sort of bonus. He felt as if she was showing him what he'd be losing if he didn't stop trying to seduce her. And his guts felt raw and exposed by the lesson.

She's just a woman, he reminded himself. There's an entire sea of them out there. But his soul rebelled. There wasn't another person in the world like Jayne, and something deep inside him knew it.

"There are a few surprises along the way, but for the most part, we want our guests to find it," Didi said.

There had been a little tension between Didi and Ray at the beginning of the meal, but Jayne had managed to put them both at ease. She had real talent for making everyone comfortable and happy.

Except him. The brighter she shone at the dinner table, the worse Adam felt. He knew he'd acted like a bastard earlier and he knew that a better man would have apologized. But he wasn't going to.

"So, *compare,* what is it you want more than anything else?" Ray asked him.

Jayne, he thought. But instead he smiled like the salesperson he'd been when he first started out in this business. "Perla Negra."

Ray laughed. "Nice. Truly, what is it you desire most? We had a couple here last month who wanted nothing but wealth."

That pissed him off. People always wished for money, as if it was the answer to the world's problems. But the truth Adam had learned as a young man was that unless you worked for the money it was empty, and left a man feeling like a hollow shell.

"Adam?"

He shook his head to clear it and reached again for his water glass. "I'm already a wealthy man. I don't need a 'treasure' to bring me what I want. I know how to go out and work for it."

He felt Jayne's hand on his thigh under the table— a small warning pinch—and then she started to pull away. He clasped her hand in his and held it in place. It was the first time she'd even acknowledged he was at the table. Despite the way she'd sparkled, she'd left him alone in the shadows.

''Allowing that, then Perla Negra will be yours by effort and not treasure hunting. What's the one thing you want but can't have?'' Didi asked.

Adam rubbed Jayne's hand against his thigh and glanced over at her. She stared up at him, her wide blue eyes, darker than midnight, watching him with a kind of expectation that made his heart beat faster. ''I want Jayne.''

Her sexy mouth parted and her pink tongue darted out to wet her lips. She tilted her head to the side and said nothing, but he could see her pulse wildly beating at the base of her neck. Unable to resist, he touched that pulse with his free hand. Caressed the spot where her life pounded through her body.

Her skin was soft, and gooseflesh spread out from his fingertips, letting him know she was exquisitely sensitive. He made a decision he wasn't aware he'd been mulling over: he was going to have Jayne as his mistress.

''Presumably she's already yours,'' Ray said.

The spell was broken and Adam turned his gaze to their other dinner companions. ''She's the only unpredictable thing in my life.''

Ray nodded and Didi pursed her lips. ''What about you, Jayne? What do you want?''

She shrugged. And Adam realized that while she seemed to be frank and up-front, letting the world see her as she was, there were a lot of layers to this woman. "I'm not wealthy like you are, honeybun. So money would be nice. That way I could sleep in every morning and get up when I wanted to, but…"

He turned away from Didi and Ray, looking down at Jayne, watching her as she bit her lip and closed her eyes for a second. When she opened them he wasn't sure whether she was going to tell them what she really wanted, or what she thought they would like to hear.

"I've always wanted a real family."

"Kids?" Adam asked.

She nodded. "I want the whole shebang. Kids, husband, in-laws. I want to be part of a big family."

"I'm an only child," Adam said.

Her smile turned so sad that for a minute he felt as if he'd been punched in the gut. But that didn't make sense. Jayne was his assistant, and if he played his cards right, maybe his mistress. Why should he ache because he knew he could never give her the one thing she craved?

"Then you better get busy with the babies," Ray said.

Didi punched him in the arm and gave him a warning look. "Babe…"

"Never mind. We have a jazz band playing in the lounge later. Will you two join us for dancing?"

"Not tonight. I promised Jayne a walk on the

beach. She likes to be outdoors, since we spend so much time in the office usually.''

Didi nodded and Ray looked pleased with himself. Jayne's hand turned under his and he wrapped his fingers around hers and held them with a desperation he wasn't sure he liked.

The night breeze was warm and steady as they walked down the tiki-lit path toward the beach. ''It probably would have made more sense to go with the Angelinis to the bar. You could have made more notes.''

''I know what I'm doing, *chère*. I've been running the company for a long time.''

''Sorry. I guess I'm too used to being your assistant. And Ray and Didi both seemed to be buying us as a couple. I was worried about that for a while.''

''I wasn't.''

''Why not? How could you be so confident?''

''You've never let me down.''

She wanted to smile but knew he was being evasive again. ''You go from being this dream man to being a cold robot quicker than I can snap my fingers.''

''I'm not cold, not around you.''

''But I am,'' she said.

He didn't respond to that. Jayne felt a little of her determination waver. They arrived at the beach. ''Still want to go for a walk?''

''Do you?''

"Yes."

Adam sat on a bench to remove his shoes and socks and roll up the bottom of his pants. She slid off her sandals and set them next to his on the bench. The sand under her bare feet felt wonderful, grainy and textured and a little cold.

Then Adam grasped her hand loosely and they started walking down the beach. The only sounds were the roar of the surf and the call of a night bird. It was a Hollywood moment—a couple under a full moon walking along the surf. But in her head Jayne realized that nothing was picture-perfect. Not her, not Adam and not the dreams she'd had as a girl alone in her room.

There was a reason why she had a million to-do lists in her life. And that reason was she had to be in control of everything. Too much of her childhood had been unpredictable.

"Do I really leave you cold?" Adam asked.

"Sometimes. I guess that wasn't very fair. But I'm not feeling myself."

He tilted his head and looked up at the stars. "I can't give you more."

"Why not? Powell's fraternization policy?"

"Partly."

She waited.

"I've seen lives destroyed because of lack of control, *chère.* And I don't want that to happen to you."

"That's the second time you've mentioned destruction. But you don't destroy anything. In fact, you build some of the most luxurious resorts in the world.''

He stopped, dropping her hand and facing the ocean. ''I'm careful in my personal life. You know that. I pick women who don't…''

''Want more than you give them?''

''Yes.''

''Why? I can't imagine you grew up thinking you'd just have a string of mistresses—they're easier than wives.''

''But I did.''

Suddenly she felt chilled and stepped a little closer to Adam. He sensed her shiver and slipped his dinner jacket off, draping over her shoulders. Then he wrapped his arm around her and pulled her close to his side.

''Why would you choose that? It's such a cold life.''

''You sound like you know something about it.''

She shrugged. She wasn't going to tell him her feelings on mistresses.

He tugged her into his arms. ''This is a night for romance and I don't want to waste it talking.''

He lowered his head, but she pulled back. ''I'm not going to be blinded by sex.''

''Blinded by sex,'' Adam said with a chuckle. ''Jesus, Jayne, you kill me.''

She smiled to herself. But she wanted some answers. "You were trying to distract me. Why?"

"I'm not sure," he said. He slipped his hand into hers again and tugged her toward the water. "Let's play."

"Okay, but I still want to know more about your relationships."

"That's not a very nice topic to bring up with a new lover."

"But we're not really lovers."

"I think we will be."

"Me, too," she said softly.

The waves ran over their feet, cool but not too cold, and they stood there staring at each other. Finally, Adam leaned down and brushed his lips against her cheek. "I saw what cheating and infidelity can do to a family. I vowed to never put anyone in that position."

"You're so strong. I don't think you'd ever do that."

"I'm my father's son, Jayne. We haven't been out of New Orleans an entire day and already I'm contemplating breaking one of the company's rules and my own vow to never get involved with a woman who works for me."

He removed his hands from her body and stepped back. She watched him for a long moment and realized that shadows of the past were once again reaching out to darken the future. She'd felt it every day of her life, but never thought about Adam that way. Until now.

"I think you're better than that."

"Sure you do."

"I do."

"Prove it," he said.

"How?"

"Kiss me and make me believe it."

"Okay," she said. Leaning up on tiptoe, she pulled his head down to hers and whispered his name against his lips. "Honeybun, prepare to be wowed."

Six

Jayne's mouth seduced him with light brushes of her lips and then tentative touches of her tongue. A shudder ripped through him. God, he needed her with a desperation that compared to nothing else he'd ever experienced.

He hardened in a rush and slipped his hands under his jacket, which was draped over her curvy body. He ran his palms up and down her back, cupping the lush shape of her hips and pulling her closer.

The game that he'd started back at the airport in New Orleans now spun totally out of his control. There was little he could do but react to this woman who embodied everything he'd ever wanted but never dared take. Except here she was and tonight they'd sleep in the same bed. And steps would be taken that couldn't be undone.

She felt small in his embrace. Without the sandals adding to her height he was reminded once again that Jayne, for all her damn-the-torpedoes attitude, was a rather slight woman.

A woman who brought springtime to his lonely soul. And though it might be his downfall, he knew he wasn't going to turn away from her.

He returned her kiss with the passion that had been banked earlier when he'd made that phone call. He told her with his body all the things he'd never say with words. He thrust his tongue deep in her mouth and explored her secrets and let her do the same to him.

She caged his face with her hands, her fingers stroking against the stubble on his chin before slipping to the back of his head to hold him still for her kisses.

She pressed her bosom to his and he felt his chest swell. He put his hands around her waist and lifted her against him, holding her with desperation and need. He gentled the embrace, knowing that if he didn't, he'd either take her standing up right here, or lying down on the sand. Which, despite the way movies portrayed it, would be damn uncomfortable.

''Wow,'' he said, lifting his head.

She smiled at him and his heart melted. He felt too

much and didn't like it, so he hugged her close and tucked her head under his chin. He turned them so that they were looking out over the ocean.

"You know me, boss. When I put my mind to something there's no stopping me."

"Have you set your mind on me?" he asked lightly. But in his soul he felt hope, and it scared him. He was so defenseless where this woman was concerned.

She nodded. "I don't think I have a choice in the matter."

The surf continued to roll over their feet and Jayne looked down at it. "I'm not a big fan of the ocean. I always hated the water," she said.

"I'm the exact opposite. When I was a boy I used to dream of sailing away," he murmured. "Can you swim?"

"I can now. It wasn't fear, it was a real loathing. My mom was always dropping me at school and sailing away to Mexico or the Keys. And to me it represented her leaving."

He took Jayne's hand and led her up the beach. Sinking to the sand, he pulled her between his legs and held her. "Tell me about your childhood."

"Why?"

"Because I want to know you inside out."

Jayne sat there in the moonlight looking like an ethereal creature from another world. He knew that the only way to protect himself would be to learn all he could about this woman. And find a way of exorcising her from his system without forming a deeper attachment.

"This isn't an act for the Angelinis, is it?" she asked, and there was a hint of vulnerability in her voice. Not an Amazon, he reminded himself.

He hugged her closer for a second. Leaning down, he nibbled on the lobe of her ear and dragged his teeth down the side of her neck. Sensual pleasure rippled through her and he pulled her hips tighter against him, arching his back to rub his cock against the curves of her butt.

"What do you think?" he asked.

"Too much is at stake for guessing."

"You're right. I want you, Jayne. I want you for my mistress. No more games or play-acting. I want the real thing." Mentally he knew the impact of this moment was going to be felt for a long time. But one of the first business lessons he'd learned was that some actions were inevitable and the price would have to be paid.

"Me, too. But I want more than just your body."

"Good."

"Good?" she asked. "You know this will impact our working relationship."

"I told you I want to know all your secrets."

"That would leave me with nowhere to hide."

He stroked her face. He'd give anything to be rid of the lust that was running rampant through his body.

No, that wasn't true. As much as he enjoyed Jayne in his office, he knew that he'd enjoy her as a lover even more. And he realized that all these long months when he'd thought he'd done a good job of ignoring her as a woman, he'd been fooling himself. He'd been waiting for her. Waiting for the right moment to do this.

''Don't you think we've done enough hiding?''

Her fingers kneaded his thighs. ''Is this an equality thing?''

Instead of answering he pulled her more firmly against him and swept his hands over her, lingering at the full curves of her breasts. Cupping them in his hands and rubbing his palms over their tips until he felt them bud and nestle against him.

Her breath caught in her throat and she shifted against him. He plucked at her nipples and lowered his head, suckling the side of her neck. Her fingers clenched against his thighs and he grew painfully hard. He knew that if he didn't have Jayne soon, he was going to self-combust.

''Let's go back to the room,'' he said.

''Yes.''

Jayne stopped analyzing and just enjoyed being with Adam. She fairly pulsed with need and couldn't wait until they got to their room to make love. She'd seen a very exquisite negligee in her new wardrobe and wanted to see Adam's reaction to her in her gown.

"On a night like this I can easily imagine that pirate Antonio sailing into port here with his beautiful maiden."

Adam's stride was loose and relaxed. It was the first time she'd walked anywhere with him that wasn't at a clipped paced. This was a side to him that she hadn't seen before, and she wanted to explore it more. She wanted to make sure this time on the beach and the magic it wove around her included him, as well.

"I'm sure she wasn't a maiden when they arrived here," he said in a wry tone.

"Unless she was in love with him, I bet she was," Jayne said.

"Don't put too much stock in love, *chère*. Passion would have made her change her mind."

She remembered what he'd said about his father earlier. But she couldn't believe that Adam didn't believe love existed.

All of his relationships were designed to insulate him from feeling anything. The part of her mind that loved puzzles wondered if there were other variables that his mistresses of the past had in common. Physically, she'd noticed they all tended to have long legs and full breasts.

"Passion's overrated. A few pheromones and some scanty clothing are all it takes to evoke passion."

"That's lust," he said.

"Made a study of it, have you?"

He lifted one eyebrow in a very wry expression that made her feel as if she were a naive schoolgirl. She didn't like the feeling, but knew in this instance she was. She didn't have any of his sophistication. To her, sex was more than pheromones, which was why she'd had so few lovers.

"Are you asking me about my love life?" he inquired.

"No. I know you have a revolving door on your bedroom."

He said nothing, but dropped her hand. She stopped and cast her gaze toward him. With one glance she knew he was angry.

"Do you really think so little of me?" he demanded.

Yes and no. Mostly, she was angry at herself for not really understanding what he wanted. "No, I was being flip. I'm sorry. I don't understand why you've chosen only brief affairs."

He tipped his head back and a warm breeze blew around them. The smell of the sea and the night-blooming jasmine surrounded them both, and she wondered how something she'd meant as a nice romantic conversation had gone so wrong.

"Because they are safer," he said softly, his deep voice a whisper on the wind.

"Safer than one-night stands?" she asked, really wanting to understand this complex man.

"No. I can live without sex for a few nights."

"Couldn't prove it by me."

He drew one finger across her collarbone and she shivered at the touch. "That's because you've been a fire in my soul for a long time."

A fire in his soul. The words echoed through her head and her heart. And she threw her arms around him and kissed him. He held her gently and let her control their embrace.

"Thank you for making this sound special."

"It is, Jayne. Don't ever doubt that."

He held her hand loosely and led her toward the path to the hotel. For a moment it felt as if all of her dreams, past and present, melded together. She forgot that she'd been hurt by her father and Ben, and really believed that this time, with Adam, love might stay. Love might blossom. Love might be right.

Anticipation burned through her, making her tremble with desire and a crazy belief that something wrong was being righted. Adam drew her to a halt under a tiki lamp and pulled her close to him. She stretched up on tiptoe to meet his mouth as it descended toward her.

This time it was a sweet embrace with no rushing. It was as if by agreeing that they'd make love in their suite she'd given him permission to linger over her as if she were a gourmet feast.

And he did linger, rubbing his lips sensually against hers until they were so sensitized she couldn't imagine her mouth without his pressed to it. He tilted his head and forced her mouth open, but only filled it with his warm breath.

Pulling back, he glanced down at her with a slight smile, then took her mouth again. He thrust his tongue past her teeth and tasted her deeply. She returned the embrace.

His hands swept up and down her back. Then his left hand slipped around the curve of her waist and caressed her stomach and midriff, working its way slowly up to her breasts. They felt heavy, and she didn't know if she could stand another caress there right now.

But as he cupped her and rubbed his finger around the edge of her nipple, never touching the engorged flesh, she realized that she needed his touch. She whimpered in the back of her throat, wishing for more, needing him to take her nipple between his fingers or even in his mouth.

His lips left hers to slide down her cheek to her neck. He nibbled the column of her throat, then bit gently at the spot where her neck and shoulder met. She arched against him and dug her fingernails into his shoulders through the cloth of his dress shirt.

"*Chère,* I can't wait."

"You don't have to."

He put his hand on the small of her back and pushed her toward the hotel. His pace was definitely quicker now.

"There you two are," Ray said as they reentered the main building. He'd shed his dinner jacket and had the stub of a cigar clamped between his teeth. He took a quick puff on it and then removed the cigar from his mouth.

"Here we are," Adam said.

Angelini must have been standing on the large veranda at the back of the hotel for some time. Jayne tried to determine if Adam had noticed Ray standing there before or after he'd kissed her.

One glance at Adam's face revealed nothing. It was the second time she'd realized that he had an innate ability to hide what he was feeling. She tried not to let the knowledge get to her, like some kind of warning.

"Our jazz band is going to be starting their second set in a minute. I was hoping to catch you on your way back from the walk and change your mind. Want come see them, *compare?*"

"Sure. I want to make some notes on the entertainment. And Jayne likes to dance."

I do? "Not tonight. I've got a headache."

"Are you okay?" Adam asked.

"Yes. I think it was the traveling and the long day at work."

"Well, starting tomorrow you won't have anything to do but relax," Ray said.

"Go ahead, Adam. I'll see you later."

The band started playing and Angelini stood in the

doorway of the hotel. Adam was at a crossroads, one path leading toward the man who held the keys to a deal he wanted to close, and the other leading to Jayne. She tried not to place too much importance on that fact. She also told herself it didn't hurt when he walked away.

Adam was uncomfortable the moment Jayne left. The last thing he wanted to do was spend the evening in a bar with Angelini. The lobby decor hadn't changed in the last twenty years. There was that sixties-style furniture and large paddle fans that kept the air circulating.

Was Jayne okay? She'd seemed fine on the beach a few minutes ago. He would stay for one drink and then make an excuse and leave. The ceiling fan teased his memory and he knew he'd seen it or one like it before.

Ray seemed annoyed when they entered the smoke-filled lounge. The act on the stage was a jazz trio and their music was good, but all Adam saw was Jayne's wide blue eyes filled with a kind of hurt that he hadn't realized he could inflict on another person.

Angelini signaled the waitress when Didi joined them. His wife didn't have much fashion sense. She wore a long skirt in some shade of olive-green. Adam was pained to see a woman dressed so...shabbily. He made a mental note to have the boutique send Didi some new clothes.

"Where's Jayne?"

"Hey, babe. She couldn't join us. Something about a headache."

Didi didn't say anything, but glared at Ray. Those two had the strangest relationship. Adam didn't sense true love between them at all. So he wasn't sure why they were insisting on it from their potential buyers.

"I'll leave you two to discuss business," Didi said with a pointed look at Ray.

"Babe, you're cramping my style," Ray said.

But Didi just walked away. Adam didn't want to sit here and schmooze with Ray for the next thirty minutes. The band slid into an old Miles Davis tune. Adam wished Jayne were here. She'd like this band, and he knew he could coax her onto the small dance floor.

"That one is always sticking her nose in my business. She gives me *agita*. Is Jayne like that?"

"No. Well, sometimes. If I ask her to do something she thinks is ridiculous or not good for business." Adam didn't mind her interference, because nine times out of ten she was right on the money. Jayne had a way of looking at life and situations with clear eyes, and sometimes she saw things that he didn't with his single-minded focus on getting the job done.

"How long you two been together?" Ray asked, taking a sip of his drink.

Adam knocked back his single malt. Not long

enough, he thought. "She started working for me eight months ago."

Ray gave him a man-to-man look. "But you knew you wanted more?"

"What are you, my father confessor?"

"*Madon'*, you have no idea. I guess that was pushy."

"Yeah, it was. I know how important it is that a couple buys this place."

"Not any couple," Ray said. "A couple in love."

"Jayne and I are committed to keeping Perla Negra as one of the Caribbean's premiere resorts."

"That's not good enough. I thought I was clear when we spoke on the phone. Perla Negra isn't just a resort. It's a legend."

"Legends make a nice selling point," Adam said.

"Yes, they do," Ray said. He took a puff off his cigar. "But it has to be more than that.... Perla Negra is a place where couples come for romance and to reaffirm the bonds between them."

Perla Negra... The way Ray spoke of it made it seem like something mystical and otherworldly, the perfect place for love. Two things that couldn't survive in the real world, or at least in Adam's world.

"I hate to break it to you, Ray, but some of the couples who come here are adulterers."

Ray shrugged.

Adam knew that not everyone felt the way he did about adultery. He also acknowledged that if his fam-

ily hadn't been shattered by it he might not hold the
act of being unfaithful in such disdain. But he did.
And it was the one thing he couldn't forgive or tolerate.

"We provide a place for them to be together. We
never stand in the way of true love."

"No matter what kind of mess it leaves behind?"
Adam asked.

"I don't follow."

Adam finished off his drink. "Never mind. I think
I'd better go see about Jayne."

"No problem," Ray said. "We'll meet you for
breakfast on the veranda. I've arranged for you both
to take a tour around the island on a boat."

"I can handle the boat myself, so we won't need
a guide. Good night."

"Buona notte, compare."

Adam walked through the lobby, intent on getting
back to Jayne. Something was wrong and he should
have picked up on it earlier instead of letting business
distract him. The only reason he had was that business
was easier to manage and deal with.

The suite was dark when he entered it except for a
small coffee table lamp. He was surprised to see the
red file folder sitting in the middle of the desk, the
one that held his action items. Jayne must have done
some work when she returned to their suite.

Relieved that she must be feeling better—not only
because he hoped to persuade her to become his

lover—he flipped open the file folder and skimmed the printed e-mails and faxes. Nothing urgent.

He loosened his tie and toed off his shoes as he approached the bedroom. He hadn't worked out the details yet, but he knew he wasn't going to be able to let Jayne leave her job, despite what he'd always believed about lovers working together. He knew that he functioned better when she was around.

He opened the door to the bedroom carefully. Moonlight spilled in from the window, and Adam stayed in the shadows, searching the bed for Jayne's small form. But the bed was empty.

"Chère?"

"Out here," she said. Her voice drifted in from the balcony.

Adam stepped out there, ready to pull her into his arms and finish what they'd started too long ago on the beach. But one look at the way she held herself and he knew something was terribly wrong with Jayne. And it wasn't a damn headache. It was something he'd done.

He suddenly remembered why he preferred having a mistress to actually dating. There was none of this kind of emotional turmoil.

Seven

Jayne had focused on work when she'd returned to their suite. She'd changed out of the wraparound silk skirt—not into the one-of-a-kind negligee that Adam had so thoughtfully provided, but a large T-shirt she'd picked up in the gift shop after Adam had left with Ray.

Jayne realized that the bridge wasn't appearing. She'd leaped off the precipice and had been in a free fall. But she was recovering now. She'd say it was moonlight madness or the sea breeze. A temporary aberration in an otherwise sane person. She and Adam could never be lovers, because she knew without a shadow of a doubt that nothing could ever compete with Powell International in Adam's life. Especially not a lover.

Earlier she'd had some hope in her heart that she could teach Adam to love her, but not anymore.

"Is your head still bothering you?" he asked from the doorway. He was hidden in shadow and she couldn't really see him, just hear his deep, sultry voice. And sense the tension that emanated from him.

An answering tautness sprang to life inside her. She shook her head. "I lied. I didn't have a headache."

He stepped out onto the balcony and leaned next to her at the railing. He crossed his arms over his chest, looking to her like a relaxed man with nothing but time on his hands.

"Why?" he asked. There was a dangerous softness to his tone that she knew from hearing it in the office meant he was close to losing his temper.

She didn't place too much importance on that. She probably should have stayed and acted her role for Ray and Didi, but she couldn't. She'd been exposed there in his arms. And if Adam had been watching her instead of Ray, Jayne feared he'd have seen her heart in her eyes. "I needed to get away."

"From me?"

She nodded. From him and from herself. But there'd been no escaping her own thoughts. So she'd tried to work, and then she'd tried to call her mom, figuring that Mona would know how to keep a man like Adam in her life. But her mother hadn't been home, and in the end Jayne hadn't been able to leave a message.

Adam watched her with an intensity that made her remember his hands on her breasts earlier. She forced her thoughts back to the conversation. "I didn't want to talk to Angelini. I don't think I'm cut out for this, Adam."

"You're talking about becoming my lover."

"At least you didn't say mistress."

He cursed under his breath and pivoted to face the sea, his hands braced on the railing and his head bent. This was the Adam she wanted to wrap in her arms and comfort. Except she knew now the price was too high, and that she wasn't to pay it for a few weeks with him.

"I knew it. What the hell happened?"

How could she explain without revealing her own vulnerability where he was concerned? "I just got a wake-up call."

"Am I supposed to follow that?"

"I guess not. I think the island was working its magic on me. I was falling for the romance of the legend of Perla Negra. And casting you in the role of a swashbuckling hero."

He rested one lean hip against the railing, his expression now forbidding and dark. And she shivered, wrapping her arms around herself.

"But now you've decided I'm not a hero?"

She'd hurt him, she realized. "I think you'd make a wonderful hero, Adam. Just not for me."

"Why not?"

"I need more than you can give me."

"Jayne—"

She reached up and touched his lips to stop the words. "Don't say anything yet. I'm not even sure what I need, but I know it's more than you give your women. And I thought I could make you understand that."

She dropped her hand and tilted her head to study him in the moonlight.

"What happened to change your mind?"

"That kiss with Ray watching. I forgot that even though you want me in your bed, we are playing a part."

"Dammit, Jayne I wasn't playing to Angelini."

She wanted to believe him, but she knew better. Adam was always aware of everyone and everything. "I'm not mad about it. I'd have done the same thing in your position."

"How gracious you are. What if I wanted to make love to you out here on the balcony?"

"I'd have to draw the line there. I just told you I'm having a hard time keeping up with the pretense."

"Exactly what is your difficulty? The hero thing?"

"Yeah, the hero thing."

"There isn't another woman in the world I'd have this conversation with," Adam told her, exasperated.

"Should I be flattered?" she asked mockingly.

"Hell, yes. Dammit, Jayne. For the first time I'm willing to break my own company rules."

"I know. It means something, but not enough. Even though I'm blaming the island resort, that's not what's wrong with me."

"What is it then?"

"I believe in love and want a family. And you don't."

"Would it help if I lied to you?"

"God, no."

"Then I don't know *what* you want. I do know if we both crawl into that bed together the point will be moot."

"Really?"

He raised one eyebrow. "Now who's not being honest?"

Swallowing carefully around her tight throat, she realized that maybe that was why she'd been standing out here waiting for him to return. She wanted to force him to make a decision. And maybe force herself to make one, as well.

"You're right. I guess that's why I left before."

"Don't think about it too much, *chère*. This isn't something either of us is used to or can control."

''It's magic, isn't it, Adam?''

He pulled her into his arms and lowered his head. ''You're the magic.''

Adam scooped Jayne up in his arms and carried her into the bedroom. Her mouth moved under his with a tentative sweetness he knew was branding him deep in his soul. She let him set the pace, and that was so different from the feisty woman he'd come to know. But he didn't question it.

He set her on her feet and framed her face in his hands. Forcing her head back with the motion of his, he compelled her mouth open. Her tongue greeted his with a tentative foray, but Adam was past the point of foreplay.

He had an erection that was almost painful, and he desperately needed to be inside of Jayne's body. He needed to spread her bare on the bed and then taste every inch of her from head to heels. And only when she'd reached the same fevered pitch that burned through him would he move up over her and claim her as his own.

He left her lips and let his mouth slide down the side of her neck, encountering that thick terry-cloth robe once again. He set her on her feet next to the bed and reached out to turn on the lamp on the nightstand.

He undid the sash at her waist and pulled back the terry cloth, expecting to find her slim, curvy body.

Instead he found a large T-shirt with the resort's logo printed on it.

"What are you wearing?" he asked, the clothing jarring him from the sensual spell he was weaving them both in.

She shrugged. "Something to sleep in."

"I know I ordered a nightgown for you."

"You ordered something for me to wear to bed with a lover."

"Then why aren't you wearing it?" he asked. But in his heart he knew the answer. She'd thought he'd used her to make Ray believe they were a couple. She'd thought he could call passion and interest from his body at will. She'd thought he'd been using her, and she didn't want to be exposed in front of him.

That hurt him in a place he didn't even like to acknowledge he had—his heart. So he ignored that and focused instead on the woman. He would use his skills as a lover to make up for the hurt and pain he'd caused her.

"Why are you making a federal case out of this, honeybun?" she asked in that smart-ass way of hers.

He had to hide a smile because he knew she sassed him only when she was uncertain. And he didn't want Jayne to be unsure of him in the bedroom, or of herself. To his knowledge she hadn't dated anyone in the last eight months since she'd started working for him. He tucked that tidbit away for later.

Right now, he set about seducing her with all the

skill he'd learned since he was a boy on the cusp of manhood. Skills he'd first honed to keep from feeling alone, and then later used so that he didn't have to feel anything other than physical gratification with women. Lately those skills had made him feel jaded. But tonight he was glad for the knowledge, because the only thing that mattered was giving the most pleasure he could to Jayne.

He leaned down, scraping his teeth against the side of her neck and then nibbling at the tender flesh there. Her taste was addictive. Instead he lingered there as if he'd been famished for a long time and she was a full-course meal.

Her hands clutched at his shoulders, fingernails scoring him through the cloth of his shirt. He lifted his head and started unbuttoning it. When he shrugged out of it he felt her appreciative gaze on his body.

"Like what you see?"

"It's okay," she said, and when he started toward her with mock menace, she giggled. Really giggled, and despite the ache in his groin, he felt lighter than ever before.

He scooped her up in his arms and dropped her on the bed. "Let's see if I can change your mind, shall we?"

"It's going to take some work on your part," she said, rolling onto her side and propping her head up on her elbow.

"I'd probably work harder if you showed me a little flesh."

She bit her lip and then lifted the hem of her shirt a little so that it rested on the top of her thighs. "How's this?"

"You've got great legs, *chère*. But…"

She lifted the shirt quickly and flashed him. He had a brief image of a nest of brown, curly hair at the apex of her thighs and a smooth flat stomach. Unless he was mistaken he'd seen a birthmark on her left hip. He reached under the shirt and rubbed the spot.

"What's this?"

"Tattoo," she said.

"Show me?"

"What are *you* going to show *me?*"

"I'm already bare-chested."

"So, convince me," she said.

He sat sideways on the bed, his hips resting next to her stomach. He took her hand from where it gripped the hem of her shirt, bringing it to his mouth. He nibbled the tip of each finger and then kissed the palm of her hand.

He took her hand and stroked it down his body, rubbing her fingers over his sensitive skin. He hardened even more and tried to shift on the bed to relieve some of the pressure between his legs. Damn. He should have removed his pants.

While her hand explored his chest, her fingernails scraped down the center of his body. He lifted her

T-shirt and then bent down to examine her tattoo. It was a pretty little flower that wasn't open, but tightly closed, and a drop of rain lay on the leaf below it.

He traced the pattern with his tongue. Later he'd question her about it, but now he was too close to her body. He could smell the scent of her arousal, and a red mist settled over him. He wanted her, dammit.

He ached to have her.

"Convinced?" he asked, but his voice now was little more than a growl.

She looked up at him from under her lashes. "I'm naked under this shirt."

"Hot damn."

She threw her head back and laughed. He gave up all pretense of playing games, shedding his pants and briefs in one quick motion.

He took the hem of her shirt and pulled it up over her head, tossing it aside. His breath caught in his throat when she lay spread before him in the golden glow of the lamp. She shone with an effervescence he wanted to claim for himself. But he knew at best all he'd have were these moments in her bed.

First Adam caressed her with his eyes and his words. "You're the most exquisite woman I've ever seen."

And when he looked at her the way he was now, she felt as if she really were. For the first time in her life, she didn't feel plain and ordinary. A flush spread over her body and she pushed her shoulders back against the bed, thrusting her breasts into greater prominence.

"Your skin is like the sunrise, warm and golden. And my fingers ache to touch you."

"I ache to be touched," she replied.

He smiled softly in acknowledgment. Then he bent over her, tracing the line of her body with his hands. His touch was so light it felt like a breeze, and she thought she was imagining it. But when he paused to explore her belly button she knew it was real.

He licked a path straight down her center, but when he reached her pubic hair he turned his attention to her thigh, nibbling his way down her left leg and then back up her right.

He avoided the areas of her body that ached most for his contact. Her nipples stood erect waiting for his mouth, but each time he came close he didn't touch them. She writhed on the bed.

He stopped and lingered at her tattoo. With his tongue he traced the pattern again, over and over until she reached down, tunneling her fingers through his hair and holding him to her.

Her tattoo was a big part of who she was—a reminder that she never wanted to be a blossom that had bloomed too many times, like her mother. Jayne had had it done when she was seventeen. It had been painful, but she'd learned that most things in life were.

Adam lifted his head, watching her. He palmed both of her breasts, rubbing their centers in a circular motion until her hips lifted from the bed. His hands moved downward then, skimming her sides and squeezing her hips.

She was helpless to do anything but lie there like a sexual feast prepared for his delight. He stood over her like a god from ancient times. He was like a powerful and successful warrior, she realized, and as she studied him she saw another scar. Unlike the small mark near his nipple, this one ran across his lower belly and down his hip.

She touched the scar gently, tracing over lines that were white with age. He reached down and moved her hand away, bringing her touch instead to his pectorals. How many times had she sat in the boardroom and imagined opening his shirt and touching him?

Now she could. And she did, leaving no area unexplored. She scored his chest with his fingernails when he reached the center of her body, tracing a path with one blunt finger, then dipping inside to test her warmth.

He stretched her carefully, adding a second finger to her opening. She clenched around him, needing more. He bent and she felt the brush of his breath for a second before his tongue tickled her bud.

His fingers moved inside her and his tongue continued its relentless assault until her hips bucked and she grabbed his head, holding him to her hot body.

Her orgasm when it broke over her left her convulsing around him.

Sweat gleamed on her skin and she throbbed from head to toe. She tugged him up over her, skimming her hands down his back. "My turn."

She pushed against him until he was on his back, then knelt next to him on the bed. She kissed him first, exploring that bold, sensual mouth. She could taste herself on him, and it made her feel a little wicked and naughty. And deep in her center she felt an answering pulse.

She scratched his small nipple carefully with her fingernail. He closed his eyes and then reached for her hand, smoothing open her palm and rubbing it over his nipple the way he always caressed her. She watched as his own back arched and his hips jerked toward her.

She took his hard length in her hand. He was hot to her touch and hard. Grasping him at the root, she circled him with her hand and stroked him.

She brought her other arm down and reached between his legs to cup him, squeezing gently until she felt a spurt of moisture at his tip. She rubbed at it with her finger.

Glancing up at him, she realized he was watching her. She lifted her finger to her lips and licked away his taste.

Something primitive lit in his eyes and he rolled over, taking her beneath him. He pinned her to the bed with his hips, his member hot and hard at her entrance. She groaned at the feel of him there and couldn't help thrusting her hips toward him.

He held her still and rubbed his length against her. It felt good, but she was still so empty, and desperately needed him inside her.

With a muttered curse, he pushed away from her. "Are you on the pill?"

She blinked a few times before she understood what he was asking. "Yes."

"Thank God. I hate condoms."

"Me, too," she said. She preferred skin to skin. Especially with Adam.

"I'm healthy," he muttered as he shifted on the bed. He draped her legs over his arms and pushed them back toward her body. "Okay?"

It was way more than okay, but she couldn't speak. He was at her entrance, pushing inside her. He thrust forward until he was fully seated. She relaxed her lower body, trying to take him deeper, and was rewarded when he slipped in farther.

He kissed her, his tongue thrusting into her mouth in the same rhythm as his body took hers. She was on fire and there was little she could do but lay beneath him, an instrument of his pleasure. She'd never had an orgasm more than once in an evening and didn't expect it to be different with Adam.

But then she felt that tingling at the center of her body that signaled one was coming. She gripped

Adam's shoulders, digging her nails into his back as her entire body started to throb and clench around him. When she came this time lights flashed before her eyes, and she felt Adam's body empty into hers at the moment consciousness dimmed.

He roared her name and then continued to thrust a few more times before pulling her into his arms and rolling to his side.

She couldn't think and could barely breathe. But her heart overflowed with emotions and she realized that despite what she'd said earlier at dinner, having a family was no longer her heart's desire. Having Adam in her life forever was.

Eight

Adam woke up alone in bed. The sunlight streamed through the open window and the sound of the surf called him. For a moment he didn't remember where he was, but then the bathroom door creaked open and Jayne tiptoed across the floor.

"Come back to bed, *chère*."

"In a minute."

She went to the wardrobe and tucked something into one of her drawers. Once again she was wearing that heavy terry-cloth robe. Her lips were still swollen from his kisses and her eyes had a lambent light in them as she gazed at him.

He knew he was existing in a kind of limbo, but

he didn't care. He'd taken Jayne to his bed and it was too late to go back. Hell, he wouldn't even if he could.

Standing next to his side of the bed, she dropped her robe, revealing the naked curves of her body. It was a perfect form, but he'd never been as aroused by just the sight of a woman as he was with Jayne.

Reaching up, he traced her side from her shoulder to her waist, lingering on the tattoo on her hip. Jayne had never struck him as a tattoo person.

"When did you get this?"

"I'll tell you if you take off the sheet," she said.

He was willing to play along. "It had better be a good tale."

"I'll make it worth your while," she said.

There was something about Jayne in this mood that intrigued him. She glowed, though maybe that was from the early morning sun streaming into the room. However, her smile was brighter, and that had nothing to do with Mother Nature. Maybe something to do with him?

He gripped her hips and drew her forward. He didn't want to hurt her. Not that he ever intended to hurt the women in his life, but for some reason he'd never really been able to get things right with females.

Sitting up, he wrapped his arms around her and rested his head against her breast. He heard her heart beating strongly under his ear. His vision was filled with her creamy curves and one pale pink nipple.

"Tell me," he whispered against her flesh. And then watched as her nipple budded and her hands tightened in his hair.

"I got it when I was seventeen."

"Wait," he said. After placing a kiss on her breast, he piled all the pillows behind his back and kicked the sheets to the foot of the bed. Then, grabbing her by the waist, he leaned back, lifting her up over his body. "Now tell me," he said.

"I can't talk now," she said, her voice breathless. She rubbed herself sinuously against him, her warmth sliding over his erection and her nipples brushing his chest.

And he didn't want to talk, either. Later he'd find out the story of why she'd gotten that tattoo and discover the source of that mysterious light inside Jayne. But right now he needed her.

She tipped her head back, bracing her hands on his shoulders, and lifted just the tiniest bit. Sliding his hands between their bodies, he positioned himself.

She opened her eyes and looked right at him. As she slowly sank down on his hard-on. Adam knew he'd never be the same. Her dewy center caressed him like a velvet glove. She paused once he was fully sheathed, and squeezed him with her inner muscles.

When he groaned her name, she smiled. She relished her power over him. "Like hearing me moan?"

She bit her bottom lip as he took her breasts in his hands, pinching her nipples carefully and then scraping them with his thumbnails. She moaned and her hips flexed against his. He soothed the small pain with his palm before angling his head and sucking one nipple into his mouth.

Her hands left his shoulders to hold his head to her. She rocked slowly over him and he knew she wasn't torturing him this time, but simply lost in the sensations he was calling forth.

"Moan for me," he said against her skin, nibbling his way to her other nipple and suckling there.

"Not yet," she said, and pushed him back against the pillows. She braced her hands against his chest, nails scoring his skin mildly. And she lifted herself off of him. She let him slide all the way out of her body, and paused while he hovered at her entrance.

He wanted to let her run the show, but enough was enough. Adam yearned for her with a desperation he would never acknowledge. He longed to once again bathe in her warmth and forget about the hunger that had been festering in him for too long.

Wrapping one arm around her, he thrust upward with his hips, then rolled them both over so that she was under him.

"Hey, I was in charge," she said, but her eyes drifted closed as he started thrusting inside her.

When her back arched to receive each of his thrusts, the slim expanse of her neck was revealed and he lowered his head to suckle at the point where her collarbone met it.

Her hands moved up and down his back. She clenched him with her muscles deep inside every time he retreated, and from her mouth came a litany that was his name.

Stroking her back, he took the full curves of her butt in his hands and caressed the crease. She arched toward him, seeking her release. With a thousand electric sparks, Adam felt his own climax sweep over him in one continuous wave, and after that he couldn't move. Lowering his head, he rested it on her chest and held her. She clutched him to her breast and didn't say a word. But Adam knew that something had happened between them and that the world outside had changed for them, as well.

They'd both drifted back to sleep after their early morning lovemaking, and in her dreams, Jayne had never had to let Adam go. He woke her the second time with a sweet kiss and a joining that was so deep and forceful that she felt certain he'd branded her soul. Once their heartbeats had settled down, he'd urged her into the shower, promising her a surprise.

The craft that Ray and Didi had provided was a high-speed motorboat. Adam was like a kid with a new toy. He raced it into the surf away from the island, doing tight turns and making sea mist spray over them both.

And Jayne was definitely surprised. Adam seemed years younger out here. He was more at home on the ocean than anyplace she'd observed him. This seemed a more natural side of him.

He was wearing his swim trunks and sunglasses, his head tipped back to the sunshine. She wore only her bikini, because once they'd left the marina, Adam had refused to allow her to wear the cover-up she'd brought.

Neither of them had discussed the future or her position within Powell International, and Jayne wasn't sure how to plan her next step. So she was doing something decidedly un-Jayne and ignoring the urge to make a plan around this. Because if she started planning it would mean that she'd given up on the fantasy of making him fall in love with her.

And after last night it was clear to her that she had no other goal. She scanned his strong, muscled body, watching him control the vessel and remembering his hands on her body.

''Why are you staring at me?''

She blushed and he raised one eyebrow, then slowed the boat. She was sitting in the captain's chair and Adam stood next to her, his powerful legs braced as he maneuvered across the water.

''You seem very at home on the ocean,'' she said at last.

He shrugged. ''I am.''

''Still dreaming of sailing away?'' she asked lightly, remembering what he'd said on the beach.

And she wondered if he dreamed of doing so alone or if now she was there with him.

"Sometimes."

"Now?"

He shook his head. "Not with you at my side. Want to try piloting the boat?"

"No," she said.

"Chicken."

"Ha. I'm not scared to learn how to drive this boat."

"Prove it."

"I don't have to prove it. I'm too self-confident to rise to your bait."

"What if something happens to me and you have to find your way back on your own?"

"I brought my cell phone."

He killed the engine, dropped the anchor and spread his arms wide, and she couldn't help but imagine him as Poseidon, king of all he surveyed. "There's something about being at sea."

"Yeah, fish smells and motion sickness."

He rested his hips against the railing of the boat and crossed his ankles. "The next time some woman tells me I'm not romantic..."

Jayne tried to laugh, but the thought of him with another woman wasn't a comfortable one. So she forced her mind away from that. Instead she stood and smiled sweetly at him before pushing him overboard.

He came neatly to the surface. "Oh, you're going to pay for that."

"Is the boat safe here?"

"Yes, my practical Jayne, it is."

"Good." She dived overboard, bobbing up next to him. She'd no sooner surfaced then she felt his hand on her thigh, strong sure fingers slipping under her suit to caress her. She stopped treading water for a minute and he gave her a wicked grin before tugging her under.

That dirty dog, distracting her with sex! They played a rough-and-tumble game of dousing each other, but each brush of his body against hers made her want him locked deep inside her again.

After twenty minutes had passed, she surfaced and glanced around to find Adam. When he reappeared, she swam behind him, wrapped her arms around him and whispered the most deliciously sexual things in his ear until he grabbed her wrist and hauled her back to the boat.

As soon as he got them both out of the water, he laid her down on the bench seat at the back of the cruiser. "Get naked."

He stripped off his own swimsuit and watched her. She'd shed her top but was still struggling out of her bottoms. He reached for the fabric and tugged it down her legs. Then he lowered himself to her, kissing her as he slid deep inside. She wrapped her legs around his hips and held on to him. "Talk dirty to me again, *chère,*" he murmured.

She did, telling him in explicit detail what he did to her and what she wanted to do to him. Her words lit a raging fire inside Adam. Their coupling was fast and furious.

In the aftermath, she clung tightly to him, her mouth resting on his chest. He tasted faintly of the sea and of man.

He cradled her in his strong arms, slipping one of his thighs between hers. One hand cupped her breast and the other her hip. The boat rocked them gently and the sea breeze cooled their flushed bodies.

"I don't want to sail away. I'm enjoying myself too much."

"Me, too," she confessed.

He drew his finger down her cheek and under her chin, tilting her head back for his kiss. He lingered over her mouth for a few minutes and when he lifted his head she wanted to pull him back to her.

"I'm glad. Did you bring that treasure map?"

"Ray gave us one as we were leaving. Are we going hunting for our heart's desire?"

Something warm lit his eyes, and though she knew it wasn't practical and made no sense, she couldn't help thinking that Adam had found what he'd been searching for in her.

Adam and Jayne dropped anchor in a small cove. He took ashore the picnic lunch that the hotel staff had provided and then returned to carry Jayne to the beach.

He should've stayed in the boat and continued to survey the island from the sea. He should be checking on neighboring property that might be available for sale. He should be concentrating on work, but he didn't want to.

"I could have walked."

"I know," he said. His arms felt empty without her, but he didn't tell Jayne that. He had the feeling she saw too much, anyway. He set her on her feet and together they spread out the blanket and food. Because Adam didn't believe in drinking and driving—even a boat—he didn't drink any of the wine that was in the cooler.

Jayne was careful to steer the conversation away from personal topics and onto current events, which they both shared similar views of, and movies, which they didn't. The sappier the storyline, the more Jayne liked it. And she wasn't above arguing with him to make a point.

There was a gleam in her eyes as she asked him about his favorite book. Though he liked true crime and biographies, he didn't want to debate his personal choices anymore.

"*Lord of the Rings,*" he said.

"Finally. I thought we had nothing in common."

"I can't believe you like those books, Jayne. They aren't sappy enough."

"You're in trouble now, honeybun."

"I'm scared," he said.

She dived for Adam, mercilessly tickling him. They wrestled on the blankets until somehow she ended up under him. Then he couldn't resist lowering his head and kissing her mouth. The fact that he had rights to her seductive lips pleased him.

He lifted his head after long moments and then sat up.

"Adam?"

"I want to know more about you," he murmured.

"What do you want to know?" she asked. Jayne sat up in turn, leaning back on her elbows.

He traced the bottom edge of her tattoo with his finger. "You never told me about this. You said you got it when you were seventeen. Why?" He'd never noticed until now that there was a core of herself that Jayne kept hidden. Adam had the feeling she was dancing just out of his reach, and that no matter how many times he claimed her body, part of her soul remained untouched. But she'd scored him deeply with her presence in his life and he wouldn't tolerate not affecting her as strongly.

"My mom has one similar to it. But it's a fully open flower."

"Why isn't yours?"

"I've always wanted to be her opposite."

Adam tugged the side of her suit down so that he could see the entire design again. There was something very restrained about Jayne's tattoo. "Tell me about your mom."

"She's sophisticated and chic. She always has the hottest new car. She's well traveled and speaks three languages fluently."

"Is she American?"

"Yes, but her father was from Colombia. She started modeling when she was fourteen."

"Do you look like her?"

"I have her eyes and that's about it. She towers over me and she's very voluptuous."

"Then you get these from her, as well," he said, cupping her full breasts.

Jayne batted his hands away playfully. "I guess. We don't really have that much in common."

"Why not?"

"She is a rich man's mistress."

"Are you sure it's not a relationship?"

"Very. She's living with Hans for six months. It's her standard arrangement. You have that in common with her."

"My arrangements usually don't have a time limit," he said. He tried to imagine what kind of upbringing that would be for a child. Especially one as sensitive as Jayne.

Adam stood and seated himself behind her. Wrapping his arms around her waist, he pulled her back against his chest. "What about your dad?"

"I don't know him."

Her neck was tempting him once again. It was long and slim and very elegant, and she tasted sweeter there than anywhere else. Did she really? he wondered. Deciding to test his theory, he bent and nibbled at her shoulder.

"Does he know about you?" Adam asked. It was one of his fears, and why he was also so careful when he slept with a woman. The thought of having a child out there he didn't know about made his gut clench.

He didn't particularly want kids, which was why he had short-term affairs. He knew that children needed a father who'd love and protect them, a dad who would dedicate himself to his family. Adam had dedicated himself to business and a quest for vengeance against a man who was no longer alive.

"My mother left him before I was born. I saw him only once."

She shuddered in his arms and Adam tightened his grip around her, wanting to protect her from painful memories. "What was that like?"

"You don't want to know."

"Of course I do," he said. He didn't understand it, but he needed to know everything about her.

"I…I hid in my closet. And he tried to talk to me but I wouldn't come out." She rubbed her arms, because she couldn't seem to stop shaking all of a sudden.

"I'm sorry."

"Don't be. I was a mistake neither he nor my mother had anticipated."

"Someone called you a mistake?"

"Not in so many words. But I felt like it."

He lowered them both to the blanket. Curling himself around her, he carefully made love to her, trying to erase the memories of her childhood with his body. He knew in his heart that any kind of relationship that he might propose would be intolerable to Jayne. She needed a man who could commit himself to her and brand her with his name and his ring.

Adam refused to acknowledge the desperation in his actions as he brought Jayne to one shattering climax after another. He found he was sated himself only when she was covered with sweat and calling his name in a hoarse voice.

And after his own orgasm ripped through him, leaving him shattered and weak, he cradled her close to his body and prayed for something he couldn't put into words.

Nine

Adam docked the boat smoothly that afternoon. Ray waited for them in the marina lounge. The rotund little man smiled when he saw them and offered Adam a cigar.

"Go ahead, Adam. I want to try my hand at the treasure map, now," Jayne told him.

"I'll go with you."

"Are you sure?" she asked. The Adam she'd come to know as her boss would never pass up an opportunity to meet with a prospective buyer.

"Yes," he said, and there was a conviction in his expression that warmed her heart.

Ray waved them off, and Adam took her hand. He

led her up the path toward a cave in the hills where the treasure of La Perla Negra supposedly resided.

"Why are you doing this? I know you don't care about the treasure," Jayne stated.

"Maybe you don't know me as well as you think you do."

"That's doubtful. After all, I've been overseeing your office for almost a year now. I think I know the kind of man you are."

"What kind am I?"

She wanted to keep things light, but every action that Adam had taken today had been something out of a dream. No, not a dream—her secret desires. The romantic picnic and their lovemaking had made her feel as if there was hope. That her love for Adam wasn't necessarily one-sided and that the future might hold more for them than she'd ever dared imagine.

"You like the finer things in life."

"True. What else?"

"You're very determined and stubborn."

"Not that you share that trait."

"Be quiet. I'm the one talking here."

"Sorry, *chère*. What else were you going to say?"

"I think you might be lonely and that you've found a way to disguise that from the world. Those gorgeous mistresses of yours give you the illusion that you have a successful life."

He stopped on the path, dropping her hand. She

wondered if she'd gone too far. But then he cupped her face and lowered his head, sipping at her lips as if they were a fine wine.

"You're right. But I have my reasons," he whispered.

"What are they?"

"I don't want to ruin any illusions you might have of me."

"You won't," she said. Nothing could dim the love she felt for Adam. It was strange to think that when they'd left New Orleans he'd been her fantasy lover, and now he was the real thing.

He led her to a wrought-iron bench facing the resort, and beyond it, the ocean. "When I was fourteen my dad ran off with his secretary, leaving Mom and me on our own."

That explained Powell International's policy against workplace romances. Jayne wondered if Adam even realized he was trying to protect the families of all his employees from the same hurt he'd endured. Did he realize he couldn't?

"That must have been hard," she said.

He shrugged. "Mom had never worked a day in her life and was totally lost. She locked herself in her room and cried for three months. I took a job at a fast-food joint and started working to support us.

"I made a vow, Jayne, to never hurt anyone the way my mom was hurt."

Jayne slipped her arm around his waist and held him tightly. "What about you? Didn't your father's leaving hurt you?"

"No. I was almost a man. Strong enough to stand on my own."

But Jayne sensed he hadn't been. For all his demanding nature at work, Adam was still an extremely fair boss. He valued his workers and took a personal interest in their lives, especially those on his executive staff.

"Fourteen's still a boy," she said.

He hugged her close to his side. "You sound so fierce. Going to beat up everyone who's hurt me?"

"If I could."

"Oh, Jaynie. Don't care too deeply about me. I don't think I could endure hurting you."

"Because I care so deeply, you won't."

"I will. I'm not meant for...happily ever after."

"That's crap. Everyone is meant for bliss. You're just afraid because your parents' relationship went sour."

"Everyone? I don't see Mr. Right in your life."

She pinched him because he'd angered her. He was Mr. Right, and if he'd just open his eyes he'd see it.

"Ouch," he said, rubbing his side.

"Come on. Let's find that treasure."

She started down the path, trying to gain control over her emotions. Adam grabbed her arm, stopping her.

"I didn't mean it that way. I just...I've tried marriage before."

"I didn't know that."

"Not many people do. She left me for a man she worked with. We'd only been married six months."

"Oh, Adam," Jayne said.

"Don't pity me. I expected it to happen and it did. Modern people aren't meant for marriage. It's an institution that's outdated."

"You don't really believe that. You're just lashing out."

"What are you, an amateur shrink?"

"Ha! You know it's true. I have a hard time with relationships because of my mom. And because I'd never talk to my dad. I wanted to, you know?"

"Why didn't you?"

"I was so afraid of him. I figured he'd left before my birth because he didn't want me. And I was so scared that once he saw me he'd remember that and leave."

Adam tightened his arm around her. He muttered something under his breath that she couldn't understand, but she felt safer than she ever had before. And a certainty that they were meant to be together.

They found the treasure chest just inside the cave. Inside were polished stones carved with the resort's logo. There was an incantation on the wall that visitors were supposed to repeat for the next three days after being at the cave, and then they'd find their heart's desire.

Jayne reached for a stone and then pivoted to face Adam. "Aren't you taking one?"

"No. I don't believe in all that mumbo jumbo."

"This from the man who has a voodoo doll on his desk."

"That's a joke and you know it."

"Yeah, sure it is. That's why if someone moves it from the right corner you have a fit."

"A fit? Jayne, men don't have fits."

"What do they have?"

"Nothing but a desire for perfection and a well-ordered life. My office is my domain and as such everything in there shouldn't be touched."

"Was that a royal decree? Should I send that in memo form to the staff?"

"No, Miss Sassy Mouth. You're the only one who thinks she can charge around in my life and make changes."

"Well, someone has to. You're stuck in a rut."

Not anymore. He didn't know if he should thank Jayne or curse her, but she'd definitely upset his routine. "What are you wishing for?"

"We're not supposed to tell," she said. Then closed her eyes and made her wish.

She then read three times the incantation that was printed on the wall, as the instructions said.

"Aren't you supposed to spin around and spit on the floor next? Say some word like *abracadabra?*"

"Don't scoff at me," she said. She moved away from the chest toward the back of the cave, stopping in front of the display area, which held a table and chairs. Next to it was a canopy bed with heavy velvet drapes. According to the legend, the pirate and his bride had lived in the cave while building their home.

Adam took a stone when Jayne wasn't looking and slipped it into his pocket, feeling like an idiot the entire time, but unable to stop himself. He wanted Jayne to stay with him even after they returned to their real world. And he'd do anything to make it happen—even wish on a stone.

He knew that asking her to be his mistress wasn't an option. There was no way she'd ever agree to it. Adam was honest enough to admit he wouldn't really be happy unless she held a more permanent position in his life.

He was going to ask her to move in with him and be his lover. In his mind there was a distinction. He'd ask her to live with him and, most of all, he'd allow her to still work with him at Powell.

"I wonder what it was like living here back then."

"Kind of damp and moldy."

"That sounds so romantic, Adam. Frankly, I expected better from you. Aren't you the man who is known for his candlelight dinners?"

"Candlelight is one thing. Living in a cave is something else. Don't tell me you'd be happy here."

"If I was with a man who loved me, who risked everything for me, I think I would be."

"Is that what you wished for?" he asked, hoping she hadn't. Because of all the things he could give her, love wasn't one of them. He'd always been afraid to trust in love because every example he'd seen had left destruction in its path.

"I'm not supposed to tell anyone," she repeated, turning aside. Adam knew she was hiding from him, but he let it go.

"I wish I'd paid more attention in school to geology," she continued. "This cave is fascinating."

"What do you want to know?" he asked, walking over to her. There was a small pool in the center of the cave. The Angelinis had done a decent job of making the grotto look like a spot where a pirate would leave his lost treasure. They had flickering sconces on the rock walls and the stones were kept in a carved wooden chest.

"What are those?" she asked.

"Stalagmites?"

"You didn't pay attention in school, either?"

"I usually sat in the back of the class and slept."

"How did you get into college?"

"A lot of hard work. I flunked out of high school and realized that the kind of success I wanted wouldn't come from working in restaurant management. So I studied and took the GED. My mom started coming out of her shock by then and we sold real estate. That combined with my earnings from drag racing gave us a financial base. When I had enough money, I went to college.''

''Where's your mom now?'' Jayne asked after a few minutes. He knew Jayne well enough to recognize that she was organizing facts and forming opinions. She always did an inordinate amount of research.

''Living in Tucson with her second husband, Al. They retired there four years ago.''

''Arizona is next on my list of states to visit. What about your dad and the secretary? Where do they live?''

Everyone knew about Jayne's fifty states. In her office she had a big map of the U.S. and she'd put a smiley face sticker on the ones she'd been to.

She'd asked about his dad. Adam wanted to ignore the fact that he had a father, even though in his mind he saw the two of them playing football in the backyard of that big old house where they'd lived outside of New Orleans when he was a boy.

''Adam? What about your dad?''

''He died in a plane crash.''

''I'm sorry.''

''It didn't matter,'' he said. He didn't tell her that the crash had happened when his dad was returning from this resort with his secretary. Adam would never let Jayne know the devastating sense of loss he'd experienced when he'd learned his dad had died. And then three days later, when they'd received the letter he'd sent them saying he was running off with Martha.

Jayne slipped her hand into his, and he felt the rock in her palm, warm from her skin. "What are you doing?"

She closed her eyes for a moment. "I'm sharing my heart's desire with you."

"Even though I scoffed at you."

"Yes. I don't want to be happy if you're not."

His gut tightened and he felt weak in a way that wasn't physical. His heart raced and he realized that he had the power to hurt Jayne. Not just because of the habits ingrained from a lifetime spent not forming attachments. But because she had a soft side under her modern exterior, and he was the man she'd let see it.

"I have to make a few phone calls before dinner. Would you do me a favor?" Adam asked when they returned to their suite a few hours later.

"What kind of favor?" she asked. She was pleasantly tired from walking and being in the sun all day.

"A charity mission. Didi Angelini has the worst taste in clothes of any woman I ever met. I think that might be part of the problem between her and Ray."

Ray did have a bit of a roving eye, and there was

a strange sort of tension between the two of them. "I noticed he can't keep his eyes off the island women."

"Me, too." Adam reached into his back pocket and took out his wallet. He pulled out his platinum card and handed it to her. "Get her a totally new wardrobe on me."

"Why are you doing this?" Jayne asked. Not that she minded the task. She just wanted to understand this facet of the man she loved. He was always unfailingly polite to women, and though he only involved some in his life as mistresses, he seemed rather protective of the women he knew.

"I can't stand to see a woman in an ugly dress," he said, going to the fax machine and sorting through the papers piled there.

"I'm not buying it, stud muffin. Tell me why."

"Jayne," he asked, as if bored with the conversation, "do you really want me to spank you?"

He stepped toward her with mock aggression, and it was all she could do not to throw her arms open and say, *take me, big boy.* But she knew Adam wasn't above using sex to distract her, and she wanted to know why this was important to him.

"Yes, but not now. I want to know why. You've done this two other times that I know about, and as far as habits go, this is a fairly odd one."

He stopped halfway toward her and thrust his hands into the pockets of his pants. His gray eyes were cold and steely, and she had the feeling if she didn't handle this properly he'd clam up.

"I don't want any lip about this," he warned her.

"I won't give you any. I'm just curious. I want to know more about what makes Adam Powell tick."

"Guilt, greed and lust make me tick," he said, self-derision lacing his words.

"There's more to you than that."

He shrugged. "Some days it doesn't feel like it."

"Stop trying to distract me."

Finally he looked up at her. "It sounds stupid when I say it out loud."

She closed the gap between them. Wrapping her arms around his ribs, she nestled her head right over his heart, and listened to its slow, calming rhythm.

"Whisper it to me."

He said her name and closed his hands over her shoulders. Tipping her face up to his, he dropped one small kiss on her lips. His erection nudged against her stomach and she knew he wanted her. But she also knew that he was hiding something.

"I want you, stud muffin, but I want answers, too."

"God, Jayne, if you call me that in front of anyone I really will turn you over my knee."

"Promises, promises. The clothing?"

He lifted her in his arms and carried her to one of the overstuffed chairs in the living area, where he sank down and settled her on his lap. Then he tucked her head under his chin. She tried to move so she could see him, make eye contact, but he was having none of it.

"My mom had the worst sense of style. One of the reasons my dad left us was that he was embarrassed by her. My mom had no idea how to change that about herself, and frankly, I didn't either. Then I met Susan. She was very fashionable and knew how to dress right. So Mom picked up a few tips from her."

"Who's Susan?" Jayne asked. He'd never talked about that time in his life before and she had a hard time picturing Adam as anything but the successful CEO he was today.

"She was my wife."

Jayne still had a hard time coming to terms with Adam as married. It didn't fit with the man she'd come to know. Even in her wildest dreams she didn't picture the two of them married.

She ached to wrap her arms around him but couldn't because of the way he held her so tightly.

"How old were you? You didn't say before."

"Twenty when we married. Twenty-one when she left. The only good thing she did was help Mom with her sense of style. After that if I saw a woman whose marriage was on the rocks and her clothing wasn't exactly fashionable, I'd help out."

"You can't fix everyone's marriage."

"I'm not even trying."

"Then what are you doing?"

"Leveling the playing field."

"That is one of the—"

"Don't say it. I warned you."

"—sweetest things I've ever heard."

"Oh, God, give me a break. I also can't stand to see a woman hiding from her natural sensuality."

"Damn, why didn't you say so earlier?"

He cupped her chin and lifted her toward him for a long, lingering kiss—at first just the soft brushing of lips against lips. Then Adam angled his head and let his tongue slowly enter her mouth, tasting her deeply.

When he lifted his head, there was more than just lust in his eyes. She saw affection and caring and a slew of other emotions she'd never expected to see when Adam looked at her.

"I *have* to call Sam this afternoon," he said at last.

"Apparently I have some shopping to do," Jayne replied, getting to her feet.

"I'll be done in thirty minutes," he said.

"No, you won't. You can't get Sam off the phone in less than forty-five."

"If I had the right incentive I could."

"I'll see what I can do."

He stopped her halfway to the door, kissing her again. This time it wasn't the sweet lingering embrace of earlier. His hands cupped her butt and he drew her hard against him. His mouth ravaged hers.

When he set her back on her feet she felt as if she'd

just lived through a class IV hurricane. "What was that?"

"Incentive for you," he said with a wink, steering her toward the door.

Jayne walked out of their room and paused for a minute on the gravel path. Adam was changing. He was no longer the unemotional man she'd worked for a few days earlier, and though she knew it might be foolhardy, her heart beat a little faster at the thought of why he'd changed.

Ten

"Where are the women?" Ray clamped the butt of a cigar between his teeth and glanced around the room. He checked his watch one more time and then scowled.

Adam wasn't concerned. Jayne had called earlier and said that she and Didi would meet them at the restaurant. He'd missed her while he'd been working. Sam, his vice president, hadn't been expecting a call, but Adam had needed some space from Jayne.

He'd told her things he'd never meant to reveal. He had a lot of difficulty keeping her in the neatly labeled slot he'd assigned her to.

They were dining in the small town at a chef-owned restaurant that Jayne had discovered when she'd researched the island. She'd suggested Adam check it out and maybe hire the chef for the resort's restaurant. As charming as Perla Negra was, it lacked the amenities guests of Powell International were used to.

"Relax. Jayne is the most organized person I know. They'll be here in time for our reservation."

"You're right, *compare*. Jayne's a firecracker."

"She is. I'm lucky to have her. Didi's not exactly a slouch, either."

"That one likes to make my life uncomfortable," Ray said.

"I think women are meant to do that to a man."

"Makes life damn disturbing," Ray said. His mouth fell open and he dropped his cigar. Adam glanced over his shoulder and felt his own jaw sag. Jayne and Didi stood in the doorway.

Ray muttered something in Italian that Adam couldn't understand, but the sentiment was one he shared. The women both looked breathtaking. Jayne's eyes sparkled when they met his and he couldn't help smiling back at her. Didi was finally wearing something that wasn't butt-ugly and actually fit her body.

But Adam couldn't take his eyes off of Jayne. It scared him to realize how important she was to him and to his life. He couldn't take the risk of letting her be that vital, and he wondered for a second if he shouldn't just distance himself from her now.

Actually, he didn't think he could.

Didi started to look a little apprehensive, and crossed her arms over her chest. Jayne gestured for her to drop her arms to her sides, which the other woman did.

"Well, aren't you going to say anything?" Jayne demanded.

Adam recovered first and crossed to the ladies. He took Didi's hand in his and brushed a kiss against the back of it. "You look beautiful. Ray and I are going to be the envy of every man in the place tonight."

Then he turned to Jayne, and smooth words deserted him. He pulled her close and kissed her fiercely, needing her with a desperation that made his soul wary. When he lifted his head, her made-for-sin mouth was dewy and swollen from his kisses. Adam wanted to say the hell with dinner and retreat back to their room.

"Babe...I...you..." For the first time since they met Ray was almost speechless.

"Cat got your tongue, Ray?"

"You look nice. I think our table is ready."

"It's a wonder you're any good at your job," Didi said.

Ray wrapped his arm around Didi's waist and led her toward the hostess stand. Adam and Jayne followed, listening to the bickering couple.

"I'm much better at it when I don't have you sticking your nose in my business."

"Babe," Didi said in a good imitation of the way Ray always said it. "I'm not sticking my nose in, I'm making sure you do things properly."

Luckily, they soon reached the table and were seated. It was one of the best in the house, in front of a large open window that let in warm sea breezes and had a view of the ocean equaled by none. Adam kept his hand on Jayne's back even after she sat down. He liked the feel of her silky smooth skin.

He also liked the fact that he had the right to touch her. That Jayne belonged to him. And dammit, she did belong to him, in a way no person ever had before. He shuddered a little as he realized it was too late to guard against caring for her. He already did.

Their waiter was a young Jamaican man with a smile a little too friendly when he turned it on Jayne. Adam leaned over and kissed her mouth in a way that told the world she belonged to him. Then he calmly ordered for both of them.

Jayne pinched his leg under the table and he reached over to her thigh and caressed it. Ray and Didi excused themselves to talk to a couple who were staying at the resort.

"What was that about?"

"What?" Adam took a sip of his drink, continuing to caress Jayne's leg under the table.

"That male territory thing you did. Why don't you get out a Sharpie pen and write your name on my forehead?"

"You'd let me do that?" he asked.

"You're hopeless," she said with a laugh.

"Only where you're concerned."

Her breath caught and she looked up at him with...
Oh, God, don't let it be love in her eyes. His heart
speeded up and he knew the situation was quickly
spinning out of his control.

A small band took the stage and soon the sounds
of reggae and calypso music filled the joint. Adam
watched Jayne humming along under her breath and
swaying to the music.

"Want to dance?"

"Yes, but you need to talk to the chef and then I
think you should—"

He quieted her by sliding his hand down her neck
to her collarbone and holding her carefully. "Come
on," he said, tugging her to her feet. "It's been too
long since I held you."

She said nothing as he led her to the dance floor
and pulled her into his arms. She nestled there trust-
ingly, laying her head on his heart as she always did,
and he prayed that she couldn't hear its frantic beating.

The rest of the week flew by and Jayne spent every
hour of the day with Adam, learning more about him.
She realized he loved to be on the water and had
rented a sailboat for them to use every afternoon.
She'd always known that he was intensely private and

very driven, but on the island she learned why. She thought she finally understood why he limited himself to relationships that were clearly defined. He wanted to protect everyone involved.

She'd never have guessed the man who was ruthless in the boardroom and who was known as a shark in the hotel world would have a hidden depth of caring that would make her heart ache.

Today he was on the beach playing a game of coed volleyball with a group of singles that had come to the resort looking for some fun. Adam had been casually studying the resort demographics. She knew because she'd spent as much time at her computer, making charts and graphs and compiling reports, as she had with Adam.

But she didn't mind it. In fact, she found that their relationship had added a dimension to their work life that she hadn't expected.

He valued her opinion, and he took breaks more frequently now just to sit quietly with Jayne. Sometimes they'd go for a walk, other times she'd tease him by calling him stud muffin and he'd fall on her, making love to her with a fierceness that convinced her he must love her.

Adam planned to take the charming resort and make it into an all-inclusive vacation destination for families. She'd just concluded a call with a treasure hunter who'd agreed to redesign the treasure map.

Ray had all but said that Adam could purchase La
Perla Negra.

Jayne thought that might be why Adam looked so
relaxed today. She sat on the sidelines, watching him
play. He was bare-chested and sweaty, and when he
looked at her she felt the intensity of his gaze even
from beneath those dark sunglasses of his.

The game broke up. Adam perched on the arm of
her chair and took a sip of her margarita. "Where
were you?"

"Talking to Guy O'Bannon."

Adam raised one eyebrow in question.

"The treasure hunter."

"What kind of name is Guy O'Bannon?"

Jayne shrugged. "I think he made it up. He was
funny as anything. I made arrangements for him to
come down to the island. For a fee he'll redesign the
treasure hunt and add some false trails as well as help
us with the legend."

"Great. Now all I need is for Ray to sign that contract and everything will be in place."

Adam signaled the waitress and ordered a Corona.
Then he lifted her from the chair. He took her place
and settled her on his lap, curving his hand around
her waist and caressing her with languid strokes of
his fingers. "I like this place. I never expected to."

"Why not?" she asked, trying to focus on the conversation and not the delicious tingles spreading over

her body. She rested her head on his shoulder and wished that this special closeness never had to end.

"This is the resort that my dad brought his secretary to when he left us."

"Oh, Adam." She tried to turn to face him but he held her tightly in his arms. Then he leaned down to glare at her.

"Don't say my name like that. I'm not a broken-hearted fourteen-year-old."

"I never thought you were. It's just... I wish you never had to suffer," she said, speaking from the heart. She knew that there was no way to protect Adam from being hurt, and to even think that this strong man needed her protection was almost ridiculous. But it didn't change the way she felt.

"At least I had my dad for those fourteen years. I'd forgotten all the good memories for a long time," Adam said at last. He cupped her face, tilting it back so he could sip from her lips. She tasted of salt and lime from her margarita.

His fingers feathered over her skin, as light as the sea breeze, and her body responded. She would never get enough of him. She'd stopped thinking that they would ever be apart, because it was too painful to imagine a time when he wasn't in her life. He owned her, body, heart and soul, and she suspected sometimes that he knew it. It didn't really bother her because she felt as if she was coming to own him in the same way.

He lifted his head, his lips wet from her kisses, and his eyes narrowed. Under her buttocks she felt him hardening. She had the feeling they weren't going to be sitting in the sun for too much longer. But anticipation was exquisite, and she knew he felt the same when he rubbed his hard-on against her and then leaned back against the chair.

She cast around for something to distract them. "How do you feel about your dad now?"

"I can't forgive him, Jayne, and I don't think I ever will be able to. But at least now I can remember the good times before."

"I'm glad. Childhood should leave lots of good, lasting memories."

He opened his eyes and she smiled up at him. "You sound like a sappy old greeting card," he murmured.

She knew she'd gotten too close with her probing, and didn't want to back down, but knew she had to. "Yeah, you bring that out in me, stud muffin."

"I thought I warned you not to call me that," he growled.

"Don't get all bristly. Here comes your beer."

"I'll take it with me."

"Oh? Where are you going?"

"Back to our room, to paddle that sweet backside of yours."

"I don't think so."

"Then you should have been paying attention."

Adam lifted her against his chest and stood up. "Be a good girl, Jayne, and grab my beer."

A river of anticipation swelled inside her. She didn't fear him and knew he'd never hurt her. So she reached for his beer and cradled the cold bottle against her stomach while she signed their tab with one hand. Adam walked up the path to their room with sure steps. And Jayne knew in her heart that she and Adam were going to be together forever.

Adam had Jayne open the door of their suite, and walked into the sun-filled room. He wasn't seriously thinking of spanking her, though with her sassy mouth she'd tempted him more than once to turn her over his knee. What he wanted more than anything was to make love to Jayne. Their time at the resort had been the most ideal fantasy of his life, and at the same time the most tense.

He knew it couldn't last and was afraid for the first time that he wouldn't be able to manage this properly. That somehow Jayne would slip through his fingers and his life would once again be filled with cold beauties instead of the fire that Jayne brought to his soul.

Adam walked into the bedroom. The drapes were drawn and only a little dappled light filled the room. He settled Jayne on the edge of the bed.

She offered him his Corona, and he took the beer and set it on the nightstand. Turning back to her, he slid his palm down her leg, cupping the flesh of her calf and then pushing the delicate sandals off her feet. Then he slipped his hand under the skirt of her sundress, caressing the firm flesh of her thighs. She shivered, her eyes drifting closed. Her legs parted and he slid his hand closer to her center.

He teased her through the silk of her panties, feeling it dampen in response to his touch. He slid one finger under the elastic leg band of her underwear and traced her opening. Her legs thrashed.

Her breathing was rapid now, her breasts straining the buttons on the bodice of her dress. He leaned down and tongued her nipple through the fabric. She gasped his name and held his head to her.

"Open your dress, *chère.*"

She fumbled with the buttons and he watched her. Finally she had them all undone down to her belly button. The fabric shielded her from his gaze except for a thin strip of creamy flesh visible through the opening. The rounded curves of her breasts moved with each breath she took.

"Bare yourself to me," he said, his voice a growl.

She nodded and pulled the bodice open. Her nipples were starting to harden, the pale pink flesh becoming darker. He pushed her skirt to her waist and looked down at her, spread before him like a sensual feast. God, he was hungry for her.

He kissed her abdomen and then moved lower, to the very heart of her. When her hips lifted in response, he parted her and thrust his tongue into her body. She tasted exquisite and he felt himself hardening almost painfully. The need for her was too demanding to resist. She moaned his name.

He kissed his way up her body, scraping his teeth over her until he found her mouth, all the while thrusting his fingers deep inside her. He sucked her into his mouth and pulled, needing to quench the thirst he had for Jayne. She was gasping his name now, her nails biting into his shoulders.

He felt her tightening around him and then she screamed as her body convulsed. He lifted his head and looked down at the woman in his arms. She met his gaze with a totally unguarded expression, and he felt sucker-punched by the emotion he saw shining in her eyes. He was unworthy of her love. He wasn't the guy she needed to make her dreams come true.

Adam stepped back and stripped off his shorts, then pulled her panties down her legs and tossed them aside without saying a word. She bit her lower lip and watched him, the emotions on her face joined by something else. Fear, pity, anger? He wasn't sure, but he sensed she knew he was running.

He didn't want to think or feel anything other than the hot desire pulsing through his veins. This was the one thing he could count on.

He took a pillow from the head of the bed and pushed it under her hips. Knowing this was the best that he could give her, he brought her to a second climax with his mouth on her.

Shuddering, she reached for him, taking his erection in her hand and pulling him toward her body. "I need you."

He needed her, too. He needed her to promise she'd never leave him, but he knew he couldn't ask for that. And he sensed her keen eyes saw that desire inside him. He flipped her over on her back.

Adam used his teeth to pull her dress down her body and drop it on the floor. He held his hand at the small of her back when she would've turned over.

He traced her spine with his tongue, then dropped nibbling kisses there, caressing the rounded curves of her hips and tracing the seam between her cheeks with his tongue. He parted her legs and slid up over her body, rubbing himself against her until she raised her hips.

Adam lifted her slightly and slid into her body from behind. Clasping her hands in his, he moved slowly, though he clamored for release. His penis was so hard he felt as if it had been years since he'd found satisfaction instead of the few hours since they'd left their suite this morning.

But he wanted this to be more than just release. He wanted to give Jayne more than she'd ever experienced with any other man, so he kept his thrusts slow and steady. He bit her neck at the base and tickled the flesh there with his tongue.

And when he knew he couldn't hold back any longer, he slid his hands down her sides and held her hips while he thrust harder and harder into her. He felt her body clenching around his a second before release surged through him and he emptied himself into her.

He collapsed on top of her, shutting his eyes so that he wouldn't have to see what Jayne was feeling. But as he lay there in a euphoric haze, he prayed that she'd agree to live with him, for the glimpse of heaven he'd just had in her arms was the closest thing to paradise he'd ever found.

Eleven

Jayne spent the afternoon of her second to last day on the island with Didi in the spa, being pampered. Adam had given her the time off and said he didn't want to see her until she relaxed. Jayne couldn't believe the changes that their time here had wrought in him. He was a different man than she'd known before, and he'd put to rest her girlish dreams of Mr. Right. Adam was so much more compelling.

Still, much of their relationship was up in the air. She didn't know what he planned to do when they returned. Jayne had already drafted a resignation letter in her head and knew that she'd gambled her heart for Adam. But she felt confident she was going to come up a winner.

Though he was careful to never make promises he couldn't keep, she knew that Adam didn't want to let her go. He'd told her as much last night in bed, in the quiet hour just before dawn when life seemed almost perfect.

"I can't believe we're leaving here in a few days," Jayne said to Didi now. "You must love living here. It's like heaven on earth."

"Not really," the older woman replied with a small smile. "But I do like it."

"Why are you selling it?" she asked. Didi and Ray weren't really old enough to retire, and they seemed to enjoy the resort. Ray was always in the beachfront bar, telling stories and entertaining the guests.

"Ray and I have to travel a lot with our jobs. So staying here isn't an option anymore."

Jayne wondered about the couple. They kept their lives private, but Jayne had been studying couples since the second grade, when one of the girls at her school had asked if Jonathon O'Neil, her mother's current lover, was Jayne's stepfather. She hadn't realized until that moment that other families didn't have a rotating male in their households.

"What is your job? I hope you aren't offended if I say so, but neither of you seems to know a lot about the hotel industry."

"We don't. We're more experts on human nature. That's why finding a couple in love to buy the resort is so important."

"I can see how that would be nice, but from a business standpoint it lacks a little credibility."

"Are you always business-minded, Jayne?" she asked.

Jayne tried to be, because life had proved easier that way. But lately she seemed to be more family-minded. Her head filled with images of her and Adam and a brood of kids that belonged to them. Of she and Adam creating the family they'd both always craved and never had. Of them living in a big house and growing old together.

She sighed. "Usually. Lately, though, not as much."

"It seems to me humans use business to occupy their lonely lives instead of seeking out comfort in each other."

"Perhaps. But there is a very nice feeling that comes with success."

"Yes, there is."

A timer went off at the drying station, letting them both know the nail polish on their toes was dry. Jayne slid her feet into the spa thongs she'd brought, and stood. "I'm glad we got to spend the day together."

"Me, too. I'll see you at dinner," Didi said, exiting the spa.

Jayne took her time gathering her bag and walking up the path toward their suite. She would miss the island. Even if Adam purchased it she probably wouldn't be coming back here for a while. She thought about her travel goals and decided she'd add in all the countries she wanted to visit, not confining herself to the fifty states. She could get used to island living.

When she reached the suite, she opened the door and found Adam on the phone. She observed him as he talked, making notes on the pad in front of him. His wore a pair of shorts and a Hawaiian print shirt that he'd left unbuttoned.

She dropped her bag inside the doorway. Adam looked up and smiled at her, gesturing that he'd only be a few more minutes. She took a bottle of seltzer water from the minibar and settled on the love seat, watching him. She didn't listen to his conversation, just let the sound of his voice wash over her.

Closing her eyes, she tried not to put too much hope into thoughts of the future, but knew it was too late. She'd fallen hard for Adam.

"How was the spa?" he asked, dropping down on the cushion next to her.

He put his arm around her shoulders and hugged her close to his side, then bent down and kissed her. He'd told her a couple of times how her mouth enticed him.

"Relaxing. I enjoyed it. Thanks for insisting I go," she said, when he lifted his head.

"No problem. I know I can be demanding sometimes, but I wanted you to see that I can also be generous."

Adam was acting a little odd. She couldn't put her

finger on it, but something was different about him. "I already knew that."

"That's right, you're the—what did you call it?— facilitator of my generosity?"

"That's right. You're usually very generous toward women at the end of your affairs. Should I be worried?"

"No. This isn't like any relationship I've had before."

Me, either, she thought. He opened his arms and she sank against him. Sometimes she felt so vulnerable around him that she thought she'd break into a million pieces. But when he held her she felt safe and that her love was a good thing. She closed her eyes now and breathed deeply of his spicy masculine scent.

"I have another present for you."

"Where?"

"On the bed."

"You don't have to keep buying me things."

"I like to spoil you, Jayne."

"Why?"

"Do I need a reason?"

"No," she said, but it worried her. She knew Adam well enough to realize he used his money as a shield.

"I want tonight to be special for you, and my present is just part of that."

He ushered her into the bedroom, where she found an exquisite cocktail gown lying on the coverlet.

Adam left her to dress, saying he had plans to make. Her heart beat faster as she realized he must have something important on his mind if he was going to all this trouble just for her.

"Buona notte," Ray said in a greeting when they arrived in the lounge for a predinner drink. Adam would be happy to have the resort business out of the way so he could concentrate on Jayne. He no longer felt a burning need to destroy this place and make it into something it wasn't. He could appreciate the charm of the resort and separate that from the betrayal he'd felt with his father.

"I've made arrangements for us to dine on our private veranda," their host announced. "The sunsets are spectacular there."

"Thanks, Ray."

"Nothing but the best for our ladies tonight."

Didi rolled her eyes, but a smile lingered on her lips, and for the first time since Adam had met the couple, they seemed to be almost at peace with one another.

"Our ladies should always have their heart's desire."

"Jayne said you'd found the treasure box?" Didi asked as Ray led the way through the public rooms to their private quarters.

"We did. The trail isn't that hard to find. Even if you decide not to sell to me I think you should jazz it up a bit. Jayne spoke to a professional treasure hunter and he'll help embellish the tale and make the search a little harder.''

"Good suggestion, *compare*. I've implemented many of things you recommended. You really know your stuff when it comes to resorts.''

Getting the resort didn't matter as much as it once had. Adam was happy to have had this time on the island with Jayne. If they didn't acquire Perla Negra, he'd buy some land and develop his own resort based on a legend. Maybe he'd bring Jayne with him to oversee the construction. ''It's what I do. And frankly, I love it.''

Ray nodded. He took a cigar out of his pocket, but Didi reached over and snatched it out of his hand before he could light it. ''I've always felt the same about my job. Sometimes this one gives me *agita*. But otherwise things aren't so bad.''

"I can tell. Not many owners would hold out for the kind of buyer they want for their resort. I can tell the property means more to you than just a quick buck.''

"Well, you can't take it with you,'' Ray said with a laugh. Didi joined him.

They arrived at a large veranda, where a table was set for four. An ice bucket stood next to the table with a magnum of champagne in it.

"We got off track,'' their hostess murmured. ''Did you like the cave? Did you read the incantation?''

"I did. I took a stone," Jayne said quietly.

"I'm not surprised. What about you, Adam?" Didi asked.

"I did, too."

Jayne glanced at him from under her eyelashes, and he felt her reproval. When Didi excused herself to check on the dinner, and Ray followed her inside, Jayne turned to Adam. "You don't have to lie to them about it. They know you're too...practical to believe in that legend," she stated.

He said nothing, just reached into his pants' pocket and pulled out the stone to show her. She swallowed hard and stared at him. Adam felt that strange feeling in his chest again when she gazed up at him, this time with her heart in her eyes.

He caressed her face, tilting her head back and capturing her lips with his own. Sipping carefully at her mouth, he treated her like the rare treasure she was. He found it hard to believe that feisty, sassy Jayne was the answer to the empty part of his life.

"What did you wish for?" she asked after a minute.

"I'm not supposed to tell."

"I hope it comes true, Adam," she said fiercely.

"You're the only one who can make that happen."

She trembled under his hands. "Same here, stud muffin."

"Woman, you are asking for it."

"When have I ever pretended not to be?" she said.

"Let's have a toast," Ray said, stepping back outside before Adam could respond.

But Adam reached down and pinched Jayne's backside surreptitiously as they walked to the table. She gave him a look over her shoulder that made his blood flow heavier and his body stir to life.

Didi joined them a moment later, carrying a tray of hors d'oeuvres. Setting it on the table, she took a flute from Ray. Once they all had a glass in their hand, Ray slipped his arm around Didi and looked at Adam, raising his flute. "To the new owner of La Perla Negra. May he find love and happiness as well as prosperous times ahead."

Adam felt a queer sensation in his stomach as he realized what Ray was saying. He couldn't lift his glass and drink, but turned to Jayne and took her in his arms. She stretched up and gave him a kiss that shook him. His hands were trembling with desire when she sank back onto her own chair.

"Now we drink," Ray said.

"Now we drink," Adam agreed. They all sipped the Asti and Adam took it as a sign. They sat down at the table. Everything in his life was coming together. After years of working and struggling to right the wrongs of the past, he was going to have the resort that had led his father to ruin. Adam had a woman by his side who he knew was a partner in business as well as in life. And he was finally coming to terms with the fact that his heart wasn't as well-guarded as he'd always believed.

Dinner went by in a haze of pleasure, and Adam realized that the only thing missing from his life was a commitment from Jayne. But in a few hours, he'd have all the pieces in place.

Jayne emerged from the bathroom wearing her one-of-a-kind negligee.

"Close your eyes," Adam told her.

She did as he asked. Beneath her feet she felt something soft and cool, and peeking from under her lashes, she saw rose petals. Their fragrance filled the room.

"I can't keep my eyes shut for long," she warned, crossing the room toward the sound of his voice. She hated not being able to see. It made her feel exposed.

"Sure you can, *chère*. It's worth it, I promise," he said. This time his voice came from a different direction.

She turned toward it, sliding one foot at a time in front of her to make sure she didn't run into anything. "I can't stand it. I want to see."

Large and warm, his hands covered her eyes. "I had no idea you were so impatient."

"It's not really impatience as much as vulnerability. I hate that feeling."

She felt his lips brush hers, with a back and forth motion that made her stand on her toes and try to pull him closer. But when she reached for him, he wasn't where she'd expected him to be.

"You don't have to seduce me. I'm already yours," she said, knowing the words were true. There was no other man who could make her forget the painful lesson she'd learned as a child, and remember her secret dreams. No other man who tempted her to believe that those dreams might have a chance of coming true. No other man who made her forget a time when they hadn't been together.

"Are you?" he asked. He touched her face, tenderly tracing her cheekbone and the line of her nose. She wished she could see his expression. Adam gave so little away and she was tired of trying to guess at the depth of his feelings.

"You must know that I am," she said. She wasn't going to hide from him.

They were scheduled to go home tomorrow afternoon, and she knew that once they returned to New Orleans, reality would come crashing down. She'd prayed that reality might mean a marriage of her life with Adam on the island and the one they'd had before. But she couldn't tell what he felt. She thought he loved her...well, knew he cared deeply for her. The way he held her at night, so close and tight, told her it had to be more than sex.

"Good," he said, quiet satisfaction in his words.

He wrapped a length of silk around her head, covering her eyes. "How's that?"

"Adam…"

"What?" His mouth was against the back of her neck, moving slowly downward. "You can't see and my hands are free."

She swallowed her doubts and said, "Do your worst, stud muffin."

He chuckled and then wrapped her in a tight embrace. "I intend to. But first…"

He lifted her in his arms and carried her somewhere. She felt the warm sea breeze a minute before he set her in one of the rattan chairs on the balcony. She loved his strength and the fact that he was a toucher. She'd never been petted like this by any man, but Adam was always reaching for her.

"Wait here a minute. I have to take care of a few last-minute details."

She heard him leave, and leaned her head against the back of the chair, tilting her face up to feel the breeze more fully on her skin. The roar of the surf was a pleasant accompaniment to the wind rustling through the palm trees and bushes.

"Miss me?" Adam asked a moment later, speaking directly into her ear.

Before she could answer, he tugged her to her feet and removed the blindfold. She blinked a few times and realized that all around her candles flickered. Not just on the balcony, in wall sconces and tiki lamps that had been mounted to the railing, but also behind her, in the bedroom.

"Are we celebrating Perla Negra?"

"No, *chère*. I'm celebrating you."

Oh, God. Her heart started beating so fast she thought it might burst from her chest. She'd hoped and prayed that he might come to care for her, but she'd never expected a gesture this big. This grand. But she should have, because Adam wasn't a man given to subtlety.

"Jayne, I have something important to ask you."

"Yes?" She could scarcely breathe as he turned toward her. Her heart raced, and for a moment she was afraid to believe the dreams she'd harbored for so long were at long last coming true.

"Will you live with me?"

She shook her head, unsure she'd heard him correctly. Adam gave her the gentlest smile she'd ever seen grace his face.

"*Chère,* we're great partners in the office. I think blending our personal and professional lives is...the perfect solution."

Jayne was still trying to understand what he'd said. But she didn't doubt his sincerity. Adam was offering her the one thing he'd never offered any other woman. And she wanted to accept. But her own dreams were hard to let go of. "I'd like nothing better," she said.

"Great. I knew you'd see it my way."

Sadly, she realized she hadn't been clear. This conversation wasn't something she'd anticipated. She wished she'd had time to make a plan of action for it. "I'm sorry, Adam. I didn't mean that the way it came out. If we're going to live and work together, why not get married?"

"Marriage is the one risk I won't take."

"Being your mistress is the one risk I won't take."

"Dammit, woman, I'm not asking you to be just a mistress."

Her heart ached for him. And she almost changed her mind and agreed to be his, whatever the terms. But in the end she knew they'd both end up hating each other. Adam watched her and she shook her head at him.

"Dammit, you think this is easy for me? You know how I feel about office romances and yet I'm willing to do this for you."

"Don't make this about me. What you're offering is designed to give you everything *you* want."

He took her in his arms. "Don't say it like that. This is the best I can do right now."

Tipping her chin back, he stared into her eyes. "Please, *chère,* give this a chance. I'm not ruling out marriage forever but I need more time."

She stared up at him, cupping his jaw in her hands and, standing on tiptoe, kissed him with all the love she had in her body. "I don't need more time, Adam. I already know I love you."

"And I care deeply for you. I know our relationship can be a successful one."

"Being your mistress or live-in lover will kill me, Adam. I've spent my entire life, built my entire self-image around not being like my mother. And I have to be honest here—I want kids." She didn't need a marriage certificate to stay with the man she loved if he was committed to her. She could tell by the look in his eyes that he didn't want them. But she held her breath for his answer.

"No."

Her heart broke then and she realized that she'd fallen in love not with Adam, but with the man Adam could be if he'd ever let go of the past and start to dream of the future.

She shook her head and pulled out of his arms, backing away from the man that had seemed like her future.

"Oh, *chère*."

She went to the dresser to find her clothing. Pulling them on carefully, praying she could finish dressing and get out of there before she started crying. She refused to let Adam's last image of her be one with tears running down her face.

"So this is it?" he asked.

"Yes. You'll have my notice on your desk Monday morning."

"I thought you loved me," he said, quietly.

She stared at the man she knew. The man who'd carefully crafted a life of loneliness because he be-

lieved that was the only safe way of living. She
wanted to reach for him. But didn't.

"I do. But that doesn't mean I don't value myself."

"What's that supposed to mean?" he asked. He
grabbed his pants from the floor and shoved his legs
into them.

"Nothing. I was being nasty." And she had been.
In fact, she'd hurt herself with the words. She knew
that Adam felt more for her than the other women
he'd seen. And if she were a different kind of person—one who didn't need order and structure—she
might be able to accept the offer he'd made, and hope
that some day he'd come around.

He crossed the room, but when he reached for her,
she took a step back. She didn't want him to touch
her now. She felt as if she might break into a million
pieces with very little provocation.

"Please, don't go. I'll give you anything you want
if you stay."

"Anything?" she asked, knowing he wasn't offering his love and that she'd never ask for it.

"Yes. Name it—a new car, a fur, jewelry. *Anything.*"

She knew then that despite the fact that she'd laid
her soul bare to him, Adam had never seen the real
her. Or he'd know that the trappings of a mistress
were the last things that would make her stay with
him.

"There's nothing you have that I want," she said.

And this time she meant it. She had wanted his love, but knew that he didn't have enough in his cold soul to give her.

"You don't mean that."

"I do. You've surrounded yourself with material objects and status symbols. I need more than that to be happy. Actually, I need a lot less than what you have. What I want doesn't cost anything."

"No, you just want my soul," he said.

Until that moment she hadn't realized that she'd asked him for his soul. But she did want it. After all, he already owned hers. "I thought it was an even trade."

"Well, it's not. I'm not like you, Jayne. I don't look at the world through rosy glasses. I've lived in the real world my entire life and I know what you're looking for is a fairy tale."

She stalked to the door. She wasn't talking to him anymore. "I'm not giving you two weeks."

"I'm not giving you a reference."

"I don't need one from you."

She took her purse and ran out, slamming the door behind her. She didn't look back, but let the tears run unchecked down her cheeks.

Twelve

Adam punched the wall nearest him and cursed savagely. How had things gotten so out of control? His hand throbbed, and as he surveyed the room he realized that he couldn't stay here another minute. Every time he saw those candles and the rose petals he was reminded that his seduction had gone terribly wrong.

Why had the setup that had worked in the past failed him? Probably because Jayne wasn't like every other woman who'd been in his life. She was so damn stubborn.

He knew what she wanted. In fact, if the burning in his gut was any indication, he already loved her. But he wasn't saying the words out loud.

And he wasn't marrying her. He couldn't. He'd tried to make her understand that if she just waited a little longer, gave him time to adjust to having her in his life, he might be able to. But that wasn't good enough for Jayne.

He sank into the armchair, gazing around the hotel suite, which was like so many others. But in the last ten days, Jayne had made this feel like home. She'd given him someone to share not just the business of his life with, but also the other things. The part that no one had ever been interested in before. Jayne actually cared that he loved being on the water, and had arranged for them to go sailing every afternoon, even though she was still afraid of the ocean.

But did that mean she would stay with him? Did that mean that once he married her she wouldn't get bored and move on? And did that mean that he'd always want her in his life?

His fear was not that Jayne would leave him, he acknowledged. His real fear was that someday he'd leave her. And he couldn't stomach the thought of hurting her that way.

Hell, he needed a drink. He grabbed a shirt from his closet and shoved his feet into a pair of loafers, heading out the door and straight for the bar.

His hand still throbbed, but he felt as if he deserved the pain. God knew it was less painful than the feelings deep in his gut, feelings that he refused to acknowledge came from Jayne's leaving.

He ordered a glass of single malt and sat down at one of the deserted tables in the back of the smoky lounge. The band had long since finished their last set and the place was almost empty.

"Eh, *compare*, still celebrating?" Ray sat down across from him.

The waiter brought his drink, and Adam downed half the glass. "Bring me another."

"Where's Jayne?" Ray asked.

"I have no idea," he stated. He could guess, though, and the images in his head made him want to get drunk so that he couldn't see them anymore. He didn't want to picture Jayne as he'd last seen her—face pale, tears glistening in her eyes. She'd run from him, and he cursed himself for making her go.

"Women problems?" Ray asked.

Adam sneered at the older man. "Not me. I'm the expert when it comes to relationships."

Ray leaned back in his chair and reached in his pocket for a cigar. He lit it and then glanced around the room. "Don't get me wrong, pal, but what kind of expert is sitting in a bar an hour before closing time, drinking alone?"

"Not much of one," Adam said, downing the rest of his drink. He knew nothing when it came to women or relationships, which was probably why he'd lost the one woman he wanted to keep.

"Want to talk about it?" Ray asked, exhaling a thin veil of smoke.

"You really get into that father confessor thing?" Adam said with derision.

"Nah. It's just that I've been there."

"With Didi?" Adam asked. It would make him feel better to know that he wasn't alone.

"No, not with her. I let someone else slip away because I didn't realize that the love of the right woman can make a man stronger. You know, a better man."

"Well, Jayne doesn't see that. She can only see…" Adam didn't know what Jayne saw when she looked at him. He suspected it was some romanticized version of him. But he'd bet his business that she didn't any longer.

"What can she see?"

"That I'm not the kind of guy to give her what she wants in order to be happy," Adam said at last. He toyed with his highball glass, rolling it in his palms.

"Oh, hell."

"Listen, if you no longer want to sell me the resort, I'll understand. You should know that I was setting you up from the beginning. Jayne was my assistant, not my mistress," Adam said.

"But that changed."

"Not for long," he answered.

"This has nothing to do with the resort. Listen, you go after Jayne and talk to her."

Adam wished it were that simple. But he wasn't

willing to lay his soul on the line for her. And she'd settle for nothing less. "She won't listen to me."

"You have to try," Ray insisted.

"You're taking this father confessor thing too seriously. It's over between Jayne and me. The only thing left to do is move on."

"*Madon'*, why the hell did I think this would be easy?" Ray said, stubbing his cigar out in the ashtray.

"What are you talking about?" Adam asked. What in blazes was he thinking, discussing this with a man who was nothing more to him than a business acquaintance?

"Look, *compare,* I'm not really a resort owner. I'm a matchmaker sent from heaven to make sure that you and Jayne fall in love."

"Well, you screwed up," Adam said, not believing what Ray said for a minute.

"You're telling me! But you're not leaving me any options here. If you won't talk to her…"

Ray might be a little bit insane, Adam decided, flinching when the older man took his hand. Then, suddenly, the walls around them were spinning, and when they finally stopped he and Ray were outside a bar in New Orleans.

"This isn't real."

"Keep telling yourself that, *compare,*" Ray said.

"Why are we here?"

"I don't know. This is the place you brought us to."

Adam recognized the bar. He hadn't been in there since the night of his divorce, when he'd gotten rip-roaring drunk. "Take me back to Perla Negra."

"Not yet. Let's go inside."

Ray nudged him toward the door and Adam went in. He scanned the dimly lit interior and had no trouble finding himself seated at the bar. He looked so damn young and scared.

"Another round?" the bartender asked.

"Keep 'em coming," the younger Adam said. He downed the glass of cheap whiskey. In those days he hadn't been able to afford the good stuff.

"Here you go," the bartender said.

"Thanks, man."

When the bartender turned away, Adam stood and announced to the room in general, "From this moment on, I will not be a victim to women and their emotional traps."

Glasses were raised in support, and the younger Adam sat back down and finished his drink.

The older Adam stared in shock. He'd built his life around a vow he'd made when he was twenty-one and not sure of himself, he realized at last. He knew what had happened the next day: he'd made a solid business plan and used the impetus of Susan leaving him to start Powell International. He'd worked hard for six months before he met Rhonda, his first mistress. He'd still been too raw to really want more than sex from a woman.

So they'd come up with an arrangement that had worked for both of them. And what had been a temporary stopgap in his relationships had become the norm.

In an instant, Adam found himself back at his table in the lounge at Perla Negra. Ray was nowhere to be seen, and Adam wondered if he hadn't dreamed the entire episode. He rubbed his forehead. The liquor had given him a buzz. And something Jayne said kept echoing in his head.

Just because I love you doesn't mean I don't value myself.

Adam realized that he hadn't been valuing either of them, but letting the past keep him in the dark.

He left the bar, hoping it wasn't too late to find Jayne. The only chance either of them had for happiness was together, he was certain. He loved her, and not saying the words out loud didn't keep him safe, it kept him out of the sunlight that was Jayne.

Jayne had asked the bellman to call her a cab. Waiting outside the resort, she refused to cry. She was angry at Adam and at herself. How could she have misjudged him?

But had she? She'd spent her entire life hiding from the men who scared her. She'd been engaged to Ben because he was safe and didn't make her heart beat faster. Only now, looking back, did she acknowledge that his leaving her didn't hurt as badly as this moment with Adam.

Was a ring really that big of a deal in the big scheme of things? Her heart said no. But having a family was. And not just for herself. Adam needed it, too. He needed to have his own children so he could shower them with that unconditional love that she knew was buried deep inside him.

Was she a coward for leaving like this?

"Jayne, thank God, I caught you."

"I'm not going to change my mind," she said softly.

Adam glowered at her and she felt the force of his determination. "Yes, you will. I'm going to convince you."

"With another practiced seduction?" she asked sarcastically. She still ached from their last encounter, and she wasn't sure she was up for another one.

He shoved his hands in his hair, looking almost frantic. Her heart beat a little faster as she realized that he'd come after her. Adam had never gone after any of his women before. He just moved on.

"No. That was a mistake."

Her cab pulled up in the driveway and the driver got out. "You called for a taxi?"

"Yes. I'm going to the airport."

"No, she's not," Adam stated.

"Yes I am."

"Listen, it's late, and I don't want to sit here while you two fight it out," the cabbie said.

Adam took some money from his pocket, shoved it at the cab driver and said, "You're free to go."

As the man got back in his car and drove away, Jayne glared at Adam. She hated that he thought he could use his money to arrange life to suit him.

"Come with me," he said to her.

"Not now. When you get home, come to my place and we can talk."

"Forget that," he said. Reaching out, he lifted her over his shoulder, then snagged her bag in one hand.

"Put me down!"

"No."

She struggled and he smacked her butt with the flat of his hand. "Stay still, dammit."

He stalked through the nearly empty lobby. Jayne stopped struggling and instead fought the urge to wrap her arms around his waist. She didn't want to leave, and it seemed he didn't want her to go.

He set her on her feet once they were in their room. She stared up at him, not recognizing this man. There was something in Adam's eyes she'd never seen before. Something that looked like...love.

He took her face in both of his hands and lowered his head, whispering something against her lips. Tracing them with the tip of his tongue, he deepened the kiss when she opened her mouth. She sighed, lifting her hands to his chest.

She didn't want to live the rest of her life without Adam. Tears started falling, and Adam brushed them away with tender fingertips.

"Don't cry, *chère*. Don't cry."

He rocked her in his arms, and she knew that she'd stay no matter what he offered this time. And that hurt her deep inside, because she'd always believed that someday she'd meet a man who'd want her for herself and want all of her.

"I love you."

She stared up at him, sure she hadn't heard him correctly. "I don't need the words."

"Really? I think you do. And I know you deserve them."

"Adam, I've only been gone thirty minutes. How can you love me?"

"I saw the light, and it was a scary experience. I'll tell you about it later. I think I've loved you all along, Jayne."

"I want to believe you," she said.

"But you don't. Hell, don't leave me again, *chère*. If you go, I'll become the hard shell of a man that you think I am now.

"I need you, Jayne. You make me a better man and I think I make you a better woman. You shouldn't have run away from me."

"I couldn't stay. I was afraid."

"Well, you don't have to be anymore. No more hiding for you, Jayne."

"Do you mean it? Because if you changed your mind—"

"I was afraid of that, too. But I can't change my mind. Woman, you own me heart and soul."

She swallowed against the tears burning the back of her eyes. This time they were tears of joy, for she knew that Adam didn't say things he didn't mean. If Adam committed himself to her, he'd stay with her.

And there was no mistaking the love shining from his eyes.

"I love you," she said at last.

"I love you, too. And I always will."

He lifted her in his arms and carried her into the bedroom. He settled her in the center of the big bed and then reached into the nightstand drawer for something.

It was a long, narrow jeweler's box. "I ordered this for you. It's not traditional, but then, neither are we."

He piled the pillows against the headboard and sat back against them, then pulled her onto his lap. He held her loosely in his embrace while he removed the sapphire tennis bracelet from the black velvet case. He fastened the clasp around her wrist.

"We're getting married," he said.

"You're not asking me?"

"Do I really need to?"

"Yes," she said. She wanted to have a really good story to tell her grandkids one day. Though it'd be hard to top him carrying her through the lobby over his shoulder.

"Will you marry me?"

She wriggled her eyebrows at him. "Only if I can call you stud muffin."

He groaned. "Okay."

Her heart felt incredibly light and she turned on his lap, wrapping her arms around him. "I can't wait to be your wife."

He took control of their embrace and they didn't talk for a long time as clothing was hastily discarded and they sealed their vows of love and commitment with their bodies.

Afterward Adam curled himself around her and held her fiercely in his embrace. They talked of the future and of their dreams for their life together. Jayne realized that Perla Negra had worked its magic and she'd found her heart's desire.

Epilogue

I looked out over the ocean. All my life I'd lived near it, but never really seen it. I'd only thought that the beach was a good place for a smuggling drop and that water was a dangerous place to dump a body because sooner or later it washed up on shore.

But today, with the sun setting on the horizon and the minister saying words of love and lifetime commitment, I realized there's a lot of beauty on earth. Too bad I didn't learn that lesson while I was still alive.

Adam gave a Jayne a kiss that was too intense for public viewing. I turned away and felt Didi's hand slip through my arm. I'd never admit it, but I'd enjoyed her company on earth.

And once she'd stopped dressing like my maiden aunt, she looked great.

"Nice job," she said softly.

I took her hand in mine and started walking down the beach. "I know."

"Pasquale, you need to work on humility."

"Babe, I never really grasped why pretending you don't know you're good at something was a good thing."

"I thought I warned you about calling me babe."

"You might have," I said.

She chuckled. "You've got too much charm for your own good."

"Ah, babe, I didn't think you'd noticed."

"Save it for your couples," she said. And I felt my body start to dissolve. She might think she'd had the last word this time, but she'd gone soft against my side before she disappeared. Maybe it was the fact that I spent so much time around couples falling in love, but I was starting to like Didi.

* * * * * *

THE WIFE
SEDUCTION

MARGARET MAYO

Margaret Mayo is a hopeless romantic who loves writing and falls in love with every one of her heroes. It was never her ambition to become an author, although she always loved reading, even to the extent of reading comics out loud to her twin brother when she was eight years old.

She was born in Staffordshire, England, and has lived in the same part of the country ever since. She left school to become a secretary, taking a break to have her two children, Adrian and Tina. Once they were at school she started back to work and planned to further her career by becoming a bi-lingual secretary. Unfortunately she couldn't speak any languages other than her native English, so she began evening classes. It was at this time that she got the idea for a romantic short story — Margaret, and her mother before her, had always read Mills & Boon® romances and to actually be writing one excited her beyond measure. She forgot the languages and now has over seventy novels to her credit.

Before she became a successful author Margaret was extremely shy and found it difficult to talk to strangers. For research purposes she forced herself to speak to people from all walks of life and now says her shyness has gone forever — to a certain degree. She is still happier pouring her thoughts out on paper.

CHAPTER ONE

'ARE you happy?'

Anna snuggled up against Oliver, feeling the exciting heat of his body, and nodded. This was a holiday romance come true. Two weeks in her sister's cottage with the handsome Oliver Langford and she was head over heels in love. They were now on the ferry on their way home to England and he'd asked her to marry him and she truly was the happiest girl in the world. She wasn't sure Oliver even needed to ask whether she was happy. Wasn't it there in the glow on her face, in the way she looked at him, kept touching him, kept rubbing her body against him? He was incredible. He was magnificently male, and she never wanted to let him go.

Meeting him on the outward trip and then having him turn up on the doorstep a few days later had been totally amazing, like something out of a movie. How he'd found her, she didn't care. It was sufficient that he had. She'd had no hesitation about inviting him in and then asking him to stay for the rest of her holiday.

He was totally, mind-numbingly gorgeous. The proverbial tall, dark handsome stranger, with an incredible magnetism and the most amazing tawny-gold eyes.

That never-to-be-forgotten crossing from Fishguard to Rosslare had been rough, the ferry objecting to the buffeting waves, and when Anna cannoned into

5

Oliver Langford in the gift shop his arms had come instinctively and protectively around her.

Immediately, without any warning, an electric current had shot through her. She felt an instant and unaccountable response, a scary response. Nothing like that had ever happened to her before.

'I'm sorry,' she'd stammered, finding it hard to even speak. It was as though the air around them had thickened, making it impossible to breathe—as though a cloud had shut out everyone else in the gift shop, insulating her and the stranger in a cocoon of sensuality.

'The pleasure's mine.' There had been a gruffness in his voice as though he too had felt his senses stirred by the sudden impact, as though he too was aware of no one around them.

He couldn't seem to drag his eyes away from her; they were dipping deep into her soul and searching for answers to questions that she knew nothing about. They were looking hungrily at her mouth and back to her eyes again.

'Would you like me to walk you back to your seat?' And still his golden eyes were locked into hers. It was as though he were consuming her, filling Anna with a fever of desire such as she had never felt before.

How could a perfect stranger do that? It didn't make sense. Why should the impact of a man dressed all in black spin her into a sexual frenzy?

There was no answer.

She'd wrenched away from him. 'I can manage,' she'd said with quiet dignity, not realising how much fire there was in her emerald eyes, or what it was doing to the man who had saved her from falling.

She'd gone quietly back to her seat and hadn't seen him again until he turned up at the cottage. Not that she hadn't thought about him. She had, constantly, and the shock of seeing him had almost sent her into a blind panic, it was as though she had conjured him up by simply thinking about him.

But those two weeks had been the most unforgettable of her life. She'd gone to that beautiful corner of southern Ireland for peace and relaxation after a job gone wrong and instead had found passion and excitement beyond measure, which had climaxed in Oliver asking her to marry him.

'What are you thinking?' Oliver stroked Anna's delightful retroussé nose with a gentle finger. Fate was at last being kind to him. Anna was so much the antithesis of other women he had known that he couldn't believe his good fortune.

She turned her face up to his, her green eyes smiling, her silky red hair a perfect foil for her porcelain pale skin with its scattering of freckles which he had kissed—every single one of them—and thoroughly enjoyed doing so.

'I was thinking about how we met,' Anna admitted. 'About the stunning quickness of it all. Two weeks ago I didn't know you, and now I've promised to marry you. Am I out of my mind?'

'If you are then so am I,' he told her with a tender smile. 'Two weeks ago I was off women altogether. You are a very special person, Anna Paige, do you know that? I think you must be a witch in disguise, casting your magic spell over me. And I think we should make our wedding arrangements the moment we get home.'

'You don't think we should wait and make sure?' she asked softly.

'I am sure,' he declared. 'I want to spend the rest of my life with you. I want to make babies with you. I want—everything. Your love, your devotion, your friendship, your commitment. It's what I'm prepared to give you. Am I asking too much?'

He held his breath as he waited for her answer.

To his relief Anna smiled and offered her mouth for his kiss. 'It's what I want as well,' she whispered and he could feel the passion trembling through her.

If they hadn't been in a public place he would have made love to her. Contenting himself with a kiss was a poor second. She was so ravishing, he couldn't keep his hands off her.

It had been blind panic that had made him follow her off the ferry. The thought of never seeing her again had made him feel quite ill, and he had cursed the conference that kept him away from her for three days.

He had told himself he was crazy because he'd never felt such an instant mind-blowing attraction to a woman before, and he'd kept imagining her with another man. He couldn't believe that someone as radiant and beautiful as Anna did not have a boyfriend.

It had been with a great deal of trepidation, therefore, that he had knocked on the cottage door. And a dream come true when he discovered she was alone—and equally as pleased and excited to see him.

'Quite how soon are you proposing we should get married?' she asked huskily.

'At the very first opportunity,' he growled, savouring the sweetness of her mouth, breathing in the very essence of her which drugged his senses every time she was near. In fact, she continually drove him crazy. Even thinking about her when they were apart, for no matter how short a space of time, minutes even, his male hormones rioted. He was in a constant state of excitement. 'I can't take the risk that someone else will come along and snatch you from me.'

'There's no chance of that,' she told him with a sweetly confident smile. 'You've bewitched me too.'

But he intended taking no chances. Their wedding was going to take place as speedily as he could arrange it. Never before had he met a woman who he safely knew he wanted to spend the rest of his life with. Anna was different, he knew that instinctively, and he didn't want to waste precious time.

As soon as they docked he planned to take her home to Cambridge to meet his father, and he was hoping Anna would stay overnight before returning to her rented London flat. He was terrified that out of sight would mean out of mind, only reluctantly accepting that she needed to sort and finalise things before she came to live with him.

These two passionate weeks in Ireland had taught him how precious she was to him, how much a part of him she had become, so that without her even breathing was difficult.

What he wasn't prepared for, but on hindsight knew that he should have been, was his father's reaction.

*   *   *

'Father, I'd like you to meet Anna Paige, the girl I'm going to marry.'

Anna beamed at Edward Langford. He was not quite as tall as his son and much heavier set, but he had the same lion's eyes and a mass of long thick white hair brushed back from his face like a mane.

She held out her hand but to her amazement he didn't take it. Instead his eyes were fierce and condemning, visibly rejecting her.

She had no idea why. And after looking her up and down with a contemptuous curl to his lip, as though she were not fit to even be in the same room, he directed his attention back to his son. 'Are you out of your mind, Oliver?'

She felt Oliver stiffen and her hand sought his. What was going on here?

'No, Father, I'm not,' he answered firmly. 'I love Anna.'

'Love! Bah! How long have you known her?'

'Two weeks.' Oliver's hand tightened over Anna's, reassuring her, silently telling her that his father's bark was worse than his bite and not to be alarmed. 'But time doesn't enter into it. I love Anna, and it doesn't matter what you say, Father, I'm going to marry her—as soon as I can arrange it. I see no reason to wait.'

'You're a fool.' The older man's face was furiously red by this time.

Anna finally spoke. 'If he is then I'm a fool, too. I feel the same as Oliver, I want to marry him without delay. I'm sorry you feel this way, Mr Langford, but I can assure you that—'

She was interrupted by Edward's housekeeper saying that he was needed on the telephone urgently because there was trouble at one of the sites.

'You see to it,' Edward ordered Oliver peremptorily. 'Heaven knows, there have been enough problems while you've been away.'

Oliver looked down at Anna and frowned and she knew he was worried about leaving her. 'It's all right,' she said with a confident smile. He'd already told her that his father had retired from his property development company because of heart problems and handed over the reins to him, so it was only right and proper that Oliver deal with things now.

'Have you any real idea why my son's asked you to marry him?' Edward thundered, the moment Oliver left the room.

The question sent her brows sliding up but she refused to be intimidated. 'Because he loves me, Mr Langford, as I do him. Are you suggesting there is any other reason?'

'I'm not suggesting it, I know it,' he told her grimly. 'He's in love with someone else. Admittedly they had a dispute and Oliver told her it was all over, but he's said that before, more than once, and they've always got back together.'

'Would her name be Melanie, by any chance?' asked Anna sharply.

Edward Langford's bushy brows rose. 'He's told you about her?'

Anna inclined her head. 'Naturally. We've kept nothing from each other. A good marriage has to be based on trust and understanding and we've been perfectly open about our past lives.' She had told Oliver about Tony, the guy she was once engaged to, and he'd told her about Melanie, the girl his father wanted him to marry.

'You've caught him on the rebound.'

'I don't think so,' Anna retorted. 'Oliver said it was definitely all over.' He had added that he was glad to get rid of her. She was the daughter of a close friend of Edward's, and his father's god-daughter to boot. Oliver had found out that she was bragging to her friends about what a good stud he was and that she could get as much money as she liked out of him.

'How do you know that I'm not just after your body as well?' Anna had taunted. And even as she spoke she'd rubbed herself against him, slid down the zip on his trousers and slipped her hand inside. He had groaned and succumbed and it had been a long time before they finished their conversation, a very long time.

'My son's had enough fortune-hunters on his tail for me to be able to spot them a mile off,' insisted Edward Langford, looking at Anna with such dark intent that she shivered.

'You're just a little more clever than most,' he snarled. 'You got in when he was at his most vulnerable. But his money is my money. He's worked his way up in my company, I made sure he did it the hard way, but every penny he earns is indirectly from me, and I will not allow some—hussy—to come along and take it from him.'

Anna eyed the old man coolly, not allowing the light to fade from her eyes for one millisecond. 'When I met Oliver, Mr Langford, I didn't know he came from a wealthy family, or even that he had money himself. I fell in love with Oliver the man. He could have been unemployed, for all I cared. Money doesn't interest me, except as a need to buy clothes for my back and food for my stomach. So long as I have enough for that, I'm quite happy.'

Faded golden eyes looked hostilely into her sparky green ones, her words not impressing him in the slightest. 'I'm expected to believe that, am I? Well, let me tell you, miss, there's not one woman alive who isn't impressed by money.'

He crossed to a desk, whipped out a cheque book and scribbled in it before ripping out the cheque and offering it to her. 'Here, take this, and let that be an end to this impossible situation.'

It was for an indecently large amount, enough to set her up for the rest of her life, but Anna wasn't interested. In fact, she was insulted by his offer. All she wanted was to marry the man she loved.

Her eyes flashed her indignation; her spine stiffened. 'I don't want your money, Mr Langford. I realise that you don't believe in love but I do, and so does Oliver, and all we want is to be together.' Slowly and deliberately she tore the cheque into tiny pieces and let them flutter to the ground. 'This is what you can do with your money.'

The golden eyes leapt with fire, but to give him his due the old man remained coldly distant. 'You're a silly little girl,' he spat. 'You're making the biggest mistake of your life.'

'I don't think so,' she told him calmly. 'But you're entitled to your opinion.'

Wide nostrils flared even wider. 'If I cannot persuade you to change your mind about this impossible marriage then be warned, if you ever do anything to

hurt my son, Miss Paige, anything at all, then you'll
have me to contend with. Make no mistake about
that.'

When Oliver came back into the room she was alone,
the torn cheque tucked into the bottom of her bag for
disposing of later.

'Where's my father?' he asked with a frown.

Anna shrugged. 'I guess he found something else
to do.' She didn't want to spoil things by telling him
what his father had done.

'I'm so sorry he didn't give you the welcome you
deserve,' he said, pulling her close and looking worriedly into her eyes. 'I truly never expected he'd react
like this.'

'It doesn't matter,' she said. 'You're the one I'm
marrying; you're the one I love.'

'Let's go home,' he growled. 'There are things I
want to do to you.'

Anna's body leapt in response and she wasn't sorry
to be walking out of Weston Hall. It was the family
home, a daunting square brick house built on a vast
estate on the outskirts of Cambridge.

Oliver lived at Weston Lodge in the grounds. Near
enough to his father in case Edward needed him, but
far enough away to live his own life.

'I like it here,' she said happily as they walked
inside. It was still a fairly large house but nothing like
the Hall. It had a warm and welcoming atmosphere
with spacious rooms and plenty of plump comfy armchairs. 'Is this where we'll be living when we're married?'

'It certainly is, and it's where we'll be spending

tonight. In fact—' his eyes darkened dramatically '—I think I should show you the bedroom straight away.'

Anna had no qualms about that. She pushed the unhappy episode with his father out of her mind and got on with the job of loving Oliver Langford.

CHAPTER TWO

IT WAS a perfect spring morning, daffodils nodding, birds singing, the sky a deep heavenly blue. The church was massed with flowers—white flowers, every sort imaginable, roses, lilies, carnations—and white satin bows and trailing ribbons; as Anna walked up the aisle on her father's arm she had never felt happier.

Oliver had taken so much trouble to ensure their marriage was perfect in every detail. All she'd had to do was choose her wedding dress and her young niece's bridesmaid's dress. Oliver and her parents had done the rest. How they'd achieved so much in a week she wasn't sure.

There was a vast difference between the welcome her parents had given Oliver to the way Edward had threatened her. She had deliberately pushed his hostility to the back of her mind, telling herself that it was only a matter of time before Oliver's father accepted her, but she couldn't help thinking about it sometimes.

Oliver turned as she reached him and the light of love in his eyes had never burned so bright. 'You look beautiful,' he praised softly, 'like one of Titian's mythical figures. I am the world's luckiest man.'

'I'm lucky, too,' she whispered. 'I love you, Oliver Langford.'

His father didn't attend their wedding but it didn't

16

mar the day for Anna. In fact if Edward had been
there she would have been too aware of his resentment to relax. Instead everything was perfect.

As Oliver had important business commitments
they postponed their honeymoon but Anna didn't
mind. She felt as though they'd honeymooned already. Those magical days and nights in Ireland
would live in her memory for ever, and in the months
that followed she had never been happier.

Oliver was completely happy too. He showed it in
so many ways. He certainly wasn't pining for a lost
love.

Her brother had been unable to attend their wedding
because of business commitments in Europe, but now
he was back and she was delighted when he paid her
a surprise visit.

They looked nothing like brother and sister. Chris
was older by five years, had blond hair rather than
red, and eyes which were a deep navy blue. He was
tall and seriously good looking.

He ran his own advertising company and adored
his younger sister. 'What a pity Oliver isn't here,' she
said. 'I really want you to meet him. Come in, sit
down: we have so much to catch up on.'

Chris looked surprisingly serious all of a sudden.
'I actually knew Oliver wouldn't be home. It's the
reason I came now, while you're alone.'

Anna frowned, some of her happiness evaporating,
a vague unease taking its place. 'Why? Don't you
approve? Have you come to warn me about him? Is
there something you've found out that I don't know?'

He gave a faint, tight-lipped smile, an awkward

smile. 'Of course not, silly. I need to ask you a favour, a big one.'

'Oh?' This was a turn-up for the books. It was usually Anna asking Chris for something. She was the baby of the family and he'd always been good to her.

'There's no easy way to say it.' He bit his lip reflectively and recrossed his ankles several times. 'I need money, Anna.'

'What?' She'd never known Chris short of money.

'My business is in trouble,' he announced unhappily. 'Although—' he added quickly, before she could say anything '—I'm expecting a big order which will set me right back on track. It's just a hiccup, but—' he spread his hands expansively '—without financial help I could go under.'

Anna shook her head, desperately sorry for Chris. 'I don't see how I can help—unless you were thinking that Oliver might?' she asked in a moment of enlightenment. 'In fact, I'm sure he would; he's the most generous man I know. I could ask him.'

'No!' Chris virtually jumped down her throat. 'You must never tell your husband.'

And when Anna looked shocked, he explained ruefully, 'You see, the order I'm hoping to get, which I'm sure I will get, is from your husband's company. And if he knew I was having difficulties then he'd never put the business my way. Unless—' a sudden thought struck him '—he already knows who I am? If so, I'm sunk.'

'He knows I adore you,' she answered with one of her wide sparkling smiles, 'and he knows you're in advertising—but I don't think I've ever mentioned the name of your company.'

His shoulders relaxed and he let out a long-held breath. 'Thank goodness.'

'I could give you a few hundred, I suppose,' she said slowly, thoughtfully. 'What were you thinking of?' But when he told her how much he needed, more if she'd got it, she gave a groan of despair. 'I don't have that kind of money. Have you tried Mum and Dad? They had an endowment policy up recently, I bet—'

'I can't,' he said, running his fingers agitatedly through his hair. 'You know how much Dad was against me going into business for myself, said I hadn't got the head for it. If I told him I was in trouble I'd never hear the last of it.'

Anna sighed. 'There is one possible solution. Oliver puts some money into an account for me each month, I don't know why; I told him I don't need it. There's enough in there. Although actually I'd promised myself I'd never touch it; I don't want him to think I married him for his money.' She didn't want to be tarred with the same brush as Melanie, or to give Oliver's father the ammunition he was looking for.

'Anna, I promise you'll get it back.' Chris leaned forward eagerly, his navy eyes brightening with hope. 'Oliver need never know.' And he'd gone on pleading until in the end she'd reluctantly given in.

And no one would have been any the wiser if Edward Langford hadn't seen her brother leaving the house, hadn't seen him giving her a hug on the doorstep...

A few days went by before Oliver confronted her. He'd given her no clue over dinner as to what was to come, but when she got up to clear the table—something she always did for Mrs Green—he said, 'Sit down again.' And his tone brooked no refusal.

Anna stared at him in amazement because he never, ever, spoke to her like this. 'What's wrong?' His face was frighteningly grim all of a sudden.

'I hear you had a visitor a few days ago, a male visitor.' Well-shaped brows rose questioningly. 'I've been waiting for you to tell me about him, but since it's clear that you're not going to, then I'm afraid I shall have to insist on knowing who it was.' His golden eyes were accusing and hard and in that moment he looked very much like his father.

Anna gave an inward groan. This was what came of promising to keep secrets. 'Who told you?'

'My father, as a matter of fact,' he answered icily. 'Not that it really matters who told me. The point is, you didn't.'

She might have known Edward would find out. He probably permanently spied on her, or had someone do it for him. 'And what did your father have to say?' she asked defensively. 'That I'm having an affair?' It was exactly what Edward Langford would like her to do. Anything to end their marriage.

'I'm asking you to explain who he was. It stands to reason that if it was something innocent you'd have told me.'

'As a matter of fact it was innocent,' she claimed, her green eyes sparking angry fire. 'It was my brother.' And that was as much as he needed to know.

There was a sceptical lift now to those dark brows.

'Your brother? And you didn't tell me?' He made her sound stupid.

'I guess it slipped my mind,' she replied with a faint shrug, wondering why she found him amazingly sexy when he was angry.

Oliver shook his head in disbelief. 'Your brother comes home after months abroad and it slips your mind? Do you take me for an idiot? It would be the first thing you'd tell me.' He stood up and hauled Anna to her feet, his hands gripping her shoulders so hard that they hurt. 'I want the truth. Who was it? Was it that swine of a man you were once engaged to? Is he hanging around again?'

'Tony?' Anna was dismayed that Oliver would even think this way. 'I've not seen him since we split up and that's the truth. I should have said something, I know, but you weren't here when I thought about it, and when you were—well, we had other things to occupy our minds.' She moved her body suggestively against his. 'Much more interesting things. I love you, Oliver, far too much to be unfaithful. I'll never, ever, do that to you, I promise.'

He groaned and his mouth came down on hers. 'I told my father he was wrong, I said you weren't like that, but—oh, Anna—' and words weren't needed to express his sorrow for doubting her.

'You'd better invite your brother over here one evening,' he muttered between kisses.

And Anna agreed, while knowing she would keep putting it off until after Chris got the order.

Their lovemaking that night was quick and intense. The argument had heightened their senses and the instant Oliver touched her she exploded, feeding herself from his mouth in a frenzy of sexual hunger.

His hands were all over her, fierce and encouraging, and Anna's nails clawed Oliver's back as he found the moist, throbbing heart of her. She arched her body in glorious wild abandonment. 'Take me now, Oliver. Now!'

It was the best time ever. She jerked and bucked beneath him and thought the waves of pleasure would never stop. Oliver too groaned and shuddered, and they went to sleep in each other's arms, completely satisfied.

A week or so later an excited Chris phoned her. 'I've got the business, Anna. Can you meet me? I want to take you out for a celebratory lunch.'

That lunch proved her undoing.

The very same evening Oliver came home from work with his face grim, his eyes so hard and condemning that Anna knew exactly what he was going to say. And he didn't fail her. 'I want to know who you had lunch with today.'

Her shoulders stiffened. 'How do you know I had lunch with anyone?' And because attack was always the best form of defence, she added angrily, 'Have you been spying on me? Don't you trust me any more? If this is what I'm going to get from you every time I go out, then—'

He sliced through her words. 'Who was he?'

A feeling of unease seeped into Anna's bones. 'It was Chris again, as a matter of fact.'

'The mystery brother who you seem determined I shouldn't meet?' His voice was loaded with sarcasm, his golden eyes razor-sharp. 'I don't believe you, Anna.'

Her hackles began to rise. 'I'm sorry, but it's the truth.'

'So when were you planning to tell me? Or was this to be another of your little secrets?' he asked sarcastically. 'I suddenly don't understand you, Anna. In fact, I feel I don't know you at all.'

Anna sighed deeply and unhappily. Even though her brother had asked her to keep quiet a while longer, she knew that it wouldn't be wise, that it was time to tell Oliver the truth. It couldn't hurt, surely, not now that Chris had got the order?

She hadn't liked keeping it a secret from her husband, and she liked even less the way he was accusing her. But before she could even open her mouth, Oliver sprang another surprise accusation.

'Not only are you dating another man but you're giving him money.' His golden eyes blazed with fury. 'Money that I, out of the generosity of my heart, have given you.'

A flash of righteous anger ripped through Anna. 'You've checked up on me? How dare you? You had no right.' If she was a man she'd have punched him. It was an invasion of privacy, that's what it was— even though he'd given her the money in the first place.

'Unless what you're saying is that the money isn't really mine,' she flared. 'Is that it? It's just a token thing to make you look good and feel good, but you never intended that I should spend any of it. And now that it's gone you're wishing you'd never given it to me in the first place.'

'My actions are not in question,' he retorted coolly. 'What is, is why have you given away thirty thousand pounds. It's what I'm assuming you've done with it. Or have you spent it on some flash piece of jewellery that you've not yet shown me? I don't think so. There's a man involved and I want to know who he is and what he means to you. And don't continue to give me that brother rubbish, because it won't wash.'

Before Anna could say anything in her own defence, he added, 'It's that rat you were once engaged to, isn't it? An ambitious but penniless young man, you said, who didn't want to be tied down into marriage before he'd made his millions. Is this his way of doing it, sponging off other people?'

'You're crazy, Oliver Langford.' There were two spots of high colour in Anna's cheeks, her eyes were brilliant with anger. 'This has nothing to do with Tony. Actually, it has nothing to do with you, either.' Brave words. 'That money was mine to do with as I liked—or so I thought. If you have a problem with that, if you can't trust me enough to accept that I had a very good reason for doing what I did, and that one day I would have told you, then you're not half the man I thought you were.'

'Oh, so you would have told me?'

'Eventually.'

'In my book, husbands and wives don't keep secrets from each other.'

She tossed her head, red hair flying magnificently. 'If you hadn't been nosy enough to check up on me, you wouldn't have known. And if you saw me at lunchtime, why the hell didn't you come and speak to me? Or do you get some sort of savage enjoyment out of spying on me?'

Anna couldn't believe they were having this conversation, that their idyllic marriage was in danger because of a promise she'd made to her brother.

'It wasn't me who saw you, it was my father.'

'Ah!' She needed to hear no more. 'And I suppose he couldn't wait to tell you? To blacken my name? I suppose he also made a point of saying that he saw my companion with his arms around me as we parted? It must have looked a very cosy scene to him.'

She shook her head in wild and furious resentment. Edward Langford would have her hung, drawn and quartered without an ounce of compassion, or any thought that he could have been wrong. She'd played right into his hands.

This was exactly what he'd been hoping for.

Their argument raged long and loud until eventually Oliver walked out. Where he went she didn't know, but he didn't come home that night. And the bed felt cold and empty without him.

At lunch time the next day he turned up and began ramming clothes and toiletries indiscriminately into a holdall. 'You'll see me again when you're prepared to tell me the truth,' he said icily, almost viciously, 'and not a minute before.'

The days that followed were the blackest of Anna's life. She was aware that her husband had moved in with his father because she'd seen his car whizzing past, and she kept expecting Oliver to walk through the door and say he'd made a mistake, that he loved her and couldn't live without her, but he didn't. And she had too much pride to go after him.

Besides, she was hardly likely to be made welcome there. Edward would continue to feed his son's distrust and anger—until in the end he'd have no love left for her at all.

When Edward himself came to visit she wasn't surprised, in fact, she'd been expecting it. But what he had to say most certainly did shock her.

'I want you out of this house,' he said bluntly.

'I think that's up to your son.' Anna surprised herself by managing to keep her voice cool and calm, her chin high. 'As far as I'm concerned, we're still married and I have every right to live here. I'm afraid it has nothing to do with you.'

'Really?' Shaggy brows rose to meet the mane of white hair. 'Perhaps Oliver omitted to mention that this house actually belongs to me. And in that event I have every right to evict you. I'm giving you seven days to find somewhere else to live.'

Anna felt as though he'd stabbed her between the shoulder blades. Oliver had never breathed a word about his father owning Weston Lodge. For pity's sake, why had he never bought a place of his own? It wasn't as though he couldn't afford it. It didn't make sense.

But it was herself she had to think about now. She was jobless and virtually penniless and in a week's time she would be homeless. Edward must have laughed his head off when Oliver walked out on her.

Anna supposed she could move in with her own parents, but they'd been so pleased she'd found such a wonderful man after her disastrous engagement to

Tony that she couldn't bear to tell them it was all over so quickly.

She could also go to see Oliver and plead with him, go to see him at the office in order to avoid Edward, but pride stood in her way. Oliver had made his position very clear and if he wanted her back then he was the one who had to do the running.

So she moved to her sister's holiday cottage—the very place where she'd first met Oliver. Damn him! She'd expected at the very least a courtesy call before she left Weston Lodge—but no. Nothing. Not a visit, not a phone call, not even a hastily written note on a scrap of paper saying good riddance.

Actually this cottage was the worst place she could have come to. It was filled with too many memories. It was here that they'd introduced themselves properly, here where they'd first made love, here where they'd fallen in love. Just the thought of Oliver making love to her sent her into a tizzy.

But she'd had little choice of where to live at such short notice. She'd taken her sister into her confidence and Dawn had offered her the cottage for as long as she needed it.

'Although if I know Oliver,' Dawn had said, 'he'll be after you in no time at all, begging you to go back to him. That guy's deeply in love with you. You can't tell me that some stupid misunderstanding will change it. Once Chris's business is on the up, and you're free to tell Oliver the truth, then—'

'I don't think so.' Anna shook her head with fierce determination. 'I'm certainly not going to run after him with explanations.'

'But—' began Dawn.

'But nothing,' interrupted Anna. 'I've made up my mind. And I don't want you to tell Chris what's happened either, or he'll feel truly awful. Tell him, if he asks, that Oliver has business in Ireland and we're using your cottage. Tell Mum and Dad that as well.'

In the weeks that followed she tried to convince herself that she was well rid of Oliver, but the truth was she missed him more than she had imagined possible. She missed their nights of passion—sleeping alone was crucifying her, she missed his companionship, their long, interesting, sometimes heated conversations. In those six short months he had become so much a part of her life that she found it difficult living without him, it was as though half of her was missing.

Time would heal she supposed—but...

It was obvious his love for her had died—if he'd ever truly been in love with her. Maybe his father was right and he had turned to her on the rebound.

Perhaps it had been lust that drove him, some sort of physical cleansing to rid his mind of the woman who had hurt him. The physical side of their marriage had certainly been a very high priority—not that she'd complained, she'd been as eager as he to satisfy their pagan needs.

And then came the phone call. Only Dawn ever rang so it was a distinct shock to hear Oliver's deeply attractive voice. A surge of something approaching excitement catapulted through her but she stamped on it because it would be fatal thinking along those lines.

Physical reactions were ruinous and negative and must never be allowed purchase. If it was his intention to try and patch things up, he was in for a big disappointment. Oliver Langford had definitely burned his bridges the day he walked out on her.

'Anna, sad news, I'm afraid.' There was no pre-amble.

'Oh?' This wasn't what she'd expected.

'My father died yesterday of a massive heart at-tack.'

For a few seconds Anna was too stunned to say anything. Edward Langford, dead! The ebullient old man who'd done his best to stop her marriage, gone! She was saddened to hear it even though she hadn't really liked him. The truth was, she'd never been al-lowed to get to know him.

'I'm sorry to hear that,' she said finally, softly. 'It's hard to take in. He seemed such a vital man, as though he had years of life left in him.'

'My father was his own worst enemy,' Oliver growled. 'He constantly disobeyed doctor's orders. I was wondering if… I—I'd like you to come to the funeral.'

'Of course.' She said it instinctively, then won-dered if it would be wise. Edward had turned Oliver against her. Meeting again could invoke friction—and she would hate there to be any of that on the day of his father's funeral. It was likely he was inviting her to keep up a front for the sake of family and friends. He had numerous cousins and aunts and uncles whom she'd never met, who would all be coming to the funeral. And of course there was Melanie!

Anna couldn't help wondering whether Melanie had wormed her way back into Oliver's affections.

CHAPTER THREE

OLIVER'S palms were moist and there was an unnatural thudding in the region of his heart. Ridiculous when Anna no longer meant anything to him, when he had washed his hands of her and his next planned step was to instruct his solicitor in divorce. How could simply hearing her voice trigger such a juvenile reaction?

He shook his head and forced himself to continue with the very disturbing job of arranging his father's funeral. Edward Langford had died as he had lived. Railing at change, surmising he knew better than everyone else. He'd been arguing with Oliver over the way he was applying new management techniques when he'd keeled over. By the time the ambulance arrived he was dead.

Oliver couldn't bear to remain at the Hall with his father gone and he moved back into the house he had shared with Anna, which wasn't much better because there were memories here of a different kind.

For six months he'd been a completely happy man. He'd found the girl of his dreams, he'd totally adored her and then, like a bullet shattering a crystal vase, his heart had been smashed into a million tiny miserable pieces.

If anyone had warned him that Anna would turn out the same as Melanie, the same as other girls he'd dated, he would have told them they were off their head. Anna was perfection personified; she could do no wrong. Or was that where his problem had lain? He'd stood her on a pedestal, been unprepared for her to have human failings the same as everyone else.

He'd been surprised by her ready acceptance to come to the funeral, and hoped she wasn't trusting he'd had a change of heart. So why, he wondered, had he asked her, if it wasn't to use the opportunity to try and patch things up?

His father had never approved of Anna, the same as he'd never approved of anything Oliver did. All his life it had been like that.

And it would have been perfectly reasonable for him not to ask Anna to come to the funeral. In fact, it would be hard for her to try and pretend sadness for a man who'd never attempted to welcome her into the family.

Technically, though, she was still his wife and he wanted her by his side. None of his family knew that they'd split up, and a funeral was hardly the place to tell them. He steadfastly refused to accept that there was any other reason.

Anna left her car behind and flew to London where Oliver sent a car to pick her up. She'd half-expected that he'd come himself, had felt a flurry of anxiety at the thought, but instead one of his company drivers met her.

Her heart zinged into overdrive as they neared Cambridge but she deliberately hardened it, refusing to accept that she had any feelings left for this man who had so callously walked out on her.

The driver dropped her off at the Lodge, for which

she was grateful. She'd half expected, half dreaded, that Oliver would want her at his father's house with him. And that was something she felt she couldn't face.

If she hadn't been welcome there in his father's lifetime, he wouldn't have wanted her there after his death, that was for sure. But also she needed some breathing space before she confronted Oliver. Time to accustom herself to being back here where she had once been so happy.

His housekeeper was there to greet her. 'It's sad news about Mr Edward,' she said as she busied herself making tea and buttering scones.

'It certainly is,' Anna agreed. 'Is Oliver up at the house? I suppose I ought to—'

'Out on business somewhere,' interrupted Mrs Green. 'There's such a lot to organise.' When the tea was made, the scones pushed towards Anna with a pot of homemade strawberry jam, Mrs Green sat down at the kitchen table and leaned towards her.

'Tell me to mind my own business if you like, but I don't understand why you two split up. I thought you were the perfect couple. Oliver's been like a bear with a sore head. He misses you terribly.'

He had a strange way of showing it, thought Anna. If his father hadn't died, she wouldn't be here now. The next step would have been divorce. She had no doubt in her mind about that.

'He was the one who did the walking, Mrs Green,' she pointed out, not quite meeting the other woman's eyes. 'There's no chance of us getting back together. If that's what you were hoping I'm sorry.'

The woman looked disappointed. 'And I'm sorry it came to this. I'm very fond of you, Anna.'

No more was said and after Anna had nibbled half a scone and drank a cup of tea she got up and began to wander around the house. Nothing had changed. Pictures that she'd chosen were still on the walls, little ornaments, things they'd selected together—everything was exactly as she'd left it.

Upstairs she trailed through the bedrooms, dumping her overnight bag in one of the guest rooms, coming to a sudden halt in the doorway of what had used to be their room.

Anna felt a mixture of trepidation and resignation as she slowly pushed open the door. It turned swiftly to shock. Oliver was back! His leather slippers were tucked beneath the dressing-table stool, a tie hung on the back of a chair, but more potent was the lingering musky smell of his cologne.

When had he returned? After his father's death, or immediately after she had left? What sort of thoughts went through his head as he lay here each night? Was he remembering her and the amazing lovemaking they'd shared—or the way things had used to be before she moved in? Was this what he preferred—the life of a bachelor?

Even as her mind tried to make sense of what she'd just discovered, Anna heard a movement behind her, and whirling round she came face to face with Oliver.

It was a heart-stopping moment. He was as gorgeous as she remembered, his black hair short as though he'd just had it cut, his face a touch gaunt perhaps, his eyes shadowed, but that was perfectly natural under the circumstances. She could imagine how she'd feel if she lost either of her parents.

'Mrs G said I'd find you here. Thank you for coming, Anna; it means a lot to me.'

'It was the least I could do.'

There was an awkward silence and to break it Anna impulsively hugged him. 'I'm sorry about your father.' It was the sort of hug she would give Chris.

But it was a mistake. She had thought she could make it impersonal. Grave error. There was nothing impersonal about her feelings for Oliver. Her mouth ran dry and a mountain of pulses jerked into overtime.

Even Oliver looked stunned, though she couldn't accept that he'd felt anything. More than likely he was wondering what had made her do it, praying she wasn't intent on trying to revive their marriage.

He needn't worry. Whatever feelings ran rampant inside her, she intended to keep them hidden.

'I didn't realise you were living back here,' she said in an effort to defuse the sudden tension.

He offered no explanation, simply saying, 'If you want this room I can easily move—'

'No.' Anna stopped him before he could go any further. 'I've already claimed one of the others. I was just passing the time. I'm sorry if I've intruded.'

She could easily imagine what it would be like sleeping in the bed they had once shared. It was bad enough at the cottage, but here, where they'd spent so many long, deliriously happy months, it would be unbearable. How could he do it?

'So long as you're comfortable.'

Such forced politeness. Best put an end to it. 'I think I might go and unpack and take a shower.'

But he seemed not to want to let her go. 'Carl met you all right?'

'Yes, the plane was on time.'

'I would have come myself but—'

'You had other obligations,' she cut in. 'I understand. This is a sad time for you, Oliver. If there's anything you want me to do, any help I can give, you only have to say.'

'Thank you,' he said and, with an expectant lift of one eyebrow, added, 'Will you have dinner with me this evening?'

This wasn't what Anna had meant and her eyes widened in dismay.

'I'm sorry,' he said at once. 'It's just that I could do with some company right now. But it's all right, I understand how you must feel. I'll cancel the booking and—'

'No, I'll come,' she insisted, feeling sorry for him then.

But later, when she joined Oliver downstairs, when her insides sizzled at the mere sight of him, she began to wish that she'd refused. It was going to be hard hiding the attraction she still held for him.

She guessed that part of it would never go away. She could hate him for what he'd done, the way he'd accused and distrusted her, the way he'd simply abandoned her, but the physical magnetism—that lethal attraction she had felt on the ferry—would always remain.

He was wearing a white shirt and close-fitting dark trousers; his matching jacket lay casually over the arm of a chair. His tie was black and she was reminded how fiercely he must be missing his father.

She herself had chosen to wear a black dress—not purposely in respect for Edward but because it was the only outfit she had brought with her which was suitable for dining out. It had long sleeves and a scoop neck, was fitted to the hips and then flared gently to mid-calf.

Oliver's eyes roved lazily over her, lingering on her mouth, the same sort of appraisal he'd made when they first met and it sent the same sort of dizzy feelings through her, but he made no comment, simply enquiring, 'A drink before we leave, perhaps?'

Anna shook her head. 'No, thank you.' The sooner they went, the sooner they'd be home.

It was a restaurant he'd taken her to before, quietly elegant with tables set far enough apart for conversations not to be overheard. There was no lounge, the bar was in a corner of the dining room, and they were shown straight to their table.

'How did you know where to find me?' she asked after they'd ordered drinks and made their choices from the extensive menu.

'I rang Dawn.' His lips twisted wryly. 'I know you asked her to tell no one but I gave her little choice. Don't be too hard on her.'

Anna actually already knew what he'd done. She'd phoned Dawn last night after Oliver's news about his father, and discovered that Oliver had contacted her sister not long after she'd left for Ireland. The fact that he'd known for all these weeks where she was but done nothing about it spoke volumes.

After the funeral tomorrow he would politely thank her for coming, wish her a safe flight back to Ireland and that would be the end of her marriage.

She had also asked Dawn whether Chris knew that she and Oliver had split up. But her sister had kept her promise in this instance. Anna was aware, though, that the time had come to contact him, her parents too. They had a right to know what was going on.

She'd rung them a couple of times from Ireland but they'd been under the impression that Oliver was with her, and she'd never told them otherwise.

During the meal Oliver steered the conversation away from all things personal, talking mainly about his job, which suited Anna down to the ground. But as he talked she gained the impression that he wasn't happy in his work any more. It wasn't anything he said, just his general attitude. There wasn't the fire and enthusiasm that he'd always had.

Maybe it was because of present circumstances, but somehow she didn't think so. Something had gone wrong that he wasn't telling her about. Which made her sad because he'd always told her everything. She'd congratulated him when things were going well, commiserated if he'd had problems, calmed him when he was angry over something. And now she was no longer a part of that life.

They were halfway through their main course when an attractive blonde wearing a skirt only just long enough to be decent, stopped at their table. 'Oliver, what a surprise.' And, in a very loud aside, 'What's she doing here?'

'Melanie,' he said, politely standing up but not answering her question. 'I thought you were in Egypt.'

'I came back this morning. I couldn't believe it when Daddy told me about Uncle Edward.' There were tears in her eyes as she spoke. 'I tried to phone you. You poor darling, you must be devastated.' She wrapped her arms around him. 'You shouldn't have to bear this alone. If only I'd been here, I—'

'He isn't alone.' Anna heard herself say the words, though they either didn't hear or ignored her. She'd met Melanie a few times and on no occasion had the girl enamoured herself to her. In fact, she had treated Anna with icy disdain.

Anna had always assumed that Oliver continued to put up with her for his father's sake—but when he held her now, when he stroked her hair, almost as though he were comforting Melanie instead of the other way round, Anna felt he was taking things too far. This girl had treated him scandalously, for pity's sake. Why was he behaving like this?

Fury zipped through her veins. Would either of them notice if she got up and walked out? Melanie shouldn't be allowed to do this to Oliver, not after all she'd put him through. Goodness, he'd not even welcomed her, his own wife, with this much fuss.

She stood up, picked up her bag and was halfway across the dining room when Oliver caught her up. 'Where are you going?' he asked quietly.

'To the Ladies.' Because I suddenly feel sick, she added silently.

'You're not walking out because of Melanie? I know she can be a bit full on at times, but for my father's sake I can't ignore her at a time like this.'

'You're a free man,' she tossed airily. 'You can do whatever you like, be with whomever you like. It really doesn't matter to me any more. If you'd prefer Melanie at your side, now she's home from her holiday, then—'

'No!' He said the word sharply and loudly. 'I want you. You are my wife.'

'You walked out on me, Oliver.'

He closed his eyes for a second as if to say, I know and I shouldn't have done. But when he looked at her again his expression was blank, his feelings well hidden. 'Whatever I did, I want you with me now.'

For appearances' sake? she felt like asking, but she didn't. It was the wrong time to goad him. 'I'll be back in a minute,' she said coolly, and carried on to the cloakroom.

But she didn't hasten, taking time to dab powder on her nose and reapply her lipstick. She was running a comb through her hair when the door opened and Melanie waltzed in.

Anna saw her through the mirror, saw the calculating gleam in the blue eyes, and knew immediately that there was trouble brewing. Melanie wasn't here to touch up her make-up, she was spoiling for a fight. Anna turned to face her.

Melanie spoke first. 'I think you have a cheek coming back for Uncle Edward's funeral when Oliver chucked you out.'

'Since Oliver doesn't mind, I hardly think you have any say in the matter,' Anna said with quiet dignity, wondering exactly how much he had told this girl about their break-up. She had no intention, though, of getting into a slanging match. Melanie wasn't worth it.

'Oliver doesn't love you any more.'

It was a childish statement and Anna's finely shaped brows slid up. 'He's told you that, has he?' It was the truth, yes, he had stopped loving her—but she didn't need it ramming down her throat.

'Not in so many words,' Melanie admitted with a careless shrug, taking a brush from her bag and dragging it needlessly through her long thick hair. 'But we've spent a lot of time together since you split up. He needed someone to soothe his ravaged breast,' she added dramatically. 'You could say we're back on to our old footing. He's a fantastic lover, isn't he? The best. I've made sure he's not missing out.'

Surely this couldn't be true? Anna felt her heart take a dive. Oliver wouldn't jump from her bed to Melanie's when he'd declared so strongly that he no longer felt anything for this other girl, would he? Not when Melanie had ruined their relationship with her outrageous bragging.

On the other hand, he was a healthy male with a good appetite for sex; she couldn't expect him to remain celibate for long.

It hurt, though, accepting that he might have turned to Melanie in her absence and it was difficult to remain calm. Somehow she managed it. 'Good for you,' she said with a cool little smile. 'Now, if you'll excuse me, Melanie, I'll get back to Oliver before he thinks we've both deserted him.'

It took even more of an effort to walk to their table and pretend there was nothing wrong. She saw Oliver watching her, frowning, wondering. And she was determined she would give him no cause to ask questions.

'Sorry I took so long,' she said, pasting a brilliant smile on her face.

'What did Melanie have to say?'

'Melanie?' she asked innocently. 'Not a lot. She's very distressed about your father, of course. Is she here on her own? Is she joining us?' She tried to make it sound as though she didn't mind, that she would welcome the other girl.

'I believe she's with a friend,' Oliver told her, his attention distracted as Melanie emerged from the cloakroom. They both watched as the blonde made her way to a table the other side of the room and sat down opposite her male companion with an apologetic smile.

He was a dark-haired, I'm-good-looking-and-I-know-it individual who Anna wouldn't trust as far as she could throw him. A typical rake out for a good time.

How could Oliver bear to touch a woman who went out with men like that? wondered Anna.

'Do you know him?' she asked.

'Who?'

'Melanie's friend. You seemed to be watching them very closely.'

Oliver shrugged. 'Just curious, that's all. I can't say I've ever met the guy—but then, Melanie has lots of friends.'

'She's a very attractive girl.' In an artificial sort of way.

'Mmm, I suppose so.'

'Do you still fancy her?'

'What is this, a third degree?' he asked sharply. 'I've invited *you* out tonight. I don't want to talk about Melanie.'

'But you are very close?' She noticed he hadn't answered her question.

He shrugged. 'She's almost one of the family. I'm glad she's back in time for my father's funeral. She'd have been terribly upset if she hadn't found out until too late.'

'Didn't anyone think to phone her—leave a message at her hotel?'

'No one knew exactly where she was. In Egypt, yes—but precisely where, no. Not even her own father. She has a habit of taking herself off on a whim and telling no one.'

'I see. Did she perhaps holiday with that guy she's with now?'

'I don't know.' Oliver began to sound distinctly irritated. 'And I don't really care. It's no business of mine.'

Oh, but it was, thought Anna. He was getting too worked up to be completely disinterested.

'I want to talk about you,' he said, fixing his eyes steadfastly on hers. 'I want to know why you left so suddenly. I couldn't believe it when my father told me that you'd gone. It didn't make sense. Why didn't you come and see me first?'

So Edward had said nothing about ordering her out, and she could hardly lay the blame now with his father not yet buried. Anna lifted her shoulders in a dismissive gesture. 'What was there to discuss?'

'There was absolutely no need for you to leave,' he declared firmly. 'And why Ireland? I know I was angry with you—damned angry, as a matter of fact— but you didn't have to shoot off like that.'

'I thought it best,' she said quietly.

'And you're happy there?'

Anna shrugged. 'It's temporary.'

'And the boyfriend?'

'What boyfriend?' she asked coldly.

'The one you gave the money to. Is he with you?'

Anna closed her eyes. This was most definitely the wrong time and the wrong place for this kind of conversation. 'You're wrong about Tony but I have no wish to discuss it. I think actually I'd like to go home.' How easily the word slipped out. 'I mean back to your house,' she corrected quickly. 'I'm tired.'

'Very well.' He beckoned the waiter for their bill and surprisingly he never once looked in Melanie's direction as they left the restaurant. But Anna did, and the look of venom in Melanie's eyes was enough to send icy shivers down her spine. The message was clear, this was not going to be the last she saw of her.

CHAPTER FOUR

ANNA had insisted on going straight to bed when they got back to Weston Lodge despite it being only a little after nine. The fact that Oliver still refused to give her the benefit of the doubt, that he still thought she'd given the money away for personal gain, hurt too much for her to put herself in line for any more accusations. She wanted to spend as little time with him as possible.

She heard him come upstairs a little before midnight, heard him pause at her door, and she waited, wondering if he'd turn the knob and walk in. Her hammered heartbeats echoed in her ears as seconds became a minute and a minute became two.

But finally, much to her relief, he moved on. She heard the faint squeak of the bedroom door—it had always done that and they'd always promised to get it oiled—and the gentle click as it closed. Only then did she realise that she'd been holding her breath.

What had he been thinking as he stood outside? She would have liked to believe that he'd been tempted to come in and make love to her with that driving animal passion which had always set her body on fire. But she knew differently. That part of her life was most definitely over.

Would she ever, though, really know what was going on inside Oliver's head? Was he glad or sorry that their marriage had ended? Was it his intention to file for divorce as soon as the funeral was over? Or did he strongly regret them breaking up but was far too proud to go back on his word?

Dawn was breaking when she finally fell asleep, and when Anna didn't go down for breakfast Mrs Green brought a tray to her room. 'Oliver's orders,' she said firmly as Anna sleepily pushed herself up. 'You have to eat. He said you hardly touched your meal last night. A waste of money, that was; I could easily have cooked you something nice and light.'

'You're very kind, Mrs Green,' said Anna as she lifted the silver cover and saw scrambled eggs, bacon and mushrooms, as well as crisp toast and butter and a pot of marmalade. 'But I'll never get through all this.'

'You've lost weight,' the housekeeper said warningly. 'I bet you haven't been eating properly. Now tuck in like a good girl. I'll put your tea here on the side. Would you like me to pour it?'

'I can manage, thank you.'

No sooner had Mrs Green gone than Oliver walked in. His hair was still damp from the shower, and he was dressed in black trousers and a white silk shirt. He looked sombre and pale and her heart went out to him. 'Did Mrs G pass on my orders?' he asked gruffly.

'It depends what they were,' she replied, taking a fork to the scrambled egg.

'You didn't eat enough last night to feed a sparrow,' he muttered uncompromisingly. 'You haven't been down for breakfast and the funeral's in a little over an hour. What game are you playing?'

Anna felt a pang of horror. 'I hadn't realised how

late it was. I haven't time for breakfast now.' The
fork went flying. 'I'll—'

But Oliver was adamant. 'Eat!' he thundered, 'I
don't want you fainting on me at the funeral.'

'Only if you leave,' she agreed. 'I can't possibly
eat with you standing over me.' Not when it tortured
her heart to even look at him.

Family, friends, business colleagues, all were gathered in a hushed group at the cemetery when a lone
figure made its way towards them, a tall, elegant,
slender woman in her early fifties wearing a smart
black suit and a black hat with a wide brim shadowing
her face.

Anna had no idea who the latecomer was but she
saw Oliver's relatives, especially the older ones, begin
to nudge each other and whisper—and not one of
them smiled or greeted her.

Oliver was the last to see her, and when he did
Anna saw the narrowing of his eyes, the indrawn
breath of disbelief, the sudden tightening of his
mouth. And when she looked down at his hands they
were curled into fists. But it wasn't until they got back
to Weston Hall that she found out who the stranger
was.

Mrs Green, together with Edward's housekeeper,
Mrs Hughes, had prepared a hot buffet and Anna and
Oliver stood to one side while everyone helped themselves. Suddenly the woman who had caused such a
stir at the cemetery appeared in front of them. Until
that moment Anna hadn't even realised that she'd returned to the Hall with the rest of the mourners.

'Oliver,' she cooed, her scarlet lips drawn into the

semblance of a smile. 'What a handsome young man you are. You don't know who I am, of course, but—'

'I know exactly who you are,' he declared in a hard, tight voice. 'What I want to know is what you're doing here?'

The woman laid scarlet-tipped fingers soothingly on his arm. 'What's Edward been saying to you about me? I've come to pay my last respects to my departed husband. There's no crime in that, is there?'

Anna felt her mouth drop open. She'd been given the impression that Oliver's mother was dead. How could this be her?

And yet, looking at her, Anna could see a strong resemblance, especially the fine straight nose and the pronounced shape of their ear lobes. There was no mistaking they were mother and son. In fact, Oliver looked more like his mother than he did his father.

'Except that you're no longer Edward's wife,' he reminded her quietly.

The woman smiled, her vivid lips almost evil. 'Didn't your father tell you, sweetheart, we never got divorced? I know it was more than thirty years ago but we somehow never got round to it. I never married again and neither did Edward so we just—' she gave a shrug of her slim shoulders '—let things drift. You know how it is.'

'No, I'm afraid I don't know how it is,' Oliver retorted, his face visibly paling at this piece of information. 'And I think it would be much better for all concerned if you left—right now.'

But still the woman smiled. 'I can't do that, Oliver. I want to hear what's in the will. Unless you already know the contents?'

Oliver was forced to admit that he didn't. 'My father's solicitor will be coming along later this afternoon to read it.'

'I rather thought that was the way things would be
done,' she said. 'Edward had charming old-fashioned
views on many things. Why don't you introduce me
to—' her pencilled brows rose '—your wife, I believe?'

Reluctantly and gravely Oliver did so. Anna shook
the woman's ice-cold hand but as soon as she left to
mingle with the others, Anna couldn't help asking,
'Oliver, I thought your mother died when you were
little?'

'To all intents and purposes,' he admitted grimly.
'It's what my father wished to believe. Rosemary
walked out on him when a business gamble failed;
she said he was no good to her without money.'

The money problem again!

'And you remember her?'

'I kept a photograph,' he admitted. 'I've also seen
her in the society columns of *The Times*. She's rarely
short of male companions.'

'Do you really think that she and your father were
never divorced?'

'It's something I fully intend asking Charles
Miller,' he answered quietly. 'I think she's lying. She
knows my father's estate will be vast. There've been
a couple of times over the years when she's attempted, unsuccessfully, to get back into his good
books.'

'She doesn't look as though she needs money
now,' said Anna. 'That's a cashmere designer suit

she's wearing. Perhaps we're doing her an injustice? Perhaps she *has* come to pay her last respects?'

'I'd like to believe that,' he said, 'but somehow I don't think so.'

Later, as they sat in the vast drawing room waiting for the will to be read, Anna asked quietly, 'What did Charles Miller say about your mother?'

Oliver winced. He'd cornered the solicitor earlier and taken him into his father's study and the news he'd heard hadn't pleased him. 'There was no divorce. My father seemed to think it would serve Rosemary right if she wasn't free to marry anyone else.'

Anna frowned. 'But she could have divorced him, surely? She didn't have to remain married.'

Oliver shrugged. 'I guess they were both playing games.' Rosemary's name had been a taboo subject in the Langford household; instead, Edward had vented his anger on the child she'd left behind.

Anna took Oliver's hand in sympathy, just that and nothing more, yet it created a rush of feeling so intense that it shocked him. How could something as simple as a touch make a mockery of his determination to end their marriage? She'd proved that she was no better than either Rosemary or Melanie. What was wrong with him? Why couldn't he get her out of his system?

When the will was read, the bulk of Edward's estate was naturally left to his son. There were smaller bequests to various relatives, and a modest amount for Melanie. To Anna there was nothing, and to Rosemary there was nothing either—which didn't please Oliver's mother.

The woman's face turned a startling shade of puce and she jumped to her feet. 'I intend to contest the will.' She directed her comments to the solicitor, but they were loud and clear for all to hear. 'Edward and I remained married. He cannot cut me off without a penny.'

'That is your choice,' said Charles gravely, running a finger round the neck of his collar. 'But I have to tell you now, Mrs Langford, that I don't think you'll get very far.'

Oliver took Anna's arm and led her from the drawing room. 'Let's go home. Mrs Hughes will lock up here when everyone's gone.'

It was the way he said home that warmed Anna's heart—it was as though he meant it was her home too. If only. Her six months of marriage had been so full of happiness, so full of love and laughter, that it was difficult to accept it was all over. Perhaps, if she tried very hard, she could pretend for a few more hours that nothing had happened, that they were still deeply in love.

And once inside, when he took off his jacket and tie and unbuttoned his collar, when he flopped down on his favourite armchair in the sitting room, she could almost believe it.

He began to relax, the lines of strain on his face seemed to fade, when suddenly there came a sharp rapping on the door.

Oliver stifled a curse.

'Don't answer it,' said Anna, not wanting to spoil these precious moments.

'It might be Charles, as anxious to escape as I was. I must speak to him.'

But it wasn't Charles' voice Anna could hear as Oliver opened the door—it was Rosemary's, an extremely furious Rosemary.

'Running away is a fool's game,' she shot at her son viciously. 'What's the matter, couldn't you face the thought of me upsetting your precious little tin god of a solicitor?'

'I doubt you'll upset Charles,' he told her calmly.

'Well, he needn't think that I shall sit back and do nothing,' she shrieked. 'I have a right to some of Edward's money.'

'You think what you like,' said Oliver, and Anna was proud of the way he kept his cool. 'It has nothing to do with me.' And she noticed that he didn't invite her in. Not that she could blame him. His mother must be his least favourite person.

'It has a whole lot to do with you,' retorted Rosemary. 'If you were a good son then you'd see me right. I wouldn't need to go through a solicitor. It's going to cost me money to—'

Oliver cut her short. 'I'm sorry but, the way I see it, you gave up the right to being my mother the day you walked out.'

Anna waited with bated breath to hear what Rosemary was going to say next. Perhaps she ought to show her face, give Oliver some support.

But Rosemary had clearly decided she'd said enough. She walked back down the path, turning as she reached the roadway. Anna could see her through the window, her back ramrod straight, her chin high, her lips a slash of angry scarlet in her pale but beautiful face.

'You've not heard the last of this,' she flung icily. 'I shall be around for a while longer. Don't think I'm going to quietly run away; that isn't my style.'

There was more of her in Oliver than he knew, felt Anna. Not only did they resemble each other but they both had the same tenacity of purpose when they thought they were in the right.

When he came back into the room his mouth was set. 'I'm sorry about that.'

And Anna knew that their comfortable togetherness was gone. Oliver was hurting, hurting badly, and she wished there was something she could do to ease his pain.

'Hopefully,' she said soothingly, 'Rosemary will accept that there's no point in fighting this particular battle and will fade gracefully into the background again.'

Oliver crossed to the drinks cupboard, poured himself a large whisky and downed it in one swallow, then poured another before taking it back to his chair. 'Rosemary is one of the world's takers. The only thing she ever gave in her entire life was birth to me. And little good that did her—or me, for that matter.'

Anna frowned. 'What do you mean?'

He shook his head. 'It doesn't matter.' Then he drew in a ragged breath. 'What a day.'

'Funerals are always harrowing occasions.'

'Some more than others,' he growled. 'Come here. I need you.'

His request startled Anna but it didn't enter her head to say no. Instead she moved slowly towards him, locking her eyes into his, ignoring the throb of her pulses, the heat that torched her suddenly sensitive skin, the hammer beats of her heart.

When Oliver pulled her down on to his lap and tucked her head into the hollow of his shoulder, curving an arm about her and holding her close, she felt an echoing beat inside him, a tension he couldn't disguise.

Her heart pounded in excited anticipation. They'd sat like this a hundred times before and always it had led to one thing.

An electric finger stroked her cheek; hot golden eyes watched her mouth as she ran the tip of her tongue over lips that were uncomfortably dry, and quietly he asked, 'When are you going back to Ireland?'

Anna groaned silently. Did he have to talk about such things when she was in a temporary seventh heaven? She didn't want to spoil these precious moments with conversation.

What she really wanted was to slip her hand inside his shirt and feel once again that electrifying hair-roughened skin. She wanted to lift her mouth for a mind-shattering kiss. She wanted—oh, so much.

'Anna?'

She stifled a sigh. 'Tomorrow.' Much too soon if he was going to treat her like this. Much, much too soon. 'But it's only temporary. I'll be moving back to London shortly. Finding myself a job.'

Now shut up and carry on holding me.

For a moment the stroking continued, unsteady fingers moving slowly from her cheek to her throat, brushing back stray strands of hair, pausing thoughtfully on the erratic tell-tale pulse at its base. The tension inside her built into a throbbing inferno.

Then he spoke again. 'Would you be happy in London? I remember you telling me that you were glad to be out of the rat race.' And his fingers moved to touch the swell of one aching breast.

'So I was,' she said in a strangled voice. Dear Lord, did he know what he was doing to her? 'But a girl has to earn a living.'

The wrong thing to have said.

'Or find a rich husband who can feed your fantasies,' he jeered. 'Come to think of it, you're not much different to Rosemary.'

Anna shot off his lap, fury in her eyes now, tension of a different kind zinging through her limbs. 'How dare you? How dare you compare me to that woman?' She was about to say a whole lot more when common sense warned that Oliver had gone through a lot today and perhaps wasn't thinking rationally.

He picked up his drink and took a long, slow sip, watching her through narrowed eyes. 'So you think there's no comparison? Perhaps you ought to look at things from my side of the fence.'

'I think you're tired and you don't know what you're saying.' Anna endeavoured to sound calm, though heaven knew she was furious inside. 'And if the truth's known I'm tired too,' she added with forced quietness. 'I think I'll go up to my room and take a rest.'

Surprisingly he let her go but as she left she heard the clink of bottle on glass. Let him drink himself stupid, she thought. As if I care.

But she did care. She didn't like to see Oliver up-

set. Burying his father was bad enough but for
Rosemary to add to his torment by putting in an appearance and causing a scene was dreadful. And now
he'd lashed out at her, and she'd been on the verge
of fighting back—which would have created even
more problems.

Anna didn't know what time it was when Oliver
came to her room. She'd fallen asleep on the bed and
in her dream Oliver was chasing her round and round
a lake at the dead of night.

Her own screams woke her and Oliver was standing by the bed. It was dark except for the ghostly
light from an almost full moon. She wasn't sure
whether she was still dreaming. 'Get away from me!'
she yelled.

Instead he sat down on the edge of the bed and
gathered her to him. 'It's all right,' he said gently,
soothingly. 'You were dreaming.'

'I was dreaming about you,' she admitted, more
quietly now. 'Actually, it was a nightmare.'

He grimaced at that. 'I guess I said things I
shouldn't have.'

'Don't apologise.' Held once more in his arms,
Anna felt that she could afford to be magnaminous.
Certainly she didn't want to argue—although he
wouldn't have said the words if he hadn't thought
there was truth in them. He was never, ever, going to
accept that her reasons for giving away that money
were altruistic. It was futile of her to hope that they
might have a future.

As Oliver continued to hold her his eyes glittered,
an intensity in their depths that Anna found deeply
disturbing. She could feel the heat of his body through

the thin silk of his shirt, and the erratic beat of his heart.

There was more to just holding her—he was aroused! The discovery caused her breathing to quicken and she closed her eyes, trying to shut out the sight of this man who was her husband in name only. It wouldn't be wise to let him make love to her, and yet how could she stop him when her need was growing apace with his?

And even though she couldn't see the desire in his eyes she could feel it and smell it. A rampant male. That particular musky smell was Oliver's alone. She'd always claimed it was an aphrodisiac.

And nothing had changed!

CHAPTER FIVE

WALKING out of Anna's room was sheer torture. Oliver wanted her like he never had before. The way she'd been there for him today, rarely leaving his side—comforting him, even—had triggered emotions he'd thought long since dead.

Physically and spiritually she was all he'd ever wanted in a woman, his ideal mate. But, unfortunately, like the rest of the female sex, her sights were set on other things. Why was it that money always meant so much to a woman?

When Anna had told him off for opening her an account, declaring that he was being too generous, that she could manage on her housekeeping allowance and didn't need any more, he'd believed her. He'd thought how truly wonderful she was, how refreshingly different. It had made him love her all the more.

But she wasn't different at all; she'd just had a different approach. She'd let the money build up into a distinctly healthy amount, which she'd promptly handed over to her ex-lover—if ex was the word.

He might still be her lover for all Oliver knew. Was it something she had plotted from the beginning? She'd said Tony wasn't with her in Ireland but it was mighty suspicious. First the money disappeared and then she did.

Every time he thought about it his blood boiled. He

didn't believe her brother story for one second. Her brother was a successful businessman.

The man in question, according to his father, had been tall and blond and good-looking—and that was how she'd described Tony. It had to be him; it could be no one else. Oliver slammed his bedroom door behind him.

He was glad now that he'd walked out of her room, that he hadn't given in to those insane urges that crept up on him whenever he was alone with her. The trouble was, she was such a vital person. She glowed with energy, her red hair a perfect foil for those sparkling green eyes, and he couldn't resist her. From day one she'd exerted her magic over him.

Admittedly some of the sparkle had dimmed when she turned up for the funeral. Was it the sadness of the occasion or because her source of ready money had dried up? He'd like to bet it was the latter.

Anna packed her bag before she went downstairs, she saw no point in delaying her departure. Oliver, she discovered, had already breakfasted and left.

'Did he leave a message?' she asked as the housekeeper brought in a fresh pot of tea. 'Has he gone to work?' He didn't normally leave this early.

'I've no idea. Would you like scrambled eggs and mushrooms, or bacon and tomato?'

'Just toast, please.'

'Mr Oliver won't like it,' warned Mrs Green with a wag of her finger. 'He gave me strict instructions that you were to eat a good breakfast.'

Then he should have stayed and made sure she did. Anna felt decidedly disgruntled by his absence. He knew she was leaving today. Didn't he want to say goodbye? Had she misinterpreted the signals last night? And what had that slammed door been all about?

She'd thought it was sexual frustration. Obviously she'd been wrong. He didn't want her any more; he'd come to his senses, realised she was the enemy. Well, that was all right with her. When he came back, she'd be gone; he would never see her again. She poured her tea and stirred it so furiously that it spilled into the saucer.

But before Anna had even left the breakfast table Mrs Green announced that she had a visitor.

'It's Rosemary Langford,' she informed Anna through pursed lips. 'I told her Oliver was out but she said she'd like to speak to you. I've put her in the drawing room.'

Anna didn't want to speak to Rosemary—not now, not any time. But there was no getting out of it. 'Very well, Mrs Green. Give me five minutes and then come and rescue me.'

The housekeeper's thin face broke into a smile. 'With pleasure.'

Rosemary wore another black suit in fine wool with a much shorter skirt and high-heeled suede shoes. Anna grudgingly admitted that Rosemary had a good pair of legs for her age. In fact, she was one very smart woman, her jet-black hair brushed severely back this morning and tied in a loose knot in her nape. She most certainly didn't look as though she was in need of a cut of Edward's fortune. And she made Anna feel distinctly underdressed in her cotton shirt and jeans.

The woman had been standing near the window, surveying the autumn tints in the garden. She turned as Anna walked into the room, gold hoop earrings swinging, her smile artificial, her grey eyes wary and calculating. 'So good of you to see me.'

Good didn't enter into it, thought Anna bitterly, she'd had no choice. 'I'm sorry Oliver's not here.'

'It wasn't Oliver I came to see. I want you to speak to him for me, Anna. I want you to persuade him that I should get a share of Edward's money.'

There was nothing like coming straight out with it. Anna wanted to laugh right into the woman's face. 'I'm sorry, I can't do that.'

'Whyever not?'

'Because it has nothing to do with me.'

'Because you've been left out of the will, too? I wonder why that was?' There was a mean gleam in Rosemary's narrowed eyes. 'Did Edward have it in for you, the same as he did me?'

Anna shook her head firmly. There was no way she wanted this woman lumping the two of them together, making out they were both casualties of the will. 'I think my circumstances and yours are miles apart.'

'Oh, I don't know.' Scarlet lips twisted into a meaningful smile. 'I hear your marriage is on the rocks. Your little charade yesterday didn't fool me for one second.'

'And what has that got to do with it?' asked Anna, her eyes flashing, her composure slipping for a second. She'd seen Rosemary latch on to Melanie, seen them looking across at her, so it wasn't hard to guess where she'd got her information from. But she was not going to give the woman the pleasure of knowing how bad the rift was between her and Oliver.

'It means we've both suffered at the hands of the Langford men,' spat Rosemary. 'And, believe me, whether you help or not, I intend fighting for what I believe is rightly mine.'

The gall of the woman was incredible. How could Rosemary even think for one second that she deserved to benefit from Edward's estate? 'Then you'll fight alone,' declared Anna. 'I want no part in it.'

'Actually, I've already begun. I've moved in to Weston Hall.'

The note of triumph in her voice, the toss of her head, the gleam in her eyes, made Anna look at her sharply. 'You're not serious?' In the background the phone rang but it barely registered. This was much more important.

'When I went back there yesterday, everyone was leaving. No one took any notice of me. I simply wandered upstairs and found myself a comfortable bedroom. To think I once thought Edward would lose that magnificent place. I underestimated his business acumen. And it's in even better condition now than it used to be. Is Oliver thinking of moving in?'

'The phone is for you, Anna.' Mrs Green appeared in the doorway.

'Is it Oliver?' Anna prayed it was, she must tell him straight away what Rosemary was doing.

'No, it's the call you were expecting.'

'Oh, yes, I see. Thank you. Rosemary, this may take some time. I think it would be best if you went.'

The woman didn't look bothered; she'd said all

she'd come to say. 'You will pass on the information to Oliver?'

'Naturally.'

'Thank you for seeing me.' And she sailed out with a satisfied smirk on her face.

'Did I do right?' asked the housekeeper. 'You looked mighty worried.'

'Perfect, Mrs Green. Is there anyone on the phone?'

A smile softened the woman's anxious face. 'No. I rang from the other line, the one Oliver had put in his study for when he's sailing the Net.'

Anna grinned. 'I never knew you were so devious. And it's "surfing", Mrs Green.'

'Well, whatever. It did the trick, didn't it?' she asked, her smile even wider.

'Without a doubt. Now I must find Oliver and quickly. Have you really no idea where he is?'

'I've a feeling he planned to see his solicitor,' the housekeeper answered uncertainly.

When Oliver heard the news he was livid, and in no time Anna saw his car shoot straight past Weston Lodge and up to the main house, skidding round the corner as he went. She hoped he hadn't driven like that all the way from Cambridge.

It was a good hour before he returned. Anna had waited impatiently and met him at the door. Her heart went out to him when she saw the deep lines etched into his brow, the distress in his eyes. She wanted to comfort him, hold him—take him to bed. This last thought shocked her. Where had that come from?

'I'm sorry she dragged you into it,' he said. 'I've managed to get rid of her—for the time being.'

'Do you think she'll stay around while she's contesting the will?' asked Anna in concern. 'Where does she actually live?'

'I've no idea on both counts,' he answered shortly. 'And I can't say that I'm interested. I could murder a coffee, though. Ask Mrs G, will you, while I get changed?'

Ten minutes later, the pin-striped suit replaced by black jeans and a thin crew-neck sweater, a mug of coffee cradled between his palms, Oliver sat looking at her. 'Who'd have thought things would turn out like this.'

'What did Charles have to say?' Anna's coffee was on the table at her side, her hands folded neatly on her lap. She sat still and calm but inwardly she was furious over Rosemary's behaviour. Oliver's mother had no right doing this to him.

'That she hasn't a leg to stand on. But I don't think that's going to stop her. She's set her mind on getting something out of this. She does the same with every man in her life, and there have been many. I've done some digging. I really don't like what I've found out,' he added grimly.

Anna didn't feel she could ask for details; it was no longer any of her business. 'Are you going to live up at the Hall yourself?'

'Not on your life.' His answer was quick in coming and very definite. 'I'll never live there. I'm putting it on the market—this house as well.'

Anna stopped in the act of picking up her coffee

cup. 'But Weston Hall's been in your family for generations, Oliver. How can you do that?'

He shrugged unconcernedly. 'Home can be the humblest cottage. That place is a pile of bricks and mortar, far too big for me. I don't know why my father carried on living there.'

'Have you told Rosemary?'

'No. She'd be back in there like a thief in the night, taking everything she could lay her hands on. She thinks I'm moving in and hopefully she won't find out any differently until it's too late.'

Anna finally drank her now almost cold coffee. 'It will be a mammoth task sorting everything. I could help, if you like?' Her heart pitter-pattered as she made the offer. Quite why she'd done it, she wasn't sure. It had come from deep within her.

Oliver's eyes narrowed. 'I thought you were leaving?'

'I don't have to,' she said with a faint smile and a lift of her slender shoulders. 'And with Rosemary possibly still lurking I thought maybe you could do with some support?'

Oliver looked at her for a long suspended moment. Anna felt a faint eruption inside her, a quivering response to the query in those golden eyes.

No! That wasn't the reason she'd offered, she told herself firmly. She felt sorry for him, that was all.

'Well, thank you, Anna, that's kind of you.' But a raised brow suggested that he wasn't altogether sure of her motives.

'It's not because I'm hoping to get anything out of it,' she pointed out swiftly and firmly. 'I'm doing it solely to help you.'

'Why would you want to do that?' And still the golden eyes watched her.

Desire began to pump, sensual liquid desire that found its way into every vein and every nerve, heightening her awareness, warming her skin. 'Because,' she said slowly, 'I'm not entirely insensitive to your needs. Maybe our marriage didn't work out, but it doesn't mean to say I hate you, or wouldn't do anything to help you.'

'And what needs would those be?' His voice deepened, his eyes burning into hers in such a way that she felt sure he knew her every thought, her every emotion.

She drew in a deep, steadying breath. 'It will take many weeks to sort through your father's stuff, to decide what to get rid of and what to keep.'

'And you're prepared to live here with me while all of this goes on? Without asking for anything in return?' He paused long enough to let his question sink in, and then added bitterly, 'In my experience, no woman does anything for nothing.'

In other words, he still didn't trust her. He probably thought she'd bag the family silver while he wasn't looking. 'If that's what you think,' she snapped, her eyes a vivid flash of emerald in a pale, distraught face, 'then forget I offered. I'll go and tell Mrs Green I won't be here for lunch. I have a plane to catch.' Her head was high as she pushed herself out of the chair.

But before she reached the door, Oliver leapt up and laid a hand on her shoulder. 'No, Anna, don't leave. I'm sorry; I'm touched by your offer. You took me by surprise, that's all.' He smiled wryly. 'I would like your help.'

His smile did something to her—melted her anger, made her smile back in return. 'I promise you won't be disappointed.'

And nor was he. In the days that followed, Oliver truly enjoyed having Anna around. There was an enormous amount of work to be done, much more than he'd first thought, and they worked steadily side by side, hour after hour, day after day.

They separated everything into various categories. Some to be kept for his own personal use, although there wasn't much of that—he wanted no reminders. Stuff to be dumped, some to go to charity, and the rest to either be sold separately or with the house.

And the more time they spent together, the more difficult he found it to remain detached. His feelings for Anna had not faded one little bit. She'd let him down, she'd disappointed him, she'd angered him— made him furious, in fact—but working beside that delectable body day after day soon began to tell on him.

He couldn't sleep at night for thinking about her, wondering whether he dared go to her room. What would happen if he did? If he took her into his bed now, she would think he'd forgiven her, would believe there was hope—whereas he still wasn't sure that he trusted her motives. He wanted to, he really did, but past experience had taught him that it was safest to let his head rule his heart.

But all his good intentions went by the board one morning when she tripped over the flex of a lamp and fell against him. It was like a replay of the day they'd first met. His arms instinctively went around her and the same sensual perfume had the same drugging effect.

With a groan, his arms tightened and everything he'd held in check came pulsing uncontrollably to life. The feel of her tempting, exciting body burst open the floodgates of desire.

And when she didn't resist, when he felt her tremble, when he saw the difficulty she had in breathing, he knew that he was not going to let her go.

He cupped her face between his palms, looked for several haunting, meaningful seconds into her incredible luminous eyes, and with a further agonised groan his mouth closed over hers.

Anna was beyond stopping him. She was amazingly helpless. His lips burned where they touched. It had been so long since he'd kissed her, really kissed her, that her limbs had gone fluid and if he dared let her go she feared that she would melt into a pool on the floor.

'Oh, Anna!' he breathed. 'What you do to me.' And his tongue darted between her lips, seeking and finding the pleasure he desperately desired.

It was Anna's turn to moan, to feel a need so deep that it scared her. Her tongue played games with his; she tasted the never-to-be-forgotten maleness of him, ground her hips against his, felt the damning evidence of his arousal.

More excitement, more fear. She ought to stop him but how could she? How could she deny herself such exquisite pleasure? It had been inevitable from the moment she offered to stay that something like this would happen. The surprising part was that it had taken so long.

All the emotions she'd kept bottled up rushed to the surface. She returned kiss for earth-shattering kiss, deeply, wantonly, and when he picked her up and carried her effortlessly towards the stairs she did nothing to stop him.

Her body needed his; it needed to be loved, it begged fulfilment. Neither of them spoke, tension building, breathing becoming difficult, painful even, and in the bedroom—she assumed the one Oliver had used when he was staying with his father—he dropped her on to the bed and raced to get out of his clothes.

Anna watched with fascination the frenzy that was driving him. The burning desire, the jerky movements as first shirt and then shoes and socks were ripped off. Belt, zip, and he almost tripped in his haste to get out of his trousers.

Her stomach tightened when a pair of black briefs was all that was left between him and his modesty. And there was nothing very modest about what they were hiding.

It was time to get undressed herself. She'd lain almost trance-like as she watched Oliver's frantic actions, but now her hunger got the better of her. Consumed by fire, pulses racing, heart thudding, her breasts already aching for his touch, she leapt off the bed and began to lift her sweater.

'No! Don't! That's my job.' His urgent voice reached into her unconscious.

She hadn't even realised that he was watching her. His briefs were gone. He stood tall and totally male in front of her, perfectly at ease with his nakedness. 'This is all right, Anna?' he asked quietly, almost anxiously.

No words would come so she swallowed hard and nodded instead. He took the bottom of her lambswool sweater. She raised her arms and he stripped it off in one fluid movement. Her jeans followed with not quite so much patience.

His breathing was ragged and Anna felt his tremors as he unclipped her bra and tossed it across the room, quickly followed by the matching black lacy briefs.

They fell on each other then, and Anna felt herself land with a thud on the bed. Oliver sucked first one and then the other burning nipple into his eager mouth, while his hand explored and tortured other regions.

Anna writhed beneath him, her hand seeking and finding what she wanted most.

'Don't touch,' he groaned, 'or I promise you I'll never make it.'

But he did make it, and as he entered her, as their bodies fused, as passion took over, he wondered how he was going to live without her. And as they lay in throbbing silence afterwards, their limbs too heavy to move, their hearts slowly getting back to normal, Oliver knew that this had been the best time ever—and, judging by Anna's wild climactic response, the best for her, too.

It wasn't until she cuddled into the crook of his arm, making little cooing sounds of satisfaction, stroking her fingers over his sweat-slicked chest, that it occurred to him that maybe this was what had been behind her offer of help. Maybe this had been in her mind all along—maybe she'd seen it as a way of getting through to him, of getting their marriage back on track.

So that she could wheedle even more money out of him!

His blood ran cold.

CHAPTER SIX

ANNA couldn't sleep. She lay in bed and watched a silver crescent of moon move slowly across the velvet darkness of the sky. She had thought, mistakenly as it turned out, that after their fantastic lovemaking Oliver would suggest she move back in to his bed. She had stupidly hoped it was the beginning of a reconciliation.

She could still feel the touch of his hands and mouth on her body, still feel a churning in her stomach, a pulsing through her veins. She clenched her thighs tightly together, nursing the sensation at their apex. How could Oliver do this to her? How could he leave her in limbo like this?

After their fast and furious enjoyment of each other's bodies, they'd gone back to their sorting and packing, but the atmosphere between them had changed. It had become charged with electric tension, she was far too aware of him to concentrate on her task.

All she'd wanted to do was feast her eyes on him. She'd wanted to touch, to share, to feel, to continue this unexpected togetherness. But Oliver, sadly, seemed to regret his actions, beginning work with renewed vigour, practically ignoring her, not stopping until it was time for them to go back home to the meal Mrs Green always had ready for them.

After they'd eaten, he shut himself in his study to

read his emails and check on the days running of his business. His computer was networked to his various branches and he'd explained to Anna that without it he would not have been able to take so much time off work.

He finally surfaced at half past ten and there were deep lines of strain etched into his face. 'I'm going to bed,' he announced abruptly.

Anna had been reading a book while she waited for him, and now she looked up in disappointment. 'Don't you even want a drink?'

'No, nothing.' But the look he gave her didn't suggest nothing. It suggested he'd like to make love to her again and a quick heat invaded her limbs. She wanted to say, I'll come to bed with you, but she knew that the suggestion had to come from him.

It didn't. He'd gone straight to his room, and here she was unable to sleep for thinking about Oliver, thinking what it would be like to share his bed again, to have him make crazy, passionate love to her every night, the way he used to.

He had proved this afternoon that he found it hard to resist her, so why was he ignoring her now? Did he deeply regret what had happened? Was he castigating himself? Was he still of the opinion that she was after his money?

It was going to be difficult working together with sexual tension like this sparking between them. Had he thought of that when he let his male urges get the better of him? If it was to be an on-off thing, she would rather it had never happened—in fact, she wouldn't have gone along with it had she known.

Anna was down to breakfast before Oliver, and

when he joined her his shadowed eyes suggested that he hadn't slept much either.

And when they got to the house he carefully busied himself in a separate room. He was making it very obvious that there was going to be no repeat of what had happened yesterday.

When, a short time later, she heard a sound behind her Anna couldn't stop her heart skipping several beats. It did it automatically whenever he was near. She whirled around with a smile on her face, but her smile faded and her heart crashed dangerously when she saw who stood there.

'What are you doing here?' asked Melanie, her blue eyes coldly questioning. 'Where's Oliver?'

'He's around,' Anna told her calmly. 'I'm helping him sort his father's stuff.'

'And what gives you that right?' she demanded haughtily. 'I thought you only came for Uncle Edward's funeral. Why are you still here? I sincerely hope you're not trying to worm your way back into Oliver's life, because it won't work. Oliver doesn't love you any more—if he ever did.'

'I think what Oliver and I do is none of your business,' retorted Anna, straightening her back and eyeing Melanie coldly. She was relieved when Oliver chose that moment to come into the room because she didn't relish this type of conversation. She wasn't up to discussing her husband with his ex-girlfriend. Or was it current girlfriend? She suddenly wasn't sure.

When Melanie flung herself into his arms and lifted her face expectantly to his, and when Oliver obediently kissed her, a stab of jealousy pierced the shattered pieces of Anna's heart. She couldn't bear to see them together, especially as less than twenty-four hours earlier he'd been making love to her.

Why had she given herself so eagerly? she asked herself. Why hadn't she remembered Melanie? Why had she let her feelings run away with her? Why hadn't she been stronger?

The brief kiss over, Melanie pouted delicately. 'You should have asked me to help you, Oliver. I had no idea you were getting rid of any of Uncle Edward's things. In fact, I can't see the point unless—' she frowned '—you're planning to buy yourself a whole heap of new stuff. Rosemary said that—'

'Rosemary?' he interrupted harshly. 'She's still hanging around?'

Anna saw the way his eyes narrowed suspiciously, the way his body froze.

'I don't know what you mean hanging around. But I did see her the other day,' Melanie admitted.

'She's staying locally?'

'In Cambridge, I believe,' she answered. 'Why, is it important?'

'Which hotel?' he snapped, not bothering to answer her question.

'I don't know, but we're having lunch together tomorrow. I could—'

'No need; I have nothing to say to her.' But the grimness of his jaw suggested quite the opposite.

Melanie shrugged her narrow shoulders. 'She's still pretty worked up about the will.'

'Is that what she said? Has she asked you to put in a good word for her?'

'Of course not,' said Melanie. 'Don't fret yourself, Oliver.'

He turned away impatiently. 'Anna, how about some coffee?'

He was asking *her* to make coffee for him and Melanie! It was like asking her to accept that they were lovers. Anna wanted to refuse but what good would it do her? Her face was darkly furious, though, as she left the room, and all the while she was out she kept picturing the two of them together.

And her misgivings were justfied when she returned and found them sitting on the leather chesterfield. Oliver's arm was about Melanie's shoulders and she looked as though she'd been crying. But when she looked at Anna there was a light of triumph in her eyes and it wasn't hard to see that they'd been crocodile tears.

'Here we are.' Anna tried to sound cheerful as she put the tray on the table, but it was all she could do to pour Melanie's coffee and hand it to her civilly.

And when Oliver announced that he was taking Melanie out for lunch and probably wouldn't be back, she gave an inward groan of despair. 'She's very upset over my father,' he explained. 'Coming here has brought back memories.'

I bet, thought Anna. Memories of what she'd once had with Oliver, what she wanted again, what she was going out of her way to get.

'There's no need for you to stay, either,' he said, with a note of concern. 'You deserve some time to yourself, you've been working hard.'

As far as Anna was concerned, it wasn't work. It had been pleasure simply being in Oliver's company.

She'd begun to hope for something more from their relationship; she'd begun to think they were mending bridges that had once seemed beyond repair, especially after yesterday.

But Melanie had swiftly put paid to that—and, if Melanie was to be believed, she'd been looking after his needs anyway. Perhaps the reason for Oliver making love to her was frustration because the blonde hadn't been around. He'd been using her as a substitute.

The thought was like a solid punch in the stomach; it almost had her doubling over with pain. 'Thank you, but I think I'll stay,' she said tightly. 'I have nothing else to do.'

'No, you can't do that,' protested Melanie with surprising vehemence. 'You need to take time off as well. You know what they say about all work and no play.'

Anna glanced at Oliver and saw him nodding his agreement. Did that mean he thought she was dull? There had certainly been no dullness about their love-making yesterday. She had responded uninhibitedly—she'd had no choice—it had been like instantaneous combustion. She'd had no control over her actions. And nor had he.

So what game was he playing?

'I might. I'll see,' she said.

'You really ought to make some time for yourself,' declared Melanie firmly.

'My sentiments entirely,' added Oliver.

When they had gone, Anna found that she didn't want to stay after all. She wandered up to the bedroom they'd used but simply looking at the still crumpled sheets aroused a torrent of anger.

All that had driven him had been need. He'd used her. She ought to have realised that last night when he didn't even kiss her before he went to bed. She smoothed the sheets automatically, resolving never to let herself get into this situation again.

She returned to Weston Lodge but it was Mrs Green's day off and she didn't feel like making herself any lunch so she decided it was time to pay her parents a visit—until she remembered that she didn't have her car, that it was still sitting outside the cottage in Ireland.

Her parents lived in the depths of the countryside on the other side of Cambridge, not even on a bus route. A taxi would be horrendously expensive, so what other course did it leave her?

There was Edward's car, of course, tucked in its garage up at the Hall—his Land Rover, too. Why not take one of those? Oliver had said he was going to sell them but he'd done nothing yet and she felt sure he wouldn't mind. He'd left the keys to the Hall with her and she'd seen the car keys hanging up in the kitchen.

In the end she took the Land Rover, feeling that the Rolls was a little too much for her, but when she got to her parents' they weren't in and she cursed her stupidity. She ought to have phoned. Mindless going all that way on the spur of the moment.

It wasn't her day, she decided. She'd try her brother, and if he wasn't at his office then she'd—what would she do? Lunch somewhere alone? Go to the cinema? Do what? It was amazing how lost she felt.

During the last few days she'd come to rely on Oliver's presence, had almost begun to feel secure— in his friendship, if nothing more. Now she wasn't so sure. Melanie had only to lift her finger and he'd gone running. What did that tell her?

She shook her head to try and clear it of such unwanted thoughts and headed back towards Cambridge.

Chris was in and pleased to see her. 'I thought you were still in Ireland. I'm about to have a late lunch. Do you want to join me or have you eaten?'

'It's what I was banking on,' she said, giving her brother an extra big hug.

'Hey, what's that for? Do I sense a need to talk? Is all well with you and Oliver?'

Anna grimaced, she hadn't realised that she was giving herself away. 'I'll tell you over lunch.'

And she told him the whole sorry story.

'Oh, Lord,' he exclaimed. 'I never realised it would cause this much trouble.' Chris put down his knife and fork and looked at her anxiously. 'You have told him what the money was for?'

Anna shook her head.

'Why not? Heavens, Anna, you can't put your marriage in jeopardy because of me.' He shook his head, his navy eyes worried.

'He wouldn't listen,' Anna admitted sadly. 'He thought the worst. And dammit, Chris, if he can think that of his own wife then it doesn't say much for the state of our marriage, does it? I thought trust came into these things. Huh!' she exclaimed contemptuously. 'He doesn't trust me any further than he can throw me. Besides, his old girlfriend's back in his life.'

Anna hadn't realised exactly how much she was giving away until her brother put his hand on hers across the table. 'Calm down, sis,' he said anxiously. 'I'm sure you must be mistaken. Dawn said she'd never seen a man so much in love as Oliver.'

'Maybe Oliver was, but Oliver's not any more,' she retorted bitterly.

'You're sure of that?'

'Positive.'

'I still think you should tell him. I've had a part payment; I'm back on track and I'll soon be able to repay the money.'

'It's not the point, Chris.' But how she wished her brother had never asked for help in the first place. It would have saved her so much heartache. On the other hand, it was best she'd found out what Oliver was like sooner rather than later.

She'd heard of girls who had control freaks as husbands, men who demanded to know where every penny was spent, what they'd been doing with their time and who with. Wanting to run their lives for them. Was Oliver like that? Was this the tip of the iceberg? Would things have got worse? Was she well rid of him?

'I think it's entirely the point,' insisted her brother. 'You're as unhappy as hell. You've changed since I last saw you. You were so vibrant—now look at you. You look like death warmed up. Do Mum and Dad know your marriage is on the rocks?'

'No,' she answered with a wry grimace. 'I've just been over there, actually, but they were out.'

'It will gut them.'

'I know,' she said with a heavy sigh. 'It's why I've kept quiet.'

'You mean you were hoping it would blow over, that you might get back together?'

'Something like that.'

'He's an idiot if he lets you go.'

'Maybe Oliver never loved me,' she said ruefully. 'His father said he married me on the rebound, I'm beginning to think he was right.'

'So why did he finish with this other woman?'

Anna's eyes flashed. 'The money thing again.'

Chris's breath hissed out loudly and he shook his head. 'The man has a complex. No wonder you're confused. Do you still love him?'

Anna lifted her slender shoulders. 'I don't know.'

'Which means you do. I think you should give him one more chance. Tell him about me, tell him I asked you to keep it a secret, and if that doesn't work then...' He spread his hands expansively. 'Then send him to me. I'll make him see sense.'

'But don't you see, Chris? I don't want him back on those terms. He should never have doubted me in the first place.'

'I agree. I've met the most wonderful girl in the world and I'd trust her with my life. I really would. I guess that's true love.'

'Oh, Chris.' Anna's eyes opened wide. 'You must have been dying to tell me and I've been rabbiting on about my own woes. I'm sorry. What's her name and where did you meet her? Tell me everything.'

* * *

When Anna eventually got home Oliver was waiting for her. His eyes were hard and cold, his whole body as taut as a violin string. 'Where the hell have you been?'

Anna frowned as she felt a cold shiver run down her spine. The words 'control freak' sprang to mind. 'What does it matter to you?'

'I see you took my father's Land Rover.'

'So that's the issue, is it?' she asked with lifted brows. 'I was supposed to have asked permission.'

'Now you're being ridiculous,' he snapped. 'You did say you might stay on at the Hall, I couldn't find you, I was worried.'

Oliver worried! That was a laugh. 'I'm sorry, but there was no one to ask,' she tossed coolly. 'I've been prisoner here long enough; I thought it was time I went out.'

'Prisoner?' His brows curved into a disbelieving arc.

'In that I don't have my car.'

'I see. I can't recall you saying that it was an inconvenience.'

And it hadn't been, up until now, but she wasn't going to tell him that. 'I decided to visit my parents. Do you have a problem with that?'

Oliver's eyes narrowed. 'How are they?'

Anna shrugged. 'Actually, they weren't in. So I had lunch with Chris instead.'

'The phantom brother?'

Anna didn't like the sarcasm in his voice and her eyes flashed. 'The very same.'

'When am I going to meet him?'

'I think never, considering our marriage is over,'

she retorted sharply and angrily. She had thought on the way home that perhaps Chris was right and she ought to make Oliver listen to the truth. But his attitude now made her swiftly change her mind. He wouldn't believe her if she wrote it in blood.

'That's a pity. I think Chris and I would have had plenty to talk about.'

'Like whether I gave the money to him or Tony, is that what you mean?' she asked caustically, while trying to ignore her fierce swell of unbidden desire.

What was it about Oliver that whenever they argued she felt this insane urge to make love to him? It always happened. Was it the fire in his eyes, the slow burn in his cheeks, the tautness of his body? Whatever, it was doing things to her that shouldn't be allowed to happen, not any longer.

'Mmm, Tony,' he said thoughtfully. 'Have you seen him recently?'

Her eyes shot sparks of fierce anger. 'You know damn well I haven't. I've been nowhere since I got here.'

His look was disbelieving but for some reason he didn't press the issue. Instead, he said, 'Maybe you should keep the Land Rover as a runaround. I hadn't realised that you felt tied. Why didn't you take the Roller? It would have created much more of an impression.'

'For whom? There's no one I want to impress, Oliver.' She'd had enough of this conversation. 'How did your lunch with Melanie go?'

He smiled for the first time since she'd got home and Anna felt swift daggers of jealousy. She tried to tell herself that she couldn't possibly be jealous when

she wasn't in love with Oliver any more, but it made
no difference. She was jealous. The green-eyed mon-
ster reared its head every time she thought about
Oliver and Melanie together.

'We went to The Riverside. They serve excellent
food and—'

'Yes, I know. You used to take me there,' she cut
in shortly. They had agreed it was their special
place—and now he'd taken Melanie. How cruel could
he get?

'So I did,' he said, with a self-conscious laugh as
though he'd just remembered.

'So where is she now? I expected you to spend the
rest of the day with her.'

'She had other plans.'

Anna thought he sounded disappointed. 'Have you
mended your differences? Are you two an item
again?'

'Why do you ask?' Dark brows rode high. 'Does
it bother you?'

'Not in the least,' she lied. 'I'm only mildly curious. You don't have to tell me.'

Nor did he, which piqued her beyond measure.

Mrs Green had prepared everything for their supper; all Anna had to do was grill the chicken breasts
and toss the salad. Oliver shut himself in his study
and told her to give him a call when it was ready.

She was unprepared, therefore, when she turned
around from the sink and found him watching her.
Her hand flew subconsciously to her throat. 'You
gave me a fright. How long have you been there?'
For a fraction of a second she'd seen a gleam in those

golden eyes, gone in an instant, possibly imagined, but it nevertheless made her jittery inside.

'Long enough to know that you'd look even better in that overall if you wore nothing underneath.'

Anna had donned one of Mrs Green's tabards to protect her silk blouse and she had a quick mental image of herself in that alone. It would cover front and back—but from the side…?

She felt herself blushing furiously. She didn't want Oliver thinking this way about her, not now he was friendly with Melanie again. What was he trying to do, play one off against the other? And for what reason?

'I thought you were working.'

'I couldn't concentrate.'

Because he was thinking about Melanie? Wondering who it was she had gone off to see? But if she was planning to use her again in the other girl's absence, then he was in for a big disappointment. She wasn't going to make the same mistake twice.

Except that her insides had already begun to sizzle at the mere thought of him touching her, of his hands sliding beneath the tabard and touching her breasts which had peaked beneath the thin silk.

'Supper won't be long,' she said coolly, surprising herself by the steadiness of her voice. 'If you want to go and pour yourself a drink and relax while you're waiting…'

'Good idea. G&T for you?'

'I don't think so.' She needed a clear head to get through the next hour or so; she had to be on her guard lest she weaken and let him slip through her defences the way he had yesterday.

She was still puzzled as to why he had made love to her so wonderfully one minute and then virtually ignored her the next. Admittedly, they'd always been good in bed together; it had been a dream part of their marriage, perhaps the best part. Perhaps that was all they'd had—a sexual attraction which they'd mistaken for love. And perhaps he still was sexually attracted to her, and sometimes he fought it, sometimes he didn't.

Oliver returned bearing two tall crystal glasses chinking with ice and a slice of lemon. 'I don't like drinking alone.'

She had to admit that the gin and tonic was both delicious and refreshing. The heat in the kitchen wasn't entirely due to the cooker and she swallowed her drink more quickly than was wise, making her head feel fuzzy and her mind not quite as sharp as it had been a few minutes ago.

'Another one?' Oliver was only halfway through his.

'No, thank you.'

'Shall I open a bottle of wine to go with our meal?'

She looked at him sharply. 'What is this? Are you trying to get me drunk?'

'Perish the thought,' he said with a flicker of a smile. 'I like my women to know what they're doing.'

My women! How many did he have? Were there others besides herself and Melanie? Or was it a figure of speech and she was overreacting? She guessed the latter—hoped it was the latter. 'I prefer to be in control of myself as well,' she said primly.

'Except that you don't always manage it.'

He lifted a knowing brow and Anna's cheeks

flushed again. Did he have to remind her how easily she gave way to desire? But it was only with him, never anyone else—didn't he know that? Tony hadn't aroused her even half as much as Oliver did—as Oliver used to, she corrected herself quickly.

'Don't be embarrassed, it's one of the things I like most about you.'

'Still?' she asked, managing to inject a note of scepticism into her voice.

'Some things never go away, Anna.' There was a deep suggestiveness in his tone that had her looking at him quickly. But his face was impassive. 'Like the smell of burning. It takes ages for it to—'

With a shriek Anna turned to the grill and pulled out the charred remains of the chicken. How could she have let him distract her to this extent?

'It's your fault,' she exclaimed crossly. 'Why couldn't you have kept out of the way?'

'You look delightful when you're angry.'

She groaned inwardly wishing he wouldn't play up to her like this.

'You won't think I'm delightful if I throw it all over you,' she declared fiercely. 'You'd best get out while I dispose of the mess.'

'Why don't you let me do it?' He put down his glass and took a step towards her.

But Anna didn't want him interfering; she wanted him out. 'No! Just go, will you?' She was overreacting again but she couldn't help it. He'd worked her up into such a state that if he came any nearer she would explode.

But he did come nearer. And he tried to take the

grillpan out of her hand, and when she resisted the two pieces of burnt chicken skidded to the floor.

'Now look what you've done,' she yelled, and to her dismay she burst into tears.

CHAPTER SEVEN

OLIVER was horrified to see Anna crying.

He hated any woman to cry. It made him feel helpless. Should he console her or do as she'd asked and get out of the way? Sanity said he should go; instinct made him take the pan off her and pull her into his arms.

'It's not the end of the world,' he said soothingly. 'We'll eat out. It's not a problem.'

'Where? The Riverside?' she snapped.

He winced as she drove home the mistake he'd made in taking Melanie there. It had been Melanie's idea and he hadn't been thinking straight. All he'd known was that he'd been tormented ever since he'd lost his head and made love to Anna.

It had made him crave more, crave the life they'd once had, but his marriage had gone badly wrong. And so he'd grasped Melanie's suggestion as the diversion he so badly needed.

Melanie was devastated by Edward's death—she'd loved her godfather dearly—and despite her faults Oliver felt he couldn't completely abandon her at this critical time. But he hadn't enjoyed himself and he had in fact been relieved when Melanie announced that she had somewhere else to go.

When he got home and found Anna missing, he'd gone crazy. He'd been so looking forward to spending more time with her, even though he knew it would torture his soul.

What he'd really wanted to do when she did return was sweep her up in his arms and kiss her senseless. But he knew that would solve nothing, so he'd conjured up his anger in order to distance himself from her—and had succeeded for a short time.

But in his study, he'd been unable to concentrate. All he could see on the computer screen was Anna's gorgeous face, those wonderfully alive eyes, that flamboyant hair, the wide, infinitely kissable mouth.

It had forced him to find her and he'd stood in the kitchen doorway for a good couple of minutes before she spotted him. His fantasy of seeing her in the bright yellow tabard and nothing else almost had him pouncing on her and ripping her clothes off. Maybe if she hadn't turned when she did he would have done.

Even now, holding her, soothing her, there was nothing calm about the parts of him that she couldn't see. He felt tortured by fire, by a need so intense it was painful. 'We can go wherever you like.' Bed, preferably.

'I'm not hungry.'

Nor was he—except for love. Or was it lust? He hated that word and yet he knew deep down inside that it was lust that drove him, that had always driven him where Anna was concerned. He'd committed the cardinal crime of letting his heart rule his head when he'd asked her to marry him. Not even his heart. It was the bit between his legs that was the problem.

His father had done the same thing with Rosemary. He'd been besotted by a pretty face and a nice pair

of legs and look where that had got him. No wonder
Edward had been appalled when he saw his son making exactly the same mistake.

'You need to eat,' he told Anna firmly. 'You've
lost weight; you can't afford to lose any more.' And
still he held her, and still his damned male hormones
played riot.

'As if that matters to you.' Anna finally tried to
struggle free.

But he needed to hold her, he needed to feel her
exciting body against him. He needed to dream a little
longer. 'I care whether you're looking after yourself,'
he said gruffly, forcing the words past a choking knot
in his throat.

'I can't think why,' she retorted.

That hurt, her thinking that he didn't care any
longer. He supposed he deserved it, considering he'd
walked out on her. It had been a bad move, but he'd
needed time to think about what she'd done. Before
he'd reached any decisions, though, she'd upped and
left—and he hadn't a clue where she'd gone. The discovery had left him stunned.

He'd wanted to look for her immediately but his
father had persuaded him that to do so would create
more problems in the future. 'Women only ever want
what they can get out of a man,' Edward had said
firmly. 'They never change. They might promise you
the earth, you might even think for a little while that
they've changed, but it never lasts. They're like leop-
ards.'

And so Oliver had bowed to his father's wisdom.
It hadn't stopped him from ringing Dawn and per-
suading her to tell him where Anna was, and maybe

if Melanie hadn't revealed the same flaw in her nature then he might have gone after her, it had made him think twice and then three times and then four, and in the end he had convinced himself that he'd done the right thing.

'If you don't want to go out, Anna—' he lifted her chin so that he could look into her face '—then at least let me do us something to eat.' The tears were gone but her eyes were still pink-rimmed. Lord, how he wanted to bed her. 'What were we having with the chicken?' he asked, wondering how he managed to keep the longing out of his voice.

'Salad,' she answered thinly, 'and potatoes.'

'So how about I make us a potato omelette to go with the salad?' he asked, deliberately cheerful. 'You run along and freshen up, and I'll sort everything out here.'

He was afraid she'd refuse, that she'd race up to her bedroom and stay there for the rest of the evening. But finally she heaved a sigh and gave him a weak, tremulous smile. 'OK.'

When she came back down Anna had changed into a rust-coloured all-in-one trouser suit. It fastened with a zip down the front and he wondered if she knew how tempting that zip was.

At first glance, the suit looked demure and safe with its high neck and short sleeves. It was probably the reason she'd worn it. But that zip! He couldn't take his eyes off it.

Oliver imagined himself pulling it down and revealing slow inch by slow inch her delicately scented skin, skin so pale and soft and smooth that it excited him just to touch it. And the thought of exposing those perfectly rounded breasts which fit so beautifully into his palms caused an ache deep in his groin.

He groaned—he couldn't help himself—and Anna looked at him with a swift frown. 'Is something wrong?'

Everything! Don't you know that? From somewhere, he managed to drag up a wry smile, and he patted his stomach. 'Excuse me, I'm hungry.' He wasn't so sure she believed it was a grumble of hunger, though.

'I thought we'd eat in here,' he said. 'Less trouble.' And less chance of intimacy. There were no cosy seats to relax in afterwards, just two kitchen stools and a granite breakfast bar.

But it was still a mistake. The seats didn't have to be comfortable, there didn't have to be candles and music—the very fact that he was sitting next to Anna was enough. They could have been anywhere, in an igloo in the frozen wastes of Siberia or in the most romantic of restaurants in the most romantic place in the world and it would have been the same.

He should never have insisted they eat together. He should have gone out; he shouldn't have come back. How was he going to get through the rest of the evening without giving way to the ferocious desire that was twisting him into knots?

'Nice omelette,' she said. 'Your cooking skills have improved.'

He knew she was referring to a disastrous meal he had cooked them early on in their marriage. It wasn't that he was a bad cook—he'd always liked to cook for himself whenever Mrs G let him anywhere near the kitchen. But on that particular day—when he'd wanted so much to impress Anna—everything had gone wrong.

From the overdone pheasant to the collapsed soufflé. Anna had gallantly eaten everything he'd put in front of her, but they'd ended up in fits of laughter. One thing had led to another, kisses had led to making love on the dining room floor, and it was yet another fantastic memory to add to his store. 'That was a day I shall never forget,' he admitted.

Anna stilled for a fraction of a second.

'I've never cooked soufflé again, or eaten pheasant,' he admitted.

'It wasn't a complete disaster.'

It was his turn to stop breathing.

Was she referring to them making love?

'I'd have probably ended up in tears if it had happened to me,' she said, 'whereas you simply laughed.'

And was that all she remembered? 'You laughed at me first,' he reminded her.

'Because you looked so stricken. I had to do something to lighten the moment.'

'How about some of that laughter now?' He hadn't meant to say that; he didn't want her to think that he intended the day to end the same as that other one had. 'I mean, I'm sorry if I laid into you earlier. I seem to make a habit of ruining things.'

'It's all right,' she said with a vague shrug and an even vaguer smile.

'No, it's not all right,' he said, bouncing his palms off the worktop to give emphasis to his words. 'I shouldn't have yelled at you for going out. I'd not given a thought to the fact that you had no transport. I'm sorry, Anna.'

'You're forgiven,' she said demurely. 'Finish your omelette before it goes cold.'

But he was the one who didn't feel like eating now. Sitting so close that their elbows occasionally touched, so close that if he opened his legs just that little bit wider his thigh would brush hers, was doing dangerous things to him.

With an effort, he turned the conversation to everyday subjects, and they both managed to finish their meal. 'Would you like another gin?' he asked as he put down his knife and fork.

Anna shook her head. 'I'd prefer a coffee.'

'You're not turning teetotal on me?'

'You know I don't drink much.'

'But another one won't hurt. Come on, Anna. Let's relax at the end of a wearing day.'

'It hasn't been wearing for me,' she said. 'In fact, it was quite relaxing until…'

She'd come home and he'd given her a third degree. He felt suitably chastised. 'In that case, you make your coffee while I mix my drink.' He left the kitchen gasping for air. It was stupid, he knew. This was the woman he was going to divorce. What right had she to make him feel like this?

That's right, lay the blame on Anna, accused his conscience. She hasn't done anything; it's all in your mind. A mind which was as filled with confusion as the endless wires in a telephone junction box.

When he returned to the kitchen, Anna had stacked the dishes in the dishwasher, spooned instant coffee into a china mug, filled the kettle, and was waiting for it to boil.

'You didn't have to clear away,' he said.

'We couldn't leave it for Mrs Green.'

'I would have done it later.'

Her eyes flashed in exasperation. 'Will you stop fussing, Oliver? It's done now.' She turned to the kettle and poured water over the coffee, added milk, stirred it, and then looked back at him.

Even those simplest actions fascinated him, made him realise what he was giving up. And all of a sudden he didn't know whether he could.

'I think I might take it up to my room,' said Anna.

'No, Anna, don't.' And without even stopping to think what message his actions would convey he reached out and took her into his arms.

CHAPTER EIGHT

ANNA had the distinct feeling that if she didn't push Oliver away she was going to regret it.

He'd been on edge all evening, right from the moment he'd consoled her for dropping the stupid chicken. She hadn't been married to him for six months for nothing. She knew perfectly well how aroused he was, how much he wanted to make love to her.

The heat from him as they'd sat eating dinner had been tremendous. If they'd touched, he would have set her on fire. In fact, on the few occasions when his arm accidentally brushed hers, it had taken all her self-control not to move away. She'd almost expected to see her skin sear and shrivel.

'I think we should make ourselves comfortable in the sitting room,' he said, his voice a low warning growl that should have had her running for safety, but instead she allowed him to lead her from the kitchen.

Once in the other room, however, Anna quickly twisted away from him and dropped into one of the deep, plump armchairs. She saw from his frown that this wasn't exactly what he'd had in mind, but he said nothing, taking the matching, facing chair instead.

A fatal mistake, Anna realised at once. Oliver had always professed that he enjoyed watching her more than any other pastime. She too had once enjoyed being the object of his desire, had liked the feelings he aroused in her simply by looking at her. He could undress her with his eyes, make love to her with his eyes. It was a form of foreplay that she'd never experienced with anyone else, and doubted she ever would again.

Even now she could feel a stirring deep in her womb and deliberately she kept her eyes averted. But Oliver never took his eyes off her. Those wonderful tawny-gold eyes that had been her downfall in the very beginning.

Her coffee was growing cold but she didn't want to move for fear their eyes might meet and he would discover that she was as aroused as he, that she wanted to make love as much as he did. What a fateful night this was turning out to be.

'Drink your coffee.'

It was as though he had read her thoughts. She glanced across at him before she reached for it. Fatal. She couldn't drag her eyes away. They locked into his with all the force of a magnet on steel.

'Come here,' he whispered.

Anna swallowed and moistened her mouth, and her eyes darkened. 'What for?'

'As if you need to ask,' he growled.

The magnet pulled and Anna followed, her steps slow and resisting, but her eyes never leaving his. She was going to drown in them, she knew, and yet slavishly she went to her doom.

When she reached him he gave a groan and pulled her on to his lap. 'You're a witch, do you know that? An irresistible witch. You make me do things I hadn't planned to do; you make me break my own rules.'

Their mouths came together, a slow, sensual tasting

that lasted for ever. And then Oliver bade her kneel in front of him and he took the tab of her zip between his teeth and began to slowly draw it down.

It was one of the most erotic things he had ever done and Anna arched instinctively towards him, her breath coming in short, sharp gasps.

Oliver shuddered and his trembling fingers followed the line of the zip, stroking, appreciating, reacquainting, sending her female hormones into panic. And when he reached the bottom he finally lost patience.

He grabbed a handful of material in each hand and yanked it down over her shoulders, disposing of her bra with equally indecent haste, not content until her breasts were free of the restraining fabric, free for him to take into his palms, free for him to stroke his thumb deliciously over her erect and hungry nipples.

His teeth nipped and tortured, making her whimper with pleasure and ache for more. She held his head against her, loving the feel of his thick springy hair through her fingers.

It was wrong to let herself get carried away when there was no hope for the future, but wrong went out of the window when Oliver kissed her like this. It was almost as though he was worshipping her breasts.

He touched, he stroked; he licked, he sucked, and when he looked up at her there was a feverish light in his eyes. They were a more intense gold than she'd ever seen them, filled with such hot desire that it sent fresh shivers right through her.

'Oh, Oliver.' It was a cry she couldn't contain.

'Oh, Oliver, what?' he asked, still suckling.

'What you do to me.'

'What *I* do to you?' He lifted his head then. 'Have you any idea how I feel? You've worked your spell on me again, made me realise what I've been missing. This side of our marriage was never in dispute.'

Anna stiffened, their rare moment of togetherness in danger of being ruined—if it wasn't already. 'Are you saying that this is all you've ever wanted me for?' She sucked in her breath as she waited for his answer.

'It was an important part of it, Anna,' he admitted, his thumbs still stroking her now screamingly sensitised nipples. 'A very important part. I firmly believe that if the physical element goes out of a marriage it quickly disintegrates.'

Which told her precisely nothing. Theirs had disintegrated regardless of the fact that they still excited each other. It put his theory firmly out of the running, and suggested, even though he hadn't actually put it into words, that the delights of the flesh was all he'd ever wanted her for.

And she would be a fool to let it continue when he'd kick her out again as soon as she'd served her purpose. It made her wonder which purpose. Helping him sort his father's belongings? Or satisfying his carnal desires?

Surely he had Melanie for that? Or was it because he'd been with Melanie and she'd left him frustrated that he was doing this now? The thought was like a bitter pill too large to swallow and she shook her head. 'I can't go on with this, Oliver. You're right— sex is good between us, but it's not high on my list of priorities.'

Much!

'This is a mistake,' she added more quietly now as

she tried to back away from him. 'I don't know why I let myself get into this situation.'

Some of the light went out of his eyes. 'I thought it was because you wanted to?'

'I did, I do, but—it isn't right. We're on the verge of a divorce, Oliver. Have you forgotten that? How can we still make love?'

'I guess some things become a habit,' he admitted ruefully.

'Well, it's one habit you'll have to get out of,' she retorted, as she jumped to her feet and began tugging her suit back into place. Her bra was ignored. All she wanted to do was hide her pulsing breasts from his greedy eyes.

But it was the most awkward piece of clothing she owned and as she struggled to get her arms into the sleeves Oliver sprang up. 'Here, let me help.'

And begin the torture all over again!

'I can manage,' she said determinedly.

But it wasn't easy, especially as he stood and watched, especially when she saw the way his fingers clenched as she finally slid the zip back into place and there wasn't an inch of her body left for him to feast his eyes on. And yet she felt oddly sad that the evening which had promised such excitement had ended like this.

'I think I might go and catch up on some more work, after all,' he announced gruffly

Their eyes met and held and Anna saw sadness but she hardened her heart. She'd done the right thing. Emotional blackmail wasn't the answer. 'Don't do it on my account. I'm going to bed.'

But not to sleep, not for a long time. She'd had so

many sleepless nights since their marriage ended. So many nights when she'd lain awake thinking about Oliver and the good times they'd had. Could still have, if their experience earlier was anything to go by. But what good would it do? How would it help when at the end of the day he'd still divorce her?

The next morning Oliver was waiting for her at the breakfast table. He looked devastatingly casual in a pair of grey linen trousers, a blue shirt and a grey and blue cotton sweater—certainly not as though he was going to work up at the Hall.

Had he decided that their close proximity would be too much for him if she was going to insist that he keep his hands off her? Had he decided that putting distance between them was the only solution?

Anna didn't know whether to feel happy or sad. When she'd stopped him making love to her she hadn't wanted him to back off altogether, she'd simply wanted to cool things between them.

'I thought we'd have a change today,' he said cheerfully as she took her seat at the table.

Anna frowned, her heart spinning. So he wasn't rejecting her! 'What did you have in mind?'

'Maybe a trip on the river? Though it could be a tad cold. We could go into London, perhaps—shop, sightsee, take in a show?'

'I think you're forgetting I used to live in London,' she reminded him.

'As if I could forget anything about you.' His voice seemed to go down an octave as he spoke, his eyes warm as a summer day as they looked into hers.

Anna felt a tremor run through her. 'Actually, I am

homesick for the city. I think I'd like that.' There would be safety in crowds, unlike if they went river cruising when it would be just herself and Oliver. In London they'd be jostled and pushed and there'd be absolutely no chance of intimacy.

Even sorting Edward's stuff, there was always a forced togetherness which did nothing for her state of mind. A day away from it, a day doing something different, was exactly what she needed—what they both needed.

They caught the train and were in London by mid-morning and Anna thoroughly enjoyed strolling through the streets with Oliver. They explored the food hall in Harrods, ate lunch in style at Rules, one of London's oldest restaurants, and she tried on a blue and green chiffon evening dress which would be perfect around Christmas time. Although it was horrendously expensive Oliver persuaded her to buy it, and then settled the bill himself as she changed back into her street clothes.

'You shouldn't have done that,' she declared huffily. The expression on his face when he'd looked at her had frizzled her insides. It had suggested that he would get as much pleasure in stripping it off her as he would in seeing her in it.

Dark brows rose. 'I can't buy my wife clothes, is that what you're saying?'

'I'm no longer your wife,' she retorted.

His face shadowed but the next second he smiled with apparent unconcern. 'I can still buy you a present, can't I?'

Anna's pleasure was bittersweet. It wasn't quite the answer she would have liked.

They went to a show afterwards, an obscure musical that Anna didn't understand but which she pretended to enjoy, clapping energetically in all the right places and flashing Oliver approving glances.

All the big shows had been fully booked, this was the only one they'd been able to get tickets for, and over dinner afterwards Oliver said, 'You were very enthusiastic over that musical. I wasn't altogether sure it was your type.'

Anna wrinkled her nose. 'It wasn't. It wasn't yours either, was it?' They knew each too well to hide their true feelings.

'So has it spoilt your day?'

'Not at all,' she said immediately, fervently. 'I've thoroughly enjoyed myself. I feel guilty, though. You took time off work to organise things at the house and instead you're squiring me around.'

'Which I wouldn't have suggested if I hadn't wanted to do it. You're still a pleasure to be with.'

So why had he kicked her out of his life? Was this the moment to tell him about Chris, to explain exactly what she'd needed that thirty thousand pounds for? Would all be forgiven? Would she be satisfied with that? Or would she still feel disillusioned because he'd thought the worst of her in the first place?

'You're the sexiest woman in here, Anna, do you know that?' His voice had gone so low it sent shivers down her spine, her toes curling in her shoes 'I want you in my bed tonight. I can't live with you and not have you; it's driving me insane.'

Anna's hopes took a massive nosedive. He couldn't have made it any plainer what he wanted from her if he'd spelt it out in letters ten feet high. And once the house clearance was finished, it would be goodbye Anna.

Her eyes flashed a heated, brilliant green. 'If you can't handle my presence then perhaps I shouldn't stay. I'm not here for your convenience, Oliver; I thought I was helping with a particularly unpalatable job. If it's sex you're after, then ask Melanie—from what I can see, she'd be only too willing to oblige.'

He was clearly stunned by her reaction, his head jerking up, his eyes narrowed and questioning. 'You can't mean that, Anna?'

'Why can't I?'

'Because—because things are good between us.'

'You mean physically?' she asked sharply. 'If that's the only reason you accepted my offer, then I'll leave in the morning. You can finish off yourself or get Melanie to help.' She couldn't help throwing in the other woman's name again. 'She'd be delighted, I'm sure.'

'Let's leave Melanie out of this,' he growled.

'Why should we?' she shot back. 'I think she's very much a part of your life, despite what you say, and I don't think you need me.'

He closed his eyes for a moment as if trying to shut out her words. 'You really think that Melanie and I have got back together?'

Anna shrugged. 'It's how it looks.'

'Would it bother you if we had?'

It would hurt like hell, but she wasn't admitting it. 'Why should it when our marriage is over?' she asked instead. 'You're free to see whomever you like, do what you like with whomever you like. It has nothing to do with me any more. I think I'd like to go home,

Oliver.' She'd hardly touched her meal but it would choke her to try and eat now.

He didn't argue. He paid the bill and they left. They took a taxi to the station and neither of them spoke. But there was a half-hour wait for the train so they sat and drank coffee.

'Today was meant to be a happy occasion,' declared Oliver, swirling his drink vigorously in his cup. 'I wanted you to have a good time.'

'Which I have.'

'Until I spoiled it by admitting that your body drives me crazy,' he said with self-derision. 'Would it help if I apologised, Anna? If I said it was crass and insensitive of me to confess to such feelings— even if I felt them?'

Anna pulled a wry face and lifted her shoulders in a vague gesture. 'I'm flattered, but I don't understand. We're supposed to be separated. Why are you doing this to me?'

It was his turn to grimace. 'I guess there are some things that never go away.'

'Like sex, you mean?' she asked acidly. She tried to forget that it was all she'd thought about when she first met him. There had been an instant chemical flare of attraction, of desire, of goodness knew what, which they'd both mistaken for love.

Which was still there!

But it wasn't enough. A marriage needed more and she wasn't going to be sidetracked by that incredible passion again.

Oliver didn't answer her question. He looked pensively into his cup instead, holding it still now, and Anna guessed she had hit on the truth. She drank half of her coffee and then declared she needed to go to the loo. She didn't hurry and when she got back it was time for their train.

The journey was uncomfortably silent. There seemed nothing more to be said. It wasn't until they got home that Oliver asked whether she was still determined to leave.

'I'll stay and help until it's all done if you promise to behave,' she declared, looking him straight in the eye, making sure he knew she meant what she said. 'If you want me to, that is.'

Though why she was offering Anna had no idea. She had to be insane. It would be far safer to put as much distance between them as possible because, if the truth were known, she wanted his body as much as he wanted hers. And she had no doubt in her mind that it would always be that way.

'I'd like that.' Oliver nodded his agreement. 'But I can't—'

'Make any promises,' she finished for him. 'You don't have control over your male testosterone, is that what you're saying?'

'I guess I am.'

'So it will be up to me to keep you at arm's length? Very well, I can do that.' She spoke with confidence but her tingling nerves betrayed her real emotions. Keeping Oliver at bay would be like trying to ward off a hungry crocodile.

But, surprisingly, in the weeks that followed all went smoothly. Oliver never crossed the barriers she had rigidly imposed, though on several occasions she spotted him watching her hungrily.

His very real need of her caused her skin to burn

mercilessly, it sent a rash of scary emotions through her veins, and she had to busy herself elsewhere until the feelings went away.

Melanie came to see Oliver several times but on each occasion he told her that he was too busy to take her out, and that he didn't need any further help. Anna wondered how hard it was for him to deny his body what it craved.

If it was pure sex that drove him, surely Melanie could fulfil those needs? Or had she misjudged him? Did he want to give their marriage another go? Was that behind everything? And, if so, why hadn't he said? Why didn't he tell her what he was thinking, feeling, expecting?

Instead, most days he worked in silence, talking only of the work in hand, sometimes saying he'd never realised what a large task it was.

'You're forgetting that Edward's lifetime is here,' she said as Oliver sorted through file after file in his father's cabinets, while she kept busy packing the hundreds of books which Oliver wanted to keep.

'Are you telling me his whole life is being packed into carboard boxes? That this is the way we all end?'

'I guess it's something like that,' she agreed. 'It's sad, isn't it?'

'And I've had enough for today.' He lifted his arms above his head and stretched and Anna had an imbecilic urge to go to him, to press her hungry body close to his. This constant togetherness was telling on her, making her wonder whether she'd made the right decision.

And if it was telling on her, what was it doing to Oliver? She'd heard him prowling his room at night and once she'd heard him come to her door. He had stood there for a long time before he'd quietly gone back.

She'd become very tense, holding her breath, straining her ears, and wishing, much to her disgust, that he'd give up on his promise and come and make fantasic love to her.

Of course, if he had come in, she'd probably have ordered him straight out again—but the things it did to her simply thinking about it were enough to spin her mind into orbit.

But at least they never fell out. He was politeness itself, always courteous, always thoughtful, almost too much so. Sometimes she could have screamed at the correctness of his behaviour.

Then one day the perfect veneer crashed. She was on her knees on the upstairs landing carefully sorting sheets and pillowcases into sets when he came storming towards her, eyes like twin flames of fire. 'I should have known I couldn't trust you.'

Anna looked up at Oliver in frank amazement. 'What are you talking about? What am I supposed to have done now?' And she knew by the look on his face that it had to be something dire.

CHAPTER NINE

'I'M TALKING about family heirlooms.' Oliver didn't take his eyes off Anna's face for one single second. 'Diamonds and sapphires that belonged to my grandmother. My great-grandfather's gold hunter watch.'

'And what have they to do with me?' she asked indignantly, feeling an unhealthy chill steal down her spine.

'Do you dare to ask?' he thrust, his face red with rage, 'when you're the only person who's been left alone in this house since my father died?'

Anna went very still and very cold. 'You're suggesting I took them?'

'Who else?'

'Perhaps you'd like to search my room?' She found it hard to believe that Oliver was accusing her of theft. One minute he'd wanted to take her to bed; now he looked as though he'd like to strangle her with his bare hands.

Perhaps it was as well their marriage had ended.

This was a side of him she'd never seen before, at least not to this degree. He'd been angry about the money, but this time he was so enraged he was dancing on the balls of his feet and his golden eyes leapt with fire.

'As if that would turn up anything,' he tossed scornfully. 'We both know what's happened to the stuff, don't we? That little story about seeing your brother again was nothing more than a cover-up. Well, let me tell you, lady, this time you've gone too far. You had a legitimate excuse where the money was concerned, but not now.'

Anna tried her hardest to keep her dignity because she knew that yelling back at him would get her nowhere. But it was difficult when confronted by such a fierce and unrelenting condemnation.

'Oliver—'

'Don't!'

'Don't what?' she asked with a quick frown, wishing she hadn't felt the usual rush of adrenalin. She didn't need anything that would let her down.

'Don't try to get out of it.'

'You're jumping to conclusions.'

'I wish I was.'

'I haven't been anywhere near your father's precious jewellery. I didn't even know it existed.'.

'And I'm supposed to believe that, am I?'

'It's the truth.'

'So where the hell is it?'

'I don't know. If you don't want to believe me, that's your prerogative, but I've not seen it, I've not taken it, and I've not given it to Tony.'

For a fraction of a second he looked as though he wanted to believe her, but then his face hardened again, the rage continued. 'Tony's address—please.'

The 'please' was an afterthought, but he could have dropped to his knees and begged and it would have got him nowhere because she had no idea where Tony was. There had been no contact between them since he'd called off their engagement.

'I don't have it.'

'Liar!' he ground through his teeth.

Anger welled in Anna like a pan of milk on the boil. 'I have never lied to you, Oliver, and I'm not lying now. I don't know where your damn jewellery is. Maybe your father got rid of it. Have you seen it since he died? Where did he keep it?'

'In the safe—and yes, I've seen it.'

'So how was I—' Anna touched her two hands to her chest '—supposed to have taken it?'

'Because the key to the safe was with the rest of the house keys. It was labelled "cellar," apparently to confuse any potential burglar—but you had plenty of time to try all the keys before you took off in the Land Rover.'

'Are you sure it doesn't have a combination lock as well, which I'm miraculously supposed to have known?' she asked scathingly. 'This is ridiculous, Oliver. I'm not going to listen to any more of your accusations.'

Anna was so incensed she could have hit him. Had their relationship disintegrated to such a degree that Oliver thought her capable of stealing? She swept savagely past him, shaking off his arm as he tried to stop her, running quickly down the stairs, and storming out of the house.

At the Lodge she phoned for a taxi. Then she ran up to her room, snatched her case from the top of the wardrobe and flung her clothes into it. By the time she had finished, when every last possession was packed, the taxi had arrived.

Anna was still spitting fire as she left behind the house where she had once been so happy. The sad part was, Oliver hadn't even come after her.

She had a long wait at the airport. Turning up without a ticket or with any thought as to what time the next plane to Dublin was hadn't been a very good move. What it did do was give her time to think.

And at the end of all her thinking she knew that she was doing the right thing. Trying to mend bridges never worked. Twice Oliver had hurt her; he was not going to get the chance to do it again.

She was extremely bitter and deeply hurt that he'd thought her capable of stealing his family heirlooms. It proved that he'd never really loved her. Sex had, as she'd suspected, been the only common bond between them.

If he had loved her, he'd have trusted her implicitly; he wouldn't have thought for even one second that she was responsible. She was well rid of him.

It was late evening and dark when Anna arrived at the cottage. She was cold and tired and considerably out of sorts. She switched on the electric fire in the living room, filled the kettle and put that on to boil, then went upstairs and switched on the electric blanket.

That done, she emptied her suitcase unceremoniously on to the spare bed, telling herself that she would put everything away in the morning. She sorted out a nightdress and dressing gown and undressed in front of the fire downstairs. She made herself a mug of drinking chocolate, ate half a packet of biscuits, because she was suddenly starving, and then went to bed.

And amazingly she slept for ten hours. When she opened her eyes she couldn't remember where she was, but it didn't take long for the whole sorry affair to come flooding back.

Was Oliver glad to be rid of her, she wondered sadly, or would he come chasing after her demanding to know what she'd done with the jewellery? He'd be in for a big disappointment if he did, because she hadn't a clue what had happened to it.

What she did know was that her marriage to Oliver was definitely over; it was a part of her life best forgotten, a closed chapter. Today she was going to make a fresh start.

She jumped out of bed, showered and dressed, plucked a loaf out of the freezer, toasted a couple of slices, made a big pot of coffee, and spent the next hour thinking about her future.

For the time being, she'd stay here. She'd get a temporary job again in Wexford, and once she felt up to it she would return to London and settle back into her old life.

She'd made a big mistake in marrying Oliver, the biggest mistake of her life. Love at first sight, marrying on an impulse, rarely worked. She should have known that; she'd heard it said enough times.

Anna spent the day settling in, shopping for food, and generally making herself comfortable. Tomorrow she planned to go job-hunting.

Oliver couldn't believe he had accused Anna of stealing. The Anna he had married would never do something like that. Not in a million years. The money that she'd taken was a different matter altogether—she'd seen that as her own and he shouldn't have judged her now on the strength of what she'd done then.

But what was he to believe? Where had the jewellery gone? Who had taken it? Looking at the situation logically, Anna was the only one who'd had the keys to the Hall, who'd had the opportunity.

He'd seen the gems in the safe in the days after the funeral—and now they were gone—and Anna had paid a visit to her mysterious brother again! Everything pointed to her—and yet deep down inside him he knew that she wasn't guilty. He should never have accused her; he was the world's biggest idiot.

The trouble was she'd been driving him insane for weeks with her tempting body and her enticing green eyes. Every time she looked at him he'd felt a surge of hunger, a very real need to take her to bed again and make wild passionate love.

It kept him awake at night and tormented him during the day and the time had been drawing close when he could hang on to his emotions no longer. It was why he had snapped. Why he had accused her. Why he hadn't been thinking straight.

And now it was too late.

Oliver had wanted to stop Anna on that fateful day; he'd wanted to go after her, tell her he'd been mistaken, that he'd made his accusation in the heat of the moment and he knew he was wrong. But he also knew that he needed to give her time to calm down.

So he'd waited a couple of hours before returning to the Lodge—then had the shock of his life when he discovered that she'd disappeared and taken everything with her.

He had thought she meant that she wasn't staying at the Hall, not that she was leaving him altogether. Damn! What was he to do now? Was there any chance for them or had he well and truly ruined any future prospects?

Accusing Anna had been a moment of madness. His blind fury had killed her love for him. Killed it stone dead.

He poured a whisky and tossed it down his throat. In fact, he had several whiskies and he spent the rest of the day in a self-induced alcoholic haze, trying to convince himself that he was better off without Anna.

In the cold light of dawn, he knew differently. His head throbbed, his mouth felt like a sewer, but he knew that he had to find her. He loved her too much to let her go without a fight. She was sure to have gone to the cottage to pick up her car. With a bit of luck, she'd stay a few days and he would find her there.

When Melanie phoned just as he was about to ring up and book his flight, he cut her short. He didn't want Melanie hanging around any more. He'd done his duty; he'd been nice to her while she was grieving over Edward, but enough was enough.

And when it rang again immediately afterwards he barked fiercely, 'Melanie, I thought I'd told you—'

'I don't know who Melanie is but it's definitely not me.'

Oliver was momentarily taken aback by the man's amused voice. 'I'm sorry, who is this?'

'Chris Paige, Anna's brother. Is she there?'

Anna's brother! The mysterious brother whom he'd never been allowed to meet.

'No, she isn't,' he said perhaps more sharply than he intended, but he could do without these calls at this precise moment.

'When will she be home? I really would like to speak to her.'

Oliver closed his eyes and leant his head back against the chair. 'Never.' Had he really said that, or was it only in his mind?

'What do you mean never?'

Oh, Lord, he had said it. He'd have to tell the truth now. 'She's left me.'

There was a short, palpable silence before Chris said slowly, 'Because of the money she lent me? Were you still hassling her over that?'

So it was her brother after all that Anna had given the money to, and she'd told Chris about his reaction. What sort of a fiend did that make him? And while Oliver was still wondering how to answer, Chris spoke again.

'Did she ever tell you the real reason she lent it to me?'

'No,' Oliver admitted quietly, rubbing a hand over his throbbing brow.

'It was because I made her promise not to,' admitted Chris. 'I did eventually release her from that promise but it was my fault all the same that you never got to hear the truth.'

'A promise?' What was the man talking about?

'I needed money; my business was in trouble. I knew it was only a temporary thing, but—'

'And you made Anna promise not to tell me?' cut in Oliver impatiently. 'For goodness' sake, I'd have lent you the money myself if I'd known, if Anna had spoken up.' None of this made any sense.

But when Chris finished explaining, Oliver had to admit that Langford Properties probably wouldn't have put the business his way if they'd known he was in financial trouble.

'So what are you going to do about my sister?' asked Chris, swiftly dismissive of talk about work.

'I'm going after her,' Oliver declared firmly. 'Though whether she'll have me back is another story. I've said some distinctly terrible things to her.'

'I guess you have plenty of humble pie to eat. Anna has lots of pride, you know. But, for what it's worth, I think she still loves you. Good luck.'

As Oliver put down the phone he knew he would need all the luck he could get. Chris didn't know the whole story. He'd probably never have suggested attempting a reconciliation if he did. He would have told Oliver to keep well away from his sister with his ridiculous and unfounded accusations.

CHAPTER TEN

ANNA had been expecting Oliver ever since Chris's phone call; she'd even stood at the window most of the day watching and waiting. At first she'd thought about scooting off somewhere, to London maybe, somewhere where he wouldn't find her.

But she'd decided ultimately that the confrontation had to be made, final decisions reached. Divorce was her only option. There was no point in remaining married to a man who didn't trust her, who would never trust her.

Chris had tried to persuade her to give it another go, but Anna knew that she daren't, couldn't, wouldn't. 'He's not getting the chance to hurt me again,' she'd declared fiercely.

She gave up her vigil when it grew dark. He wasn't coming. Not today, anyway. Thank goodness. All this nervous agitation for nothing. She was in the kitchen preparing a light supper when Oliver pounded on the door. The sudden sound frightened her but she knew instinctively that it was him.

Her legs felt as though they were filled with lead as she made her way to the front door. It took an age for her to get there. And when she opened it she didn't stand back for Oliver to enter but waited for him to speak, snapping on the outside light so that she could see him more clearly.

He looked dreadful. His golden eyes were sunk into

deeply shadowed sockets, his cheeks were drawn, and it pleased her that he'd been suffering, too. Why should she be the only one to feel like hell?

'Anna.' He nodded.

So he wasn't going to make the opening move; he was leaving it up to her. 'Hello, Oliver. I've been expecting you.' She deliberately kept her voice icy cold and impersonal. 'A pity you didn't phone, first. It would have saved you a journey.'

'I understand that I'm not welcome,' he said, his eyes narrowing on her pale face. 'But surely you're not going to turn me away?'

'Is there any reason why I shouldn't?' she asked sharply. 'Didn't I make it clear that it's all over between us?'

'We need to talk,' he said.

'Why?' she asked heatedly. 'Because you've found out about the promise I made Chris? That I really do have a brother? It makes a difference, does it?' She was ready to spit fire. If he thought he could come here and apologise and it would make things all right again then he was deeply mistaken.

'It doesn't make a difference—of course not,' he retorted. 'I was in the wrong and I admit that. Now can I please come in?'

Anna could see that she was not going to get away with keeping him on the doorstep so she reluctantly stepped aside, though she heaved a sigh to show her disapproval. 'You've wasted your time. Nothing you can say will make any difference to how I feel.'

No man truly in love with his wife would accuse her of stealing family jewellery, he would at least discuss it first. But not Oliver. Oh, no, he'd acted first and thought last. And now, having realised that he'd made a mistake, it looked as though he wanted to put matters right.

And pigs might fly!

Anna closed the door behind Oliver and followed him through to the sitting room. It was a tiny room, nothing at all like the handsomely proportioned sitting room at Weston Lodge. And there was no escaping him.

His devastating masculinity filled the cramped space; his cologne invaded it; his very presence was a threat to her sanity. 'Now say what you've got to say and then go,' she said crisply, trying not to look at him, but it was impossible.

Oliver Langford could not be ignored. He wore the same black squidgy leather jacket that he had on the fateful day they'd first met, black sweater, black jeans. Sexy, dismayingly exciting.

He stood, apparently waiting for her to be seated before he took a chair himself. And Anna, who had been determined to remain standing, who had no intention of encouraging him to linger, found her legs would hold her up no longer. Please don't let him stay long, she prayed, as she slid down on to the nearest chair. I'm not up to this.

Oliver sat too. 'I made a huge mistake.'

'I won't argue with that,' she said. 'Is that why you're here, to apologise?'

'Something like that.' And then he frowned. 'Are you all right, Anna? You look very pale. Are you eating properly?'

Oh, Lord, she hoped he wasn't going to question her over her health. There were some things she'd rather he didn't know. 'Of course I'm eating,' she snapped. 'As a matter of fact, I was just making myself some supper.'

'Then make it supper for two. I'm famished.'

Anna groaned. Did he have to add to her torment? 'It's only a tuna sandwich.'

'I like tuna.'

'And some salad.'

'That's good.' He pushed himself up. 'I'll come and help, shall I?'

Help or hinder? She needed neither. 'There's not really room for two in the kitchen, as you very well know. I can manage on my own. You stay here. I'll bring it in on a tray.'

'I seem to remember we worked well together at one time,' he said with a sudden gleam in his eye. 'It was a very cosy arrangement.'

Yes, so cosy that their bodies continually brushed against each other. It had been an exercise in physical excitement. They'd even made love in the kitchen. But that was then and this was now, and she didn't want any reminders.

'Cosy arrangements are no longer the order of the day,' she told him coolly. 'You'd best remember that. I'd rather you stay here.'

He shrugged. 'You're the boss.' And reluctantly he sat down again.

When Anna reached the kitchen she stood with her back to the wall and took in several deep, steadying breaths. Although she'd been expecting Oliver, had decided exactly what she was going to say to him, she hadn't been prepared for this adrenalin rush.

She had thought that every single one of her feelings had been destroyed, she'd thought all that remained was hatred. How, then, could she explain the fact that her insides had sizzled simply by looking at him?

Or was she receiving mixed signals? Was it sizzling hatred and not desire? Was it resentment that pulsed through her veins not hunger? How could she be sure? She did know, though, that if she didn't hurry and finish the sandwiches he would come in search of her.

The thought electrified her into action and ten minutes later all was ready. Oliver had thoughtfully moved the coffee table between the two chairs and she set down the tray, congratulating herself on appearing calm and untroubled when it was a far cry from the feelings churning inside her.

They spoke little over supper although Anna knew it wouldn't be long before Oliver started on what he'd really come here for. Was it to apologise? Was it to beg her forgiveness? Was it to say he'd made a grave error of judgement? Or was it to sort out their divorce?

'What are you thinking?'

Anna looked across at Oliver. He had stopped eating and was watching her intently with those devastating golden eyes.

'You were very deep in thought,' he said. 'Troubled thought. Did it concern me?'

'Naturally.' It would have been stupid to claim otherwise.

'We have a lot of talking to do,' he admitted.

'Yes.'

'It was wrong of me to accuse you of taking those heirlooms.'

'I'm glad you realise it.'

'I should have known you'd never do a thing like that.'

'Yes, you should have.'

'I should also have known that you had a very good reason for using that thirty thousands pounds.' His lips twisted wryly. 'I shouldn't have tarred you with the same brush as Rosemary and Melanie.'

'And do you feel better now you've said all that?' she asked tartly.

Oliver's hands gripped the arms of his chair until his knuckles gleamed white. He clearly hadn't expected quite so much antagonism. But his voice remained calm. 'I'm asking your forgiveness.'

'No you're not.' Anna shook her head firmly. 'You're trying to make amends. But it won't work. You've hurt me far too much. You could get down on your knees and it would make no difference.'

'Anna—'

'Anna, nothing,' she shot. 'We're finished; it's over. I doubt we ever really loved each other. If we had there wouldn't have been these problems, you'd have trusted me, you'd have let me explain. We enjoyed good sex but that was all. Your father was right to oppose the marriage. He was the only one with any sense.'

Oliver rubbed his fingers over his brow. 'You've changed, Anna. You were never this hard before. You always—'

'Is it any wonder I've changed,' she cut in, widening her eyes and looking at him scornfully, 'after the way you treated me? I don't want you in my life any more, Oliver. If you've come here to grovel and beg me to go back with you, then forget it, because I won't. I'd actually prefer it if you left.' Please, God, she was doing the right thing.

'At this time of night?'

'Yes, at this time of night. It's your fault for coming so late.'

'I couldn't get an earlier flight.'

'Then you should have waited until tomorrow.'

'I was hoping you'd let me stay?'

Anna groaned. This was the last thing she wanted. 'I don't think so.'

'Not even if I promise not to hassle you? If I promise to be a good boy?'

He pulled such a forlorn face and it was such a ridiculous thing for him to say that Anna's good intentions went flying out the window. 'Provided you leave at first light,' she reluctantly agreed. 'I don't want you here, Oliver. It's over between us and the sooner you accept it, the better.'

He winced at her harsh words. 'There must be some way I can get you to change your mind?'

'None at all,' she retorted. 'If you want to go to bed now, you know where the spare room is. I'll clear away here.'

'No, please, let me help.' He sprang to his feet and picked up the tray.

'In that case, you can do it all. I'll go to bed,' she said tightly. 'Goodnight, Oliver.' He didn't look pleased but she didn't care, and she was safely tucked up under the covers when she heard him mount the stairs.

She had brushed her teeth and washed her face in record time so that she wouldn't bump into him again. But she wasn't able to relax and she found herself listening and waiting.

Her fingers curled and her whole body stiffened when he reached her bedroom door, even her heart thudded, but he passed on by without a falter in his step. He went into the bathroom, which separated the two rooms, she heard water running and the toilet flushing, and then she heard him go into the spare room. After that there was silence but still she didn't relax.

She imagined him undressing. Stripping off his sweater and jeans, his shoes and socks, the brief plain underpants he always wore. And as he hadn't brought an overnight bag she imagined him sleeping nude between the clean cotton sheets. The very thought of his magnificent firm body was more than enough to send her into spasm.

It was a long time before she slept.

The next morning she hoped and prayed that Oliver would have taken her at her word and gone before she ventured downstairs, but she had no such luck. He even had breakfast ready. But the smell of crispy bacon as she walked into the kitchen was more than Anna's stomach could stand.

She rushed back up to the bathroom, desperately hoping Oliver hadn't heard her. When she finally rejoined him breakfast had been cleared away. There was a coffee pot on the go but that was all. He looked at her in concern. 'I know there's something wrong with you, Anna. Why don't you tell me what it is?'

'I must have picked up a bug,' she said airily. 'I think I'll have some toast.' She needed action, anything so that she wouldn't have to look at Oliver. Whether she would eat the toast was a different matter altogether.

'I'm expected to believe that, am I?' he asked shortly. 'You've seen a doctor? He's told you it's a bug?'

'Not yet, I haven't,' she answered with a shrug. 'It's only just come on. Don't worry about it, Oliver, I'll be all right.'

But she could feel his eyes boring into her back as she popped bread into the toaster. And while she was waiting she filled the kettle. 'I think I'd like tea rather than coffee. Do you want a cup?'

'No, thank you, Anna.' Such polite words.

She would have liked to turn around and look at him but knew that she daren't. Her heart pumped uneasily. Then she told herself that she was being silly because how could he possibly have guessed? When her toast was made and the tea poured Oliver took it from her and carried it through to the sitting room. In those idyllic days when they first met, they'd always eaten at the window table where they could watch the birds in the garden, the freshness of spring, the weather over the Wicklow Mountains. So there was nothing unusual in him carrying her breakfast there.

And yet Anna still had this peculiar feeling. It was probably guilt, she decided, as she sat down and picked up a piece of toast. Guilt because she'd made a conscious decision to hide her condition from him.

She nibbled a corner and kept her eyes averted.

Oliver sat the other side of the table, the pot of coffee in front of him.

'I think it's more than just a bug,' he said quietly. 'Don't you think you ought to tell me?'

Anna frowned and felt her stomach begin to churn again, though for a very different reason this time. 'I don't know what you're talking about.'

'Oh, I think you do. Look at me, Anna. Tell me truthfully what is wrong.'

'There is nothing wrong,' she insisted, but she still couldn't bring herself to look at him.

'I looked in your bathroom cabinet this morning for a spare toothbrush.'

Alarm bells rang. Big alarm bells.

'And guess what I saw, Anna?'

She remained silent.

'A pregnancy testing kit.'

She wanted to slide beneath the table, she wanted to disappear into a hole in the ground. She could brazen it out and say, So what? She could say that she'd used it and it had proved negative. She could say lots of things—but at the end of the day he would find out.

Oliver wasn't stupid. He could see the state she was in. Her morning sickness had come on early and there was no way she could hide it.

If only she hadn't stopped taking the Pill that first time she left him. She'd been experiencing problems and intended trying a different one. Meanwhile, she had decided to give her body a rest.

Stupidly, she hadn't given it a thought when she let Oliver make love to her. They'd both been fired with the passion of the moment and contraception had been the last thing on their minds.

A fatal mistake. One of many she had made where this man was concerned.

She eyed him bravely. 'And do you know what, Oliver? It tested positive. Not that it's going to make very much difference to you, because this baby's mine.'

It was a decision she'd made when she first discovered that she was pregnant. She didn't want him as the father. He had well and truly given up that right. 'I'm not coming back to you. I'll naturally let you—'

'The hell you aren't coming back!' It was a mighty roar and almost lifted the rafters. Then Oliver must have realised that this was no way to get what he wanted because his voice went much quieter.

'This baby is mine as much as yours, Anna. I presume it is mine?' He said it as an afterthought, not really believing that it was anyone else's.

'Of course.'

'Therefore I want to be a part of it, I want to be there for you, help you through this bad time. You must see a doctor. It will be best if you come home with me and see the family doctor. I'll make the arrangements, I'll—'

'Oliver.' Anna's tone was firm. 'I'm not coming back to a man who thinks I stole the family jewels.'

She was pleased to note that he had the grace to look ashamed. As well he should.

'I'm not giving you any choice, Anna,' he said, fingers strumming on the table. 'The truth is that I accused you without thinking. I realised immediately that you would never have done such a thing. You're too honest, too straight, too good.'

He added these last two words with a wry twist of his lips. 'Too good for me. I know I can never repair the damage I've inflicted, but for the sake of our baby—' he smiled as he said the words '—I'm begging you to give me one last chance. I promise I will never, ever, accuse you of stealing again. Or of marrying me for money.'

'You're right—you won't, because you won't get the chance,' she told him surely. It was no good him making promises because if he'd done it twice what was to say he wouldn't do it a third time? She refused to take the risk.

He frowned harshly. 'You really mean that you won't come home with me, Anna.'

'Yes.' She had thought it through very carefully and decided it was the right thing to do. 'I'll let you have access, I shan't be petty enough to deny you that, but—'

'For God's sake, woman, what do I have to do? Get down on my knees and beg?'

'That I would like to see,' she tossed the words at him bitterly, 'but it still wouldn't be enough. Nothing will. I don't think you have any idea how much you've hurt me. I shall never forgive you, not as long as I live. So I can't see the point in us living together. It would put us both into an impossible situation.'

CHAPTER ELEVEN

OLIVER couldn't even begin to describe his feelings when he'd seen that pregnancy testing kit. Shock at first, complete and utter shock. He'd stared at it for several minutes, his heart banging against his ribs, before deciding it was a relic left behind by Anna's sister.

But maybe not.

Maybe it was Anna's!

Alarm set in then—but only because their marriage wasn't working. The thought of Anna having a baby, his baby, brought a rush of paternal warmth, a joy he had never experienced before.

And he'd known as soon as he'd seen how ill Anna looked when she came downstairs that she was pregnant. She'd been pale the night before but he'd put that down to exhaustion. This was something different.

He'd quietly followed her up to the bathroom and heard her retching, and so he'd returned to the kitchen and got rid of everything that could induce nausea.

He knew when it had happened but he didn't know how when she was on the Pill. But if anything could mend their marriage, bring them back together, it was surely this. He had been unprepared, therefore, when she'd flatly refused to go home with him.

An impossible situation she had said and he could see how her mind worked. What he needed to do was somehow, some way, persuade her to return with him. And once he'd got her home he could work on her. Convince her that he would never let her down again, that it was the worst mistake he'd ever made in his life, and that this was the best thing that could have happened to them.

It might be a long haul but he loved Anna so desperately that he was prepared to do anything to save their marriage.

'You can't stay here alone, Anna,' he said quietly. 'Not in your condition.'

'I shan't feel sick for ever so why shouldn't I?' she snapped, her emerald eyes glaring magnificently.

She was so beautiful, so desirable, that he couldn't imagine why he had endangered their marriage by accusing her of crimes that he knew she wasn't capable of committing. He could only plead insanity due to sexual frustration.

'I want you home because you're my wife,' he said patiently. 'I want to look after you, take care of you, make things easier for you.'

Her eyes flashed again. 'Belated concern, Oliver? Are you forgetting that you're the one who made things hard for me?'

She couldn't have hurt him any more if she'd struck him with an axe. 'You think I don't know that? You think it won't haunt me for the rest of my life?'

He was aware that the pain he felt filled his voice. He wanted her to hear it, he wanted her to know that he truly regretted what he had done. 'Anna, I want to make it up to you. You must give me that chance.'

He saw the way she looked at him, the flash of indignation, followed by uncertainty as their eyes briefly met, the way she averted them again quickly as though she was afraid of giving something away. Hope flooded through him. It looked as though she wasn't as immune to him as she was trying to make out.

There had always been a strong chemical attraction, a raging fire that had drawn them irresistibly together and in that one tiny instant he had seen it again. Admittedly, a faint spark only. But in that spark there was hope. Her fire wasn't dead—he hadn't killed it—and if it was the last thing he did he would nurture it back to precious life.

He pressed home his minuscule advantage. 'Anna, you have my word that I will never hurt you again. This is our child you are carrying, conceived through an act of love.' Hopefully she wouldn't negate that. 'Will your conscience let you deny your child its father?'

He wanted to go on and say it would want for nothing but that would mean bringing the money issue into it again—and this was something he needed to avoid like the plague. It would be like holding a red rag to a bull. She would turn on him again and all hope would be lost.

'My conscience has nothing to do with it, Oliver,' she told him coldly. 'You're the one who's made me feel this way. You can't go around flinging accusations and then expect to welcome me back into your arms the next minute as though nothing has happened.'

'I know that,' he admitted ruefully. 'Don't you think I've paid the penalty? But we're not talking about you, now, we're talking about the child. It's not only me who needs you—it's our baby, too.'

They had spoken of having a family many times, though they hadn't planned it quite this soon. And they had agreed that a child needed both parents—they had said that if ever the unthinkable happened and their marriage foundered they would stick together for the sake of any children they might have. Had she forgotten that?'

Anna took a long, deep breath, closed her eyes and for several long, never-ending seconds, appeared to consider his words. Faint hope rose in him, but when she spoke it wasn't what he wanted to hear. 'I'm sorry, Oliver, it wouldn't work.'

'We could make it work,' he said softly. 'I cannot envisage life without you. I'm not using our baby as blackmail—well, maybe just a little,' he added with a self-deprecating grimace. 'But I need you, too. You mean the whole world to me. These last two days have been the blackest of my life.'

'Oliver,' she said with a touch of impatience, 'I've already given this a lot of thought. I don't see how I can live with a man who distrusts me. It wouldn't work. I'd be forever waiting for the next time.'

'There won't be a next time,' he promised her firmly. It hurt deep in his gut that she should even think this. Hadn't his apologies been enough? Hadn't she believed him? What more could he say?

Anna shook her head. 'It's easy for you to say that, Oliver. I've discovered a side to you that I hadn't known existed, and one that I don't like. Have you really no idea how I feel? I have never stolen so much as a penny in my life. You have hurt and humiliated me, you made me feel like the lowest of the low, and yet you now expect me to come back and live with you, put myself up for more of the same, just because I'm carrying your baby. It's not on, Oliver. I can't do it.'

His faint spark of hope died. Short of using caveman tactics and physically carrying her back home, what was he to do? He had never seen Anna so determined. And so magnificently beautiful in her anger.

He wanted to bed her there and then, make exciting, uninhibited love like they had in the early days of their marriage. Would that work? Would she agree to anything once they were locked in each other's arms, unable to get enough of each other?

But he knew that emotional blackmail wasn't the answer. Anna had to come back because she wanted to, because she knew it would be best for her and the baby.

He poured himself another cup of coffee while he decided what to say next, noticing as he did so that Anna hadn't touched her toast; there was still only one tiny bite gone from the corner. She hadn't touched her tea, either.

'How can I prove that I won't accuse you of anything like that ever again, if you don't give me the chance?' He was prepared to go down on his knees and beg if he thought it would help. He'd never been in a situation like this before. Most things he could talk his way around, but with Anna so stubborn...

'Maybe you should have thought of that before you made your allegations.'

Oliver groaned. 'As if I haven't done that a thousand times already. Anna—' he leant forward urgently and took her hands across the table '—I don't want you to go through this alone. I want to be there at your side. You need me. You can't tell me that you're looking forward to being alone during what should be one of the most exciting and rewarding times of your life?'

She closed her eyes, shut him out, didn't let him see whatever she was thinking. But he was almost sure he had got through to her. At least she didn't snatch her hands away.

'What would happen if you became ill while you were living alone?' he urged. 'Even now, with this morning sickness, you need someone with you. Anna, please come back with me—even if it's only until the baby's born. At least give yourself a chance, give me a chance to prove that I do truly love you and I'll never hurt you again.'

Her eyes slowly opened and in their green depths he thought he saw hesitation, uncertainty.

'If,' he went on, 'once the baby's born, you decide that you cannot bear to live with me a moment longer, then I will let you go.' Though he hoped it never came to that. He hoped time would prove to her that he meant what he said, because how could he let go the woman he loved more than life itself?

He would do whatever it took. He would demonstrate in every way possible that his love was unswerving and loyal, that he trusted her implicitly in all things.

'*If* I come,' she said eventually, 'and it's a very big if, it will be under one condition.'

The words were music to his ears. 'Name it,' he

said magnanimously. Nothing could be worse than
her not coming at all.

'That we continue to sleep in separate rooms,' she
said firmly, her eyes almost glaring now, expecting
him to object. 'It will be a marriage in name only for
the sake of the baby.'

It was not the answer he wanted but it was better
than nothing. It hurt like hell that she didn't want to
sleep with him, but hopefully she would change her
mind once she realised how deep his feelings for her
were, once she accepted that he would never hurt her
again. It was a matter, he supposed, of earning her
trust.

He nodded slowly. 'If that's what you really want.'

'It is,' she declared firmly.

Anna knew that she had to be out of her mind agreeing to Oliver's request, but the truth was she didn't
relish the idea of going through this pregnancy on her
own. Oliver had hit on the truth—she was afraid of
it. Perhaps all new mothers-to-be felt this way? She
didn't know.

And although all trust between them had been destroyed she did still, surprisingly, love Oliver. Why,
she didn't know considering the way he had treated
her, but she did. Not that she was going to let him
see it. Although how hard that would be was anyone's
guess.

They couldn't get a ferry until the following day
and it was late evening by the time they got home.
Anna hated to admit it but it really did feel like home
when she walked into Weston Lodge.

They had, after all, spent six happy months here

and it had the familiar feel of a place where love had reigned supreme. It was such a pity that Oliver had ruined everything.

Oliver put her bags into the room she had used when she was here last. 'This is what you want?' he asked with grave concern. 'You don't have to sleep in here, you know. I'd much rather you—'

'It's what I want,' she declared firmly.

'Can I help you unpack?'

'No, thanks.' Another brisk retort. 'I can manage on my own.'

'Then I'll ask Mrs G to make us a drink and perhaps a sandwich.'

Anna shook her head. 'Don't bother on my part. I'm tired. I'm going straight to bed.'

Oliver frowned. 'You are all right, Anna? It's been a long day, I know. Are you sure that—?'

'Oliver, I am very sure.' Her eyes flashed her irritation. 'All I want to do is sleep.' Last night had been stressful; she'd hardly slept a wink. All the time she'd kept thinking that Oliver might come waltzing into her room. And the truth was, she wouldn't have been able to keep him at bay. No matter what her head told her, her heart dictated otherwise. And she guessed it always would.

Oliver too had been unable to sleep. She'd heard him go downstairs just after two and had been sorely tempted to follow, hoping that a hot drink might settle her. But it had been too big a risk to take.

Her feelings ran far too high for such close contact. She would have ended up in his arms—and what good would that have done? He would have thought she'd forgiven him and she hadn't. It was doubtful she ever would.

But would she be able to sleep tonight, despite how tired she was? Would she still worry that he might come to her, that her body would give way to its cravings? They were questions she couldn't answer.

'I'll say goodnight, then, Anna.' Oliver gave her a chaste kiss on the brow. 'If there is anything you need just—'

'Please go, Oliver. I'm all right; I'm only tired. Stop fussing.'

He went then, reluctantly, and Anna flung herself down on the bed fully clothed. Had she made a mistake in allowing him to persuade her to come back here? Was he going to watch over her like a mother hen? Smother her?

She closed her eyes. She didn't want that. She wanted to be left alone; she wanted to do things her way without him interfering or fussing. He had lost all right to be a husband to her. Tomorrow she would make that very plain.

Anna fell into an immediate deep sleep, waking some time in the middle of the night with a desperate urge to go to the bathroom. Thank goodness it was en-suite, was her first thought. If she'd had to walk along the landing, Oliver might have pounced. She'd like to bet that he had one ear cocked listening for any sounds from her room.

She shivered as she threw off her clothes and pulled on a nightie, but once she had curled beneath the duvet she went straight back to sleep.

The next morning she was woken by Mrs Green with tea and biscuits. 'Eat these, my dear, and then lie down again for half an hour. You shouldn't feel sick then. It always worked with me.'

Anna struggled to sit up and pulled an embarrassed face. 'Oliver's told you?'

'Indeed he has. I'm very pleased for you both. I presume I should be pleased?'.

'We're back together,' said Anna quietly.

'But not in the same bed,' pointed out the house-keeper tartly. 'It's not a good sign. I have no idea what's gone on between you two but if you want my advice you'll patch things up, and quickly. Oliver's hopeful, I know. He was hell to live with when you went away. You two are made for each other. Don't throw your love away.'

When Anna finally made her way downstairs Oliver was waiting for her. She had hoped he'd be at work, she didn't want him disrupting his normal rou-tine on her behalf, and she hoped it wasn't going to become a regular thing.

'What are you doing here?' she asked crossly as she walked into the breakfast room, yet at the same time her senses leapt in response to him, an awareness filling her that almost had her running into his arms.

'I've made an appointment for you at the doctor's,' Oliver informed her.

Anna felt a swift stab of resentment at the way he was taking over and was glad she hadn't given in to her urges. 'I'm quite capable of doing that for myself, thank you.'

'Yes, I know,' he answered, 'but I wasn't sure how quickly you'd do it and I thought that it was important you—'

'I don't need you to think for me,' she retorted.

And then decided that maybe she was being too hard on him. He still looked as though he hadn't slept in a month, although he was freshly showered and shaven, and he was wearing a crisp blue shirt with a pair of navy linen trousers. 'I'm sorry, of course you're concerned. When is the appointment?'

'Ten-thirty. We have plenty of time. Can you manage some breakfast now?'

'Maybe a slice of toast.'

Oliver frowned. 'That isn't much.'

'It's all I want,' she insisted. 'I remember my sister saying little had often suited her better than big meals.'

The doctor confirmed that she was indeed well and truly pregnant. He shook Oliver's hand and her own and wished them a healthy baby. 'It's a pity your father won't have the pleasure of seeing his grandchild.'

Oliver nodded curtly and outside the surgery Anna, having noticed his expression, said, 'That was a bit insensitive of him, talking about your father like that.'

'You don't know the half,' he muttered. 'My father wouldn't have wanted anything to do with his grandchild.'

'He wouldn't?' And then the ugly truth hit her. 'Because of me? Because he never liked me?' Goodness, had Edward's animosity gone that far? He would have spited his grandchild because he didn't approve of her?

'Of course not,' Oliver declared impatiently. 'Because he didn't like me. Get in the car and we'll talk at home, if you're really interested.'

Edward didn't like his son? This was news to Anna

and she pondered about it as Oliver drove. She'd never seen any signs. It didn't make sense.

In the house she turned to him. 'Tell me about your father. You've never hinted that there was anything wrong.'

Oliver drew in a deep breath and let it out slowly, ridding himself of some of his tension as they sat down.

'That's because we managed to rub along together,' he admitted with a heavy shrug. 'I respected him—it's something I was brought up to do. It's why I lived here instead of moving right away. He needed me, even though he wouldn't admit it. But that doesn't mean to say I'm not resentful of the way he used to treat me.'

'He didn't appreciate having to bring you up, is that what you're saying?'

'Something like that,' he admitted ruefully. 'I only went into the business to prove that I wasn't the idiot he always said I was. Even when he retired he couldn't accept that I was doing a good job. We had many arguments.'

And one of those arguments had resulted in his death, thought Anna sadly. She might not have liked Edward, and liked him even less now that she'd heard how he treated Oliver, but it didn't mean that she couldn't feel some sort of compassion for him.

She pulled a wry face. 'I suppose that explains the way he behaved towards me.'

'Not at all,' Oliver told her crisply. 'He married Rosemary in haste, without really getting to know her, and he thought he knew where we were heading. He would have accepted you in time.'

'No, he wouldn't,' replied Anna firmly. 'He actually offered me money not to marry you.'

'He did what?' Oliver jolted upright, golden eyes shocked. 'Why didn't you tell me?'

'Because I dealt with it,' she explained calmly. 'I tore up his cheque. I told him I loved you and it would have made no difference if you were a pauper.'

There was faint admiration in his eyes now. 'I bet he didn't like that.'

'I don't think he did.' Anna went quiet for a moment, wondering whether to tell him the rest.

'There's more, isn't there?'

She had forgotten how easily Oliver could read her mind, and her lips contorted themselves into a regretful smile. 'You know me too well.'

'So out with it. I might as well have the whole awful truth in one go.'

Anna swallowed hard. 'He threw me out. He told me it was his house and gave me a week to move.'

Oliver slumped. It was as though all the stuffing had been knocked out of him. 'And you went—without coming to see me? Without telling me what he'd done?'

Then, with a swift recovery, he bounced to his feet. 'The old bastard! Maybe it's as well you didn't tell me or I might have done something I later regretted. Anna—' he spoke more quietly now, struggling to control his powerful emotions '—why *didn't* you tell me?'

'I thought you wouldn't care,' she answered quietly. 'You'd never once been back to try and talk things over and I wasn't coming up there with your father in the house. I had too much pride for that.'

'So if my father hadn't died, we'd have never got back together. Is that what you're saying?'

'It's possible. I was hurting too much for a confrontation. You'd made up your mind and that was it.'

Oliver closed his eyes in self-recrimination. 'I don't know about calling my father a swine. I've been a pretty big one myself.'

'You can say that again.' But, despite all that had gone wrong between them, Anna still felt the strong pull of his sexuality. It was something that had never gone away, and she hated sitting here with distance between them. But sex wasn't the answer, she had to remember that. It was where they had gone wrong in the first place.

'Why didn't you ever tell me this house belonged to Edward?' she asked.

Oliver shrugged. 'I never gave it a thought. But I do think we should sell up soon. I think we should be settled into our new place before the baby is born.'

Our new place! Our new place. Was this a wise move? She had a lot of forgiving to do before commitments were made, and a new house meant commitment. It meant he was expecting her to spend the rest of her life with him.

'You don't look sure about it, Anna?' She hadn't realised he was watching her, nor that her face was so expressive. She shrugged. 'You said that if it didn't work out by the time the baby was born, then I'd be free to go. I don't see the point in us moving until we're sure that—'

Oliver's eyes flashed and he sprang to his feet. 'Maybe *you're* not sure, Anna, but I most definitely am. We are man and wife and that is the way I want us to stay.'

CHAPTER TWELVE

ANNA'S first thought was that Oliver had tricked her. He had got her back here with the promise that she was free to leave if things didn't work out and now he was saying that he had no intention of letting her go.

'I love you, Anna,' he continued before she could respond. 'And I'd like to think that you still love me. The hurt hasn't yet gone away, which is understandable, but I have every intention of making amends for my atrocious behaviour. You will never again have cause to think ill of me. In fact, you'll thank me for coming after you.'

Her lips twisted wryly. 'That's a sweeping statement, Oliver.'

'I won't let you down, I promise,' he said urgently. 'Now I suggest that I find Mrs G and organise an early lunch. Are you feeling up to it?'

'Actually I am hungry,' she agreed, deciding there was no point in arguing. Only time would tell. 'I'll phone Chris while you're doing that. Let him know I'm back.'

He nodded. 'Good idea. Perhaps you ought to invite him over for dinner, one evening. It's about time I met this brother of yours.'

'You're not still of the opinion that Tony's lurking somewhere in the background?' The question was out before she could stop it.

Oliver groaned. 'Don't remind me how foolish I've been. I don't know why I thought he was involved. Well, yes, I do. You'd once said Tony was handsome and blond, and the guy my father saw you with matched that description. I never imagined that your brother would have blond hair.'

'Perhaps your mother leaving for such selfish reasons messed you up a lot,' she said. 'Made you suspicious of everyone.'

'It wasn't Rosemary leaving, it was my father's attitude,' he retorted bitterly.

Anna wanted to go to him then, to hold him, to say that everything would be all right. But she couldn't be sure. It was still far too early. How did she know Oliver wouldn't come down on her again when something else went wrong?

It wasn't easy, though, keeping her distance from him. In the weeks that followed Oliver became over protective, he was for ever asking how she was, if she needed anything, oughtn't she to rest more?

It was a constant bombardment and she was glad when he found it necessary to go to work.

He put both houses on the market and there began a steady stream of prospective purchasers. Anna kept out of the way whenever the agents came to show someone around.

Often she would go out looking for property that would be suitable for her and Oliver. 'I'll leave the choice entirely up to you,' he had said. 'If you're happy then I'll be happy.'

It was an onerous task, especially as she still wasn't sure whether their marriage would last. But at least it gave her something to do.

And when she happened upon a cottage deep in the Cambridgeshire countryside, a cottage that somehow reminded her of the cottage in Ireland where she and Oliver had been so deliriously happy, she knew that this was where she wanted to live.

It was crazy really, because why did she want reminders of a life that might have been? Or was she living in hope that one day things might work out between them? Was that really at the back of her mind?

The cottage wasn't for sale, so she didn't know why she had stopped to look. It was much bigger than the holiday cottage. It had probably started out in life as a two-up, two-down, but it had been extended over the years so that it was now as imposing as a country manor, and yet it still had that cottage appeal. Diamond-leaded windows and ivy clad walls, chimneys and gables and what looked like a massive garden for the children to play in.

Anna checked her thoughts. Children? Was she planning to have more children with Oliver? Had she subconsciously resigned herself to the fact that their marriage would get back on track?

She had no way of knowing. Half of her wanted it to happen; the other half was so deeply resentful of the way he had treated her that it was doubtful she would ever forgive him.

Even as she stood and looked at the cottage, smoke curled from one of the chimneys and Anna wanted to go and knock on the door and ask to be let in. She wanted to sit before a cosy log fire, warm her hands and her toes and dream that it was her very own house.

Over dinner that evening, she told Oliver about the cottage. 'It wasn't for sale but it's my dream house. I'd love to live somewhere like that.'

Her enthusiasm shone through and Oliver smiled appreciatively. 'If that's what you want, then that's what you shall have. Take me to see it and we'll start a search for a look-alike.'

And so on Sunday they drove out and when the elderly householder returned from taking his dog for a walk Oliver went to speak to him.

Anna got out of the car and stood and watched. She loved the cottage even more the second time. It was perfect. How would they ever find anything else like it?

Oliver came back. 'You're not going to believe this,' he said. 'But that guy's been thinking of selling for some time. It's too big for him, since his wife died, but he can't face the thought of a stream of strangers traipsing through. If we want it it's ours. He intends to go and live with his daughter in Essex.'

'Oh, Oliver!' Anna couldn't stop herself from flinging her arms around him. 'Does he mean it?'

'Absolutely. He said we can go inside and look now, if you like.'

'I don't care what it's like inside,' she said dismissively. 'I know it will be perfect. I can't believe we're so lucky.'

Oliver held her tightly against him, smiling indulgently into her glowing face. 'I've not seen you this happy since you came home.'

How it happened, she didn't know, but the next second Oliver's mouth possessed hers. It took her breath away, it sent a spiral of sensation through her entire body. And although she knew she ought to push him away, slap his face even, she somehow couldn't do it.

She let the kiss happen—in full view of the owner of the house. She let Oliver's mouth seduce hers into responding. She felt an elation that had been missing in her life for a long time.

It was a deeply satisfying kiss, a kiss that made her whole body throb and made her realise that she was punishing herself by shutting Oliver out. And when Oliver abruptly let her go she felt bereft.

She expected him to apologise, to declare that he had overstepped the mark, but he didn't. Instead he looked inordinately pleased with himself as he took her hand and led her up to the house.

Inside was as good as she'd expected, a well-proportioned living room and lounge, a dining room and a study, a kitchen to die for, and four bedrooms, two of them en-suite. It was perfect.

'What do you think?' asked the owner.

'It's fantastic,' said Anna. 'Exactly what we want. I can't believe we've been so lucky. Do you really want to sell?'

'I'd get out tomorrow if I could.'

'I'll see my solicitor first thing in the morning,' declared Oliver, and he held out his hand and they shook on the deal.

'I'm happy to let it go to two young people so obviously in love. It does my heart good to see you.' He was a white-haired, kindly-looking man. 'You remind me of my wife and myself when we were first married. We were kissing and cuddling the whole time. I hope you'll be as happy here as we were.'

Oliver's arm came about Anna's shoulders. 'I don't think there's any doubt about that.'

Anna felt a fraud but she lifted her face with the expected smile and Oliver kissed her. A brief kiss, this time, just a brushing of their lips for the old man's benefit, but it set her alight again and she wondered whether she was going to be able to keep up the game against Oliver for much longer.

'Do you like it as much as I do?' she asked when they returned to the car.

'No doubt about it,' he said, putting the key into the ignition and starting the engine. 'It will be a fresh start for both of us.'

But before he drove away he turned to her and said hopefully, 'Did your response to my kiss mean that you've finally forgiven me?'

Anna steeled her heart and shook her head. She couldn't give him false hopes. 'It was a moment of joy because of the cottage, nothing more.'

Brows lifted in disbelief. 'It didn't feel like nothing.'

'I'm not saying that my feelings for you have died, Oliver.' Far from it; they ran rampant all the time she and Oliver were together. 'But after the way you treated me, do you really expect me to jump back into your arms so quickly?' Her eyes flashed a vivid and scathing green. 'Actually, it might never happen. Having your own husband accuse you of stealing takes some getting over. Shall we go?'

He didn't say another word; he swung away and set the car in motion. A glance at his profile revealed a set jaw and beetling brows, and his grip on the steering wheel turned his knuckles white. Serves him right, she thought. He shouldn't throw stones without expecting to get hurt himself.

They didn't go straight home, as she'd expected; instead, Oliver took her to one of his favourite riverside restaurants for lunch. Anna no longer had bouts of morning sickness and was able to once more enjoy her food, so it was a treat to be taken out.

Fog hung over the water but there were people walking along the river bank wrapped warmly in scarves and hats and Anna watched them from their table near the window.

At first Oliver was quiet, deep in his own thoughts, making Anna wonder whether she had been unnecessarily hard on him. But why should she let him get away with what he had done? She was prepared to be friends for the sake of the baby, but no more, and it was best he knew that.

The fact that she was cutting off her nose to spite her face didn't enter into it. She could cope with having no one to kiss and cuddle her, no one to share her bed, no one to send her mindless with pleasure. Couldn't she?

She didn't like the answer her body gave, but sex wasn't the be-all and end-all of life. What if she hadn't got a husband or a boyfriend? She'd cope then, wouldn't she? Yes, but there was a difference when she shared a house with a man who had stolen her heart the first moment she set eyes on him.

'What are you thinking?'

Anna looked from the river to Oliver. She met the intenseness of his golden eyes and felt a dance of fire in her belly. 'Not much. This and that.'

'Would this and that be you and me, by any chance?' One dark eyebrow quirked knowingly.

Anna gave an inward groan. 'Maybe,' she acknowledged with a dismissive shrug of her slender shoulders.

'Are you regretting coming back to me?'

'No.' It was a tiny no, escaping swiftly before she had chance to think about it. But she didn't look at him, she played with her fork instead, moving a piece of potato around her plate, smashing it into tiny pieces. 'Not entirely.'

'Is there a chance that we'll get back on to the level that we so much enjoyed before I put my foolish foot in it?'

Still Anna didn't look at him, though she knew her answer would shape their future. It seemed as though he was beginning to think there was no hope. And did she really want that? Did she want to split up from him, go their separate ways, share their baby, toss it from one to the other over the years?

Her answer was most definitely no.

'I think we might, eventually,' she said in an almost whisper. But it wasn't now. She wasn't yet ready. How long it would take, she didn't know.

Oliver reached across the table and took her hand. 'If there is hope, then I can wait. Otherwise, I would prefer we ended it now.' Anna looked across and saw the pain in his eyes, the stark pain that was cutting right into him, and she almost gave in. But he needed to learn his lesson. She had to be hard for the sake of her future.

The fact that he'd apologised a thousand times—swore he would never accuse her of anything like that again—didn't altogether appease her. Words were easy; it was actions that counted.

So a few more weeks, perhaps, maybe even until the baby was born. But could she live with him for that long and still sleep in separate rooms? Already some of her resentment was wearing off; her traitorous body was reminding her of the fantastic times they'd had together, could have again.

'Anna?'

She realised that Oliver was still waiting for her answer. And, judging by the shadow darkening his face, by the rigid jut of his jaw, it looked as though he'd made up his mind that she wanted to leave.

'I'll stay with you, Oliver,' she said, her tone still quiet, 'but I need more time. I won't be rushed. If you do you'll drive me away.'

A great big smile chased the shadows from his face, his golden eyes lit up, and his hand tightened over hers. 'You won't regret this, Anna, I promise.'

She smiled faintly and gave her head an infinitesimal shake, as though not entirely sure of it herself. Tingles ran through her, congregating in a disturbing heat in the pit of her stomach. And all because he was holding her hand!

During the rest of the meal Oliver was his normal, cheerful, conversational self, and Anna found herself more relaxed than she had been in a long time. Perhaps the new house would be the answer.

Gone would be all the old memories, the old heartache. They would start again, and she'd have plenty to do arranging things, once they moved in. It didn't really need decorating but it would be nice to stamp her own personality on it.

'I was just thinking about the house,' she said. 'I still can't believe how lucky we are. It's so much of a coincidence that Mr Jones wanted to sell.'

'It must mean we were meant to have it,' Oliver claimed, eyes glowing with pleasure. 'Fate looked down on you that day, my sweetheart. It made you drive down that particular lane and made you stop and look at that particular cottage.'

Anna laughed. 'Oliver, I didn't realise you believed in such things.'

'I don't, as a rule, but what other explanation is there?' he asked, spreading his hands palms upward. 'What is to be will be—isn't that what they say?'

'Will Mrs Green come with us?'

'If you'd like her to. The idea of putting her out of a home and a job has been worrying me.'

'She's constantly talking to me about the baby,' said Anna. 'I think she's looking forward to helping me look after it.'

'It?' asked Oliver with mock indignance. 'You're calling my son an it?'

'Your son might be a daughter,' she pointed out.

He grinned. 'If she's as adorable as you, I'll be quite content. We'll have a boy next time.'

'And exactly how many children are you planning to have, Mr Langford?' But Anna didn't really mind this talk about babies. She liked to see Oliver happy. She hadn't realised how unhappy he had been, these last few weeks. She'd been so wrapped up in her own hurt that she'd hardly spared a thought for what he was going through.

'Oh, at least four,' he said airily, then raised a questioning brow. 'Of course, it all depends on whether I'm let back into your bed in time.'

Anna didn't answer that one, but she smiled as she sliced off a piece of tender lamb, dipping it into the delicious redcurrant sauce before popping it into her mouth.

Oliver watched her every move and when a speck of sauce dripped off the fork on to her chin he swiftly leant across the table and stroked it away with his finger. He then offered her his finger to suck away the offending drop.

At one time, Anna would have complied. They would have turned the whole event into a highly arousing sensual act. But although she was tempted, she wasn't quite up to that yet. He was rushing her. So she shook her head and Oliver, his lips twisting in wry disappointment, sucked his finger himself.

His eyes never left hers, though. He let her see that he was still getting pleasure out of tasting her drop of redcurrant sauce.

A tiny incident, and yet one that remained in Anna's mind for the rest of the day. In fact, this was the most enjoyable day she'd had in a long time.

After lunch they went for a drive and it was dark when they arrived home. She was laughing over something Oliver had said, wondering at the same time how she would be able to part from him when it was time for bed. They had shared so much today that she didn't want to let him go.

But her smile faded, and so did Oliver's, when they discovered a police car pulled up outside the house.

'What on earth—?' he exclaimed as he jumped out of the car and hurried forward.

Anna swiftly followed.

CHAPTER THIRTEEN

OLIVER and Anna found Mrs Green entertaining two policemen in the kitchen. A teapot and a plate with one piece of shortbread and a few crumbs left on it was in front of them. They looked almost disappointed to be interrupted.

'What's going on?' asked Oliver, looking questioningly from one to the other.

'Mr Oliver Langford?' enquired the senior of the officers.

'That's right.'

'It's about Rosemary Langford—your mother, I believe?'

Oliver's eyes narrowed. 'I think you'd better come into my study.'

Anna wanted to follow but didn't feel she had the right, so she stayed behind with the housekeeper. 'What do they want? Did they say?'

Mrs Green pursed her lips. 'They wouldn't tell me. They've only been here about five minutes. Soon made short work of my shortbread, they did. One said he'd like the recipe for his wife.'

'Do you think anything's happened to Oliver's mother?' asked Anna worriedly.

'Can't say,' answered the housekeeper, and it was clear by her expression that she didn't really care. Rosemary Langford was Mrs Green's least favourite person.

It wasn't long before Anna heard Oliver showing the policemen out. She went straight to him. 'What's wrong? Is your mother ill?'

'No,' he answered fiercely. 'She's at the station. She's been arrested.'

'What?' Anna looked at him in wide-eyed shock. 'Why? What's she done?'

Oliver sucked in his cheeks as he appeared to be making a conscious decision how much to tell her.

'It's all right,' she said. 'It's your business. If you don't want to tell me, then—'

'I do want to tell you. I was wondering how to. But there is no way round it without putting myself in a bad light.'

Anna frowned. 'What are you talking about?'

'Rosemary stole the jewellery.'

'Oh!' For some reason, her legs grew weak and she groped for the chair behind her. No wonder Oliver had hesitated about telling her. He must feel even more of a first class fool now.

'Did she take it the night she stayed there, do you think?' she asked, a further puzzled frown drawing her fine brows together. It really was a disturbing matter. 'The night of your father's funeral?'

'No.' Oliver spoke very definitely. 'I saw them in the safe after that.'

'So, how did she do it?'

'That is something I intend to find out,' he answered grimly. 'I'm going to the police station right now. I don't know how long I'll be. Don't wait up.'

But Anna couldn't go to bed without knowing what was happening and when Oliver finally came home she was curled up on a chair in the sitting room with an open book on her lap, even though she wasn't reading.

Instead she'd been daydreaming, thinking about their future. In a month's time it would be Christmas—their first Christmas together. They wouldn't have moved by then, but next year they'd be well and truly settled in their new cottage and they'd have their baby to buy presents for. And hopefully all their troubles would be behind them.

Oliver looked tired and drained and surprised to see her still up.

'Can I get you a drink?' she asked. 'Mrs Green's gone to bed.'

But Oliver shook his head. 'You've had a long day. Shouldn't you be in bed also?'

'I wouldn't have been able to sleep without hearing about Rosemary. What's happened to her? Has she been charged?'

'No.' Oliver's lips were tight and grim as he sank down into the other armchair. Wearily, he stretched out his legs and, putting his head back, he looked at the ceiling.

'I couldn't let them do it to her.'

Because, after all, she was his mother. 'So they've let her go?'

'Yes.'

'And that's the end of it? You've got the jewellery back.'

'Not yet, but I will do.'

'You've spoken to Rosemary?'

'Briefly,' he admitted. 'I'm going to see her again in the morning.'

'How did she manage to get into the house?' asked

Anna, her mind working feverishly. 'Did she creep in while we were working upstairs?'

'I know none of the details yet. All I know is that I couldn't let them jail her. God knows why. She did me no favours, but—'

'It's because you're a decent and honorable man, Oliver Langford,' she told him quietly.

He sat up straight then and looked at her. 'You really mean that?'

'I guess I do,' she said, as if finding it surprising herself, 'but I'm still not rushing things.'

'I understand.' His expression was both sorrowful and hopeful. He stood up and came to her, and he pulled her to her feet and held her against him. There was nothing passionate about it. Like two friends greeting each other after a long absence.

Anna closed her eyes and let the warmth of him seep into her, the strength of him hold her upright, and the clean, familiar, masculine smell of him assault her nostrils.

It was a brief hug, disappointingly brief. And yet it was right that it should be so, because feelings were already being awoken inside her. Feelings she had clamped down, that were supposed to stay there until she gave them permission to flood back to life.

'Go to bed now, Anna,' he muttered, stroking a stray strand of hair from her brow with an incredibly gentle finger. 'Sleep well, my darling.'

Anna wanted to ask if he was going to bed too but, afraid that he might interpret it as an invitation, she headed for the door, turning as she went through it to give him a sad smile. 'I'm sorry about your mother.'

The following day when Oliver went to see

Rosemary, Anna took the opportunity to go up to the Hall to have a last look around.

All of Edward's personal belongings had now been sorted and what needed to be got rid of had gone. Everything was ready for the sale. There was even a middle-aged couple very interested in it. Strangely, Anna felt sad that it would soon pass out of the Langford family.

And yet she could understand Oliver wanting to have nothing further to do with it. Her own childhood memories were so happy that she found it hard to imagine any father treating his son the way Edward had treated Oliver.

Every time he came up here, he must remember the misery of his childhood. She could feel his pain, suffer for him, and yet hadn't he forced her to suffer too? Was there something of his father in him that reared its ugly head every now and then? Ought she still to be careful?

She heard footsteps and couldn't help speculating why she wasn't surprised when Melanie appeared.

'I wondered who was in here,' said the other girl abruptly. 'I hoped it was Oliver.'

'I'm sorry to disappoint you.' Anna eyed the blonde suspiciously.

'Is he with you?'

'No.'

'Is he at work?'

Anna had no intention of telling Melanie where Oliver was. It was up to him whether he told her what Rosemary had done. 'Actually, he has business to attend to. Is there anything in particular you wanted him for? Shall I tell him you called?'

'I want to know why he is selling this house,' declared Melanie aggressively. 'Why he didn't tell me what he was planning. I did wonder why he was packing all Uncle Edward's stuff up but I thought it was because he was going to move in himself.' A scowl creased her brow. 'I bet it's all your doing. I bet—'

'Melanie,' Anna interrupted firmly, 'it has nothing to do with me. It was Oliver's decision. If you have a problem with it then I suggest you ask him.'

'Oh, I intend to,' she snapped. 'Your marriage still isn't going to work out, you know. He told me he's getting a little fed up of the way you're messing him about.'

'Is that so?' Anna wondered what Melanie would have to say if she knew that Anna was pregnant. Thank goodness it was too soon for her to show. 'Then answer me this, Melanie,' she said coolly. 'If that's the way he feels, why did he come after me?'

Melanie shrugged. 'Oliver's like that. Actually, no man likes to think he's been dumped; they like to do the dumping.'

'I see,' said Anna stiffly. 'Thank you for telling me. I'll bear it in mind, the next time I feel like walking out. And I'll tell him you called. Goodbye, Melanie.'

With a toss of her long blonde hair, Melanie turned and walked out. Anna shivered. Wasn't that girl ever going to get the message?

It was way past lunchtime when Oliver returned. Anna had presumed he'd gone straight to the office after visiting Rosemary and she'd accepted that she wouldn't see him again until evening. She was unprepared for the rush of warmth that enveloped her.

Whether it was because of Melanie's comments,

whether it was because of the kiss yesterday, or whether it was because she really was beginning to forgive him, she wasn't sure. But whatever, her reaction to him was almost like that in the early days of their marriage.

And it must have shown on her face because Oliver looked at her hesitantly and then took her into his arms. 'You almost look pleased to see me,' he said, still not attempting to kiss her, but holding her with the tenderness that only a man in love could.

'I am. I want to know what's gone on.'

'Is that all?' He held her at arm's length, but there was no censure in his voice. A smile perhaps, indulgence. 'First of all, tell me how you are. As a matter of fact, Mrs Langford, now that your morning sickness has passed, you're beginning to look more radiant with each passing day.'

'I feel good,' she admitted. 'I went up to the Hall this morning. You didn't mind?' she asked, as a faint after thought.

'Not at all. Did we have more viewers? I thought Mr—'

'No, I just wanted to look at it, to picture you there as a child. I—'

He put his finger gently over her lips. 'Let's not talk about that.'

'I had a visitor while I was there.'

He frowned then. 'Who?'

'Melanie.'

And his arms dropped to his sides. 'What did she want?' He moved away from her, went to stand by the fireplace where a log fire was burning. Oliver always liked a real fire in the room they used most, despite the central heating.

'She wanted you.'

'What for?'

'I have no idea,' Anna admitted. 'I said I'd tell you she'd been.'

'Right, well, I'll deal with it.' He spoke matter-of-factly, as though it were some business matter he was dealing with, but Anna couldn't help wondering exactly how much Melanie meant to him.

'Tell me about Rosemary.' Anna sat down and tucked her legs beneath her in a corner of the settee.

Oliver dropped into an armchair but he couldn't relax. He sat forward, legs parted, hands linked between them, staring at the pattern on the carpet.

He had felt bad enough about accusing Anna but now that he had absolute, positive proof that she hadn't taken the heirlooms he felt a hundred times worse. How was he ever going to face her again? How was he ever going to make amends?

'She stole a key,' he said shortly. 'My father was a creature of habit; he kept them in the same place as thirty years ago. And then she enlisted Melanie's help to get us both out of the house.'

'Oh! That was the day I went to see Chris the day—' She stopped abruptly.

'The day I thought you'd had the opportunity to take them. Yes, I know.' He shook his head, his shoulders bowed. 'How could I have got things so dreadfully wrong, Anna?'

'I suppose it was a natural conclusion.'

And how could she be so understanding after the

way he'd treated her? Admittedly, she hadn't yet totally forgiven him, but she was definitely weakening.
When she responded to his kiss yesterday, he had felt
as though he'd won the lottery. Not the big win, but
a very satisfying win nevertheless.

'No, it wasn't a natural conclusion,' he admitted
unhappily. 'It was like firing a gun without looking
at the target. It was insanity.'

'We're supposed to be discussing Rosemary, not
me,' she said firmly. 'What was her reaction when
you said you weren't going to press charges? I hope
she was properly grateful.'

'I don't think she even thought it would get as far
as her being charged,' he confessed unhappily. 'She
was busy trying to convince the officers that the jewellery was rightfully hers because she was still legally
next of kin to Edward.'

'Did it work?'

'Not when I said he'd left her precisely nothing in
his will and that it had been thirty years since they'd
lived together. But, much as I despise Rosemary, I
couldn't let her go to prison. So long as I get the stuff
back, then I'm prepared to take it no further.'

'She's very lucky.'

Oliver shrugged. 'Surprisingly, I feel sorry for her.
She made a big mistake when she walked out on my
father and me and I think she realises that now. She's
left with no family and only a handful of friends—if
she can even call them that. It's not exactly an inviting picture for her old age.'

'So she wanted to make sure she had a little nest
egg, is that it?'

'I guess so.'

'Was she planning to sell the stuff?'

'Yes.'

'I think I feel sorry for her as well.'

Anna was magnificent, decided Oliver. Only the very purest person could forgive a woman who had unwittingly caused her a great deal of hurt. He desperately wanted to go to her, to hold her, to never let her out of his arms again—ever.

But he had to be careful, he still needed to take things one step at a time. Too much pushing now and he would be back to square one. In fact, it could push her away altogether.

'I told her about the new house,' he admitted. 'I told her she was welcome to visit any time she wanted.'

Anna lifted her brows in surprise. 'That was very generous of you.'

'She is my mother,' he admitted with a wry twist of his lips.

'Most men would turn their back on her, especially after this latest episode.'

'Maybe I would have done, once. You're the one who's made me realise that it is possible to forgive, no matter how bad the crime.'

Anna didn't answer and he didn't blame her. Instead she jumped to her feet. 'I'll go and ask Mrs Green to make us a pot of tea. Have you had lunch? There's some excellent chicken soup that—'

'I'm not hungry,' he interrupted. 'Just the tea—or coffee, I think. Whatever you're having.'

Anna smiled. 'Camomile tea, then?'

He groaned and clapped a hand comically to his

brow, having forgotten that she'd gone off ordinary tea. 'Not that stuff, please. I'll have coffee.'

When she'd gone, he leant back in his chair and closed his eyes. His talk with Rosemary had drained him, but he was glad that they'd reached some sort of compromise. He didn't particularly want to be close to her—he didn't want her taking advantage of him—but on the other hand no mother deserved the cold shoulder from her son, no matter what she had done.

In truth, he couldn't clearly remember her from his childhood. He recalled a vague figure who always smelt nice and wore sparkling earrings, but that was all. It was his father's attitude that had kept alive his resentment—and, now Edward had gone, what was the point in remaining hostile?

But his thoughts didn't remain with his mother for very long. Anna was his main concern, Anna and the baby. He couldn't begin to describe how he felt about the fact that he was going to become a father.

It was a scary thought as well as an exciting one. He knew nothing about bringing up babies, or even about children in general. He'd always steered well clear of them. It was probably his own experiences that had done this to him, but the time had come for him to learn.

He'd already said he would go with Anna to her antenatal classes but he really wanted to learn more. Or did being a father come naturally? Perhaps a book on child care would be beneficial?

'What are you thinking?'

He hadn't heard Anna re-enter the room. He

opened one eye. 'About being a father.' And closed it again quickly.

'You think it's not manly to think about it?'

'It frightens me half to death.'

'Me too,' she admitted.

Immediately he opened both eyes and looked at her. 'You've nothing to be afraid of. I'll be there for you every step of the way.'

And to his enormous pleasure she came and sat on his lap. The first time she had voluntarily come to him. It almost took his breath away and he had to force himself not to read too much into it, not to smother her with love and kisses, not to scare her away again.

'I know you'll look after me, Oliver,' she said in a breathy little whisper.

'For ever,' he assured her.

And they sat like that in quiet, reassuring silence. He was afraid to do more than hold her gently, and also afraid she would feel his response to her nearness. He felt on fire, everything throbbing, everything wanting. Hunger so intense that it hurt. He didn't know for how long he could carry on being a gentleman, but he didn't want to be the first to break away.

It was a bittersweet relief when Mrs Green came in with their drinks. They both sprang guiltily apart. Though why, he didn't know except that's how he felt. Guilty. It was probably because his housekeeper knew full well what their sleeping arrangements were. What would she make of this?

The woman said nothing but her smile was broad as she looked at him. 'Here we are. Your favourite fruit cake as well.' And there was a lift to her step as she turned and went out.

'She thinks we're back together,' said Anna.

'It's a nice thought.'

'But a premature one. Cake, Oliver?'

The interlude was over. The first tiny step taken. She was not going to let him overstep the mark. But he nevertheless felt more hopeful than he had in a long time.

CHAPTER FOURTEEN

OLIVER held out his hand. 'I'm pleased to meet you at last.'

The other man shook it firmly. 'Me too. I'd begun to think it would never happen.'

They eyed each other squarely—two tall men, both broad-shouldered and good-looking, one dark haired, one blond. Anna kept her eye on Oliver, but there was no hint of suspicion. Oliver truly was pleased to meet her brother and she could tell by the warmth of his smile that he now accepted Chris without reservation.

'I'm glad also that you've met at last,' she said, her voice fired with enthusiasm. 'You spend so much time away from home these days, Chris, that you're difficult to track down.'

He shook his head in dismissal. 'You can always get in touch with me, sis, you should know that. It's a big contract I've landed in France; I can't afford to neglect them.'

'Of course not,' commented Oliver. 'Business is business. What would you like to drink? Scotch? Gin? Vodka?'

'Scotch, please, with just a dash of water.'

'And a mineral water for you, Anna?' he asked, his eyes softening as he looked at her.

'Please.'

'Have you told your brother our good news?'

She smiled and nodded happily, and Chris said, 'I've already given Anna my congratulations. I'm happy for you both.'

'We're happy, too,' agreed Oliver as he busied himself at the drinks cupboard. 'It's the best thing that could have happened to us.' He threw a meaningful look at Anna as he spoke and she felt a quick surge of pure pleasure. She knew that he was trying to tell her that if she hadn't gotten pregnant they might easily have gone their separate ways.

'My sales team tell me that your ad campaign and your attention to detail has been second to none, Chris,' said Oliver handing him his drink. 'Business is booming as a result of it. Good man.'

'Without my little sister's generosity, I'd never have made it,' Chris answered firmly. 'I have something for you, Anna.' He withdrew an envelope from his inside pocket and handed it to her. 'A cheque for the full amount of the loan. I was going to wait until the end of the evening, but since we're talking business I think you should have it now.'

'Thank you,' she said quietly. 'There was no rush.' And she would rather he hadn't done it in front of Oliver, although she guessed that it was deliberate. She had the feeling that Chris was trying to goad Oliver into apologising again.

And it worked.

'You make me feel the world's biggest heel, Chris,' he said with a short laugh. 'It's a pity I didn't meet you when we were first married. I'd have known then that I had nothing to worry about. I somehow got you confused with Anna's ex-fiancé.'

'Tony?' Chris raised his eyebrows. 'I saw him the

other day, did I tell you, Anna? He's married a rich, young widow. Her husband owned a growing chain of supermarkets. He had no relatives, so she became the very wealthy new owner. Tony's having the time of his life.'

Anna felt Oliver watching for her response, but all she did was laugh. 'So he's got his money without working for it. Amazing. He's someone else who attaches importance to money. It should never enter into relationships. I know when I met...' She tailed off, looking at Oliver from beneath her lashes. 'Forget I said that. It's not important.'

Chris frowned as he looked from one to the other. 'Is there something I'm missing, here? I thought all was hunky dory between you two again.'

'Not quite,' admitted Oliver. 'Your sister's playing hard to get, these days.'

'With a baby on the way?' Chris lifted a questioning brow at Anna.

'It makes life less predictable,' she said with a light laugh. 'Shall we go through to the dining room? I'm sure Mrs Green has everything ready.'

Chris had been going to bring his new girlfriend along tonight but at the last minute she'd been unable to come, so Anna was landed with the two men. A few weeks ago it would have been unthinkable, unbearable, but gradually she and Oliver had drawn closer until she was now almost ready to forgive him.

Almost but not quite.

Next week it was Christmas. Maybe the best Christmas present ever would be to give herself to him. Finally and irrevocably.

She smiled at the thought, and felt a swift surge of

longing deep in her stomach. Could she really wait?
The way she was feeling at the moment she wanted
to jump on him the second her brother left. She
wanted to share his bed, to experience once more a
magical night of lovemaking.

'You're looking mighty pleased with yourself, all
of a sudden,' Oliver said, glancing at her across the
table. 'Are you going to share whatever's brought that
smile to your face?'

He never missed a trick. He was always watching
her, even when she wasn't aware of it. And quite
often he anticipated her needs. He loved her so much,
and he wasn't afraid to show it, that she sometimes
felt guilty for still keeping him at arm's length. Thank
goodness he didn't know *exactly* what she was thinking.

'I'm just happy my brother's here,' she said lightly,
hugging the warm glow that enveloped her. 'I'm glad
you two have met at last. It's a pity Laura couldn't
come. We'll have to meet her some other time, Chris.'

And she remained happy and excited for the whole
of the meal. Oliver and Chris got on well, making
Anna realise that if business crises hadn't kept the
two men apart, her marriage problems would have
been solved a whole lot earlier.

On the other hand, she and Oliver had now earned
each other's trust; their ups and downs had been a
learning curve, one more step on life's difficult stair-
case.

When Chris finally left, she and Oliver made themselves comfortable in the sitting room. It was Anna's
favourite room with its deep armchairs and cosy fire.

Even in the summer she liked it because of the glorious views over the open countryside.

'I'm glad you and Chris got on well,' she said, leaning her head back, and folding her hands over her slightly swollen tummy.

Oliver inclined his head. 'He's a good man. Brilliant brain. It would have been a shame if his business had gone under.'

'That's what I thought,' she said, covertly studying him from beneath almost closed eyes. He was so gorgeous, so sexy, so desirable—nothing had changed.

All animosity had left her. She wanted him so desperately, it hurt. Why wait till Christmas? Why wait another whole seven days? Why carry on torturing herself?

On the other hand, the wait would be worth it. She'd walk into his room on Christmas morning and climb into his bed. It would be a present he'd remember for the rest of his life.

'I'm proud of you for keeping your promise to your brother.'

She looked at him then, green eyes openly questioning. 'You are?'

'Absolutely. It couldn't have been easy.'

'You can say that again.'

'Especially as it put our marriage in jeopardy,' he said gruffly.

'I would have actually told you if you hadn't offended me by checking my bank account and jumping to all the wrong conclusions.' She lifted her fine brows in censure. 'That was despicable, Oliver.'

'I know,' he admitted guiltily. 'But my father was convinced you'd only married me for my money. I wanted to prove him wrong—it's why I checked your account. I saw red when it had all gone.' He raked his fingers through his hair and dropped his forehead into his palm, hiding his face from her in self-disgust. 'I couldn't think why you had any need to take it. I couldn't think straight, if the truth's known.'

'So it was Edward again who put a spoke in our marriage,' she confirmed sharply. 'I rather thought it might have been. He must have permanently spied on me, looking for something to blacken me in your eyes. He succeeded magnificently.'

'I'm so sorry,' said Oliver, and she could see the pain etched in his face.

'Me, too,' she admitted.

'Am I forgiven yet?'

Anna smiled, secretly thinking about Christmas. 'I'm getting there.'

'Are you close enough to give me a goodnight kiss?' he asked hoarsely.

Yes please, clamoured her heart. She smiled, faintly. 'I think I could manage that.'

'Come here, then.'

Slowly, as if drawn by an invisible cord, Anna pushed herself up and closed the space between them. Arms reached out for her and she was pulled gently down on to his lap. Then those same arms held her possessively and she lifted her head to look into smouldering gold eyes.

It was almost her undoing. She found herself wanting more than a kiss—she wanted Oliver, all of him, here, now. And he wanted her! There was no ignoring his arousal. She was sitting on it!

But incredibly his kiss was gentle. It was tentative,

it was exploratory, it was humble, it was hopeful. It was so many things. His hands didn't rove, his tongue didn't beg. But even without passion he set her on fire.

Nevertheless, Anna decided to call a halt. Those extra few days' breathing space would heighten the pleasure and excitement. And it would do him good to worry a little while longer.

'I'm off to bed now, Oliver,' she said lightly.

He didn't argue, he didn't detain her, but he looked woefully unhappy and Anna knew that, for all his outward patience, all his repeated apologies, he was suffering badly—and that if she pushed him too hard for too long he might think it wasn't worth it and call the whole thing off.

Maybe waiting for Christmas wasn't such a good idea after all. Maybe now would...

But already he was helping her to her feet. 'You're usually in bed by this time. What am I thinking? Good night, sweetheart. Pleasant dreams.'

'Goodnight, Oliver.' She reached up and kissed him again—the first really spontaneous kiss in a long time. And when she lay in bed a short time later Anna found herself riddled with doubts.

Oliver had paid the penalty. The time had come for her to forgive and forget, to welcome him with open arms into her bed again. It felt so empty and cold without him, despite the electric blanket.

She wouldn't need a blanket with Oliver. He would warm her, body and soul—he would set her on fire. Another whole week of sleeping alone in this bed was going to be sheer purgatory.

The next couple of days she was so busy with last-minute Christmas shopping, decorating the tree she had insisted Oliver buy, bringing in armfuls of holly, doing all the hundred and one things that Christmas entailed, that she fell exhausted into bed each night. And Oliver laid no claims on her either, which was a help although it also surprised her.

She had thought that he would want to press home his advantage, repeat the kisses, turn it into something more. But no, he contented himself with a brief kiss each night, a kiss that meant absolutely nothing, a kiss that made her extremely disappointed—and also frustrated if the truth were known.

Two days before Christmas Oliver had a business dinner to attend. 'I'll probably be late back,' he said, 'so don't wait up.'

That was another night taken care of.

And on Christmas Eve night Melanie paid them a visit.

She brought a present for Oliver but nothing for Anna. Not that Anna minded, she hadn't bought Melanie anything either. And she was surprised when Oliver told the other girl that he had something for her.

'It's upstairs. I'll go and get it,' he said.

Melanie warmed her hands in front of the fire after he'd gone. 'We had a good time last night at the dinner. Did Oliver tell you?'

The words were calculatingly casual but Anna felt as though she'd been kicked in the stomach, as though all the breath had been knocked out of her. And her first thought was, thank goodness I didn't go to bed with Oliver.

Her second thought was that she couldn't blame

him for turning to Melanie when she wouldn't give him what he wanted. And it answered her question as to why he was so patient.

And her third thought was that she mustn't let Melanie see how surprised and hurt she was.

'Of course Oliver told me,' she replied in what she hoped was her normal voice. It didn't quite sound like it, but maybe Melanie wouldn't notice.

'We went back to my place afterwards. Oliver—'

'Melanie!'

The colour drained from Melanie's face as Oliver's appalled voice came from the doorway. 'What the hell are you talking about?'

Melanie turned slowly to face him but her eyes didn't quite meet his.

'Do you always talk like this to my wife when my back's turned?'

The blonde girl pouted and shrugged.

'Anna?'

But Anna didn't want to get involved and so she remained silent also.

'Believe me, Anna,' Oliver said, 'There is nothing going on between Melanie and myself. Not a thing, not for a long time.' He crossed the room to Anna's side and draped his arm about her shoulders.

'This is my wife, Melanie, and I love her very much. I'd like you to remember that. Whatever we once had going between us has been over a long time, and if you're going to come here to cause trouble then I'd prefer you didn't visit again.'

A slow burn flamed Melanie's face and without saying another word she turned and walked out.

'You didn't give her her present,' Anna reminded him quietly.

'She doesn't deserve it,' he said harshly. 'Does she speak to you like that often?'

'Only every time we meet.'

He groaned and his arm about her tightened. 'I had no idea. I hope you don't believe her because there's not a word of truth in it.'

'I used to,' she admitted, enjoying the feel of his hard body against her.

'It really was a business dinner. I don't know how Melanie found out about it.'

'I believe you,' she said.

'Oh, Anna, my Anna.' He held her against him for a long throbbing moment. 'What you've had to put up with. I'm so sorry. There's been nothing between me and Melanie since that day I found her bragging. I've felt it a duty to keep an eye on her for my father's sake, but that's all. I don't think I ever really loved her—not the way I love you.'

It was time.

The message rang loud and clear in Anna's head.

Time to tell Oliver.

No point in waiting until tomorrow.

The time was now.

CHAPTER FIFTEEN

OLIVER had felt appalled when he stood listening to Melanie's lies. All he could think of was what it was doing to do to Anna, how it was in danger of wrecking their still fragile relationship.

He'd worked so hard over the last weeks to ensure nothing went wrong. It was half killing him to hold back, to remain patient and attentive, when what he really wanted to do was ravish her lovely body, made even lovelier by the fact that she was carrying his baby.

This don't-touch-me rule was driving him insane. And the number of times he'd almost lost control and demanded to know how much longer she was going to keep it up were nobody's business. Only the fact that he knew he would ruin everything if he did stopped him.

But how long was a man expected to wait?

As he continued to hold Anna, his whole body burnt with a fierce flame and he didn't want to let her go. Another night in bed alone, another night of tormented dreams, and then waking on Christmas morning with no one in bed beside him. How could he bear it?

'Oliver,' Anna whispered urgently. 'I'd like to give you your Christmas present now. Will you wait here while I fetch it?'

He smiled down at her. 'Of course, but I thought we'd put them under the tree and—'

'This is only a part of it.'

'If it's what you want.'

She looked so eager all of a sudden, her eyes alight, her lips parted in anticipation. And so damned sexy, more like the girl he'd first met. Her vitality had been missing, she'd become serious and withdrawn, and it was a pleasure to see her like this again.

He wondered what the present was that she couldn't wait to give him. She looked so excited that he knew he daren't let her down, even if he didn't like it although he was sure he would since it was Anna's choice.

He stood with his back to the fire, his hands behind him feeling its warmth. He heard her light footsteps on the stairs and saw the door coming open.

After that he was robbed of speech, robbed of breath, robbed of everything.

All Anna wore was a short, sheer red nightdress decorated with gold tinsel. There was a big green and red bow in her hair and high-heeled green sandals on her feet also decked out with tinsel.

She was all seductress as she sashayed towards him, her shining emerald eyes locked into his. His heart hammered frenziedly against his breast bone, pulses pounded, but apart from that he couldn't move a muscle, not even blink.

He was completely mesmerised by this exquisite creature who came up to him and slid her arms around him and said the words he thought he would never hear again.

'Oliver, I love you. I forgive you; I'm now ready to be yours.'

He swallowed hard. '*You* are my present?'

'If you want me.'

'If I want you?' There was no doubt about that. He'd nearly died with wanting her. 'Oh, Anna,' he groaned. 'Anna. This is the best Christmas present ever.' And his head swooped and he found her mouth and this time there was no holding back, no reservations—on his part or Anna's.

Anna had almost forgotten what it was like to be loved by Oliver, forgotten the excitement that trembled through her veins, the heat that invaded her limbs, the hunger that took over.

His tongue probed with an urgency that thrilled her, it explored intimately and fiercely what had long been denied him. Oliver the lover came back to life, ruthlessly demanding, passionately taking, and her own desires leapt in abandoned response.

She could actually feel his hands trembling as they sought the contours of her body beneath the thin red layers of fabric, slightly hesitant, as though he was still a fraction uncertain.

He didn't need to be. She was his now for all time, and she wanted to reassure him. 'I really do love you, Oliver, very, very much.'

His golden eyes were dark with desire as he raised his head, his mouth was soft and moist from her own mouth. 'You've truly forgiven me?' he asked thickly.

'Totally,' she whispered. 'If I carried on the feud any longer, I'd be torturing myself.'

'Oh, Anna,' he groaned, 'you don't know how I've

longed to hear you say that. This is the best day of my entire life.'

'Let's go to bed,' she suggested quietly and huskily.

His eyes gleamed with fresh desire. 'Can I unwrap my Christmas present in bed?'

'Yes.'

'Can I play with my present all night long?'

'Yes.'

'Then let's go,' he said with a triumphant grin. 'Let's not waste a minute.' He swung her up into his arms and Anna felt the unsteady beat of his heart as he carried her upstairs to his bedroom. She felt the intense heat of his body, the urgency that fuelled him.

And it was fuelling her! This was better than when they'd first met. It had been exciting then, yes, but this was a different excitement. She knew her man, now—she knew what to expect, she knew his hard-boned body as well as her own. She knew how much he could pleasure her and she could pleasure him.

But in this Anna was mistaken. Everything was so much better than she remembered, and it all began when Oliver untied the bow in her hair.

'Rule number one,' he informed her with a slow, teasing smile, 'never tear your wrappings. Always undo with care.' The ribbon came off and was neatly folded for further use. Next he cradled her face between his palms and kissed every inch of it, slowly and thoroughly, eyelids, nose, the incredibly erogonous zone behind her ears which made her wriggle and moan, and finally he claimed her mouth.

A long slow kiss, as though he had all the time in the world. He nibbled her lips, he dropped kisses inside her lower lip; his tongue explored, it danced attendance on her own, it created havoc with her senses.

When he finally lifted his head there was a glittering satisfaction in his golden eyes. 'Rule number two,' he said. 'Make the pleasure last. Explore the gift's shape before you unwrap it completely.'

They were standing in front of the mirrored wardrobe and he stepped behind her so that she could watch every move he made—and her reaction to him.

His hands began at her throat, stroking a slow and tantalising path towards her breasts. Her head fell back against his shoulder, her breathing grew quicker and shallower, and her eyes watched with greedy fascination.

Her breasts had grown fuller during her pregnancy and were sometimes too sensitive to touch, but at this moment they ached with need, and when his large capable hands closed over them she gave a tiny moan of pleasure.

Watching through the mirror, Anna saw the way her body wriggled against him, the luminous green of her eyes, the way her face screwed up as though she were in pain. Except that the pain was pleasure—a deep, unadulterated, long-awaited pleasure.

All this she had been missing; all this he had almost thrown away. It was unthinkable.

His hands moved lower, over her rounded hips, over her slightly swollen stomach. It was his turn to give a groan of pleasure at that point, and finally he reached the hem of her nightdress.

Anna waited with bated breath for rule number three.

She tried to guess what it would be. Perhaps something like—Finally, pull off the wrapper with equal care. Fold it up carefully before proceeding.

It never came.

Oliver suddenly couldn't wait. Her nightdress was yanked over her head and their eyes met in the mirror for one brief heart-stopping second before he effortlessly picked her up and carried her across to the bed.

It was then a race to get out of his own clothes. It took him about five seconds before he landed on the bed beside her.

'Do you like your gift?' she asked with a mischievous smile.

'Do I like it?' he groaned. 'What a question.'

'I was going to wait until morning, but suddenly I couldn't.'

'I'm glad,' he said roughly. 'I wasn't looking forward to waking up on Christmas morning with my wife in another room. I think I might have come in and ravished you anyway.'

'I'm glad we're friends again, Oliver,' she said, snuggling against him.

'Tonight you're not my friend, you're my lover— my very charming, my very enchanting, my very beautiful, my very pregnant lover.'

'Take me, Oliver,' she urged. 'Make me yours again.'

'It won't hurt the baby?'

'No. He needs to know that he's loved, too.'

Oliver needed no further encouragement. They lay stomach to stomach, hip to hip, and when he entered her it was with such loving care that it was Anna who went a little wild, Anna who rolled him on to his back, straddling him, riding him, feeling herself go mindless with pleasure when her climax came.

The next time it was his turn to kneel over her, his turn to take the lead, to bring her to a peak of desire before he finally gave her the release she begged.

Most of the night they continued to play their love games. It was almost as though they were making up for lost time. But eventually exhaustion set in; their eyes closed, their bodies grew limp and sleep claimed them.

And when they awoke it was snowing outside.

As it never—or very rarely—snowed on Christmas morning, Anna saw this as a good omen. 'Look,' she said, rubbing a circle in the condensation on the window and peering outside. 'Look, Oliver. Isn't it wonderful?'

'I think you're wonderful. I would never have forgiven me for what I did.'

'Isn't there some corny old saying about love conquering all? I guess I never truly stopped loving you.'

'Nor I you,' he said. 'Come here, Anna, and let me prove it to you.'

She didn't need any persuasion, and if it hadn't been for Mrs Green cooking their Christmas dinner Anna and Oliver Langford would probably have stopped in bed for the rest of the day.

EPILOGUE

Two years later...

'I THINK we ought to go on honeymoon.' Oliver, lying in bed beside Anna, ran his hand over her swollen abdomen. 'Before Junior Two puts in his appearance.'

Anna smiled slowly. 'Mmm, I think I'd like that. Where shall we go?'

'Somewhere exotic and hot where all you have to do is lie around all day and be deliciously lazy.'

'I can't imagine myself ever being lazy,' she murmured.

They had moved house before Peter was born and although Mrs Green did all she could Anna really liked doing most things herself.

She loved looking after her darling baby and her gorgeous husband. She went cold every time she thought about how near she had come to losing him. And of course she loved her new house.

When Peter was ten months old they'd added an annexe to the cottage—Rosemary was coming to live with them!

Oliver's mother had changed. Her fright with the police and Oliver's unexpected generosity had made her do a lot of hard thinking. And today she was a gracious lady who had finally accepted that there was more to life than money.

'Do you know where I'd like to go?' Anna said,

stroking Oliver's cheek, feeling the early morning rasp of a much needed shave.

'The world's your oyster, my darling. Just name it.'

'To Dawn's cottage. We were so happy there, Oliver. It would be a perfect place for a honeymoon. And now your mother's here, I'm sure she'll help Mrs Green look after Peter.'

'I think you're right,' he said. 'She's really taken to the little guy. She says he reminds her of me at his age. I don't think she wants to miss out on his childhood the way she did mine.'

'So it's settled?' she asked, eyes shining.

'If that's what you really want?'

'I do, more than anything in the world. And Oliver, thank you for loving me.'

'Oh, no,' he said quickly, 'it's me who has to thank you for giving me a second chance. And it has worked out, hasn't it?'

Anna nodded. 'Better than I ever expected. I'm the happiest woman in the world.'

'And I,' he said with the widest grin imaginable, 'am the happiest man.'

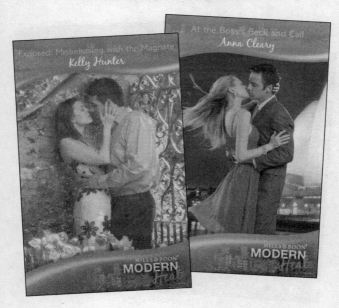

millsandboon.co.uk Community

Join Us!

The Community is the perfect place to meet and chat to kindred spirits who love books and reading as much as you do, but it's also the place to:

- **Get the inside scoop from authors about their latest books**
- **Learn how to write a romance book with advice from our editors**
- **Help us to continue publishing the best in women's fiction**
- **Share your thoughts on the books we publish**
- **Befriend other users**

Forums: Interact with each other as well as authors, editors and a whole host of other users worldwide.

Blogs: Every registered community member has their own blog to tell the world what they're up to and what's on their mind.

Book Challenge: We're aiming to read 5,000 books and have joined forces with The Reading Agency in our inaugural Book Challenge.

Profile Page: Showcase yourself and keep a record of your recent community activity.

Social Networking: We've added buttons at the end of every post to share via digg, Facebook, Google, Yahoo, technorati and de.licio.us.

www.millsandboon.co.uk

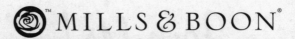